C.C. Y
Full Circle

"Being a visionary is seeing things others do not."
-Nanisca
"The Woman King"

TABLE OF CONTENTS

CHAPTER ONE	6
CHAPTER TWO	14
CHAPTER THREE	22
CHAPTER FOUR	33
CHAPTER FIVE	45
CHAPTER SIX	53
CHAPTER SEVEN	63
CHAPTER EIGHT	74
CHAPTER NINE	81
CHAPTER TEN	88
CHAPTER ELEVEN	98
CHAPTER TWELVE	112
CHAPTER THIRTEEN	133
CHAPTER FOURTEEN	151
CHAPTER FIFTEEN	165
CHAPTER SIXTEEN	180
CHAPTER SEVENTEEN	193
CHAPTER EIGHTEEN	207
CHAPTER NINETEEN	227
CHAPTER TWENTY	242
CHAPTER TWENTY-ONE	252
CHAPTER TWENTY-TWO	264
CHAPTER TWENTY-THREE	282
CHAPTER TWENTY-FOUR	295

CHAPTER TWENTY-FIVE 305
CHAPTER TWENTY-SIX 317
CHAPTER TWENTY-SEVEN 331
CHAPTER TWENTY-EIGHT 345
ACKNOWLEDGMENTS 362
C.C. Y 363

THE NIGHTMARE

He unbuckles his belt, pulls it from his pants, and strides toward my fragile and battered mother. Tears are falling from her soft brown eyes. She cradles herself on the floor like defeated prey. She is afraid to look him in the eye. It makes him angrier. "You stupid cunt," he said as he continued to walk toward her, like a predator in the wild, preparing to attack and kill its prey. "You made me this way." He swings the belt in the air and, bam, it connects with her head with a loud crack.

She falls flat onto the dirty, white kitchen floor. There's blood dripping from her swollen mouth. She remains dormant on the blood-stained floor. Mom knows how to play the prey. When she is submissive, her husband loses interest quicker. She knows what he seeks is confirmation of his masculinity, and the sooner she can help him feel that way, the faster her nightmare will cease. She continues to lie motionless, giving him all the power as he continues whipping her repeatedly. When he finishes satisfying his ego and insecurities through blows and slaps, he unzips his pants, pulls them down, and rapes her.

I, feeling hopeless, and barely seven years old, watched from the cracked door of my bedroom. The vicious thunder and rainstorm pouring outside hid any screams of pain from Mom. I wanted to cry out, but Mom told me many times to stay quiet. She knows he would come for me if she didn't endure the assault. I cover my mouth and sob as the horror continues to unfold in front of me. My inability to help her makes me feel powerless.

CHAPTER ONE

I opened my eyes to the pitch-black space surrounding me. The room was filled with nothing but silence. I lay paralyzed in bed, my breathing unbalanced, and my forehead seeped in sweat. My heart was thumping rapidly in a moment of fear; I thought I was having a heart attack. I remained frozen on the uncomfortable mattress I'd purchased from a yard sale five years ago. Perhaps the awful bed was the reason for most of my nightmares. My body temperature changed from scorching hot to icy cold. I'd experienced frequent nightmares recently, so it wasn't all that shocking to my body anymore, but I hadn't gotten used to it mentally.

Fifteen, five, one, eight, seven, one hundred, I counted in my head. My mind became briefly distracted, but my body was still in distress. All I could do was hopelessly glare at the black ceiling.

After what felt like an eternity of never-ending panic, I decided it was time to take back control. *It's okay, I'm safe,* I chanted in my head. My mom's voice unconsciously invaded my brain. *"Alina, close your eyes. Think of a place that makes you happy. Now breathe in and out, slowly. Good, now count to ten. And remember, I'll always be with you, my love."* Then she kisses my forehead and tucks me into bed.

With that memory, I forced out a smile.

I inhaled deeply through my nose, held it in for six seconds, and then exhaled. I used to laugh at people that claimed deep breathing helped with their anxiety. It was difficult for me to comprehend how such a small and simple act was beneficial. And besides, I breathed all day, every day anyway. *Or so I thought.* I underestimated the power of proper deep breathing and as soon as I took it more seriously, deep breathing became a vital support in my battle with depression, anxiety, and PTSD.

It hadn't always been perfect. There were a few times when I didn't do it properly and that led to heart palpitation, then hyperventilation, and finally a panic attack. When I was younger, I found myself in the emergency room many times, but the doctors couldn't diagnose what was wrong with me. All they did was perform a quick physical check, say I was overreacting, and discharged me. After the seventh time, I stopped going to the hospital altogether. Even now, as a twenty-four-year-old, I rarely visit the hospital. The only exception would be if I was dying, but even then I'd probably find a reason not to see a doctor.

After my fifth deep breath, my heart rate slowed, and my breathing was back to normal. I wiggled my fingers and toes a few times to ensure I was in control of my muscles again. After successfully regaining the function in my limbs, I closed my eyes, embraced the darkness, and fell back asleep.

The bright morning light gleamed through the small window, illuminating my tiny bedroom. The sun crept through like a carrier of light, lifting and brightening everything in its path. It gently skimmed across my face and slowly nudged me awake. On rare days, there was nothing better than a warm good morning kiss from the sun. On those days, I'd sit on the couch with a cup of coffee with heavy French Vanilla Cream and watch the sunshine sweep through my four-hundred-square-foot apartment. I treasured those moments because it was the only time I could relax my brain.

Shortly after the delicate wake-up nudge, my alarm clock rang. Unfortunately, the clock wasn't as kind as the sun. Regretfully, I slowly opened my tired brown eyes and stared at the white ceiling above. Even though I'd mentioned that sometimes it was nice to wake up in the morning, I was also the same person who believed "early" morning meant after ten a.m., and not six. I admired people who could wake up that early. Especially those who could wake up that early, work out, shower, and somehow cook breakfast for themselves. My best friend, Ana, was one of those people. She never once in her life purposely slept past seven in the morning, ever. She only ever slept in when she was blacked out drunk the night before. About a year ago, I attempted to live a day like her, and my body shut down before nine in the morning. Since then, I hadn't woken up that early- until today.

I bitterly stared at the number six on the clock. I wanted to toss the damn thing from my window and let it shatter against the hard concrete ground and just go back to sleep, but I knew Ana would be furious. Since I couldn't take the liberty of such a dramatic action, the only thing I could think to do was sluggishly rest in bed for another five minutes and count all the dots on my ceiling. It helped wake me up.

Eventually, I pushed myself up with my elbows and sat up straight. But instead of forcing my feet onto the floor, I leaned my back and head against the headboard. I reached over and grabbed my overly used brown journal on the bedside table and began writing.

For the longest time, no one was aware of my nightmares, not even my mother. But on one snowy night, the dream was so horrifying; that I screamed and woke her up. She busted into my room to comfort me, and I confessed what had been happening in my sleep. I remembered her arms tightly embracing my tiny body. She kissed my forehead and continuously apologized. I didn't understand why she kept saying sorry. It wasn't until I was an adult that I realized she blamed herself for my pain. My mom knew she couldn't fix my mental struggles, so she told me to journal. She said it was a way for me to cope and reflect a small portion of my pain on paper. I didn't understand at first, but each year as I grew older and wiser, I realized she was right. It helped me to write about things that I bottled up internally. So far, there were over twenty journals safely tucked away in a box somewhere in the closet.

As I was finishing up my final thoughts, adding as many details as possible, my old and outdated iPhone rang abruptly. I closed my journal, chucked it back on the table, and searched endlessly for the phone. I heard it ringing and vibrating, but I couldn't see it. *Where's the damn phone?* I asked myself, irritated. After tossing the pillows and blanket on the floor, I found the phone underneath the bed. I snatched it up and answered.

"Good morning, Ana." I tried to sound as gleeful as possible.

"Morning, my beautiful babe. Are you excited?!" she implored with a chirpy voice.

"Of course. It's about time we have our girls' trip."

"Are you all packed?"

"I am, are *you*?" I teased her.

"Hell yeah! Cancún is the one trip that I will not be late to the airport for," she giggled loudly, and then continued, "Be ready in an hour. I'll come to pick you up. Okay?"

"Sounds good," I said and hung up the phone.

Ana and I met in the cafeteria during my freshman year of high school. I was never fond of lunch in the cafeteria. I would rather get smacked in the face with a dodgeball by the overly confident football players in the gym or take another one of Mr. Zander's pop quizzes in statistics, than sit at those ugly silver picnic tables, staring aimlessly at the plain white walls. The cafeteria served as a constant reminder from Monday to Friday that I was detached from the world around me, untethered from the world. I'd concluded long ago that I'd always be alone.

That changed when Ana unexpectedly placed her lunchbox on the table and sat down next to me to eat her lunch. Her actions bewildered me because no one had done that before. I'd gone through middle school and the beginning of high school alone. What caught me off guard, even more, was her not saying a word to me. I glanced around the room before we sat silently and ate. When she finished her food, she put her hand out and introduced herself. "I'm Ana. Nice to meet you." We shook hands, and from that moment on, and since then, we were inseparable. We completed high school, attended the same college, and even graduated together. She was the small glimpse of light sent during the darkest part of my childhood. The memories brought a smile to my face.

After making my bed, I strolled to the small bathroom right outside the bedroom to get ready. I gaped at my exhausted brown eyes and pale olive skin in the mirror. There was a slight dark circle under each eye. I appeared as if I had been deprived of sleep for a few days. I grabbed my Chapstick and applied it to my dehydrated lips. The mint balm was soothing for odd reasons. I pulled up my wavy long black hair in a loose bun and washed my face in the sink. After brushing my teeth, I turned on the shower head and waited until it was lukewarm. I needed a nice warm shower to fully nudge myself awake.

Half an hour later, I heard a ding from my phone. I looked at the text message from Ana that read, "Be there in 5 minutes." I hastily curled the last section of my hair and ran my fingers through it with coconut oil. My brittle hair needed some shine. I tossed my head up and down a few times to make it seem more natural. It took me ten years to learn how to curl my hair correctly, but even then, I wasn't entirely sure that I'd done it right. I parted my hair in the middle to decrease my age, even though I was already young. I didn't bother to smear any makeup on. Well, truthfully, I didn't know how to apply makeup. It was tricky growing up and listening to Ana talk about all the times she and her mom practiced doing each other's hair and makeup. She called it their "mother and daughter special bonding time". I smiled and pretended to be enthusiastic; I was good at that. She meant no harm, but it shattered my heart when she shared those beautiful moments. It pained me because I couldn't relate to any of the memories. My mom never taught me how to do any of those things; I learned most lessons in life on my own.

Ana tried to teach me how to apply makeup once, but it was too many steps to remember. I couldn't see myself spending an hour or longer playing with makeup. I made a mistake once when I expressed to her that I had no clue about a foundation shade for my skin. After nearly fainting, she grabbed my hand and dragged me to a high-end makeup store. I remembered feeling lost and stunned. Not only was I overwhelmed that there was makeup at every corner, but I was also turned off by how costly their products were. I wasn't too fond of the idea of buying a fifty-dollar liquid foundation. I proudly told her I was more of a Walmart girl, and because she loves me, we went there instead.

I applied moisturizer and day cream on my face instead. At least then, I wouldn't look so parched. I glanced at the time on my phone and realized I had to go. I darted out of the bathroom and threw on a white T-shirt and black sports leggings. I'd never been much of a colorful type of girl. The only color clothing in my closet was black, white, nude, or gray. I couldn't imagine wearing any other color. I peeped at my reflection one last time in the full mirror hanging on the back of my bedroom door before slipping into my white sneakers. *Smile, Alina, so the world thinks you're happy.* I forced out a smile.

My phone was ringing once more. "Here." Ana's text said.

I grabbed my black luggage, the coach wristlet Ana bought for my 23rd birthday and scrambled out the door. I skipped a few steps down the stairs that lead to the parking lot. My best friend, as expected, was in chic black, high-waisted jeans, a white crop top, and completing her look with an oversized Louis Vuitton tote bag. She stood joyfully by the Uber Cadillac with her shoulder-length, blonde hair dancing gently in the wind. Her gray eyes reflected beautifully against the sunlight. Her makeup, like always, was on point. It was glamorous yet soft, and it accentuated her natural beauty. As I moved in closer, her enthusiasm dwindled. Once I stopped in front of her, she glared at the small luggage in my hand.

"That's it? One small bag?" She inquired, her voice a mix of confusion and disbelief.

I looked at the luggage that had been with me for over ten years and looked back up at her, not comprehending what she was implying.

"Alina, we are going to Cancún, Mexico, for an entire week, and you're bringing one small piece of luggage?" she asked again, still astonished.

I rolled my eyes at her and said, "You know I don't need a lot of clothes, right?"

Ana released an enormous sigh of defeat. She understood she would not convince me otherwise.

"You know what? I can't complain. It took an entire year for me to convince you to go on this trip, and I will not ruin it." After accepting defeat, she embraced me in her long arms.

Ana always smelled nice, and of course, it was Chanel 1 perfume. That made me realize I didn't spray on my cheap Burlington perfume. *Oh well, it is what it is.* At least I applied deodorant. An enormous man with spiky hair, brown eyes, and a very large nose stepped out of the car and helped with the luggage. We leaped into the back seat while he placed the bags in the trunk. Before I had the chance to settle, Ana took out her latest brand-new iPhone and snapped a selfie. The girl loved her selfies. The driver stepped back in, and finally, we were on our way to Boston Logan International Airport.

"I'm Kevin, nice to meet you guys." He said politely.

"Hi Kevin, I'm Ana, and this is Alina."

"So, where are you guys headed to?" He asked, interested.

"Cancún, Mexico, for a vacation."

"Oh nice, I've never been, but I heard it's a beautiful spot for a vacation."

"I've been there a few times with my family. It is beautiful. You should visit sometimes."

Ana was always the outgoing and extroverted one. She had no problem striking up a conversation with anyone, anywhere. I admired that characteristic trait. I sat quietly and peered out the window at the view of the world as it passed by. Even though there wasn't much to gaze at other than old buildings and cars stuck in traffic, it was enough to distract me from having to converse. Ana continued to snap more pictures, pulling me into a few of the photos in between communicating with Kevin. After about thirty minutes into the ride, she must have taken thirty or more photos.

"So, Alina, what do you do?" Kevin asked.
His question brought me back to the present moment.

"Um… I'm a case manager. I worked with the elderly population in assisted living." I often found discussing my job awkward, but truthfully, I found most dialogues unpleasant.

"Oh, nice. My grandma lives in assisted living in Providence. She hates it there, but my family figures she's safer there than staying at home alone. I admire people that can work with that population. I mean, I love my grandma, but I don't think I can handle working with ten other elderly people who are like her," he said playfully.

I didn't mind Kevin. He seemed authentic and unapologetic.

"That's what I tell her almost every day. I'd probably pull my hair out." Ana chimed in with a giggle.

The entire ride consisted of Kevin talking about his life and job. Ana primarily did the talking. But, here and there, I would share my thoughts. After a little over an hour and an annoying wait in traffic, we eventually arrived at the airport. Kevin hopped out and helped with our luggage while Ana snapped a few more selfies by the front door. After thanking him for the ride, we strolled inside. I was never a huge fan of the airport because of the headache of getting there, going through security, and finding the gate. That was one of the primary reasons I rarely traveled. I only relaxed once we sat down at our gate. I pulled out my phone and casually scrolled through my social media. It was bombarded with Ana's post. At least she posted photos of me that weren't a complete disaster. I briefly glanced over at Ana, who was also scrolling through her phone, examining all the pictures she took.

"I like this one," she said and showed it to me. She always knew how to pick the right one.

"I do too."

Before I could mumble anything else, she posted it to her social media. She was quick with that kind of stuff. She was the only person I knew who was confident enough to double post in a day. After about an hour of waiting, we finally boarded the plane. It took a few days of begging, but I convinced Ana to buy economy seats instead of first class. I anxiously walked down the aisle and looked for our seats. It delighted me that I was sitting by the oval window. I placed my luggage in the compartment above and took my seat. Ana gladly sat in the middle seat. Once we fully settled, I exhaled a deep breath and relaxed.

The plane started moving and soon we took off into the clear blue sky.

"I'm so proud of you," Ana said unexpectedly.

I stared at her, puzzled. "What do you mean?"

She clasped my hand and, with a warm smile, said, "For finally taking a risk and traveling with me. I know you're not a fan of going on vacation. But I'm so grateful that you're willing to do this with me."

Ana was good at sweet-talking. She could get out of any trouble if she wanted to. Though, her small words were a big encouragement for me.

"No problem and thank you for always understanding me."

We exchanged warm smiles. Once we were high in the clouds, I closed my eyes and fell asleep.

CHAPTER TWO

Ana shrugged me awake.

"We're finally here!" She announced jubilantly.

That was the most restful four hours of sleep I ever had. It made up for the missed hours that I didn't get from last night. I felt rejuvenated. I glanced down at the world underneath and was taken aback by the clear sea and white sand. For the first time, I was glad she kept insisting that I take this trip with her.

We walked out of the gate and straight to baggage claim. Left and right, people gawked at us like we had something on our faces. Perhaps it was strange for them to see one of us with three large suitcases and the other with one small one? Whatever the reason was, I wasn't too fond of it. We stepped outside the airport, and the hot air enveloped my face. It was good, scorching heat. I breathed in the lovely summer air as I noticed a tiny bald man with a thick beard and mustache standing in front of a white shuttle holding a piece of paper with our names on it. We joyfully made our way toward him. He pushed our luggage into the trunk while we merrily hopped into the back seat.

I was in awe of the scenery as the car drove along the highway, but more importantly, I was elated at the sight of the ocean. I observed as it moved in a subtle, soothing way. I couldn't wait to dip my feet in it.

I'd tried to find the cheapest resort possible, but Ana insisted we go to the grandest and most expensive one. I told her I didn't have the money, but she went behind my back and booked everything for the two of us. The first few times she did that early in our friendship, I felt so uncomfortable, but after ten years, it'd become a regular thing in our friendship. Money was never an issue for Ana because she was from an affluent and successful family. Her dad owned two different real estate companies, and her mom was a well-known gynecologist. On top of that, their family owned a successful wine venture. With all that wealth one would assume that Ana's family was pretentious and arrogant, but they are far from it. They were the kindest and most generous people I'd ever met. From the very beginning, they'd treated me like family. Though it took me a long while to realize that they were genuine people, it was clear to me the type of people they were when they took me in at eighteen years old. I had aged out of the foster home I was living in and had nowhere to go next. If it weren't for them, I'd have no clue where I'd be today. I stayed with them for a few months, but after a while, I wanted to be independent and survive on my own. So, I got a job, found my small apartment, and moved out.

"Oh my gosh. It's so beautiful. Even though I've been here a few times, it always feels like the first time," Ana said and pointed to the blue ocean waves crashing against the rocks.

She was right - it was breathtaking. I didn't usually do this, but I had to take out my phone and capture the magnificence of the sea. After another twenty minutes or so, we finally reached the resort's tall, white gate. It opened to what I initially thought was a castle fit for royalty. The driveway was long and spacious, and there were clusters of sky-high palm trees and beautifully trimmed bushes on each side of the driveway. I remembered admiring the resort's beauty via online photos, but to glimpse it in person was a completely different experience. I rolled down the window and listened to the sound of the tides slamming against the stone and inhaled the fresh breeze. Ana squeezed my hand in excitement like a small child. Finally, we stopped in the front entrance of the grand, white and gold hotel. The tiny man opened the door and we stepped out of the shuttle. Right away, the concierge greeted us with a friendly and welcoming smile as he led us inside to check-in. As we waited, another employee appeared from nowhere and presented us with two glasses of champagne on a tray. Ana was more than thrilled to grab both glasses and handed one to me. We raised our drinks in the air, a quick toast to the beginning of our girls' trip and headed inside.

Ana booked the most elegant and luxurious room for us to stay in. She initially wanted to do a penthouse, but I convinced her it was too much money and for once she listened. I was more than pleased with what we had. There were two large queen-sized beds, a massive walk-in closet, a balcony that faced directly at the ocean, and a bathroom that was the size of my bedroom. I paused in the middle of the massive room and stared in awe. She dove right into her bed and spread her arms and legs like a snow angel.

"Wow," I heard myself say under my breath.

"I know, right? Now come on, let's change into our bathing suits and go to the beach!" She hopped off the bed and opened one of her bags to look for a bikini.

Ana looked fabulous in her fiery red two-piece bikini. She had the ideal hourglass figure that many women only dreamt of. I guess all those hours and days working out in the gym paid off. As she was rubbing sunscreen up and down her legs, I wondered whether I should wear the black two-piece or the black one-piece. The two pieces meant my stomach would be showing, which I wasn't overly thrilled with. I reached for the one-piece because it would hide most of my skin, but Ana interrupted me.

"I forbid you to wear the one-piece." She made her way to the bed, picked up the one-piece swimsuit, and tossed it in her luggage.

"Uh, why did you do that?" I asked in disbelief.

She glared at me. "Come here," and dragged me to face myself in front of the massive full-body mirror in the corner. "Look at yourself. You're one of the most beautiful women I have ever seen in my life. And contrary to what you might believe, you have a banging body. So why are you trying to hide yourself?"

I sighed and steered away from my reflection. I turned to face her and said, "You're only saying that because you're my best friend."

She frowned. "That's not true. You know I'm honest; I tell people the truth no matter how much it hurts them. Who has time to make up lies and shit?" She said and continued, "Anyway, I remember the first time I saw you eating in the cafeteria by yourself. I thought you were gorgeous. Otherwise, I wouldn't have approached you." She teased playfully.

I unleashed a half-smile and lazily picked up the two pieces and went to change. Fifteen minutes later, we walked out of the room and straight to the beach. I loved that it was only a few hundred feet away, just behind the hotel.

There was a warm, calming sensation coursing through my body when I stepped on the sand with my bare feet. It was soft and delicate on my little toes. Ana held my hand as we strolled past multiple people sunbathing. It was a crowded beach, but a family chasing their little ones caught my attention. It reminded me of the good old days when my mother used to bring me to the beach. The kids were laughing and screaming as they continued to sprint away from their parents. They had the purest looks of joy on their faces.

"Damn, where's the empty beach chairs?" Ana asked herself while she was looking around, annoyed.

Right as she said that a football hurled in my direction and nearly took my head off. Luckily, I dodged away in time. Two young gentlemen, both with defined and sculpted bodies, in black swim trunks sprinted our way. One of them with brown hair picked up the ball and said, "Sorry ladies, didn't mean to almost hit you!"

Ana looked at him, briefly speechless from how good-looking he was. I gently pinched her hand.

"Oh, it's fine. We're still alive." She said playfully and the two giggled like high schoolers.

Their other two friends shouted at them, and they excused themselves.

"Well, I'm already enjoying this vacation more than I expected." She announced as we continued to search for empty chairs. I teasingly rolled my eyes.

Oh boy, here we go.

After what felt like a hopeless search, we finally found two seats under a palm umbrella and settled down. She snapped a few more photos of herself before leaving me to sit alone in the chair. It hadn't even been five minutes and she was already in the water. I didn't mind though because I needed a few minutes alone to take in the lovely view that was right in front of me. Just as I'd predicted, two men instantly approached her. I knew it would happen sooner or later. Ana had no problem attracting men anywhere she went. She waved and signaled for me to join, but I wasn't ready yet. I shook my head and smiled, to which she responded with a scowl.

    I laid on my back and closed my eyes. I didn't think it was possible to feel so relaxed. *Perhaps I should go on more vacations in the future.* After a few moments of solace, I decided to get a drink. I pushed myself off the chair and headed to the bar between the beach and the hotel. I felt a ripple of anxiety as I hiked through the crowded pool. I felt eyes watching as I passed, but I composed myself and made sure to watch my step. Knowing my anxiety, I'd probably trip on the air and plummet flat on my face. I thanked whoever was in charge in the sky when I made it safely to the bar. I found an empty stool, sat down, and waited for the bartender to approach me. After a few minutes passed, the handsome young bartender with curly brown hair took my order. He was wearing orange swim shorts and a colorful shirt that was completely unbuttoned.

    "What can I get you today, miss?" He asked with a soft voice and an adorable Spanish accent.

    "Can I get a long island iced tea, please?"

    "Sure, no problem."

    He turned away to do his thing. He was smooth and moved around gracefully. It was entertaining to watch as I waited for my drink.

    "Here you go. On the house." He said as he slid the drink my way.

    I stood there shyly and said, "Uh, thanks."

    He offered me the cutest smile, showing his straight white teeth. I picked up the glass, but as I turned to walk back to the beach, I slammed into another woman. Unfortunately, this resulted in me spilling my entire drink all over her curvy body. She had silky chest-length brown hair that was now covered in long island iced tea. Immediately, everyone paused their conversations, and turned their heads to watch the commotion.

"I am so sorry," I said, frightened that I had made a scene.

The woman, with her mouth open in a startling gasp, looked down at her soaked, green two-piece swimsuit, and then back up at me. She paused when our eyes met. There was anger and something else behind her eyes. I couldn't pinpoint exactly. She stared at me for a long time, almost as if she was trying to comprehend where she knew me from. I couldn't say the same. I'd never seen her in my life; I would remember a gorgeous woman like her.

"Are you serious?" She questioned with irritation. "Do you know how much this swimsuit cost?"

I remained silent, unsure of what to say. I'd never been the type of person to handle confrontation in a calm matter. My stomach was swirling with anxiety and my fingers slightly twitched with every second that flew by. My face was burning up quickly.

"Well, I guess you wouldn't know. I can tell how cheap that piece of trash *you* have on is," the woman said and laughed. That was when I realized she had a group of women behind her, chuckling along with her.

"Is everything alright?" A manly voice inquired.

A mysterious man wearing a gray swimsuit appeared from behind the stunning woman. He had short black hair, and a perfectly chiseled jawline, and his muscles looked like they had been sculpted by the Greek gods and placed on his body. He appeared around the same age as me, perhaps a few years older. He had a boyish charm to his face, and I was mesmerized by his heart-shaped lips and soft brown eyes.

He walked up next to the woman. "Are you alright?" he asked.

She rolled her eyes at him and then turned her attention back to me. "No, I'm not alright. I just bought this from Gucci, and she ruined it."

He finally shifted his eyes to me, and I nearly bolted away from his piercing stare. I waited for him to start insulting me in the same way the woman did, but instead, he just gazed at me. There was an uncomfortable silence between us. The woman and her entourage looked on, bewildered. They weren't the only ones. It was times like this that I wished I could read people's minds. I wanted to sprint away, but my legs were stuck to the ground. He continued to stare as if he recognized me from somewhere. How was it that both he and the woman had the same reaction? I'd never met either one of them before.

After what felt like an eternity, a never-ending staring contest, he blinked a few times and turned his attention back to her, "It's just a swimsuit. It's not that big of a deal. I'll buy you a new one."

The woman released a massive sigh of irritation. "Whatever. Watch where you're going next time." She warned me as she left. All of the women followed behind her like a group of lost puppies.

I remained dormant, anxious to look at him. From the corner of my eye, I noticed he was still looking at me. *Why is he still staring at me?* His fierce eyes almost drilled a hole into the side of my head.

"Hey! What's going on?" Ana asked from behind me.

Oh, thank God. I let loose a subtle breath of relief at the sound of her voice. I turned to face my guardian angel and said, "I accidentally spilled my drink on someone."

"Oh, well, are you alright?" She questioned.

"Yes, I'm fine. The woman's swimsuit, not so much."

"I'm glad you're fine," Ana turned her attention to the mysterious man who was still staring. "And you are?" she asked, intrigued.

He placed his hand out and said, "My name is Adrian."

She shook his hand and said, "Adrian? I'm Ana. Nice to meet you."

"I didn't get your name," he said to me.

"Alina," I said softly.

"Alina," he said with a soft smile. I'd never heard anyone say my name with such gentleness.

I find most men intimidating, but there was something different about him. I couldn't bring my eyes to meet his. He made me nervous in a way that I'd never been before.

"I apologize for her behavior; she's usually not this crazy." He said playfully.

"Accidents happen," Ana said.

What followed next was another uncomfortable silence. Finally, after maybe ten seconds or so, I couldn't stand the awkwardness any longer. I yanked Ana's wrist and dragged her back to the beach.

"Oh my god, he is soooo hot," she whispered in my ear. She wasn't wrong, and even though our backs were to him, I felt on the back of my neck that he watched us as we walked away.

CHAPTER THREE

Later that evening I slipped on a loose-fitting, black spaghetti-strap dress. I couldn't wear a bra underneath, so I opted for pasties to cover my nipples. If I was ever forced to compliment a favorite part of my body, I would say I was pleased with the perkiness of my boobs. I curled my hair once again and pulled it up in a half ponytail. With my hair out of the way, I was able to showcase my facial features and sharp jawline. I sat on the edge of the bed and put lavender-scented lotion on my legs.

Ana walked out of the bathroom in her tight, yet elegant, long-sleeved, knee-length red dress with a deep V neck, and red lipstick to match. The dress hugged her curves in all the right places. She'd also decided to straighten her long, blond hair.

"Why didn't you ask Adrian for his number?" She asked as she applied jasmine-scented lotion on her legs.

"Because I don't know him. Plus, I don't think his girlfriend would be happy to know that the girl who ruined her *Gucci* swimsuit asked for his number." I explained.

"How do you know they're dating? Or are you assuming?"

I perked up at her and said, "Why do you have to do that?"

"Because when you're afraid to approach a guy, you tend to make up stuff that you aren't sure whether or not is true. Don't forget Alina; I've known you for a very long time. I can practically read your mind."

Once again, she wasn't wrong. Unfortunately, I had no clever comeback, so all I could do was roll my eyes. I continued to rub lotion on my legs, defeated. Ana grabbed a small black pouch from her purse and pulled out her gold star-shaped earrings. They were given to her by her parents on her 24th birthday. She stood up from her bed, strolled to the mirror, and hooked them in her ears.

"Alright let's hurry up. My dad said the restaurant closest to the hotel is excellent, and I'm starving," she prompted.

I locked the door behind us, and we descended the stairs toward the restaurant. The beautiful night sky shimmered along the ocean's waves. The resort was even more elegant in the evening. We strolled along the stone corridor with dim, white lights as our guide. The tall palm trees surrounding us danced gently with the subtle warm breeze. There were lit tiki torches grounded in the sand every couple of steps. I heard lovely Spanish music playing in the background as we approached the restaurant, and though I didn't understand what they were saying, it was soothing. I felt like I was walking to dinner in a romantic scene from a movie.

As soon as we reached the restaurant's entrance, a hostess with her hair tight in a bun greeted us with a welcoming smile. She guided us to a round table in the restaurant's center. The restaurant had a rustic chic feel to it. It was surrounded by white long drapes, and it was massive and packed with people. Many of the women were in exquisite evening dresses. The table had simple, elegant white roses in a clear vase and was surrounded by small lit candles.

"Enjoy your dinner," she said after we sat down and then took off.

Within the next few minutes, a petite blonde waitress approached our table and handed us menus. "Hola, my name is Estella, and I'll be taking care of you ladies tonight. Can I get you started on any drinks?" she asked cheerfully, with a heavy Spanish accent.

Estella had the most radiant and glowing skin, even under the dimmest of lights. I couldn't help but gaze at her smooth face. I'd be lucky to go two weeks without my skin breaking out. I'd been praying ever since we landed in Mexico for my face to stay clear of pimples, and so far, so good.

"Can we get started with a red Exzellenz Cabernet Sauvignon wine, please," Ana requested.

"Absolutely. I will get that for you right away." Estella said and left.

"Stop staring," Ana said from behind her menu.

I was unaware of my behavior until she pointed it out. "What?"

"I know what you're doing. You're comparing yourself to her," she finally placed the menu down on the table. "How many times do I have to tell you? Stop comparing yourself to other women. Yes, she's a pretty girl, but you're hot. So, knock it off." She said, clearly upset at my low self-esteem.

I unleashed an enormous sigh. I swear, sometimes Ana frightened me with how accurately she could read my mind. Though it was tough to hear, I knew she was right, again. I'd spent years comparing myself to other women and pointing out everything I thought was wrong with me. At the beginning of our friendship, she was annoyed every time I compared myself with other women. But the more she grew to know me as a person, she understood where my low self-esteem stemmed from. After that, she was more sympathetic and encouraging. However, I knew better than to expect her to always bring me out of my thoughts. I was fully aware that sooner or later, I would have to learn to do that on my own.

Estella came back with our wine bottle and two glasses. We patiently watched as she opened the bottle and expertly poured the sweet-smelling drink. "Have we decided on what to order?"

"Yes, I'll have the steak, medium well," Ana said.

"Would you like any sides to go with that?"

"Um, I think I'm good for now."

Estella wrote down the order, and then she turned to me, "And for you, senorita?"

"I'll have the salmon, please, asparagus on the side."

"Will there be anything else for you ladies tonight?"

"We're good for now. Thank you," Ana said and handed both of our menus back to her.

"Of course. I will put the order in right away." She left for the kitchen.

Ana raised her glass and said, "Well, cheers to our first night in Cancun together."

I held up my glass, and we toasted to the *almost* successful first day of vacation. I consumed a big gulp of the delicious and smooth drink. I'd never been much of a drinker, but when I did, my go-to drink was always wine and occasionally long island tea.

"This is some good wine," Ana claimed. That was a huge compliment coming from her.

"I know, right."

I took a couple of bigger sips. With an empty stomach, it wasn't long before I felt a warm sensation course through my body, mainly in the pit of my stomach. I felt more relaxed and lighter in the head. *Damn Alina, you're weak,* I thought jokingly to myself. I guess that happened because I wasn't used to drinking. I finished the rest of the wine and poured myself another glass. As we talked about our plans for the next day, the two men that hung out with Ana on the beach earlier approached our table. They casually pulled out the two remaining empty chairs and made themselves comfortable. My body immediately tensed up in their presence. I sat in the chair uncomfortably and gave Ana a look of dissatisfaction. She must have invited them. Finally, the young man with curly brown hair and brown eyes put out his hand for me to shake. I hesitated at first but grabbed it anyway and shook it.

"Hola, I'm Juan, and you must be the stunning Alina," he smiled and showcased his perfectly straight, white teeth.

I assumed she had divulged my name to him, which wasn't a big deal. However, I wasn't too pleased that she invited them without consulting with me first. I hated whenever I was put in an unpleasant situation. I exhibited a stiff smile and nodded my head as a confirmation of my name. The other young man with blonde hair down to his chin and blue eyes also put his hand out for me to shake. Once again, I awkwardly took his hand and shook it.

"I'm Jason. Ana told us you guys are from Rhode Island. What a small world, I'm from Boston," he revealed. His voice was husky but young, befitting his baby face.

The two men had the same body type, slim but their muscles were toned and defined. If I had to guess, they probably went to the gym and worked out a lot. It wasn't hard to assume they were outgoing. The way they moved and talked exuded confidence and skill when it came to striking up conversations with random women.

"So, how long are you guys staying here for?" Jason asked me and then waved his hand for Estella's attention. She came right away.

Jason perked up at her and said, "Can we have two more wine glasses?"

"Absolutely," she said without reluctance and left.

"A week," I uttered meekly and painfully.

"Not bad. I came a few days earlier and met up with this guy," he said and patted Juan on the shoulder.

"So, how did you guys meet?" Ana asked.

"I was an exchange student at Boston University, and Jason was my roommate. We hit it off right away and fast forward to three years later, we're still buddies." Juan explained.

"Damn right. I mean, this guy is crazy. When he agreed right off the bat to play a couple of pranks on the sorority girls, I knew we were going to be good friends." Jason said proudly.

I admired the bromance they shared. Unexpectedly "Hawaii" by Maluma and The Weekend played slightly louder in the background. The song was enough for Ana to leap out of her seat and grab Juan's hand. She dragged him to an open space in the restaurant and started dancing. She loved The Weekend. I observed as she danced worry-free, but at the same time, I was troubled that she deserted me.

"She's a wild one, isn't she?" Jason asked.

I groaned, "You have no idea."

To distract myself from the uncomfortable silence, I took a large sip of my drink, hoping maybe it would ease me up even more. I kept my eyes on Ana and Juan, mainly so I wouldn't have to look Jason awkwardly in the eye. I'd never been good at striking up random conversations with people, especially at the first meeting. I played with my knotted fingers underneath the table. *Don't say anything, Jason, please.*

"You don't get out very much, do you?" he asked bluntly.

I was so taken aback by his boldness that I had to turn my head in his direction. No one had ever been so candid with me. He saw the shock on my face and apologized. Though it was inappropriate to ask such a question, the truth in that question stung like that of a thousand bees.

"How did you guess?" I asked with an uneasy smile.

"I can tell by your body language and the look you had when you saw Juan and I approaching the table. I'm sorry if we interrupted your girl's night."

"It was more of a surprise than anything. I thought dinner was going to be just her and I." I said truthfully.

"I apologize again. We honestly didn't know, or else we wouldn't have interrupted."

"It's alright. Ana tends to get excited sometimes and makes decisions without consulting me first, but I'm used to it."

"Well, since they're dancing, would you like to dance, too?" he inquired with hopeful eyes.

I tried to remember the last time I attempted to dance. *Oh right, it never happened.* "Um, I don't think me being on the dance floor is a good idea. I'd rather just watch." *Geez, Alina, you sound so pathetic.*

"Hey, look, I'm sorry if I'm making you uncomfortable…" he started.

"Oh no, it's not you. It's just…it's just I'm awkward, and that's just my personality. It's not because of you." I attempted to assure him. He looked relieved. "Oh okay, well, that's good to know."

We both proceeded to painfully sit in silence. *Screw it.* I swallowed a substantial amount of my wine and crossed my fingers that it would loosen me up. *What the hell am I doing? I'm in Cancun. A hot guy is sitting right next to me. Don't be so foolish.* I finished the rest of the drink. Jason gawked at me, bewildered and fascinated at the same time. Finally, I began to feel a warm sensation in my stomach again. My body relaxed once more, and my head started to feel lighter. Gradually, I felt all the harsh judgment and negativity leaving my body. I straightened up my posture and crossed my legs underneath the table.

"To answer your question, yes, you're right. I don't get out much, and you want to know what's even crazier?"

Jason leaned in closer and said, "What?" His eyes lit up with intrigue.

"It took Ana a *whole* year to convince me to come here," I revealed.

He chuckled in disbelief and said, "For real? Wow, that's crazy. How could a beautiful woman like you not want to get out more?" He gazed at me straight in the eyes. He was audacious, indeed.

Thanks to the magic of the wine, I squinted my eyes flirtatiously and asked, "You think I'm beautiful?"

He shifted in even closer and with a sultry voice said, "The most beautiful woman in this entire resort."

I tried hard to contain my laughter, but the longer I focused on his attempt to flirt with me, the harder it was to suppress the emotion. Eventually, I couldn't tolerate it any longer and let out a giggle.

He looked at me, perplexed. "What's funny?"

I poured myself another glass of wine and playfully asked, "How many times have you used that line?"

He collapsed his body in the chair, slightly red in the face, and ran his hand through his hair in embarrassment. "You got me," he said with a quirky smile and continued, "I like you. I think you're the first girl to call me out on it."

"I may not get out much, but I know a cheesy pick-up line when I hear one," I said with an enormous grin. I felt accomplished for calling him out.

Estella came back to our table with another bottle of red wine and refilled his empty glass. We raised our glasses and toasted to a much more relaxing evening. Shortly after we chatted about work and mostly his family, Ana and Juan returned. Both were saturated in sweat, though she was glowing in it. The two of them pulled out their chairs and sat down simultaneously. Ana poured her glass to the rim and chugged the drink in one big gulp like it was water. Juan looked on with amazement in his eyes, and after she set the glass on the table, he took her hand in his. They looked like lovers. For the first time, I saw a glimpse of genuine happiness in her eyes. That was something I hadn't seen in a long time. Well, at least not since the car accident. They stared into one another's eyes, and it was delightful to watch.

"Well, I guess you guys had a good dance," Jason suddenly said, breaking the silence at the table.

She gave him a goofy smile before filling her glass again.

"Calm down, babe. You don't want to get too drunk too fast." Juan suggested in a loving voice.

She giggled. Seeing her smile made me almost forget that she didn't talk to me first about the blind double date. But even if I wanted to stay mad at her, I couldn't. She was too loveable to be angry at for too long. The night continued with the four of us laughing and enjoying each other's company. We discussed family, college, work, goals, and dreams. Being tremendously tipsy made it easier for me to converse with the group.

Four bottles of red wine later, my bladder nearly exploded. I remembered one of the many reasons why I didn't drink often- the constant annoying trips to the bathroom to pee. Every year I drank at Ana's parents' Christmas party, and I had to run to the bathroom every hour of the night. I recalled how aggravated I was, and the party was no longer fun, but more of a hassle.

"Excuse me. I have to use the restroom." I stood up and left.

I counted five women waiting outside to use the restroom. At one point, I was tempted to use the men's bathroom. It was empty. I couldn't wait any longer and asked one of the waiters where else I could go. The kind man informed me there was a bathroom outside that was not too far from the restaurant. I hurriedly left and wandered around in circles a few times, searching for the mysterious bathroom. The resort was like a maze. Every corner I turned led me down another stone corridor. I picked a long walkway and proceeded further down with the dim white lights as my guide. The corridor felt like it was never going to end. Finally, after aimlessly walking for a few minutes, I stopped and turned back around. Either the magical bathroom didn't exist, or I was too drunk to find it.

I couldn't quite decide whether the earth was moving, or if it was just my mind feeling the full effect of the many glasses of wine. I wasn't sure if there was anything that I'd stepped on before tumbling straight down to the cold hard ground—another reason why I didn't usually drink. I exhaled a sigh of shame and pushed myself up. I inspected my surroundings, and luckily no one was around to witness my embarrassing fall. That would have been worse than the sharp pain I felt in my left knee. I didn't realize I had fallen that hard, but I guess injuries don't hurt as much when you're drunk. I tried to wipe away the dirt on the bottom of my black dress and then looked down at my bloody knee.

"That was a nasty fall," a mysterious man's voice said from the dark.

It startled me. I anxiously looked around again to see where the mysterious voice was coming from. Eventually, a silhouette appeared from behind one of the palm trees, eyes reflecting in the moonlights. I squinted my eyes to get a better view of who it was, but it wasn't until the man was under the lights that I recognized who it was.
Adrian.

He was wearing a white T-shirt under a black leather jacket and black jeans. He looked down at my bloody knee, reached into his pocket, and pulled out a handkerchief. I instinctively took a few steps back when he walked toward me.

"I'm not going to hurt you," he said calmly.
Adrian asserting that he wasn't going to hurt me didn't reassure my unsafe feelings. It didn't help that no one else was around but us. I often sought not to judge people, especially when I didn't know them, but his appearing randomly in the dark made me a little uneasy. It was even more strange that he was behind a palm tree. Numerous questions

were floating in my head, which didn't help with my already anxious self. My heart started beating more erratically and my lungs tightened. *Breathe, Alina, don't panic.*

"You're bleeding. May I wipe it away?"

I flinched at first but nodded my head anyway. He knelt and gently wiped away the blood oozing down my knee and leg. When his cold hand touched my skin, I felt goosebumps gushing throughout my body. *How could his hands be freezing when it was hot outside?* He stood back up slowly when finished, scrunched up the handkerchief, and slid it back into his pants pocket.

"Thank you," I said softly.

"I didn't mean to scare you."

I realized perhaps my worried expression was too obvious. Then I felt like an ass for judging this man without getting to know him first—*way to go, Alina,* I berated myself. "No, I'm sorry. I didn't mean to make you feel that way. I appreciate the kind gesture."

He smiled lightly and said, "You're new around here."

I glanced at him, confused. "What do you mean?"

"My father is the owner of this resort. I come here a lot for vacation, but I've never seen you around. That's all I was trying to say."

"Your father is the owner?" I asked even though he had already said it.

He bobbed his head.

"That's…uh nice."

I didn't know what else to say. I wasn't sure what his purpose was when he told me his father owns the resort. *Perhaps to impress me?* I waited to see if he would say anything else, but he didn't. I wanted to leave the uncomfortable situation, but I was drawn to his gorgeous brown eyes. His gaze was soft but at the same time firm and steady. I'd thought all the alcohol in my system would make me brave, but I was wrong. I was still shy. Once again, he stared at me as if I reminded him of someone.

"Well…thanks again," I broke the silence and turned to walk away.

He grabbed my hand without warning, and it alerted me to struggle away. *Oh no, what is he doing? Is he going to hurt me? Or kidnap me?*

With a grin, he said, "Don't forget your shoe."

I foolishly looked down on the ground to where my left black heel was. I didn't realize it had fallen off when I fell. Embarrassed, I stooped down, snatched up the heel, and plopped it back on my feet. He finally let go of my hand.

"Thank you," I said and took off in the same direction I came.

CHAPTER FOUR

The glistening sunlight caressed my face and nudged me awake. I stretched out my entire body and yawned before rubbing my eyes and fully opening them. I stared at the high white ceiling once my vision was clear. Without a doubt, the several wine glasses knocked me out like a light last night. The only thing I remember was Ana walking me back to the room. I rolled onto my side and grabbed the phone from the bedside table. I was stunned to see that it was already past eleven in the morning. *So much for trying to wake up early and eat breakfast.* I unlocked the phone and scrolled through my social media. It was bombarded with Ana's posts. I didn't hesitate to like and comment with a heart emoji in every picture. It was typical of her, and I loved it.

"What should we do today?" I asked out loud from behind the phone screen.

No answer. After a few solace moments passed by, I propped myself up and rested my back on the headboard. "Ana?" When I continued to not hear her voice, I pushed myself out of bed and walked over toward hers. The mattress was still there, but she wasn't. There was no sign of her in the bathroom or the closet. I made my way back to my bed, grabbed the phone, and dialed her. I followed the sound and found her phone under her pillow. *That's strange.* Ana never left without telling me where she was going, and she would never leave without her phone.

I ran into the bathroom, hastily brushed my teeth, and washed my face with the cold water. I grabbed a pair of black shorts and a white tee from my luggage, changed, and left the room. The cloudy atmosphere staggered me. I'd expected the entire week to be clear and bright, but I guess the weatherman was wrong after all. I didn't mind it though. Gloomy days meant fewer people outside.

I searched every corner, but still no Ana. I tried my best to remain level-headed. The only thing that kept me relaxed was the constant reminder that she was safe and somewhere in the resort. Somewhere. When I veered around the corner in the pool's direction, I spotted a familiar face.

"Jason!" I shouted and sped up to him.

"Hey Alina, what's up?"

"Have you seen Ana?"

Jason had a smirk on his face like he knew. "She left with Juan after she settled you in bed last night."

I was relieved to learn of her whereabouts but baffled that she would leave without leaving me a note. As I readied to say something else, Jason interrupted.

"Oh, hey Catalina," he called out the name of a woman walking up behind me.

I turned around to see a familiar face. Catalina was the woman I had spilled my drink on. As if the sky wasn't already depressing, she appeared. By the look on her face, she wasn't too happy to see me either. Her eyes bore into me as she approached. She didn't hesitate to insert herself right in between Jason and me. Although, her glare was fixed on me only. My body slowly reacted with an uncomfortable tremble at her intense stare. After an awkward staring contest, she finally turned her attention to him. He looked nervous. Which I didn't expect from him, especially after how confident he appeared last night. After not saying a word to him, she turned her attention back to me, and said, "You, again." Her voice was bitter and cold.

"You two know each other?" he asked.

The last thing I wanted to do was relive the horrible encounter from yesterday. All I wanted to do was vacate and disappear from the unwanted situation.

"She's the cunt I told you about," she said with an attitude.

Throughout my life, people called me many insults and I never once cared much about it. But the word cunt had always been a trigger for me. It was a word that I knew too well from a young age. One that

34

I had continuously heard my father use to call my mother, to degrade her. I felt an uncomfortable sense of rage rearing its head from deep within.

"What did you just call me?"

She flashed me a surprised look. It was as if she didn't expect a comeback. "Did you say something?" she asked.

I took a slow, deep breath and composed myself. *One, two, three, four, five.* "Look, I already apologized for what happened yesterday. I didn't intend to ruin your swimsuit. There's no need for us to continue to talk about it. It was an accident."

"Who do you think you are?" She straightened her posture and folded her arms across her chest. I knew she wanted to get a rise out of me, but I refused to give her the satisfaction. There were more important things for me to worry about than standing there and arguing with a woman I barely knew, like wondering where Ana was.

"Did you not hear me or are you tone deaf?" She asked aggressively.

"Catalina, chill. As Alina said, what happened yesterday was an accident." Jason intervened finally.

She steered her attention to him, clearly unsatisfied that he defended me. "I think you need to get over your little middle school crush."

"I think it's better if I leave." I looked at him and said, "Thanks again for telling me where Ana is."

I took off before he could open his mouth to say anything else. *Please don't follow me,* was all I could think about as I walked away. It disgruntled me to hear his footsteps heeding behind me. I sped up my steps.

"Alina, wait!" he called out.

I pretended not to hear him calling my name and kept walking. The next voice I heard was Catalina asking why he was following me. I sped up. I was relieved to see a corner nearby to which I could veer off and vanish. The last thing I heard was her shouting, "How do you know that bitch?"

After making sure he was no longer following me, I stopped in a corner to take a deep breath. Once I got my breathing under control, I figured I'd walk to the beach. There was no need to search for Ana anymore. She was enjoying herself with Juan. I couldn't even be mad at her for that. Besides, I figured it was better to sit on the beach than stare at the white walls in the room.

I slipped out of my white sneakers, held them in my hand, and stepped onto the white sand. It wasn't as warm as yesterday, but it was still soothing underneath my feet. I settled down near the ocean's edge and peered at the distant horizon in front of me. I loved gazing at the never-ending sea. There was a sense of serenity and stillness that I couldn't explain. I turned to my left and watched the waves crash against the stone. The sound of birds chattering caught my attention, and I looked up to the sky and watched as a few of them danced in rhythm. Sometimes I wished I was a bird. That way, I could fly and escape whenever I needed to. I closed my eyes and savored the peace and silence. I couldn't recall the last time I was that relaxed.

"We meet again," a familiar voice said from behind.

I instantly opened my eyes in regret and turned my head around. Adrian approached wearing only black basketball shorts. He was drenched in sweat, and his sculpted and chiseled body was impressive, but I was more puzzled by how he sneaked up from behind, making no noise. Or that he showed up in places I didn't expect. Either he was a magician or a stalker. Neither one was good. I refrained from staring at his body for too long the closer he got. Without inquiring if he could, Adrian squatted down next to me and made himself comfortable. I knew I shouldn't be uncomfortable, but I was. I couldn't explain exactly why.

"How's your knee?" he asked.

"Better. Thank you." I said awkwardly.

I turned my head back to the sea to avoid gazing into his intense brown eyes. I felt my face getting warmer and my heart rate increasing. And even though I wasn't looking at him, I could sense he was staring at the side of my face.

"I guess you owe me dinner since I saved you last night," he said boldly.

The comment was unpredictable enough for me to turn my head back, and look at him, bewildered.

"What?" I asked with an eyebrow raised.

"I'm intrigued by you, Alina. It's usually not my style to ask women out to dinner."

It mystified me. "So, what do you usually do then?"

He had a mischievous smirk on his face. His eyes hinted he had no good intentions.

"That's not important. I hope you'll allow me to get to know you more. Perhaps then we can discuss…that."

He was a confident man with a familiar cockiness that reminded me of half of the jocks in high school. Even though he was a handsome man, *no, more like the sexiest man alive*, his massive ego was bothersome. It flattered me that he showed interest, but the main reason for the trip was to spend time with Ana, not to start messing around with men.

"I don't think it's a good idea for us to get to know each other. My friend and I came here to have fun. I'm not interested in going out on dates with anyone." I said with a composure that I didn't realize I had.

"Well, that's the first," he said.

"First of what?"

He chuckled to himself in disbelief.

"What's funny?"

"This is a strange phenomenon. A woman has never rejected me before."

The words that came out of his mouth were smooth, but I was still uninterested. I wanted to say something, but frankly, I wasn't sure how to respond to him. The only thing I did was stare into his eyes with confusion.

"I'm not giving up yet. Perhaps we'll see each other around again," he said and stood up. Before resuming his run, he gave me a delicate grin.

I watched as he gracefully jogged away. *So much for peace.* I sat alone, still dazed by what had just transpired. It hit me suddenly that a man had asked me out to dinner. I'd lived in the shadows for many years, but now, someone saw me. Maybe Adrian had a dark sense of humor, and he was playing a prank on me. *You're right, who could ever be attracted to you? Well, no, you are pretty.* The constant battle between the good and the bad was exhausting. It was time to leave to avoid any more internal conflict. I inhaled and exhaled a few times before getting up and going back to the room. After that encounter, I feared if I remained too long, I'd think about different scenarios in my head, which was never a good thing.

My mom used to tell me how I felt about myself affected my behavior. She was right. The negative self-talk and hatred toward myself started when I was a young child. But she didn't find out about it until I was eleven years old. She found a small notebook under my pillow filled with nothing but abusive self-loathing. She cried and ached in pain after reading every page. I remembered the despair in her soft brown eyes as tears fell down her smooth but bruised cheeks. I could only assume there were two reasons she sobbed. One was that she felt guilty that she had failed her daughter. And two, she felt a deep sorrow that an eleven-year-old child could feel that way about herself. Either way, I had never seen her so lost and helpless. She started me on the journey of positive self-talk from that day on. The road wasn't always easy. I continued to struggle daily, but at least as an adult, I was more aware of my feelings and thoughts.

I finally reached the room and when I unlocked the door, an unpleasant scene immediately greeted me. Juan was naked, on top of Ana in the middle of the room, and he was viciously thrusting inside her like a wild animal.

"Oh my God, I'm sorry!" I panicked and slammed the door behind me. My heart was fluttering rapidly. I thought it was going to leap out of my chest. *What the hell, Ana?* I thought angrily and disturbingly to myself. A few seconds later, the door narrowly cracked open, and she gently popped her head.

"I am so sorry. We'll get dressed right now," she said with shame.

Great, now the image is stuck in my head. Even though I was disturbed, I would not be the friend that cock blocked her best friend from having sex.

"Ana, it's fine. You guys... uh... finish up. No need to rush on my account. I'll walk around and explore the resort a little more."

She looked at me with the most loving eyes. "I love you so much," she kissed my left cheek, happily thanked me, and shut the door.

The hotel was a majestic castle that never ended. In every corner I turned, I walked down another long stone corridor. I didn't hesitate to stop and look closely at the carefully carved stones. I didn't understand what the pictures meant, but I imagined it was trying to tell a story of how the resort came to be. After turning around multiple corners, I paused at a particular one that led me down a path filled with a lovely, blossoming garden. It was filled with flowers of every color of the rainbow. I'd never in my existence seen such a place. I strolled down the stone pathway and whisked my fingers over the delicate petals. They were soft and calming under my fingers.

I continued down the path until I reached the center of the garden. There was a glorious, naked male statue with no arms sitting atop a stone in the middle of the water fountain. His face was slightly tilted up to the sky. From a glance, it looked like he was contemplating something that had been on his mind for a while. I gradually made my way around the magnificent sculpture and observed his every angle. I stopped at the sight of a small bench near the fountain, made my way there, and sat down. It was quiet. Just the way I liked it.

Unbeknownst to me, Catalina appeared from the same path I walked through. It was like she had followed me. First Adrian and now her. *Why?* I let out a disappointed sigh under my breath. She gracefully approached my direction and, without asking, made herself comfortable and sat down. She was too close to my liking.

"How do you know Jason?" She inquired, without looking at me. Instead, her attention was also on the statue in front of us.

I wanted to answer right away, but I paused. Even when I did nothing wrong, I always tried to explain myself. I thought about what to say. I knew I needed to be careful with my answer. From the brief few times I met with her, she had shown nothing but bitterness and an unnecessary temperament.

So, without looking at her, I said, "I met him through my best friend's... boyfriend. I met him last night. I barely know the guy. There's nothing between us you need to worry about." Even though my attention wasn't on her, I felt her fierce eyes glaring at the side of my face.

"Really? You seem to know him pretty well from earlier."

"What?"

"I know the type of girl you are just from a glance. Low self-esteem and pathetic. There's nothing on the inside but a void. When I look at you, all I see is agony and desperation. You spend years looking for validation and something to fill that emptiness. I know what you're doing with my boyfriend. So, listen carefully. If I see you talking to him again, I guarantee your trip will end sooner than you expect." She warned me, pushed herself off the bench, and walked away.

It left me speechless. I felt my body's temperature rising and my head was ready to detonate. Catalina reminded me of all the mean, snobby, and rich popular girls I had the unlucky pleasure of attending school with. Those girls made my life in school a living hell. It took years for me to fight back and when I did, it never ended well for them. I'd suppressed that other Alina for many years, but she was making it harder every second we spoke with each other. I questioned whether coming to Cancun was a good idea. *Deep breath, Alina, deep breath.* From the brief encounter, my shoulders were tight and my whole body was tense. I scanned around to make sure that she was gone for sure. After a few minutes had passed, I slowly let my guard down.

"Alina?" a familiar man's voice said from behind.

It startled me once again, and my body instantly tensed back up. I shuddered at the thought of Adrian standing behind the bench. *Is this real right now?* I unpleasantly and slowly turned my head. He was in a black shirt and dark jeans.

"Hello again," he said with a smirk.

I blink annoyingly a few times, "Are you following me?"

He had a delighted smile on his face. Adrian came around the bench and made himself comfortable next to me again without asking. I adjusted a few inches away. I searched around for the quickest exit in case I needed to make a run for it.

"The garden is one of my favorite places in the resort. When I want to be alone, I come here. I apologize if I'm making you uncomfortable. I guess what I'm trying to say is, I'm not the best at having conversations with women."

"I appreciate that you're trying to explain yourself, but it's not about the conversation. It's about the fact that you always magically and randomly show up at the most unusual time and places. It's... weird." I said bluntly.

"I know but believe me when I say that I'm not following you."

I was speechless again.

"Say something," he prompted gently.

"I don't know what you want me to say. What is it exactly that you want from me?" I asked, genuinely curious and annoyed. I studied his face as he gathered his thoughts.

"Go on a date with me just once. That's all I ask, and after, you can decide if you want me. If you don't, I will leave you alone."

"The problem is, I want you to leave me alone now. Look, I'm flattered that you're interested in me, but I didn't come here to go on dates with men. I came to enjoy some time with my best friend." I swore I explained it to him earlier. Why was I repeating myself all over again?

I felt my patience dwindle.

"Don't you think I deserve a little gratitude for helping you when you fell?"

My eyes practically bulged out of my head. I couldn't believe the audacity and entitlement. I wondered if he heard himself and how ridiculous he sounded.

"This can't be happening," I said out loud.

Agitated, I pushed myself off the bench and walked in the opposite direction I came. I walked down another long corridor. The garden was like a maze. It irritated me greatly when I sensed his footsteps following behind. *Damn it!* I picked up my momentum, but his quick feet found themselves right at my side.

I halted my steps abruptly, looked at him, and said, "Can't you see that I just want to be left alone?"

"And I'm trying to make it better for you."

Adrian was delusional. Suddenly, his good looks weren't attractive anymore. I didn't care how sexy he was. His behavior was that of a pervert. Could he be a killer?

"Make it better for me? How? By showing up in random places and saying things, like, I owe you dinner because you saved my life? You wiped off a few drops of blood from my knee, which does not constitute saving someone's life. I do not know who you are. And who says things like, I'll make it better for you?!" I asked rapidly in his face. It inflamed me when his only response was to gaze at me, emotionless.

I blinked a few times in frustration.

"You know what? Never mind." I turned my back to him and bolted further into the maze.

It was a relief to know that he was no longer behind me, but now I feared that I had gotten lost in the maze. I kept walking and turning corners, hoping that I'd find an exit, but it was just another pathway. I tried to remain calm for the first few minutes, but after finding myself at a dead-end for the fourth time, I panicked on the inside. The dark clouds above me didn't help.

"Hello!" I yelled out, hoping that someone would hear my concerned voice.

No response.

I nearly tumbled down on my butt when I heard the first wave of unexpected thunder. I never liked the sound of thunder. It triggered vivid memories of the many nights my father beat and raped my mother. He was smart. It was easier to be loud and aggressive during a storm. He knew that even if she screamed until her lungs exploded, no one would hear her. My heart rate started increasing. My chest felt tighter with each second that passed by. It was getting harder to breathe. I picked up my pace, hoping an exit would magically appear. The sky turned darker the further I walked down the twisted pathways. I tilted my head up and saw more clouds forming, and I knew raindrops would soon pour down.

After another dead end, I turned around and walked back in the direction I came from, but I was more confused. Everything around me looked the same. I had no sense of direction anymore. *Shit!* A second wave of thunder exploded, and it was twice as loud. After that, my body froze, and my legs were stuck on the ground. I was paralyzed. Seconds later, I felt the first cold raindrop on my face, and then a cascade of bone-chilling raindrops fell from the sky. Everything around me turned blurry and all the sounds muffled together. The only thing I heard clearly in my head was the scream of my mother. The harder the rain fell, the more vivid the memories appeared in my head. I felt like a small and hopeless child all over again. The warmth of my tears falling on my face blended in with the sharp chill of the rain. I gradually fell flat on my butt, and the only thing I could think to do was place my head between my knees and cover my ears with my hands.

"Mom!" Eight-year-old me screamed. I ran out of my room and threw myself between her and his belt. My father doesn't care, as he continuously strikes me in the back and head until she pushes me away and angrily yells for me to go back to my room. "Go back to your room Alina!" Tears fell down her face. "Please!" She begs me. I listen, but not without hesitation.

"Alina?" a soft voice said.

I perked up and gazed at Adrian's delicate face. At first, I thought it was a hallucination. It wasn't clear that he was real until he knelt in front of me.

"Are you alright?" He saw the distressed look I had on my face.

I wanted to respond to his question, but I couldn't. Once he realized I couldn't bring myself to speak, he stopped inquiring further. Instead, he did what no one had done before and stayed with me. Such irony that minutes ago, all I wanted was for him to disappear, but now there was no other place I wanted him than at my side. He took my hands in his and the instant our skin touched; a sense of solace streamed through my body.

"It's alright. I'm here." He said and pulled my head into his chest. My body instinctively complied and didn't fight back. It had been years since I'd been close to a man. It was both safe and frightening.

CHAPTER FIVE

The never-ending rainfall finally came to a stop, and my body slowly regained consciousness and strength afterwards. I pulled my head away from his chest and gazed into his gentle eyes. He was still holding my hands. *What the hell just happened?* I asked myself. I unhurriedly forced myself onto my feet. Adrian followed behind. I pulled my hands away from his grip and said, "Thank you." I was relieved to find my lips working again.

"You're welcome," he answered back gently.

I caught his eyes traveling quickly from my chest to my face. I realized my white shirt was wet and see-through. Even though I had a nude-tone bra underneath, I still felt exposed. Instinctively, I folded my arms over my chest and covered the embarrassing sight. I felt my face burning red again.

"I'm sorry. I didn't mean to do that," he said apologetically.

The two of us stood uncomfortably still, like stone statues.

"I would say thank you, but I'm afraid of what is going to come out of your mouth if I do," I said truthfully, almost playfully.

"Don't worry. I won't pressure you. I know that certain things I said made you uneasy and I apologize for that. However, if it's not too late, I still really would like to get to know you better," he said with a glimmer of hope in his voice.

"Why is it so important to you?" I interrogated him.

"Because there's something familiar about you. I guess that's why I was saying things so hastily."

At that moment, Adrian had a boyish charm on his face, and it looked... almost adorable. If he hadn't soothed me down a few minutes ago, I'd have rejected him again. But I couldn't force out a "no" even if I wanted to. I also couldn't let out a "yes." *What's wrong with me sometimes?* So instead, I did what I usually do best and steered the conversation elsewhere.

"We should head back. Ana is probably freaking out right now," I suggested.

He frowned with disappointment. I felt terrible for ignoring his continuous pursuit, but what was I supposed to do? I barely knew the guy.

"Of course," he said.

Slowly and silently, we made our way out of the maze and back to the hotel. I battled internally whether I should say something, but even if I did, what would I say? Knowing myself, I'd probably say something stupid or something that made no sense. I concluded it was safer to wait for him to speak.

"Why didn't you try to run for shelter when it was raining?" He asked curiously.

Damn it! Not that question. I contemplated whether I should confide in him about the reasoning behind my non-functioning body during the rain. But that would mean diving into my childhood, which would mean talking about what happened with my family. There was no way in hell I'd let him know about my childhood traumas. So, once again, I avoided the question and changed the topic.

"I'll have dinner with you."

Hopefully, it was enough to divert his curiosity from my bizarre behavior earlier. My plan worked. Adrian displayed the brightest smile on his face. It twinkled radiantly like a child at a carnival ride or Disneyland. I didn't think it was possible, but his smile made me smile. It was irresistibly contagious. We conversed more about the trip during our continued stroll. The exchange felt normal and flowed more naturally. Frankly, I didn't exactly know how it happened.

I felt relieved when we finally exited the garden. I made a mental note never to explore the garden alone again. When we reached the hotel front entrance, a staff member in a black, vested suit rushed out and gracefully greeted Adrian. Of course, he was the son of the owner. The young man handed him and me fresh, dry white towels. Another young male staff member approached with a tray containing two glasses of champagne, and a bottle. Adrian grabbed the glasses and handed me one. I took it without hesitation. After what occurred, I needed a drink. Before he said a word, I downed the entire glass in one big gulp. He gaped at me with amazement. I placed the empty glass back on the tray and looked at him.

"What?" I asked.

He let out a small chuckle and said, "Nothing. I didn't expect that. But then again, you've been nothing but full of surprises since the moment I met you."

"I was thirsty," I said playfully.

An aggressively loud clicking against the white marble floor interrupted our brief, animated moment. Catalina, in a white body-con dress, approached us with the eyes of an angry predator. I almost forgot the two of them were connected somehow. She stopped in front of us and folded her arms across her chest. It was clear my presence displeased her. The feeling was mutual.

"Where the hell have you been?" She asked Adrian.

"I was outside," he said casually.

"Outside, while it was raining. You know I was worried sick," she said. Then her attention turned to me. "So, not only are you flaunting yourself with my boyfriend but also my little brother."

I didn't know why, but I felt a sense of relief to learn they were siblings. Things slowly started making sense.

"Are you deaf?" She asked rudely.

"Catalina, enough! When are you going to learn to watch your attitude? It's because of you we're here."

"Adrian, I know what you're doing. She's not *her*. So, you better stop with this crazy obsession before shit turns bad."

Her? Who was she referring to? I had a million questions rushing into my head.

"What are you talking about?"

"Nobody asked you to speak. So, shut your filthy mouth before I shut it for you," she warned.

"I said that's enough! Never talk to Alina like that again," he defended me with a firm voice.

I gazed at him in awe. I couldn't believe he defended me against his sister.

"Alina? You're on a first-name basis now?" She turned to me once again and said, "Wow, you are good. I should watch you more carefully. You're better than I thought."

"Alright, you're done. Let's go."

He attempted to grab her arm to drag her away, but she dodged his grip and instead came face-to-face with me. She was so close; I felt her warm breath against my skin and could almost feel the chills from her frozen heart.

"This isn't over." She snatched the champagne bottle on the tray, turned, and stomped back in the same direction she'd come from.

Adrian and I watched as she disappeared up the stairs. That was intense, for no reason. A tiny part of me wanted to know why she had so much anger toward me. I get that I'd spilled my drink on her *Gucci* swimsuit, but other than that, I had done nothing that would warrant such hatred.

"I'm sorry about her. She's just overprotective," he said and then continued, "I'll see you tonight at 7 pm, at the restaurant that you and your friends were at last night?"

I nodded my head.

"I look forward to our date."

I flashed him a half smile and said, "Thanks again for earlier," and strolled away. *Don't look back. Be cool and keep walking.*

It had been a few hours. Hopefully, Ana and Juan were finished with their… sexual activities. When I arrived in front of the room, I knocked instead of unlocking the door like before. Thankfully, she opened it and he was gone.

"Why are you soaking wet?" She examined me up and down with genuine curiosity in her eyes once I stepped inside. From the look on her face, I knew she was trying hard to think of reasons why I was drenched. After letting her struggle for a while, I felt awful and felt the need to explain.

"After leaving here so you and Juan can finish having sex, I walked around the resort and came across a beautiful flower garden in the courtyard. Its beauty mesmerized me and so I explored further. After a while, I got lost and then it started raining. The next thing I knew, the rain paralyzed me." I explained in one big breath.

She knew immediately and embraced me. "Oh no, the thunder. It brought back those memories, didn't it?" She asked as she gently caressed my back.

I pulled away and nodded my head, and shortly after, tears brimmed under my eyes. I knew the courageous face I had shown in front of Adrian would be torn down when I was safe with Ana. She hugged me in her arms once more. With her, I was completely vulnerable. She was the only person I truly trusted with some of my deepest and darkest secrets.

"Oh, sweetie. I'm so sorry. It was all my fault."

"No, it's not. You can't control the rain." I said playfully as tears rolled down my cheeks.

She walked me to the edge of the bed and sat me down. Ana vanished into the bathroom and came back with a towel. She draped it around my body and sat close to me. She didn't need to utter a word. Her presence alone brought me comfort.

"Why don't I run a warm bath for you?" she asked.

"That would be nice."

She marched into the bathroom again and started the water.

"Oh, by the way, I have a date with Adrian tonight."

Ana ferociously busted out of the bathroom and scrambled towards me. I thought she was going to trip on something and fall flat on her face.

"What! How and when did that happen?" she asked rapidly.

"He helped me when it was raining. Honestly, I don't know exactly how that came to be. One minute I wanted to get away from him, and the next, I agreed to go on a date with him. Things just kind of fell into place, I guess." I said, feeling the red flush on my face.

"You're kidding. He was in the rain with you? Oh, how romantic," she teased playfully.

"Should I be concerned that he could be a killer?" I asked her bluntly.

She chuckled and said, "Why would you think that?"

"Because it's strange how much attention he pays to me, for no reason. I mean, I've watched enough documentaries to know that sometimes killers stalk their prey. Some even strike up a conversation and form a relationship before kidnapping and killing them. So maybe that's his plan?"

Ana laughed and slumped down on the bed next to me. "Okay, first, I think it's because you haven't been with a man in so long that you forgot what it feels like to have someone show you attention. You're a beautiful woman. I'm sure he thought the same when he saw you. Trust me, I saw the way he looked at you by the pool. I guarantee you your beauty blew him away. Besides, he's too good-looking to be a killer."

I rested my back flat on the bed next to her. She had a point. It had been way too long since I shared the company of a man, or was intimately touched by one in the ways I secretly desired. Ever since I met him, my heart had been beating erratically, and a sense of longing had emerged.

"You know what? I think it's time for you to feel a man inside you again." Ana said frankly.

I propped myself up with my elbow and looked at her. Maybe she was right.

"Maybe tonight is your lucky night."

I picked up a pillow and threw it at her face. We both laughed.

"Now hop in the bathtub before the water gets cold," she pushed me up.

I undressed and slowly stepped into the bathtub. My skin felt soothed by the warm water. The bathroom light was dim, and the lavender candle provided a Zen environment. The last time I took a bath was a long time ago. I could undoubtedly fall asleep if I wanted to. I grabbed the white loofah on the small table by the tub and squeezed the lavender body washed onto it. I gently scrubbed my shoulders, arms, breasts, and stomach. I moved my way down to my sex and gently brushed against it. There was a slight tickling sensation that I had not felt in a while. I rested my head back comfortably and closed my eyes. Adrian's face instantly appeared once I shut my eyes. I imagined what it would feel like to have his handsome face between my legs. I wondered how his lips and tongue would feel against my sensitive area. The imagery was both appealing and terrifying. I'd never had a man's face between my legs before. I smiled to myself.

I remembered sweat dripping down his biceps and naked abs as he was jogging towards me on the beach. I tried to imagine what he would look like completely naked. My back arched at the thought of his manhood bulging from his pants. I drifted my right hand down between my legs. I slowly circled my index finger over my clitoris, rubbing gently. It had been years since I masturbated, the motion felt almost foreign. I slipped my middle finger inside and slid it in and out slowly. I pulled out my finger to caress my clit every couple of seconds. My toes naturally curled tightly at the motion. Because I hadn't pleasured myself in such a long time, it took less than a minute for me to climax. I kept as quiet as possible and let out a few moans to myself. I loved Ana, but I didn't want her to hear my cries of pleasure. I had forgotten what a stress reliever it was to come undone. *Wow!* I slowed my breathing once I finished and resumed my bath.

After remaining in the tub for another half hour, I stepped out and wrapped myself in a towel. I wandered out of the bathroom and saw an outfit laid on the bed for me. Ana proudly crouched next to it. I glanced at the bright-colored dress and then back at her. She had a naughty smirk on her face. Immediately, I knew I was about to become her muse.

"Really? Can't I just wear a black dress or something I don't know, not colorful?" I asked with a pout.

"Babe, you're going on a date with one of the sexiest men in the resort. I will not allow for a simple black dress. You will be lavish in this long, silky, fitted red gown and hot red heels. Trust me, when he sees you, he might have to take you from behind right at the table," she said and giggled.

The thought was both enticing and terrifying.

"Now sit down. I'm going to do your hair and makeup." She commanded, and I obeyed.

CHAPTER SIX

Two hours was the longest time I spent in one spot while being pampered for a date. My butt was numb, and it ached slightly. I was ecstatic when Ana said she was doing her final touches. My will to fight and stay awake dwindled every minute that passed by.

"Alright, just one more little section of your hair!" she exclaimed enthusiastically. Once it was finished to her liking, she yanked my hand, pulling me up to my feet. She covered my eyes with her hands and walked me to the mirror. "Open your eyes."

There was a feeling of excitement and nervousness stirring in the pit of my stomach. I slowly opened my eyes. I nearly fell back on my ass as I stared at the unfamiliar woman in the mirror. Who was that? I hardly recognized myself. *Makeup does wonders.* Somehow, she turned me into a whole different person while keeping it natural and soft. I had no clue how she did it. I was in awe of her work.

Ana took a few steps back to analyze her completed project. She almost teared up. "I don't know if I feel safe with you looking this sexy out in the world by yourself."

I twirled around and embraced her. "Thank you. I'm so glad I have you." I said and almost tearing up myself, but I knew it would ravage my makeup, so I composed myself.

"Alright, now let's get you into this dress."

We turned away from the mirror and approached the red dress, still resting flawlessly on the bed. As Ana went to grab the high heels from her luggage, I skimmed my fingers along the delicate, silky gown. Of course, Armani designed it. I should have expected that. I couldn't recall a time when she wasn't wearing anything that was not designer.

"Alright, let's do this," she said after positioning the fiery pumps on the bed.

As commanded, I dropped my towel onto the floor. Ana slipped the dress over my head, and it gently cascaded down my body, stopping at my ankles. The dress was tight on the top but loose on the bottom. It was seductive and elegant. I saw a glimpse of myself as she helped me step into the fiery red pumps. She went around the back and zipped up the dress, showcasing my curves, which I didn't think I had until that moment. The dress had a slit on the right side that went past my knee by a few inches. I was apprehensive at first, but the more I stared at myself, the more confident I became. At first glance, I was against the red color, but not anymore.

She took a few steps back to admire her completed masterpiece. Then, she grabbed her phone and went off snapping pictures.

"I'm going to cherish this moment for the rest of my life. My little caterpillar has finally grown wings." She said with a massive grin.

After all the time we spent getting me ready and appreciating my transformation, I realized I hadn't looked at the clock.

"Shoot, what time is it?" I asked.

She looked at her phone and said, "Relax, it's only 6:45. Here's the game plan. Have fun, get drunk, and get laid." She wasn't joking.

"I will try," I said, but with an unconfident smile. When she noticed my anxiety crept in, and my feet moved slowly, she gently nudged me out of the door. I appreciated the push.

"Have fun!" she said and shut the door.

I headed towards the restaurant. The sky had fully cleared up and the scorching heat returned. The bottom of my dress danced with the gentle breeze as I walked down the long corridor. I'd thought the situation would fill my whole body with anxiety, but I felt strangely calm. I realized that it was because there was no one around me. *That's weird. Where is everybody?* I halted my steps and looked around. It was eerily quiet. The only sound I heard was the ocean's waves crashing along the shore. I resumed my steps, but not without hesitation.

Once at the front door, the same hostess that greeted Ana and me yesterday welcomed me.

"Good evening, Miss Alina, this way, please." She said and led the way.

How does she know my name? I thought it was odd that no one was outside, but it was even more bizarre when I entered the restaurant. It was completely empty. The woman led me to the center of the restaurant where Adrian sat confidently in a dark gray suit, a white shirt peeking out from underneath. The only thing that made sense was how flawlessly handsome he looked. He stood up from his chair as I approached him.

"Wow," he said when I stopped in front of him.

He grabbed my hand and kissed the back of it with his soft, luscious lip. "You look stunning," he said and pulled out a chair for me to sit down.

"Thank you," I said, flattered.

A baby-faced waitress with blonde hair in a pixie cut approached the table with a bottle of champagne and two glasses on a tray. She shared striking similarities with Estella. I wondered if the two women were related.

"Good evening. My name is Maya, and I will serve the two of you tonight." She opened the champagne bottle and poured the smooth drink into the glasses. After she left, we raised our glasses and cheered to the beginning of, hopefully, a good night. I took a sip of champagne as she walked away.

I tried my hardest to concentrate on the date, but it was nearly impossible not to wonder why we were alone in the restaurant. I couldn't help but divert my attention occasionally.

"What's wrong?" He asked, after noticing my distraction.

"Why are we the only people here? What happened to the other tables and people?" I asked.

"I wanted tonight to be special between the two of us, so I had the staff clear out all the tables. There are three different restaurants in this resort. The staff instructed the other guests to choose one of those instead and I had this one shut down." He said casually.

I gazed in admiration. "Really?" I didn't want to believe it.

"Yes. I wanted this date to be more intimate and private."

"That's very thoughtful of you. Honestly, I don't know what to say exactly."

"There's nothing to say. The only thing I'm concerned with is that you feel comfortable. Besides, seeing how exquisite you look right now, I'm glad no other man is here to look at you."

"That's sweet of you. I hope this isn't too much," I said, looking down at my dress.

"You look perfect."

My cheeks flushed red. I'd never been complimented in that way. It was so strange to hear, especially from him.

"Thank you. I can't believe you did all of this for me."

"I'd do anything for you."

That caused an uneasy feeling to grow inside of me. Adrian hardly knew me, yet he was freely saying things that I imagined were meant for lovers.

"That's a strange thing to say to a woman you just met," I said bluntly.

"I agree. It's usually not my style, but somehow, I can't help it with you. I don't know how to explain it fully."

I sensed it in his tone. He, too, wasn't exactly sure what he was doing. I grabbed my glass of champagne and drank half of it. If I wanted to survive the entire date, I needed more alcohol.

A few moments later, servers filled our table with food. The assortment of seafood overwhelmed me. I loved seafood, and if I wasn't on such a lovely date, I would have devoured everything already. But to avoid embarrassing myself, I remained prim and proper. *Adrian will never find out that I can eat like a truck driver.* I'd thought all the food was out, but another server arrived shortly after and set down a plate of steak and asparagus in front of me. *Um, what? Asparagus? How does he know that it's one of my favorite vegetables?*

I was flabbergasted and slightly paranoid. Maybe I was overreacting. I picked up my silverware and gently nudged on the steak.

"So, tell me about yourself, Alina."

I rolled my eyes in my head. He asked one of the most dreaded questions that ended most dates I had with guys in the past. I always found out the hard way that most of them never really care to know about my life, but more about what I could give them after when we were alone. I kept hoping that I'd find my Prince Charming, but they all ended up being Gaston from *Beauty and the Beast*. After a few years of repeated failure, I gave up.

I placed the silverware on the table. There was a hesitation in my response, but I knew eventually I had to say something. "Well, what do you want to know?" I found that more manageable than flooding him with my uninteresting life story.

"You can be easy to read, well, at least sometimes. Did that question bother you?"

"If I'm honest, that question usually ends a lot of my dates with men. I guess my life stories aren't of much interest to many of them. It's usually easier to just let them talk about themselves."

"Then they are fools to let someone as beautiful as you go."

Indeed, Adrian was an experienced womanizer. Every word that came out of his mouth had been nothing but delightful and sweet. I nearly forgot that I thought he could be a killer just a few hours ago.

"I guess my life hasn't been the most... exciting. Truthfully, this trip is probably in the top two most exciting things I've done in my life."

"Really? What's the other one?"

"Skydiving with Ana, but trust me, it took her at least five years to convince me to do it."

I felt more and more pathetic after each sentence. I refrained from making eye contact as much as possible. When I mustered up the courage to look him in the eye, I'd expected an uninterested expression, but I saw a hint of captivation on his face. *That's new.*

"I've done a lot of things in my life but never skydiving. You are certainly braver than me. Perhaps one day we can do it together." He said, hopefully.

There were many things that I wasn't certain of in life, but I was sure that I'd never go skydiving again. There was no way in hell I'd let him see my explosive scream. Ana took a picture of my face on that day, and it wasn't pleasant or attractive.

"And what about you?"

He consumed his champagne. "What do you want to know?"

"You said your father owns the resort?"

"Yes, that is correct."

"So, what does that make you?"

"Well, right now, my older brother is in line to take control of this place and many more when my father, well... retires or passes away. I only help when needed."

"You have a brother?"

"Yes, but I rarely talk about him. He likes his business to be private."

"And Catalina?"

"My father tried to get her to handle some of the business, but she is more of a free-spirited person. She doesn't see herself taking on such a tremendous responsibility. Plus, she likes to defy our father."

Catalina, defiant? I can see that.

"Do you have any siblings?"

"I don't, but I consider Ana my sister."

"Ah yes her. She seems more...,"

"Outgoing?" I interrupted.

He let out a gentle laugh, "No, more... loud."

He attempted to hide, perhaps thinking I'd be offended, but he wasn't wrong. Ana can be obnoxious. She was undoubtedly the Ying to my Yang.

"She's... I guess like how you describe your sister, a free-spirited person. She likes to do things on her own."

"You two are very different," he asserted.

58

"Is it that obvious?" I asked painfully.

"Too obvious. But I like your innocence. It's something that I need more of in my life."

I'm not even going to ask what he meant by that.

The only thing I wanted to focus on was the fact that I had a natural conversation with a man, and I was barely tipsy. *You got this!* My worries slowly faded away. As the date continued, I became more comfortable in my skin, which was a rare phenomenon. The night couldn't be more perfect. I felt like I was having a romantic dinner in a movie; to think I used to laugh at how cheesy a movie was having a scene like that, but the joke was on me because I was there.

"So, what brought you to Mexico?"

"Ana. She had been begging me to take a vacation with her. I fought off the idea for a while, but eventually I lost. It was too hard to say no to her."

"Well, I guess I have Ana to thank then." He said with a smile.

I finished my third glass of champagne and immediately the room felt lighter, as did my head.

"I'm curious. How many girls have you taken out to dinner already?" Intoxicated me had no filter sometimes.

"I would be lying if I said none. There have been a few here and there."

I poured myself a fourth glass from the freshly opened champagne bottle. I was eager to hear the rest of his answer.

"A few here and there?"

"Nothing serious. It's usually just dinner and some other stuff," he said, guarded.

"Other stuff?" I probed. I didn't recognize this side of myself. Why was I so engulfed in his personal life?

"You got me. I should have said casual sex. Is that better?" He asked, almost as if my opinions would mean something.

I was genuinely surprised that my annoyance proved effective.

"Were any of the women… serious?"

Adrian refilled his glass and drank a decent amount before answering. "I've never had any serious relationship. Truthfully, I haven't found anyone that I've connected with."

"So, you've never been in love?" I was nosy.

"Maybe once, a long time ago."

"What happened?"

"She… left," his tone became even more guarded.

His face transitioned from tender to tense. I wondered if it was appropriate to proceed with my curiosity.

"I'm sorry. I didn't mean to pry."

I felt guilty.

"No need to apologize. But it's only fair if I ask you the same thing. Have you ever been in love?"

Great. Thank God for the alcohol.

"No, I've never been in love."

He raised his glass and said, "Well then, cheers to us for having something in common."

I smiled, picked up my glass, and clinked with his. Honestly, I wasn't sure if that was a good toast or a pathetic one. The more we talked, the more I realized Adrian and I were more similar than I thought. The major difference was that he had way more sex than I could ever dream of. It surprised me how open he was about his sex life. I'd thought men would be more cautious with that type of conversation.

I nearly choked on my spit when he asked if I ever had a boyfriend. The only unpleasant recollection of having a boyfriend was back in my junior year of high school. His name was Ryan. There were many names I could give him, but the simplest one was asshole. It explained why we were only together for three months. I lost my virginity to him, and I've regretted it ever since. There was a moment in high school when all I wanted was to fit in with the others. Ryan told me part of fitting in was having sex. I was so desperate that I listened. Just the memory alone was enough to make my skin crawl. I should have listened to Ana. She had warned me about him, but I was too stubborn. I still scolded myself for being so stupid.

"Is everything alright?" Adrian asked.

"Yes. I'm sorry. I was just thinking about something."

"What were you thinking about?" He asked, mystified.

"Nothing of importance." I looked down at my knotted fingers on the table. "I know, I'm pathetic."

He grabbed my hand and locked his eyes with mine. "I can't say that I'm upset that you've never had a boyfriend. I'm happy that you didn't. I wouldn't know how to feel if you did." There was a sense of relief in his voice.

I'd misjudged him and I felt like the biggest jerk.

"I'm curious, why me?" A burning question that I'd wanted to ask him all night.

He released his grip and finished his fifth glass of champagne by my count.

"You instantly captivated me when we first met. You have the most beautiful, soft brown eyes. And I love women with black hair. You are perfect."

"Perfect? That's a big compliment. Nobody is perfect." I flushed.

"But you are. That night I couldn't sleep. All I could think about was you, which has never happened to me before. I knew then that I had to know you." His explanation was soft and polished. It was like he had rehearsed it in the mirror before coming tonight.

It moved me. "So, what would have happened if I didn't agree to this date?"

"I don't even want to think about that. I know my approach hasn't been the gentlest, but I'm glad you still gave me a chance."

The two of us smiled at each other like two teenagers instead of the adults we were. The flawlessly prepared words, his perfectly fitting suit, and five glasses of champagne later, my sexual desire slowly emerged. I imagined what it would be like to fuck him on the table, and the thought made my legs tighten underneath the table involuntarily. The idea of his cock inside me kept invading my thoughts. *Damn, Alina! You will not sleep with this man, not on the first date.* I inhaled and exhaled, a few subtle deep breaths to suppress my hormones.

Heavy footsteps interrupted our wonderful little bubble. I turned my head and saw an enormous bald man in a black suit approaching us. He headed straight for Adrian. When he was close enough, a scar stretching from his ear to his nose on the left side of his face was visible. I tried to not stare at it for too long. He bent down and whispered into Adrian's ear. Once the man finished whatever secrets he spilled, I saw a new expression in his eyes. It was fear.

"Is everything alright?"

He stood up from his chair. "Yes, everything is fine. I need to take care of something. Stay here. I will be back momentarily." He left with the man in a hurry.

It left me bewildered. I sat patiently for the first few minutes. Surely, whatever he had to do was important, I reminded myself.

I looked at the front entrance for the fourth time, or maybe the sixth time. I lost count; the amount of champagne I'd had left my brain fuzzy. Adrian was nowhere in sight. My anger rose, and after convincing myself that he wasn't returning, I pushed myself away from the table, heading for the door. I aggressively stomped my red pumps on the floor as I walked away. *Screw this shit!* I abruptly stopped, took the heels off, and held them in my hand as I exited the restaurant.

As I turned the corner heading back to our room, I bumped into a tall, strongly built, black-haired man. His chest was so solid that it knocked me back a few steps. I tilted my head up and locked eyes with the stranger. His eyes were as dark as the night sky. I couldn't believe I managed to stay on my feet with that much alcohol in my body. The stranger said nothing. He only glared at me so fiercely, I thought it would burn a hole between my eyes. There was a hint of danger behind them. I was frightened because he had the same predatory look as my father had. It was uncanny.

"I'm sorry." I heard myself say under my breath.

Why did I say that? *Stupid, stupid.* I apologized too damn much. To leave the uncomfortable encounter, I made my way around him and walked away. Miraculously, I convinced myself not to look back at the mysterious man, but even though I wasn't looking, I sensed he was watching my every move. Perhaps the trip was a mistake after all. I knew I shouldn't have left my safe little city back home.

CHAPTER SEVEN

"Come on, Alina, get up." Ana struggled to pluck me out of bed. "It's already past noon. You can't stay in bed forever." She said for the third time as she yanked the blanket from my head and collapsed on the bed next to me. "Look, I'm sorry that motherfucker left you in the middle of your date, but don't let him ruin our vacation. We came here to have fun, remember?"

She was right. I came on this vacation to have a good time with her. I certainly didn't travel four hours to sulk in bed because some asshole manipulated me. I propped myself up on my elbow and turned to look at her. "You're right. I'm sorry. I will get my ass out of bed right now and get dressed."

"No need for clothes. I've got your bikini all set. Let's go to the beach!" She said and cheerfully hopped off the bed to change.

It was a radiant day, the complete opposite of yesterday. The sun helped brighten my depressing mood as we headed toward the beach. My best friend walked with elegance and confidence while I was behind her, trying to conceal myself from the world. How was it that I felt confident for a few hours and then had it all fallen apart in less than thirty minutes? I missed the confidence I'd had during my date with Adrian; it was freeing. Maybe I was meant to stay in the shadows forever. Ana turned, grabbed my hand, and forced me to walk beside her. She wasn't playing games with me as we stepped into the sand. She scanned around for empty beach chairs, and as soon as she found one, we made our way to it and settled in. Five minutes barely passed by when Juan came running towards us and snatched Ana up from behind. They hugged and kissed passionately. *For real, Ana?* I thought to myself, slightly bothered.

"What's up, Alina?" he said to me.

"Hey. It's good to see you again." I lied.

I had nothing against him, but whenever he was around, it was no longer "Ana and Alina time." I hadn't figured out how to tell her yet, and frankly I wasn't sure that I would. She was content, what more could I ask for? I watched with disapproval as he sat down on the other chair next to us.

"It's a beautiful day. How's vacation going so far?" he asked and then pulled Ana onto his lap and wrapped his arms around her waist.

"It's been... good," I responded.

Actually, it's been very shitty. I just went on a date, and he left without an explanation. And now I feel shitty about myself, and that I was right all along. No one wants me. That was the truth, but of course, I didn't intend to bore him with my pathetic sobbed story.

"I'm glad you're having a good time," he said, oblivious to the truth.

"Where's Jason?" Ana asked.

"With his girlfriend, Catalina. She's crazy. I have never met anyone so rude and obnoxious. She came over last night and kicked me out of my room."

Anna turned and gaped at him. "And you left?"

"Well yeah. She said if I didn't, she'd suck his dick right in front of me. I wasn't going to stay and watch."

"Wow. That's some crazy shit," Ana said.

She was astounded, but I wasn't. I wholeheartedly believed she'd have done it too if he had stayed.

"So, how was your date with her brother last night?" He inquired.

My whole body stiffened right away, and I looked at him, puzzled. "H-How do you know I went on a date with him?"

"She came into the room, pissed. It infuriated her that he went out with you. She said a lot of nasty things about you. I'm not sure I can even repeat them."

"Well, she can kiss our asses. We didn't come on vacation to be stressed out. We came to have a good time," Ana chimed in and then continued, "Let's just go in the water."

I knew she purposely changed the topic so I wouldn't have to answer his question. It was much appreciated. She stood up and grabbed Juan's hand, and she attempted to take mine, but I declined. I needed to unwind for a few minutes first. She frowned but agreed to leave me be. I watched as the two of them jogged toward the ocean and plunged into the waves. I laid back down on the chair and bathed in the sun. Less than five seconds after shutting my eyes, a shadowy figure stood above me. I opened my eyes to a dreadful presence.

"Adrian."

"Alina, I'm sorry about last night. Please, believe me, I didn't mean to leave you. Just let me explain," he pleaded.

I lifted myself up and with a bitter expression said, "I don't care about your explanation. I'm over it. Now, if you can please leave, I would like to enjoy my day." I plopped back down on the chair. Instead of leaving, he sat down on the chair next to me.

Unbelievable.

"My brother came to visit last night," he started.

I sighed. Apparently, my message wasn't clear enough for him. I closed my eyes once again and tried my best to ignore his presence.

"My brother is very protective of us. Well, I should say he is very protective of Catalina. He got word that she was messing around with Jason and he immediately made his way here. She should have known about the consequences of messing around with men."

Suddenly it enthralled me, and I opened my eyes. "What consequences?"

"My brother isn't fond of any men getting close to our sister. He can't stand any man touching her."

I looked at him quizzically. "So, your brother is in love with your sister?"

He laughed and ran his hand through his hair. "Of course not. My brother fears she would leave him and the family if she found someone. I've learned not to question his intentions anymore."

"So, he came all the way here, from wherever he was, just to check on her? Perhaps a little obsessive, don't you think?"

Adrian laughed and said, "I like it when you're honest. It's sexy."

I didn't acknowledge his compliment and instead remained apathetic and unbothered. The reason wasn't enough to justify why he abruptly left.

"But please, accept my apology," he appealed with desperation.

"What I don't understand is why you didn't come back. I waited. You have staff, right?"

He nodded.

"Okay, so why couldn't you send one of them to let me know what was going on?"

"I tried, but my brother… had other intentions." He said and restrained himself from saying more.

Ana trotted back with Juan behind her. "What the hell are you doing here?" She was not pleased to see him.

"Good to see you too, Ana," he said, undisturbed by her irritation.

"You need to leave, now. I don't know what fucked up family raised you, but in my family, men don't desert their stunning dates." Ana was never one to hold herself back. Another praiseworthy quality I admired and wished I possessed.

Adrian, unbothered by her rudeness, remained dormant in the chair. He looked too comfortable, which only infuriated her more. I could see invisible steam blowing out of her ears. Angry Ana was not pleasant. To avoid further confrontation, I stood up, grabbed her hand, and yanked her away. Juan followed behind.

"I cannot believe that bastard." She said as we walked away.

Juan found another area, far away from Adrian and other people. Ana, aggravated, sat down on the chair. He sat down next to her and gently stroked her back.

"It's alright, baby. Don't let that prick ruin your day."

"What did he say to you?" She inquired as soon as I settled down.

"He said his older brother showed up last night and that was why he left."

"That was his excuse? Wow, what an ass. What does his brother have to do with him leaving the date?"

"I'm not sure. But he said it was to check up on Catalina. I don't know. It's just all a headache. Forget about it. It's all over now."

"So, what's the deal with Jason and that girl?" Ana turned her attention to Juan.

"We got here a week and a half ago, and he ran into her on the first day we arrived. They hit it off right away and have been hanging out since then. Honestly, I'm not sure what exactly she has on him. I've known Jason for a long time and he's not the type to stay with just one girl, especially on vacation." He explained.

"Are you sure she's not holding him captive?" she asked.

"Who knows? But he seems smitten with her, at least sometimes."

"Is she hot?" she asked him straight.

I examined his face as he considered an appropriate answer. It intrigued me to hear what he had to say.

"I mean, she's not ugly. But you're way hotter than her."

Ana had a satisfied grin on her face. *Nicely done Juan*, I thought to myself.

"I think we all need a drink." He said, then stood up and left.

"I'm sorry you had to run into him," she said after a few moments of silence.

"It's alright. Let's just try to enjoy our time together."

"Trust me. If he moves his ass over here, I will knee him in the fucking nuts." She had a devious smile on her face. I knew she wasn't fooling around.

"I love you so much," I said with a smile.

She grabbed my hand and said, "I know."

Juan returned shortly after, and we raised our drinks, toasting to another day. The moment we spent together, he talked about his family and life. The more he spoke, the more I realized he was a perfect match for her. They were both strong-minded and loyal. Though, I wondered what it would be like if they ever got into an argument. Ana was never one to back down in a fight, and she always had her way.

An hour passed, and I'd had enough of the sun. "Well, I'm going to head back and change for dinner."

"Juan and I are going to stay a little longer, but I'll see you in the room, okay?"

"Sounds like a plan." I stood up, gave her a soft kiss on the cheek, and made my way back.

I was relieved that I made it to the pool without running into Adrian. Perhaps he finally got the message. Even though I was glad I didn't have to see him again, the abundance of people around me did not comfort me as I cautiously strolled back. As I walked along the side of the pool, a familiar face squatting under the black metal gazebo caught my eye. The closer I got, the more I recognized it was the mysterious man I'd bumped into last night. While everyone was in a swimsuit, he was in black pants and a loose, unbuttoned white shirt. Surrounding him was a crowd of stunning women in tight, revealing bikinis. One of them with short brown hair fed him grapes like he was a king. As if that wasn't strange enough, there were three men in black suits and sunglasses standing guard. If I didn't know any better, I'd have thought they were secret service agents. All three of them stood still, hard as stones. I dreaded every step I took. I wished there was another way to go around them, but there wasn't.

The man had silky short black hair and his dark eyes were bright under the shade. He had light, neatly trimmed facial hair and a perfectly fit body. Even from afar, he looked like a Greek God. I'd thought Adrian was the most beautiful man I'd ever seen, but he was nowhere near this man's level. *Alright, enough starring.* Fortunately, God heard my prayer, and the man didn't notice me creepily gawking at him. I breathed out a sigh of relief.

"Alina!" a familiar voice called after me.

I halted my steps and turned around. "Hi, Jason." When he was near, I noticed a bruise on his right eye.

"I'm so glad I saw you."

"Um, what happened to your eye?" I couldn't focus on anything other than the black and blue color on his face.

"It's, uh... a long story. But don't worry about it," he said, avoiding the question.

I stared at him with uncertainty, knowing there was more to it than what he told me. It didn't take a genius to see that he was hiding something.

"What do you mean, don't worry about it? You have a black eye." I pointed it out candidly.

"Trust me. It's nothing. I slipped last night in the bathroom and hit my face against the sink."

"Really? You slipped?"

"Yeah, people slip all the time. It's not a big deal." He said and turned his head to look around for something, or someone. He wasn't his normal self.

"Is everything alright?" I felt my stomach twist and turn slightly on the inside.

"Yes. Yes, everything is fine. I'm just glad I saw you. At least so that I can say goodbye before leaving."

"Leaving? Where? Back to the States?"

He nodded.

"Is Juan leaving too?"

"No, j-just me." He turned to look around once again.

"Are you sure everything is fine? I mean, you don't look alright. Are you looking for someone?"

"Oh no, I'm not looking for anyone."

"Are you looking for your girlfriend?"

"That's kind of over now. Uh, she left me last night." I couldn't tell if he was relieved or upset in his tone. It sounded like he was struggling internally to figure out how he felt.

"I'm sorry to hear that. What happened?"

"I'm not exactly sure how to explain it, but her older brother showed up last night, and after that, she just... left."

His explanation was a firm confirmation he was concealing information. A black eye didn't just magically appear on his face for no reason.

"It was nice meeting you and Ana. I wish we had more time together," he said and stepped in for an awkward hug.

I hardly had time to wrap my arms around his body before I heard a deep voice mumble something behind me. We separated, and I turned around to see the mysterious man, followed by his circus of women and bodyguards. He stood gracefully with both hands shoved in his pants pockets. His presence exuded dominance, power, and danger. He trailed his eyes along my entire body and then peered intensely into my eyes. I couldn't decide whether he was intrigued or disgusted. I wanted to leave at once, but that would mean battling my way through his army. His glare sent an unfamiliar chill down my spine. I'd been in many uncomfortable situations throughout my life, but never once like I did standing in front of him. I couldn't explain it. After what felt like a never-ending staring contest, he shifted his eyes and turned them to Jason.

"I thought I told you to leave," he said dryly.

I peeked at Jason briefly, and he was a nervous wreck. There was fear in his eyes at the sight of the man.

"I was uh... I just needed to say goodbye to my friends. That's all," he answered back nervously.

The man, dissatisfied, took a few steps closer to him and said, "I don't think you understood what I said last night. Do we need to discuss it again?"

"I'm sorry," he said and shrieked like a small child that was caught doing something he wasn't supposed to do.

Within a split second, one of his men launched forward and grabbed Jason around the neck. The incident occurred so quickly my brain couldn't comprehend what was happening in front of me. The man picked Jason up and tossed him to the ground like he was a bag of trash. Jason struggled to gasp for air as his hands tightly wrapped around his neck. I watched in anguish at the horror unfolding in front of me. I glanced around, confident that someone would jump in to help, but no one did. They all remained quiet and acted as if nothing was happening. What was wrong with people?

With little thinking, I took matters into my own hands and shove the man away. His body barely moved. *Oh, fuck it!* I jumped on his back and dug my teeth into his shoulder aggressively. He wailed, released his hands from Jason's neck, and knocked me off his back. I fell to the ground, but I lifted myself back up immediately. His wrath shifted to me and there was nothing but rage in his eyes.

"You little bitch!" He shouted and struck me across the face.

I flew into the deep end of the pool and an immediate panic surged through my body as I sank. There were many things that I couldn't do in life, and swimming was one of them. I screamed in distress underwater. It petrified me that I couldn't even hear myself. I flailed my arms around, hoping that it would somehow force my body back up, but it only made my body sink faster.

As soon as my feet touched the bottom, I pushed myself up and broke the surface. The half breath of oxygen that entered my lungs felt like a miracle. That ended quickly, and my body went back down. I looked up, and all I saw was a shadowy figure staring down. The figure stood still and calm as it watched me battle to survive.

Just let go. A soothing voice said. Maybe the voice was right. I would no longer suffer from the nightmares and other misery in my life. *You'll be free.* The voice said again. The mere thought of no longer suffering was comforting. So, I stopped fighting. I closed my eyes and allowed myself to sink. *No more pain.* I smiled to myself.

I'd thought an angel touched me when I felt a hand on my shoulder, dragging me from the pool. I gasped for air as soon as my head emerged. Even though seconds ago all I wanted was to let go, I'd never thought I was so glad to breathe in my life. Everything was hazy, and I had no clue what had just happened. Suddenly, two muscular arms wrapped under my arms, bringing me up to the side of the pool. I peeked my head up and looked through my blurry vision.

"Adrian?"

He looked so worried. He cupped my face with both of his hand and frantically asked, "Alina, are you alright!?"

Jason scrambled to my side soon after. Where was he when I nearly drowned?

"I-I'm fine. I can't, I can't swim," I said weakly.

"Yeah, no shit!" Adrian exclaimed. He pulled my head into his chest and sighed a huge breath of relief and then continued, "I'm so glad you're okay."

The two men helped me to my feet, and I was face to face with the man who had shoved me. He had a despicable smile as he stood in front of me. I wanted to punch the smirk off his stupid, pretty face. My blood boiled as I scanned my surroundings once more. Despite what transpired, nobody seems to care. This was so weird.

"Leave her, little brother," the man commanded.

Adrian promptly removed his hand from my arm and stepped away from me. I turned and stared at him, perplexed. Just a few seconds ago, he was all concerned about my life and then suddenly it vanished because his brother told him to step away from me. My head was spinning like crazy. Adrian, who I'd thought may be a killer only yesterday, was now nothing more than a scared little brother. I turned and looked at Jason. He, too, strode away from me. I was alone, but weirdly enough, the feeling was familiar, so I embraced it.

"Alina!" Ana's chirpy voice called from the crowd. As soon as I saw her bolting in our direction, a slight sense of relief coursed through my body. She jabbed at anyone in her way and hurried to the pool. Within seconds, she was at my side.

"What happened!?" she asked hysterically.

I wanted to explain everything, but my energy had disappeared, leaving me unable to open my mouth to tell her. My lips were not moving, and the only muscles I had control of were my eyes, and they hadn't shifted away from the monster in front of me. A small part of me knew opening my mouth was probably not a good idea. They were dangerous people, that much was obvious. Besides, if Ana knew the truth, she would try to kill the bastard. Thankfully, my rational brain took control. I grabbed her hand and led us through the crowd, away from them. I was stunned she obeyed and followed behind without hesitation. Tears rolled down my face and I couldn't escape fast enough.

CHAPTER EIGHT

"Tell me what happened!" she demanded as soon as she slammed the door behind her.

I didn't respond. Instead, I ripped the wet clothes off my body and angrily flung them to the floor. I slipped on black shorts and a white T-shirt. She was watching me like a hawk. I hunched down at the edge of the bed and remained still for a few seconds.

"Hello?" Ana said, frustrated at my silence.

She shifted toward the bed and sat down next to me. When she saw a red mark on my face, she nearly twisted her ankle. She bent back down, grabbed my face, and examined me. I knew she wanted confirmation that she was not hallucinating the mark on my face.

"Did someone fucking hit you!?" she asked, furious.

I laid my head on her chest and wept uncontrollably. She clutched me tightly in her arms, gently stroking my back, and allowed me to let my sorrow consume me. After a few minutes of tears, I was ready to speak. She waited patiently as I pulled my head away from her chest and wiped away my tears.

"That guy you saw at the pool. Well, apparently, he's Adrian's older brother. One of his men choked Jason, and nobody did anything to help him, so I jumped on his back and bit him. He slapped me and knocked me into the pool."

She leaped out of bed, frantic, and paced back and forth. "That motherfucker! Why didn't you tell me right then?" She asked angrily.

"I wanted to, but I couldn't. My lips wouldn't move. Plus, I didn't want anything else to happen." More tears rolled down my face as I explained.

"That doesn't matter. He fucking hit you! We should report this to the hotel staff." She proposed.

I chuckled at her suggestion. If no one bothered to do anything when a man got choked and a woman nearly drowned, there was no way the hotel staff would take action. And besides, they owned the resort. But I guess she didn't know that.

"What's funny?"

"They own this place," I finally revealed.

She was speechless, which was a rare phenomenon for her. I faced the horrible realization that they would face no consequences for their actions.

"Still, we have to do something," she suggested again, but with less confidence.

"Like what?" I asked, wary.

"I don't know. Punch him in the face, kick him in the balls? Something. I can't just sit here and do nothing. You almost died, for fuck's sake." She reminded me.

"I don't think it's going to be that easy, if it's even possible."

"Well, I don't care. I'm going to figure something out. By the way, how did you get out of the pool?"

"Adrian saved me."

She looked at me with confounded eyes. Ana made her way to my side and sat down on the bed.

"I don't understand."

I took a massive breath and said, "Catalina and Adrian are siblings. That guy by the pool is their older brother. He came to the resort because Catalina was messing around with Jason. I'm pretty sure they beat him up last night and ordered him to leave. He has a black eye. I'm surprised Juan didn't tell us about any of this."

"He wasn't with him last night. He said Jason spent the night in her room. I'm guessing that was likely when the creepy brother came."

"Can we please go home?" I begged.

I was more than ready to go back and be in my tiny and safe apartment. Ana grabbed my hand and lightly tugged my hair behind my ear.

"Alright. If that makes you happy," she said and embraced me once again.

"Thank you," I said and kissed her shoulder.

****

Ana was nowhere to be seen when I opened my eyes. I didn't realize I fell asleep. I pushed myself up straight and cleared my blurry vision. Before I got out of bed, I looked around the room.

"Ana?" I called out. The bathroom was empty. I came back out and sat on her bed and fortunately, she'd left me a note. I grabbed the letter and read it.

Alina, don't worry about me. I'm with Juan.
P.S. Let's have dinner one last time to end the trip. Love you.

I loosened up. At least I knew where she was this time. I mistakenly sniffed my armpit and realized I needed a shower. I took off to the bathroom, stripped out of my clothes, turned on the showerhead, and hopped in.

Fifteen minutes later, I got out and dried my hair with a towel. Afterward, I wrapped the towel around my body and walked out of the bathroom to get ready. I looked at my phone on the bed, and it was a quarter past six in the evening. I grabbed an outfit out of my suitcase to change into.

The door suddenly swung open after I zipped up my black, high-waisted skinny jeans, startling me. Ana marched in, disheveled. She rapidly locked the door behind her and turned to me with her back pressed against the door.

"Are you alright?" I asked as she took off her sneakers and hurled them onto the floor. She said nothing. Right away, I knew she'd done something.

"Ana, what did you do?" I asked and quickly threw on my black T-shirt.

She remained quiet and avoided eye contact. That was a second confirmation: she was guilty of something.

"Ana Maria Davis, tell me what happened." I insisted with a stern voice.

She wandered toward my bed and sat on the edge.

"Remember when we were sixteen, and I told you I would always protect you?"

"Yeah?"

"I couldn't stand knowing that you got hurt and nearly died today. When you fell asleep, I left. I ran into Jason before he took off and he helped me identify the man that hit you. I waited and followed him to the bathroom and when he came back out, I kind of..." she hesitated.

I glared at her. "You what?"

She peered at me with guilt behind her eyes. "I punched him in the face and then ran like hell." She said and concealed her face with both her hands.

I practically collapsed onto the floor on the inside. My eyes went so large I'd thought they were going to fall out of the sockets. I loved her dearly, but occasionally I wanted to strangle her.

"Oh my gosh, Ana!"

Was her behavior that surprising? Truthfully, it wasn't. She used to fight a ton when we were in school. And most of the fights occurred because she was protecting me from bullies. I hadn't forgotten all she did for me, but that was when we were teenagers. We were no longer in school anymore. The situation was not equivalent to being bullied in school. Those men were not regular bullies. They were powerful, dangerous people.

I paced back and forth in frustration. I couldn't even think of what to do. She had made us into walking targets. I blamed myself for falling asleep. I should have known Ana wouldn't let something like that go easily. I wished sometimes she'd think before she acted. I had a sick feeling swirling in the pit of my stomach, and I didn't like it. Something was coming for us.

"Why would you do that?" I chastised her.

"Because he hurt you. You know how that makes me feel," she tried to justify herself.

"I know, I know, but we aren't in high school anymore. Did you not see them? People pretended like nothing was happening. I love you very much, Ana, but sometimes you don't use your brain." I ran my hand through my hair.

My weariness was exacerbated with every second that passed. She looked down at her knotted fingers in shame. Immediately, I felt awful that I raised my voice at her. She only did what she thought was right to defend me. She stood up and slowly walked toward me and opened her arms wide for an "I'm sorry" hug. My brief disgruntled burst deteriorated as soon as she did that. All I could do was sigh a breath of relief that she struck the big man and somehow survived.

"Can you forgive me?" She asked softly.

I stepped into her hug and kissed the side of her head and said, "Of course. You know I can never stay mad at you."

An unexpected knock at the door stunned both of us. Ana and I separated from our embrace and stared at each other, terrified at who might be out there.

"Do you think it's one of them?" I asked her.

"I don't know," she whispered. She headed for the door and looked through the peephole. Then, she turned to look at me and whispered, "It's Adrian."

I wanted to see him and hear what he had to say, but a part of me screamed to run as far away from him as possible. After a few seconds of debating, I signaled with a head nod for her to open the door. My need for an answer won the battle.

"Alina," he said as soon as the door opened and then politely asked, "May I come in?"

I nodded my head, and he stepped inside. Ana looked out of the room to ensure no one else was around and shut the door behind him.

"I came to apologize for my brother's behavior," he began.

"You think that's enough?" Ana asked with her arms folded across her chest. "My best friend and Jason nearly died, and you think everything will be okay after you show up here and apologize for his behavior?"

I allowed her to take charge, but mainly because I didn't know exactly what to say to him. There was a lot of turmoil inside of me that I couldn't put into coherent words. Adrian, being himself, completely ignored her. Instead, his eyes were fixed on mine.

"I know it's not enough, but I needed to say it anyway."

"I don't care about your apology. Thank you for saving my life, but it changes nothing." I said coldly. I saw a quick glimmer of pride in my best friend's eyes.

"If it makes you feel better, I came not only here to apologize for his behavior, but to say goodbye. I figure you'll be happy to know that my family and I are leaving. You won't be bothered anymore."

I was relieved to hear those words. Finally, perhaps, Ana and I could continue the remaining four days of our vacation after all.

"Good to know. You can leave now," she commanded without mercy.

He turned to walk away, but not without turning his head to lock his eyes with mine one last time. Truthfully, I was slightly sad that I would never see him again, but I also knew that was for the best. Once he was gone and the door shut, she rushed to hug me.

"How do you feel?" she asked as she rubbed my arms up and down.

"I feel so much better now knowing that they're gone. So, I think I'll be okay to stay for the rest of the time here."

"Are you sure? Because I am okay with leaving, too. You know I just want you to be happy."

"No, I'll be okay. Besides, what's going to stop us from actually enjoying ourselves now?" I said with a smile.

"You are the best," she kissed my cheek.

CHAPTER NINE

Over an hour passed, and Ana and I were still in bed, talking and laughing about random stuff that made little sense. Soon, Mr. Davis called to check in on us. It was refreshing to hear his voice. Of course, being a father, he was telling us everything we needed to do to ensure our safety for the rest of the trip. I bet he'd forgotten that he already told us the same information before we left. But we listened intently to him anyway.

"Alright girls, your mother and I are ready for bed. Have fun and know that we love you guys so much."

"We love you guys too," we both said at the same time.

After she hung up the phone, both of our stomachs simultaneously reminded us it was time for dinner. I patiently waited as she quickly slipped on a black sundress. In less than five minutes, we were out the door.

"So, I thought maybe tomorrow we should call Jason and check in with Juan. You know, just to check on him," I suggested.

"Yeah, I was thinking the same. Will you be mad if I stay the night with him? I figure since his best friend left, he's probably lonely."

"That's a great idea. I'm sure he will appreciate that."

We arrived at the same restaurant Adrian and I had been at for our disaster of a date and sat down at a table. I strived my best not to think about the night, or about Adrian. It was refreshing to see all the people and tables were back.

I thought I would feel better since he left, but I couldn't shake off the feeling that someone was watching us. I'd felt it since we left the room. I carefully scanned the restaurant. I didn't recognize any familiar faces, but it was still unsettling. Perhaps my paranoia had returned.

"Are you alright?" she asked.

"I don't know. I have a funny feeling that someone is watching us."

Ana turned her head and looked around as well. "I don't see anything weird. Don't worry. There are people all around us. Nothing is going to happen." She assured me.

"Okay," I said, but the feeling was still present.

"I think maybe tomorrow we should explore the city. Juan's family is down there, and he would love for us to visit them," she suggested.

"Yeah, why not? I think that would be fun."

A waitress with black, wavy hair approached our table with a bottle of red wine and poured the exquisite drink into our glasses. Then, she took our order and left.

"Juan's not joining us tonight?" I asked, slightly nervous that she was going to say yes.

"No. I want it to be the two of us tonight," she said with a warm smile.

I beamed with relief. "So, what's going to happen to you two when we go back home?" I asked after a sip of dry wine.

She placed her glass on the table and thought for a moment to herself. I'd never seen her so torn over what decision to make regarding a relationship.

"I honestly don't know. I mean, I can always come back and visit, but it'll be hard to leave you in the States all by yourself," she said.

I knew she wasn't joking.

"I appreciate that, but I will not be the reason you guys can't be together. Besides, I know you like him a lot. I've never seen you so genuinely happy with a guy before."

"I mean, he's different. He's not most guys I've hooked up with while on vacation before. When we're alone, we don't just have sex. We talk about life and our dreams and goals. It's new to me."

"Wow, that's a first," I poked fun at her.

"I know, I know. That was cheesy, but I can't help it. I feel something different with him. I have a good feeling about it."

I picked up my glass, raised it in the air, and said, "Well then, let's toast for your happiness."

We celebrated and laughed some more. The paranoia slowly faded away as the night went on. The three glasses of wine certainly didn't hurt. I poured myself a fourth glass as Ana cut into her tender steak.

"You think they forced Jason to leave?" she asked after a bite of her food.

I shrugged my shoulders. "I wish I knew. He seemed pretty scared and nervous when I saw him by the pool."

"I hope he's okay. I mean, why wouldn't he be? He's not with *her* anymore."

She made a good point. If getting punched in the face meant he wouldn't have to see Catalina ever again, then I'd say that was a pretty good trade-off.

Our good night was disrupted when I noticed people leaving the restaurant in a hurry, one by one to start, but then a massive amount of people stood up from their seats and exited the restaurant at the same time. Soon, it was only Ana and me that remained. I looked around, puzzled.

"Where's everyone going?' I asked.

Ana caught on and was confused as well. She called the waitress over to the table.

"How can I help you?" the sweet woman asked.

"What's going on? Why's everybody...?"

She was suddenly interrupted by Adrian's brother and his entourage walking through the front entrance. He was in a black suit and tie with a white shirt underneath and he had both of his hands in his pockets as he led his men toward our table. His steps were confident and had an air of superiority. His two siblings appeared at his side like two lost puppies. I knew something was going to happen after what Ana did.

Oh shit, I thought to myself. Instinctively, I shifted my eyes to the closest exit.

Adrian and I made eye contact once they stopped a few feet ahead of us. The restaurant was dead silent. My heart rate started thumping rapidly inside my chest and my palms were sweating with nervousness. They stood still and said nothing. My brave and sometimes irrational best friend stood up from her chair to confront the man.

"Can we help you with something?" she asked boldly.

He paid her no attention, which only made her angrier. She took a few steps closer to him. "What the hell do you want?"

Instead of answering her question, he shoved her to the side and nearly knocked her to the floor. I grabbed the steak knife on the table and my feet instinctively pushed me up from the chair. My survival instinct kicked in, and I readied myself to do whatever it took to protect ourselves.

"Marco, can we just go?" Adrian asked.

So, *Marco* was his name.

Adrian and I locked eyes once again, and even though he wasn't talking to me, his eyes signaled us to leave. My rational thoughts told me to drop the knife, grab Ana, and head out. But my irrational side encouraged me to stay and fight. *What the hell should I do?* I tightly gripped the knife in my hand as I debated in my head. Marco took three steps toward me and assessed me up and down like I was some freak in a circus. He had an elusive smirk on his face. *Stay calm.* I chanted in my head.

"Alina, right?" he inquired.

One of his siblings must have told him my name.

"I asked you a question," he said, slowly growing impatient.

Before I had the chance to open my mouth, Ana dived in between us and shielded me from him.

"Leave her alone, fucker!" she shouted.

He was dissatisfied with her bravery. The man that slapped me earlier by the pool appeared from behind Marco, yanked on her arm, and snatched her out of the way. She fought against his grasp, but he was twice her size and didn't budge. My rational thoughts vanished, and I launched forward to push him away from her. He flicked me away like I was an insect, which only angered me more. The adrenaline helped, and I jabbed the knife into his shoulder. He cried out in pain and pulled the knife out like it was nothing, tossing it on the floor. Ana scurried to my side and held my hand. He raised his hand and swung at her across the face. She plummeted to the floor, blood dripping from her mouth. The man jerked her up on her feet and wrapped his arms tightly around her waist.

"Ana!" I screamed and attempted to help her, but Marco grabbed my arm and pulled me closer to him.

I struggled to pull my arm away from him, but he was too strong for me. His eyes turned to charcoal, and, for a brief quick second, his face morphed into my father. I became paralyzed, and an icy chill swept through my body. I'd fought for many years to erase that look from my mind. The unwanted image both frightened and infuriated me. Thanks to the adrenaline and wine, my survival instinct kicked in. I ripped my arm from his grasp, stepping away from him. He stared at me with intrigued eyes.

Ana freed herself from the other man's hold and threw herself at Marco. She threw a punch so viciously I thought I'd heard a cracking sound. But even though it was a powerful blow, his body barely moved. His men drew out their guns and pointed them directly at us. *We're dead,* I thought to myself.

"Put your guns away!" Adrian ordered. They didn't obey his command.

Marco launched himself towards Ana and within a split second, his hands wrapped around her neck. His face flared with anger as he pushed her until her back was against the dining table. She tried to fight him off, but it was of no use. I hopelessly watched as she struggled to breathe. The monster was calm as he choked her.

"Ana!" I ran toward her, but Adrian grabbed my waist and trapped me tightly against his body.

"Let me go!" I yelled at him.

He whispered into my ears, "I'm trying to save your fucking life."

I ignored what he'd said and continued my fight to get away.

"Who do you think you are, bitch?" Marco asked, furious.

Ana continued to gasp for air. I was frantic as tears fell down my cheeks. First, I failed my mother. Now I was about to fail my best friend. *Why am I so weak?* I screamed at myself repeatedly.

"Brother, that's enough. You're going to kill her!" he yelled.

"Please let her go!" I pleaded in tears.

He did not heed any of our pleas. In my last hope, I turned to his sister and said, "Catalina, please, I'm begging you. Tell him to let her go!"

She looked at me, annoyed, and then exhaled an enormous sigh. "Marco, that's enough."

He still did not let go. Ana slowly started losing consciousness. Her fight gradually faded, and the battle was nearing an end.

"Ana, fight!" I shouted louder.

My scream somehow gave her the strength to stay conscious. Her hands scrambled on the table behind her, and she grabbed another steak knife and plunged it into his upper arm. Marco groaned in pain and released her from his death grip. She dropped to the floor and gasped for air. But she didn't stay down for long, and pushed herself up, running straight to me. Adrian finally let me go. We hugged one another as tears rolled down both of our cheeks.

"I'm so sorry," I said with guilt once we separated from our hug.

Catalina bolted to her brother's side. "Are you alright?"

Ana and I took a few steps back from him but couldn't go any further because his men stood behind us, blocking our exit. We watched in fear as he pulled the knife out like it was nothing and dropped it on the floor. There was blood dripping down his arm and fingers. I expected his full wrath to come our way, but he had a smirk on his face instead. *What kind of messed-up shit is this? Are these people sick or just psychos?* How could a man who had just been stabbed stand there and smile? I felt like we were getting punked. Nothing made sense.

He said something in Spanish and his men lowered their weapons. Catalina grabbed a white napkin and wrapped it around his arm. She glared at us with the same dark eyes as his. They looked like the Ken and Barbie killers from one of the documentaries I'd watched years ago.

"What's wrong with you people?" I asked, enraged. "We've done nothing. Why can't you leave us the fuck alone?"

Marco trudged in closer toward us, but his eyes fixed only on mine.

"I can see why my little brother likes you, but you're nothing like her," he said, turned his attention to Adrian and continued, "You've picked a good one this time. Let the game begin."

He gave Ana and me one last look and then left, along with his people. Adrian stopped near the front entrance, turned his head to look at me, with terrified eyes, then exited the restaurant. He knew something else was coming for us.

CHAPTER TEN

As soon as Ana and I reached our room, we packed our stuff and got ready to leave. After what just occurred, there was no way in hell we were going to stay the night and wait until tomorrow morning to depart. I didn't bother folding any of my clothes and instead threw them all in my bag. We decided sleeping overnight at the airport was safer. The resort, which was once a magical paradise, had turned into a hellish nightmare.

"Make sure you grab everything from the bathroom." I reminded her as she scrambled to grab everything from the walk-in closet.

I searched around for my journal and nearly freaked out when I couldn't find it. Thankfully, I located it under my pillow. I picked up the small thing and held it close to my chest, and it instantly soothed my anxiety. Ana shuffled back out, threw a handful of clothes in her luggage, grabbed her phone off the bed, and dialed her dad. He didn't answer, and she attempted calling again.

"Come on Dad, pick up the damn phone," she said to herself, disheartened. Finally, after the third unsuccessful outreach, she tossed the phone on the bed in frustration and continued throwing everything in her bags.

"Fuck!" she yelled.

I looked at her, startled, and said, "What's wrong?"

"I left my bracelet in Juan's room. I'm going to run there quickly and grab it."

Before she reached for the doorknob, I grabbed her hand and stopped her.

"Are you crazy? Did you forget what just happened five minutes ago? You nearly got killed. Forget about the damn thing, and let's get out of here."

"How can you say that? You know how important that bracelet is to me. I won't leave it behind." She went to bed, grabbed her cell phone, and said, "I'll bring my phone with me in case anything happens. I'll be quick."

She ran out the door before I could open my mouth to say anything else. I knew I couldn't stop her. She was right; the bracelet was significant to her. I should have been more sensitive to it. How could I forget that Jessica, her oldest sister, had given it to her on her nineteenth birthday? She loved that bracelet. It was the only thing Ana had left of her after she died in a car accident. Immediately, I felt like a terrible best friend.

I will apologize when she gets back.

I continued with packing, and because I didn't have much it didn't take long for me to finish. I hurried around the room, grabbed whatever I found, and tossed it into Ana's luggage. I went into the bathroom and grabbed everything with both hands. My soul left my body, and I dropped everything on the floor when someone knocked on the door. I froze in place. Already, I felt my heart rate increase. I slowly and quietly approached the door and looked through the peephole. My guard went down when I saw it was Juan. I instantly opened the door.

"What are you doing here?!" I asked him. I peeked outside, paranoid that *they* were watching the room somehow. I grabbed his hand, yanked him inside, and slammed the door.

"I came to return Ana's bracelet. She left it in my room last night," he said.

"She just left for your room. You didn't see her?"

Don't panic, Alina, I said to myself.

He looked at me, bewildered, and said, "No… no, I didn't. Is everything fine? You seem distracted."

"Shit! Show me where your room is," I demanded.

He agreed, and we left the room. I sprinted as fast as I could and was at his door within less than five minutes. I stopped and took a breather. I'd never run so fast in my life. Juan came up behind me, his breathing just as heavy as mine, and examined his door. It was slightly open.

"That's weird. I swear I locked it when I left," he said.

He slowly pushed the door wide open, and it was dark inside. He turned on the light switch, and it was empty. Ana wasn't there. My breath gradually left my body. I stepped inside and conducted a thorough search but came up with nothing. I began hyperventilating.

"What the hell is going on?" he asked, confused why I was panicking.

I tried to count from one to ten but lost track after the number five. My mind was scattered, and my thoughts were incoherent. I inhaled and exhaled, but my breathing was still uncontrolled. Everything in the room slowly turned blurry. Ana was gone. The more I repeated that in my head, the more my heart rate increased.

"Alina, what is going on?" Juan asked again, growing concerned.

I turned my head and looked at him. "I think - I think they… took her." To hear myself say those words terrified me even more.

"Who? Who took her?"

"Marco and his men, and his crazy sister!" Tears rolled down my face like a waterfall. "Juan, help me find her. They took her. Oh, my gosh. I can't believe it, no no no, it's not possible. Shit. Ana."

I paced back and forth and cupped my face in frustration. I wanted to scream my lungs out.

"Hold on, slow down. Who's Marco?"

"He's… he's Adrian's brother and, uh, Catalina, she's, his sister. They came, and they took her!" I wasn't in the right state of mind to form understandable sentences.

"Why would they take her?"

"He choked her, and she almost died. And then she stabbed him, and now she's gone. It must be them. There's no one else."

"Okay, okay, just calm down, please."

I was angrier after he suggested that. *Calm down? Who can calm down after their best friend got kidnapped?* Did he not hear a word I'd said?

"No! I can't, oh my gosh, I can't...I can't breathe," I fell onto one of the beds, sitting down on the edge. My head was getting lighter and lighter with each second that passed. I placed my head between my knees and sobbed uncontrollably.

Juan knelt in front of me and placed his hands on my knees. "Alina, look at me."

I looked up at him.

"We'll find her, okay? I promise." He gently stroked my knees, and the motion instantly gave me a brief soothing effect.

I began to take a few deep breaths, and reminded myself to focus on finding her, rather than formulating every worst-case scenario in my head.

****

I sat on one of the white armchairs in the main lounge as Juan explained what happened to two Mexican police officers. I'd already explained to them my side of the story and afterward needed to remove myself to concentrate on the next move. It was frustrating because as soon as I mentioned Marco's name, the two of them looked at one another. It didn't take a genius to sense they knew more than what they were telling us. I tried my best to focus on where to start, but the more I observed their behavior, the madder I became. They didn't appear interested in what he had to say at all. They didn't even take down any notes. I couldn't stand it any longer. Finally, I pushed myself off the chair and approached them.

"What is wrong with you people? You've been here for over an hour, and not once have you written anything down. You know who they are, don't you?" I asked aggressively.

Juan pulled me back, but I pushed him away. The officer with short brown hair and boyish features looked at me and said, "We will do everything we can to find your friend. For now, I suggest you stay calm at the resort and let us do our jobs."

"Stay calm? Is that what you tell all the family members that have a loved one kidnapped and taken away from them?"

The other cop, with a bald head and the stomach of a very pregnant woman, threw up his hand as a warning for me not to speak another word. "I suggest you shut up and stay put," he said in an unsympathetic tone.

I wanted to blow up and curse at them, but Juan clutched my arm and warned me with his eyes not to open my mouth. His eyes weren't joking at all. There was genuine fear in them. So, I stopped my rambling and remained quiet.

After the two cops left, I looked at him and asked, "Why did you do that?"

"You don't understand how it works here, Alina. Those people you mentioned are powerful. Unfortunately, the police will not help us. Trust me, I've seen it happen before," he explained with a hint of sadness in his voice.

"What do you mean?"

"A few years ago, a girlfriend of mine disappeared. We went to the police for help. But they did nothing. The cops here can be useless, and many of them work for corrupt and powerful people," he revealed.

"So, what now? We do nothing? I refuse to do nothing," I said, adamant.

"We have to figure something else out."

"You said they're powerful people. Who are they?"

I studied his face as he debated the answer.

"Are you familiar with the cartel?"

"I'm familiar with the term and what it means."

"I believe the Gustavo cartel may have kidnaped Ana. I've heard the family's name before. They're known as one of the world's most powerful and dangerous cartels."

Feeling like my soul was leaving my body, I almost fainted and fell to the ground. Thankfully, he caught me before it happened. My only knowledge of the cartels was through movies and documentaries. I'd never once in my life imagined that I'd be in the presence of one. *Holy shit, I went on a date with one of them.* The unpleasant thought made me gag.

"This can't be real."

"If I'm correct, she's gone, Alina," he said with a defeated voice.

I refused to believe it. "No. I don't believe that. She's still alive, I can feel it in my bones. I'm going to find her."

"How?" he asked curiously.

I suddenly remembered she was wearing her gold star-shaped earrings when they took her. Without saying anything, I ran back to the room. Juan promptly followed me. As soon as we entered the room, I grabbed my phone from the bed and turned on the tracker app. I almost died in the first few seconds it took for the app to load. When the tracker finally turned on, it pinged her location.

"Yes!" I exclaimed. For the first time in a few hours, I had a small sense of hope.

"How did you do that?" he asked, intrigued.

"A few years ago, Ana's twin sister, Marley, was kidnapped and went missing for two weeks. When the police found her by the creek a few miles from their home, she was naked. She'd been beaten and raped repeatedly before being murdered. A year later, her oldest sister, Jessica, died in a car accident caused by a drunk driver. Her parents became paranoid after losing two daughters, so they had a tracker placed in her gold earring in case anything happened to her. I know. It's unusual for parents to do something like that but imagine losing two daughters in less than two years. That'll drive any parent insane." I explained.

"I don't think it's weird at all. I'd do the same thing if I lost two daughters."

We looked at the tiny black dot on the app. It was at a standstill for a few seconds, and then it started moving, maybe in a vehicle. I pressed the direction button, and it took us straight to the phone's GPS maps.

"That's pretty incredible," Juan said, impressed by the miracle of technology of the twenty-first century.

"Come on, we don't have much time."

We left the room and sprinted back down to the hotel's lounge. Juan told me to wait as he grabbed a cab. I wasted no time when I saw a pink taxi pull up at the front entrance. We stepped inside and asked the driver to follow the voice of the GPS.

My legs were restless as the car moved onto the main road. It was difficult to control the shaking. As I stared out the window into the pitch-black sky, various scenarios formed in my head. None of them ended well. How was I going to rescue Ana from the cartel? I was one person. Marco and his siblings probably had hundreds of men at their disposal. I fought hard to hold back my tears. It wasn't time to cry. I felt terrible that I'd dragged Juan into this. He was innocent, and he should not have come. I should have just left him at the resort.

I turned to look at him and said, "You shouldn't have come."

"I know this may sound unreal, but I care about Ana, and I want her to return home safely just as much as you do. Besides, there was no way I was going to let you go by yourself." He grabbed my hand and squeezed it tightly with a smile. I returned a warm and appreciative smile. It helped to know I wasn't alone.

Over an hour went by, and we were still driving. The road became less busy with cars and less traffic. The dot on the app was still moving. *Where are they taking her?* I looked at the time and it was a quarter after ten in the evening.

"I can't believe this happened." I said, after looking at my phone for the fourth time.

"Sometimes it's hard to imagine things like this happening. But here in Mexico, it happens more often than you think it's almost... normal sometimes."

"I'm sorry about your girlfriend," I offered my late condolence. "Were you able to at least find her... body?" I almost choked on the last word.

"No. We never found her. Honestly, we don't even know if she's alive or not, and I think that's the hardest for me. Too many girls are going missing nowadays, and nobody is doing a goddamn thing about it. This world can be so cruel sometimes."

He was right. The world was ruthless, and sometimes it makes you wonder why.

"It must be difficult not knowing."

"Yes, it is. Our family still has a lot of questions, but I don't think that we'll ever get answers. I can only pray that one day we can all heal from the pain and move on."

"They never found Ana's twin sister's killer. Her parents spent years looking for the person responsible, but they never found them."

"She's so happy and bubbly. I'd never have guessed she experienced such trauma in her life."

I smiled to myself. "Yeah, she's pretty good at concealing her emotions, but I know her. She's in pain, but she doesn't want anyone to see it. Sometimes not even me," I said and continued, "I have hope that we will find her alive." I believed in the power of hope.

"I hope so, too."

I jumped when the app notified me they had stopped. It also notified me she was twenty minutes away. The drive felt like it was never-ending. When the GPS warned us, we were five minutes away, I told the driver to stop the car. We paid him and got out. I decided that walking the rest of the way was a much better plan. I imagined wherever the place was, it was probably crawling with men armed with guns. Even though it was dark, I could feel that we were making our way up a hill. The walk took us about ten minutes. As soon as we approached a giant gate a few hundred feet ahead of us, Juan pulled me to hide behind a large rock. I gazed at the enormous mansion behind the gate. It wasn't at all what I'd expected. It looked nothing like a prison cell, but more like a castle. We ducked our heads down when two men appeared with machine guns in their hands.

"This is the place," I whispered to him.

"How are we going to get inside? This place is a war zone. The minute we step out, those men are going to empty their clips into us," he said.

Even though he made a logical and reasonable argument, all I wanted to do was run inside and scream Ana's name. It took every ounce of self-control to keep me from running to that gate. Besides, if I died, who would rescue Ana?

"We have to go back to the resort and come up with a better plan," he suggested as quietly as possible.

"Now you say it. Wouldn't it have been better to say that about an hour ago?" I scowled at him and then continued, "This is exactly why I didn't want you to come. She's in there. I know it."

"Trust me. I get that. But what can we do if we're both dead?" His logic was very annoying. Juan continued, "Listen, I have some family members that could help us."

I looked at the gate and then back at him, skeptical of his suggestion. "Would they really be willing to help?"

He stayed silent. There was very little confidence on his face, and I didn't like it.

"I don't know. I mean, the word cartel alone scares most people. But I have some distant cousins that are in a gang. Maybe they'll have the balls to do something."

"I wish you would have told me that before," I said, even though I knew I had no right to blame him. I was the one that rushed to do things and got us into this position.

Heavy footsteps approaching our hideout alerted the both of us to shut our mouths. I held my breath and remained as still as a statue. Juan signaled with his hand for me to duck my head even lower. Two men started speaking in Spanish.

"What are they saying?" I asked as quietly as possible. He covered my mouth with his hand in panic. That was very foolish of me. *Stupid, stupid.*

"They know we're here." He said, his face paled like a ghost.

Seconds later, a tall, bulky man in a black sweat suit appeared behind Juan and put a gun to his head.

"Get up, both of you," he ordered with a deep voice and a heavy accent.

Juan and I gradually stood up with our hands raised in the air. The two men were both equally buff and dressed in the same black clothes. We stepped away from our hideout and into the uncertain, open space. They spoke in Spanish some more, and then the man that ordered us to get up made his way behind Juan and hit him in the back of the head with the gun.

"Juan!" I screamed helplessly as I watched his body plummet to the ground. I knew that I'd be next, and I was right. The man walked behind me, and everything went black.

CHAPTER ELEVEN

I thought it was a dream when I felt something chewing on my feet. When I regained consciousness and slowly opened my eyes, I realized a rat was nibbling on my shoe. I panicked and kicked it across the room as hard as I could. Then I felt awful about it. It was a living thing, after all. I watched as it scurried away into the darkness.

My eyesight was hazy, and I had a pounding headache. I felt a sharp pain in the back of my neck from being knocked unconscious. The ground beneath me was a frigid concrete floor. I pushed myself up with both elbows and glanced around the dark and windowless room. The only source of light was a tiny lightbulb above my head. I forcibly nudged myself up on my feet and did a full circle of my surroundings. There was nothing but walls. I wandered to the cell bar and yanked on it a few times, but it didn't budge.

"Help!" I shouted, but only my voice echoed back. I screamed again. I slammed on the bar repeatedly, even though I knew no one would hear me. Finally, I stepped away and paced back and forth in full panic mode. *Think Alina, think. Oh no, Juan.* I yelled out his name, but silence. Everything was all my fault.

I stopped pacing when I heard footsteps approaching from outside of the cell. The lights turned on, revealing a narrow hallway. I shielded my eyes from the sudden bright lights. Marco descended the stairs and strolled toward me in a long-sleeved, button-down white shirt and dark pants. Both of his hands were in his pockets. He stopped a few feet away from the cell with a smug sneer on his face.

I stepped closer to the cell bar and asked, "Where am I?"

"Do you remember anything?"

I thought to myself until all the memories returned.

"Just because your men hit me in the head doesn't mean I forgot everything," I said with a flat expression.

"I also remembered that you choked my best friend and almost killed her. I know you took her, and I know she's here."

"What makes you so confident that she's here?" He asked, interested.

I almost blurted out how I found her, but luckily my brain hesitated. Ana's dad had the tracker app on his phone, too. I hoped he would notice something wasn't right sooner rather than later and come to our rescue.

I tightened my lips and remained mute.

"Staying silent will not help you right now" he advised dryly.

I dismissed his warning and instead asked, "Where...is...Ana?"

"I can see why Adrian is intrigued by you. It surprised me when he told me he met someone who captivated him and reminded him of Isabella. I knew I had to see who the mysterious woman was, and I'll be honest, I'm not disappointed."

"Who's Isabella?"

"He didn't tell you? She was his first love. Well, at least she was until she broke his heart. After that, he promised never to fall in love with anyone ever again. I have to say, your mannerisms and looks are strikingly similar."

So, Adrian only invested his time in me because I reminded him of a former lover. Well, on top of all the shit that happened, the news was the icing on the cake. What else could go wrong?

"I'm not interested in why your brother was interested in me." I lied and continued, "I just want to know where my friend is."

Marco pulled out a key from his pocket and unlocked the cell door. He strolled inside and made his way toward me. I continued to back away until my back pressed against the wall. He stopped a few inches away from my face and placed both of his hands on the wall. He was so close I felt his every breath on my skin.

"Don't worry. Your friend isn't dead if that's what you're wondering."

"So, you have her."

"I do."

"Why did you take her?"

"Because I can."

"If you hurt her, I swear I will kill you." I was as firm as possible with my threat. Although I wasn't even sure how I'd plot against him. The man probably controlled an army, and I had two arms.

"I have not done anything to her. But I can't say the same of my men."

"What does that mean?"

He brought his mouth closer to my ear and whispered, "I'm not sure that you want to know."

I shoved his body away from mine. The smell of him, breathing so close, sickened me. With scowling eyes, I said, "If anything happens to Ana, I swear I will…"

He interrupted me, "You will what? Tell me, Alina. I'm very enthralled by how you plan to get out of here," he paused for a few seconds and then continued, "Go on, tell me."

I hated his face. I hated his voice. I hated everything about him. Most importantly, I hated the fact that he was right. I had no plan to escape. It was a suicide mission, and I was too emotional and irrational to even realize it. All I wanted to do was punch the smirk off his face.

"That's what I thought. Right now, all your lives belong to me. And there's nothing you can do about it."

If he believed that I'd stay in this prison cell and not fight back, he was more delusional than I thought.

"You. Don't. Own us," I said, stern and clear.

His smirk tightened. "We will see."

He seized a few steps back and slowly moved back and forth with both hands shoved in his pockets.

I made my way to the junction of the cell and waited there. I observed his every movement. Amid the continued silence, I thought about Juan.

"Where is Juan?" I asked.

He stopped and glanced at me. "You came to my home with that pussy of a man?" He let out a laugh and continued, "You must have been desperate. Let me guess, the police wouldn't help?"

"So what? You own the police force too?"

He ran a hand through his hair and folded his arms across his chest, showcasing his muscles through his shirt. He glared at me carefully and then said, "You can't be surprised. I know Adrian told you who owns the resort."

"That was the furthest our conversation went before he had to leave because of you."

"The police force works for my father. So yes, we control most of their department."

Everything made more sense, and my fears were confirmed. Even if we escaped and ran to the police, who was to say they wouldn't turn us back in? I felt smaller and smaller with each second that went by in this suffocating space. My chest tightened the more I thought about how hopeless I was. When would the nightmare end?

"I applaud your effort to rescue Ana," he said, almost mockingly.

"It's called being a genuine friend. Something I'm sure someone like you wouldn't understand."

"In the world I live in, friends are a liability. It's better to not have any. That way you won't be caught making stupid decisions like you are right now."

"Are you finished? I'm done talking to you."

I quickly glanced over at the unlocked door behind him. If I timed it right, perhaps I could bolt past him and out of this hellhole.

"Don't even bother. Even if you get past me, my men are everywhere. I've ordered them to shoot on sight. So, I wouldn't try anything if I were you. How will you save your friends if you're dead?" He said with eyes that told me he wasn't fooling around.

"So, what do you intend to do? Lock me in here like an animal?"

I studied his face as he thought to himself.

"You, being here, was never part of the plan. I had other intentions for you, but I guess everything works out like fate."

"Fate? There's nothing about any of this situation that's considered fateful. You and your group of psychotic friends kidnapped Ana."

"She did something that she shouldn't have. Every action has consequences, Alina."

"We did what was necessary to defend ourselves. You choked her, and she stabbed you. I see nothing wrong with what she did. If it was me, I would've gone for your throat."

"The only opinion that matters is mine. What she did was unforgivable, and she deserves her punishment right now."

I paused and shuddered at the thought of what he meant. Finally, I brought myself to ask, "Right now?"

"I'm sure some of my men are enjoying fucking the shit out of her right now." He said nonchalantly.

My heart dropped, and everything around me gradually spun in a circle. I clenched my fists tightly and felt my sharp nails pinch the skin. My blood boiled with rage and all I saw was the color red. With little control, I launched myself forward and struck a punch. All my martial art lessons as a young girl re-emerged. Thanks to my Mom, I learned at a very young age how to defend myself. And according to her, I was a very aggressive fighter. She told me it was because of all the anger and resentment I'd buried inside because of my father. She thought it was good for me to have a place where I could vent out everything, physically. In class, I was free to hit whatever I wanted, or so I'd thought. I remember clearly the day when I punched a boy in the face and broke his nose because he thought it was funny to taunt me about my hair. I showed no mercy. After the incident, they kicked me out. That wasn't the only place I was banned from. After a while, Mom stopped sending me to classes because she was worried about my safety. Little did she know the other kids were the ones who should have been concerned about their safety.

Marco turned his head in my direction and, strangely, he looked impressed. "That wasn't bad. You have the bravery, but not the strength. Now I'm even more intrigued. The difference between you and Isabella is that she never dared to do what you just did."

I returned to my corner. I was proud of what I did, but that satisfaction only lasted for a moment. The rational part of my brain alerted me to my stupidity. *I can't believe I punched the son of a drug lord. Well, perhaps Dad was right. I* am *careless.*

He took a few steps forward and said, "But being brave around here won't get you anywhere!"

He yanked me by the shoulder and rammed me against the wall on the other side. The air was knocked out of me momentarily. He was so quick that I barely had time to react to his next move. I found my back pressed against the wall as he wrapped one hand around my throat, and the other tightly gripped my jaw. I glimpsed into the nothingness in his eyes.

"I won't kill you, not yet. But I promise I will make sure you and your friends suffer." He released his grip and took a few steps back.

I was no longer brave, but more of a frightened child. A feeling I remembered too well and was never too fond of. He made me feel helpless. *Enough with the pity party. You need to be strong for Ana and Juan.* I inhaled and exhaled a few deep breaths and composed myself. I held my tears back from cascading down my face. He was the last person on the planet that I'd ever want to see me cry.

"You're courageous," he paused and then continued, "It takes a special someone to be as stupid as to hit me in my own home. The last person to do so is dead."

He returned to the center of the prison. "From now on, you will do everything and anything I ask of you, and if you don't, there will be consequences."

"That will not happen." I bravely said although I knew it wasn't the smartest thing to say.

He smirked devilishly. "Really? Alright then, let me show you something."

He strolled forward, grabbed my hand, and yanked me aggressively to his side. He dragged me outside, down the hall, and up the stairs. We emerged from the underground prison to a magnificent mansion. I stared in awe at the unique medieval architecture of the stone mansion. For a brief few seconds, I was mesmerized and nearly forgot where I was.

Marco hauled me through the luscious green grass and down a long stone corridor. We reached the end of the long hall and entered a giant golden gate entrance and into the mansion's main foyer. Ahead of us were stairs leading to the second floor. I thought that was where he was taking me, but we walked past the stairs and further into the compound. I was oddly disturbed and intrigued by portraits of nude women of all ethnicities hanging on the wall. They looked like they could walk in a Victoria's Secret fashion show. We halted in front of an elevator, and he pressed on the letter "L" and once the door opened, Marco tossed me inside like a rag doll. He continued to grip my wrist as we descended to the lowest level. *Jeez, does one man need this much space?*

When the door opened, he pulled me out and dragged me onto an open floor with architectural stilts and a water fountain in the middle of the room. A naked marble woman sat atop a stone in the center. I felt like I was standing in a castle in Ancient Rome. The spectacular beauty of the place took me back. Never in a million years would I have imagined his mansion to be this grand.

We continued walking further into the open space past the fountain. *Where the hell are we going?* I asked myself. Finally, we stopped at a giant black wooden door. Marco pulled out a key from his pocket, unlocked the door, and pushed it open wide. I saw what was in front of me and I nearly fainted.

I counted at least over twenty women, some clothed in glamorous dresses and others in lingerie. There were women of all races and ethnicities. They looked in good health and, if I wasn't mistaken, happy? *Holy shit.* I scanned the room for Ana, but she wasn't present. All of the women stopped whatever they were doing and glared at me. Some stare with curiosity while others with what appeared to be envy. *Is this where he keeps all his women prisoners?* I'd thought the room would be dark and frigid, like the cell I was just in. Instead, it was a modern and luxurious spot. The room itself was half the size of a football field, with an open-concept floor plan. There was everything from giant white beds to a pool table and a jacuzzi. Further to my right sat a wine bar, bookshelves, and a huge TV mounted on the wall. It didn't feel like the women were living like prisoners.

"What the hell is this?" I heard myself ask.

Marco turned to look at me. "I will allow you to stay alive for now. And for the first time in my life, I will give you something that I've given no one before, a choice. You can either stay here with the rest of them and serve me, or you can spend the rest of your days in the underground cell. Whatever choice you make, from now on, you're one of my whores. And as my whore, you will obey my every command, and if you don't, you'll face the consequences. Is that clear?" he asked dryly.

I became paralyzed in place. But it wasn't because of fear. It was because I found the whole situation comical. I turned to look at the insane and delusional man.

"Are you kidding me? I'd rather die than to be forced into becoming one of your whores. You must be crazy. I won't make any choices." I said sternly.

Marco clenched his jaw tightly in frustration. I knew he wasn't fond of my response.

"Is that your ultimate answer?"

"Go to hell," I said.

He beamed before grabbing my throat with one hand and slamming me against the wall. I fought back with every strength I had, but of course, he was stronger than me. I stopped fighting when I realized the harder I fought, the faster my breathing tightened.

"Listen to me, at this moment, you are nothing. And if I want to tie, gag, and fuck you all day, I will. In fact, the more you resist, the more I want to fuck you, hard. So, keep it up. I don't do well with disobedient women. And to prove my point, I will show you what I mean right now." Marco released his grip.

Before I even took a full breath, one of his men unexpectedly showed up behind me and took me by the arm. He pulled me outside and back to the elevator, and we descended into the unknown. As soon as the elevator door opened, the man pushed me out into a dark, high-ceilinged room with a giant chandelier in the center. I stared back as the elevator door closed, and he vanished.

I looked around the windowless space and its dark walls. *What's with this man and windowless rooms?* There was nothing in the room except an enormous bed and two bedside tables. Slowly, I paced the room and noticed a door. Immediately, I bolted to it. I tried to turn the knob, but it was no use. With all my strength, I banged the door repeatedly. My body collapsed to the floor with my back pressed against the door. Once again, I was powerless. The only thought I had was of his men viciously assaulting Ana. Realizing that I couldn't help her tore me apart. I wanted to detonate into a million pieces. I brought my knees to my chest and lowered my head between them. The only thing left for me to do was sob. *What the hell was I thinking? Did I think I would somehow get inside this place, find Ana, and escape? How could I be so stupid?*

When I woke up, I was in bed and the room was dimly lit. At first, I was disoriented but then realized someone had moved me from the door to the bed. I jolted up straight. My clothes were still on. I had feared that Marco had stripped me naked and raped me in my sleep. When my vision fully cleared, I nearly jumped out of bed at the sight of him standing in the corner of the room near the door with his arms folded over his chest. He was wearing black joggers and a white T-shirt. He stood with a sense of calmness that was disturbing. From afar, his eyes were empty. When he moved toward the bed, I jumped out and ran to the furthest corner of the room. I mentally prepared myself to fight him until death.

He stopped near the edge of the bed and with a smirk said, "It was funny to watch you bang on the door." There was a hint of amusement in his voice.

I remained silent. All I could think about was how to kill him and escape.

"What do you think would happen if you could get out of this room?" he asked, curious.

I ignored his question. He took a few more steps toward me. I realized then maybe the corner wasn't such a great idea.

"I don't like to repeat myself. But believe it or not, I've been patient with you. So, don't piss me off," he warned.

Alright, Alina, be smart. Either answer his question or possibly get raped.

"I don't know. I haven't thought that far out," was the best that I could manage, but it was enough to satisfy his need for obedience.

His eyes lightened slightly. For the first time, he looked like a human being. Well, a shitty and psychopathic human being.

"How did you know I was banging on the door?"

Marco pointed his finger at a camera on the wall. That was when I saw there were cameras in every corner of the room. I wanted to puke. I couldn't believe I'd thought Adrian was a potential killer when it turned out it was his brother all along. My mother was right. I shouldn't have judged so quickly. I felt guilty for thinking so low about him. But then I remembered he could have saved Ana and me, and immediately all the guilt disappeared. I wondered if he was part of the abduction.

"Why are you doing this?" I asked him, genuinely curious.

He inhaled a deep breath and exhaled through his nose. "Because I can."

"Just because you can do something, it doesn't mean you should. Kidnapping and keeping women down in your creepy basement is wrong. They're not your whores. They're people."

Perhaps trying to justify why his actions were wrong would change his perspective. But then again, I highly doubt it. He was a psychopath, and there was no use in reasoning with him.

Marco turned his back, strolled to the bed, and sat down on the edge.

"Are you afraid of me?"

"I'm not afraid of you or your men," I lied.

I stood as tall as possible so that I wouldn't appear intimidated.

"It's remarkable how much you remind me of her."

"Isabella?"

He nodded. She was insane to be involved in such a family, but perhaps they threatened her or something. I couldn't see how anyone would willingly agree to be part of the family.

"Well, I'm not her."

"That's for sure. Isabella was more obedient and easier to control."

"Again, I'm not her. So, expect nothing."

"I know," he said, almost disappointed. "You should thank her though because when you were unconscious, all I wanted to do was strip you naked and fuck you right there and then."

"Do you even hear yourself? That is some messed up shit." I blurted it out.

Only the worst of the worst humans think in that way. Marco was indeed a terrible person, just like my father.

"The thought was tempting, and even now, all I want to do is fuck you from behind against the wall."

He was a perfect resemblance to my father.

"What you speak of is called rape. That is wrong, and you're fucked up - you need help."

"When you have power, you can do whatever you please, Alina. Don't you understand the simple rule of that?"

"Having power doesn't mean you can kidnap, trap and rape women," I said. "How many women do you have trapped in your basement?" I asked.

He pushed himself up from the bed. "Trapped isn't the word that I would use to describe those women," he said and then continued, "None of them are here against their will. They came willingly, and they all chose to be my whores."

"What crazy woman willingly gives themselves up to be your whore?"

He let out a small laugh. It was scary how normal he looked when he did that.

"Believe what you want. I don't have to explain myself to you."

"So, if they are here by choice, then how come I can't leave?"

"Because I ordered you to stay. Besides, I gave you two choices earlier, and you refused both."

"They were shitty choices," I said boldly.

He raised an eyebrow as if it impressed him.

"So, what's going to happen now?" I asked.

He thought for a moment. I wish I knew what he was thinking.

"For now, you'll stay in this room until I decide what I want to do with you."

"What about Ana?"

"I think right now you need to worry about yourself more," he suggested.

"What happens if I refuse to stay in this room?"

"You don't have that much of a choice. The door will always be locked, and I can watch your every move."

"What if I kill myself?"

"You're smarter than that. Besides, I can tell how much love you have for your friend. So, you won't risk hurting yourself." He said, confident. "My brother's taste in women is usually bland, but I'm satisfied with his choice in you."

"I don't care about Adrian and his choice. I don't care that you're satisfied. I'll find a way out of here."

Marco walked toward me, closed the distance between us, and I felt his breath on my face again. He trailed his finger down my face, throat, and shoulder with one hand and loudly swallowed his saliva in hunger. I instinctively pushed his hand away and moved my head to the side, out of his sight. His touch made my skin shiver. He did not like that I had moved his hand away. I think I awoke the beast within. I saw his eyes, and they were black and ice-cold.

"Look at me," he demanded.

I remained still. Marco grabbed my face with one hand and forcibly moved it to face him. Our noses touched. I sensed every fiber in my body, shivering with fear.

Stay calm, Alina.

"For the first time in my life, I've been patient. But now that's gone, and you've pissed me off. Do you think you're special? You're nothing. The more you disobey, the harder I get. I quite like these new feelings. I'm going to have to show you right now that every action comes with consequences." He gripped my face with both hands and forced his mouth onto mine.

I fought him off and attempted to run, but he grabbed my waist, lifted me over his shoulder like I weighed nothing, and tossed me into the bed. I kicked him away and crawled to the other side. My endeavor to escape was short-lived when he grabbed my ankles and pulled me underneath him. I continued to struggle. He pinned my arms above my head after I tried to punch him again. I was utterly helpless. I screamed, but he shut it up by forcing his tongue into my mouth. Marco devoured my mouth with force and aggression. First, I tasted his breath and saliva. Then I felt his hard cock pressing against my stomach through his pants. I was trapped and terrified. *So, that's how Mom felt every time Dad raped her.*

Once I broke free from his lips, I moved my head from side to side aggressively. I did everything I could to get away. Marco pinned my face in place with one hand. I closed my eyes in fear of what could come next. As soon as I closed my eyes, the memories appeared in my head. Unlike me, my poor mother was fragile, and she didn't fight back against my father. She had accepted that he was stronger, and fighting would only worsen the assault. *"Alina, don't be like me. Be stronger than me, no matter what happens."*

I took her advice and bit down on his bottom lip as hard as possible. It worked. He pulled away and stood up. Marco ran his finger along his lip and looked down at the red blood. It surprised me he bled red like the rest of us. I pulled myself up and hauled the blanket over my body. I wanted to cry, but I knew I couldn't.

He tightly clenched his jaw. "That was idiotic," he warned. "Let's play a game. If you want to see Ana, you'll obey and do as you're ordered."

I looked at him with disgust. "Go fuck yourself," I said.

His mind game would not work. I knew he still would not let me see Ana, even if I did as commanded.

"I'm giving you a choice again, Alina. Now, either you suck my dick, or you won't see Ana ever again. If I leave, you won't be able to change your mind."

I refused to look the lunatic in the eyes, so I just ignored him.

"Alright then," he said and left the room through the door.

I was so relieved when he disappeared. It was like the darkness had vanished, and I could finally release my tears in silence. The only thing that sucks was the damn cameras in the room. But even that was better than crying in front of him. I figured if I covered my entire body under the blanket, I could freely sob without him monitoring me, so that's exactly what I did.

CHAPTER TWELVE

The room was dark when I woke up, and I wasn't sure if it was day or night. I was still groggy. My eyes were puffy from crying. I assumed I was dreaming when a delicate hand touched my arm. I turned to the side of the bed to gaze at Ana's beautiful face, smiling at me. At first, I wasn't sure it was real. Eventually, after a few moments, I realized she was real. I jumped up with relief and embraced her tightly in my arms.

"Ana!" We held onto each other for a few minutes and the both of us sobbed like babies. I'd never been happier to see her face. I was afraid to let her go, but I had so many questions.

"What happened? You left to grab the bracelet, and then you were gone," I said rapidly.

She hopped into the bed, holding both my hands.

"As soon as I got to Juan's room, two men in black suits grabbed me, and the next thing I knew, I woke up in a room like this," she explained.

"Did they hurt you?" I asked.

"No. The men left me in the darkroom. I thought I was going to die. When I woke up, Marco came into the room and told me I was foolish and that it was my fault that I got into this position. He said he was going to sell me to the highest bidder. You were right. I should have listened. I guess stabbing him with the steak knife was not my greatest decision."

I stared deeply into her gentle gray eyes. "Listen to me. You did nothing wrong. You were protecting yourself and me. And you have no reason to feel that it was your fault. You did what anyone would do to survive." I reassured her.

"I'm so glad that I at least get to see you one last time before -"

I interrupted her. "Do not say that. We are going to escape this place. I promise."

She tightened the grip on my hands and forced out a smile.

"Did they hurt you?" She asked.

"No. Well... he tried to. He tried to rape me." I let out.

She grabbed my body and embraced it in her gentle arms. "Oh, sweetie. I'm so sorry. I'm going to kill that bastard."

"Were you raped?" I asked fearfully.

"No, thank god."

I sighed in relief. "He said his men raped you. I was so scared and hopeless at the thought that I wasn't there for you. I almost died."

"All they did was grab and toss me in the room. It wasn't until this morning that one of his men dragged me here. I didn't realize they were bringing me to you."

I was glad to learn it was the next day already but was narrowly confused because he clarified last night that I would never get to see Ana unless I obeyed his demand. *So perhaps this was another part of his mind games?*

"How did you end up here? Did he kidnap you as well?"

"No, I followed you with..." I suddenly remembered the cameras, "Juan came with me."

"What! Where is he?" she asked frantically.

"I don't know. His men knocked us unconscious and after that I woke up in a cell alone. Ana, I don't know where he is. I'm sorry. I tried asking, but he wouldn't tell me."

"Hell, Alina! Why would the two of you come after me?!" she growled.

"I wasn't going to let them hurt you," I said, angry that she was angry.

"These people are dangerous. You should have gone back to the States or called the cops."

"You don't think I didn't try?! His insane family controls the police department."

She looked confused. "They do? Who the hell are these people?"

"Juan said Marco and his family are heads of the Gustavo cartel. It explains why the police didn't bother doing anything. They're too powerful. And you think I can just go back home and live my everyday life knowing my best friend got kidnapped? You should know me better than that."

Ana stood up and away from the bed. "Wait, my dad. He has the tracker on his phone, too. So, he'll be able to find us."

"Shhhh…" I subtly pointed to one camera. She understood right away.

The thought of Mr. Davis finding us was relieving, even for a moment. The real question was, when will he find out that something wasn't right? Hopefully, by now, he noticed something was wrong.

"What do you think he's going to do with us now?" I asked.

Ana came back and sat down next to me. She took my hand in hers.

"I wish I knew the answer to that. But don't worry, we have each other. We will fight through this." We hugged once again.

"I'll put a bullet right between his eyes." She said, and the thought was comforting.

"Oh, you won't believe this, but we're not the only women here."

She separated from me. "What do you mean? There are others?"

"He has at least twenty women in the basement."

Her eyes opened wide in disbelief.

"Yes, and he said that all of them came here and gave themselves up to him willingly, as his whores."

"What the actual fuck?" She said and continued, "We need to get the hell out of here."

"I agree, but he has cameras monitoring me," I whispered.

"I can also hear you," a voice said in the air. I knew it was him.

"Bastard! Come in here so I can kick the shit out of you!" Ana yelled into one camera.

I pulled her back, afraid of the consequences she would face.

115

"Don't provoke him, Ana. You don't know what he'll do. I'm pretty sure a man who imprisons women as his whores is capable of pretty much anything."

She calmed down at my suggestion. The door suddenly opened, and a man in a black suit with shoulder-length black hair headed straight for Ana, grabbed her arm, and dragged her away. I tried to hold on, but he was too strong.

"Ana!" I screamed after her. In less than a few seconds, she was gone again. "Ana!" I shouted again.

I realized the door wasn't closed all the way, and without hesitation I bolted outside and into the hall. I ran and turned the corner, only to be stopped by his ever-depressing presence. Marco stood calmly with his arms folded across his chest.

"Nice try," he said and forced me back inside.

Once back in the room, I realized I was only wearing black lace lingerie. He closed the door behind him and casually leaned his back against the door with one hand in his pocket. His eyes trailed up and down my entire body. Even though I was covered, his stare made me feel naked. I ran into bed and immediately covered myself with the blanket.

"I hope you found that gesture pleasant."

"What gesture?"

"Me allowing your friend to visit you. I had other plans for her, but I suddenly found a better purpose for her being here."

"What purpose is that?"

"Her presence will benefit me, after all. From now on, if you accept your fate here, behave, and follow orders, I will allow her to visit you."

"You are delusional. Is this fun for you?"

"If it wasn't, why would I continue to do it?" he said like the answer was so obvious.

"Right now, I'm horny, and I'm not interested in fucking any of the women in the basement. And that's a first for me." He pushed himself away from the door, pulled his shirt over his head, threw it on the floor, and strolled toward the bed. Maybe jumping into bed was not the best idea. Marco slowly crawled towards me. At that moment, I just closed my eyes. I was paralyzed with panic.

"Look at me," he demanded in his dominant voice.

I refused.

"Open your damn eyes!" He yelled.

It scared me, so I did, but I turned my attention elsewhere instead of looking at him. He snatched the blanket away, and I was exposed. He grabbed my chin and tilted my head up to face him. His eyes were unusually black and soulless, which frightened me to the core. With his other hand, he reached back and unbuttoned my bra. My body shivered in fear like a small, hopeless animal. He pulled my bra away and threw it on the floor. I instinctively crossed my arms over my chest to cover my breasts. Marco leaned in to kiss me, but I turned my head away. Though I couldn't see his eyes, I sensed the sexual frustration in his breathing. Finally, he grabbed my arm and pulled me out of bed. I found my back pressed against the wall and I was at his mercy.

"Fighting will do you no good, Alina," he said intensely. "Now look at me," he demanded once more.

I counted to five and turned my head to face his furious glare. He attempted to kiss me again, but I declined. I picked up my right knee and nailed him in the groin as hard as I could. He released my arms and dropped to the ground. I grabbed his shirt off the floor, slipped it on, and ran towards the door. Even though I did not know where to go, I ran as fast as I could. I needed to get away from that room and the monster.

The mansion was so massive that I faced another long hall every time I turned. *Don't stop running.* I told myself—*shit, Ana.* Silence came back when I yelled out her name. I opened every door I came across, but it was all empty. I got more and more lost in his twisted world.

"Ana!"

I turned around and saw Marco running for me, furious. So, I ran in the opposite direction. I skipped down the stairs and sprinted through the main door and out into the bright sun. I'd never been so happy to see the glistening sunlight in my life. I ran down the long driveway.

"Alina!" He yelled from behind.

I did not look back. My survival instinct kicked in, and my adrenaline helped with my speed. I knew in real life I could never run that fast. The tall black gate was in sight, and I briefly tasted victory. But that feeling quickly faded when I saw four of his men near the entrance with guns in their hands. My feet automatically stopped on their own. *Shit.* I heard Marco's angry footsteps heeding behind me. The four men disappeared once their boss stopped in front of me.

"Why did you do that?" he asked, agitated.

What kind of question is that? I ran because I wanted to escape you.

"Is that a serious question?" I asked him.

He picked me up and tossed me over his shoulder.

"Marco, let me go!" I yelled.

He didn't listen and walked back towards the mansion. I aggressively shifted my entire body while on his shoulder.

"Stop moving!" He demanded.

I ignored his command and continued to shift around aggressively. Finally, he put me halfway down the driveway. I shoved him away.

"I'm not going back inside," I said sternly.

"Fine, then I will fuck you right here," he lunged forward, and forced his tongue into my mouth. Marco tripped me, and we landed on the soft green grass. His uninvited lips were once again on mine. He pinned my body down with his, forcing me to remain still. He gripped my throat in one hand, and the more I resisted, the quicker the air fled my body. Finally, he yanked his shirt from my body, leaving me half-naked in broad daylight. His mouth made its way to my breasts, and I cringed as he devoured them like a barbarian.

I shoved on his shoulders, but they were nothing but muscle. I felt his rock-solid cock rubbing against my thigh and stomach. He forced his tongue into my mouth when he finished devouring my nipples. When I got a hold of his lips, I bit down, hard, and it forced him to recoil. It reopened the wound from my last bite. Marco finally stopped and stood up and away from me.

I grabbed his shirt and covered my body. I searched around, and none of his men were present to witness the humiliation. But why was it as the victim I felt embarrassed? He knelt next to me and ran his hand through my messy hair.

"Admit it. You liked it."

I shot him an intense look of hatred and spat in his face. "Go to hell," I said.

He wiped away the saliva from his face, grabbed my arm, and forced me to my feet.

"I like your scent," he said and dragged me back inside.

We eventually reached the end of the hall and turned the corner to a familiar door. The door had a code lock; he stood in front of me so I wouldn't see the passcode. It unlocked, and he thrust me right back into my dark prison room.

"Like I told you, every action has consequences. Be prepared for later."

"What's later?" I turned around and asked.

He disregarded my question and shut the door. *Asshole.* I felt tears brimming under my eyes. *What just happened? Did he really violate me a few minutes ago?* The thoughts were almost unreal. The feeling that I was powerless was paralyzing. His shirt revolted me. I ripped it in half, flung it on the floor, and spat on it. I slithered to bed and concealed myself away under the blanket.

I had no clue how much time had passed, but I knew I had been in bed in the silence for a while. I struggled a few times to fall asleep, and every time I closed my eyes, I saw his face and body on top of me. The door unexpectedly opened, and two women, one older and one younger, both with black hair up in a ponytail, walked in. As they came closer, I noticed the older woman had an enormous scar on her face. What was it with his people and scarred faces? They stopped near the bed. The older woman had a nude gown in her hands while the younger woman was holding a giant black bag.

"Who are you people?" I asked, slightly agitated and rude.

"My name is Camila, and this is my mother, Juanita. We are maids of the mansion," Camila said with a Spanish accent and then continued, "Master Marco ordered us to get you ready for the party tonight."

I looked at them, bewildered. "What party?"

"He said you will see for yourself," Juanita said.

"No," I said simply. There was no chance in hell I'd go to a party with him.

"Please, senorita, don't make this difficult for us," Camila begged.

"You can tell him he can go to the party by himself."

"Señorita, the Master will punish us if we don't do our jobs," Juanita said with a glimmer of fear in her voice. I couldn't help but gawk at her scar. I wondered if he had inflicted that on her. Suddenly I felt terrible, and I wanted nothing to happen to them, so I agreed. They happily strolled to the bed and prepared their equipment.

A few hours passed by, and Camila finally finished curling my hair. The whole time, they didn't speak unless I spoke to them. And even when they responded, the answers were minimal.

"You two realize your *master* kidnapped my friends and me, right?"

They looked at one another. I was hoping since they were also women that they'd understand what I was going through.

"We know nothing except to do our jobs," Camila said.

I knew she was lying. "Seriously? That's your response? Okay then, if you didn't know before, you do now. Can you help us?"

"Señorita Alina, please don't do anything to upset the Master. If you just follow orders, you will have a good life, just like the rest of the women here." Juanita chimed in.

"Oh, I thought Camila said you guys know nothing."

Camila flashed her mother a glance of disapproval. She turned to look at me and said, "Look, I'm sorry that I lied. But truthfully, we only do our jobs. Everything that happens in the mansion isn't any of our business. My mother is right. The women here are taken care of. They have everything they want: money, clothes, food, yachts, clubs, and more. They live a life of luxury. Isn't that every woman's dream?"

"Not every woman."

Camila cradled my hand in hers. "Just don't do anything to upset him and you'll be fine." She gave me a warm smile.

Juanita helped me into the exquisite long-sleeved V-neck, velvet gown. The nude color matched flawlessly with my caramel skin. Strangely enough, I had the same emotion I felt when Ana helped prepare me for my date with Adrian. I was relieved when they told me they had finished. The two women took a few steps back to admire their work.

"Wow, you are such a beauty señorita," Camila said. Her kind words brought a smile to my face that I didn't think was possible.

"So much like Isabella…" Juanita said.

Camila quickly interrupted her, "Mama, be quiet."

"Can you tell me more about her?" I asked, genuinely interested.

Right after I asked, the door opened, and a familiar and unpleasant face appeared through the door—the man who slapped me. My smile quickly evaporated. All I felt was rage. He signaled the two women to leave, and so they did.

"Marco is waiting for you."

"Go fuck yourself, asshole," I said.

My insult did nothing to him. Why would it? He was a man with no soul or emotion. He grabbed my hand and pulled me out of the room. We descended the stairs, through the hall, and into the backyard. The view took my breath away. His estate sat atop a mountain overlooking the entire city. I didn't realize how beautiful Mexico was until then. For a brief second, I almost forgot where I was. The man took me down to the lower yard. As soon as I took my last step down the stairs, I saw all the women from the basement decked out in glamorous dresses with their hair and makeup done. They were partying and dancing to beautiful Spanish music. They all turned to look at me. My heart started beating so fast that I had to remind myself to breathe before I passed out.

A server approached me, and I grabbed a glass of champagne. I drank all of it in one gulp to distract myself. I spotted another server with a tray of brown liquor and walked toward him to grab a glass. All it took was one sniff for me to recognize that it was whiskey. I took a sip of the potent liquor and gagged in disgust. I forced myself to take another sip, but only because I knew I needed it to help with my confidence to face all of these stunning women. If I was drunk enough, I'd probably be able to fall asleep tonight without seeing his face. The thought was comforting, and I took another sip.

I wandered gradually into the crowd, looking everywhere for Ana. She was nowhere in sight. My head started getting lighter and everything around me felt less suffocating. I strolled further into the crowd. I knew the women were still staring, but I didn't care. I took another sip of the alcohol.

"You must be Alina," a soft voice said from the corner of my eyes.

I slightly turned my head to face a woman in a black dress with brunette hair and gray eyes. She had a delicate face. She seemed too innocent to be in a place like this. I wondered how she came to be one of his whores.

"I am, and you are?"

"I'm Lucia. Marco's number eight." She said casually. She saw the look of bewilderment on my face and so she continued, "They give each of us here a number after we sign a contract."

I nearly choked on my saliva. "A contract?"

"Did you not sign one?" She asked, slightly baffled.

"I'm not exactly sure what you're talking about," I said honestly.

Lucia grabbed a glass of champagne from one server and gave him the prettiest smile. She turned her attention back to me and said, "Each of us that agreed to be one of his possessions must sign a contract. But none of us reads about all the legal stuff. We only care about one thing." She stopped and sipped her drink.

"And what's that?"

"Why, Marco, of course." She said and stared at me as if I was an idiot for not knowing the answer sooner.

I almost puked out the whiskey after she declared that openly. She had to be under a spell or something. Maybe Marco was a witch in disguise, or maybe he brainwashed them.

"You must be different if you didn't have to sign a contract."

"You're telling me you willingly signed a contract to be his… whore?" I asked in disbelief.

"Well, I wouldn't say whore, but more of his submissive, and he's the dominant."

Of course, those words meant nothing to me, and she was insane to think I'd understood what they meant.

"You enjoy all of this?"

"Well, yes, why would we sign up for something that's not enjoyable?" She said playfully.

"So exactly what *is* all of this?" I said and looked all around.

"Oh, it's just one party he hosts for us. Sometimes it can get a little suffocating in the basement. So, we come up here, dance, drink, and watch the beautiful city lights at night," she said and continued, "My favorite thing is watching the sunset. It's so exquisite from up here."

Lucia was in awe, and I was more confused than ever. The conversation felt almost unreal. I couldn't believe she just admitted that she enjoyed being his submissive. I was at a loss for words.

"So, how did you end up here?"

"Well…" I began but was suddenly interrupted by a familiar voice from behind.

"You look stunning."

I shuddered at the thought of him standing behind me. I kept my attention on Lucia and nothing else. Marco walked up to my side in a black suit and a glass of whiskey in his hand. I felt his burning gaze on the side of my face.

"Leave us," he said dryly to her. She obeyed without hesitation and disappeared into the crowd.

He made his way in front of me and scanned my body up and down like a hawk.

"Camila and Juanita did a great job. You look perfect."

"If you're waiting for a thank you, you won't get one," I said, irritated. Even though the whiskey was disgusting, it helped with my bravery.

"You know you have a pretty sharp mouth. I wonder what else it can do."

Disgusting. It can bite you; that's what it can do. I wasn't in the mood to converse, so I walked past him and headed into an unknown area. I needed to get away. But of course, he followed behind.

"How are you liking the party?"

"Party? It feels more like a freak show." I said, forgetting that there were some women close by and probably heard what I said.

"I'm not sure they appreciate being called freaks," he warned. "Some of these women can be feisty. So, I'd be careful how you use your words when you're around them."

I stopped and turned to look at him." Where is Ana?"

"In her prison, where she belongs."

"I want to see her," I demanded. The whisky had taken complete control.

He smirked. "I don't remember that being one of our deals."

"I will not suck your dick. Besides, you have all these women that are more than willing to do it. So why not ask them to do it?"

"I could, but what's the fun in having someone that wants to do it rather than someone as stubborn as you?"

How can any human being think in that way? I asked myself in disbelief. I deliberately ignored his presence, even though I knew he didn't like that. That was his problem, not mine. Shit, all the time spent worrying about Ana and hating him, I completely forgot about Juan.

"Where is Juan?"

"I don't like how concerned you are with him," he said with unpleasant eyes.

"Why would that bother you? He's a friend."

Why was I explaining myself to him?

"The only thing that should be in your mind is how you can please me so that you can see Ana. Not him. And that is not a suggestion. It's a demand."

"I'm sorry, but who do you think you are? A God?" I asked, annoyed.

"I'm the boss."

I rolled my eyes. "Last I checked, your father is the boss, not you."

His eyes turned black, and he tightly clenched his jaw. I provoked him, *shit.* Marco finished the rest of his whisky and handed the empty glass to one of his many women. He took a few steps closer and trapped my back against the stone balcony railing. He placed both of his hands on the railing and our chests pressed against one another. I was uncomfortable but calm.

"Do you want me to rip your dress and fuck you right now?"

I shook my head.

"I don't appreciate the rude remarks. Nobody talks to me in that way. Do you understand?"

"So why not just kill me then? Wouldn't that make things easier for you?" I challenged him.

He inhaled deeply with frustration but backed away.

"Where is Juan?"

"He's not dead, at least not yet anyway. But the one thing I can tell you is I made sure he suffered."

"What did you do to him?"

"I'm not sure that you should know."

I gripped my glass tightly in my hand. "What have you done to him?"

Marco purposely turned and walked away and avoided my question. I followed behind.

"Marco, tell me what you've done with Juan."

He stopped, but his back was to me, and I knew he would not turn and face me. So, I walked up to his side. He finally turned his head in my direction.

"People who defy me never live to tell their stories. Your friend is the first. If he had cooperated from the beginning, his suffering wouldn't have been as bad, but he didn't. He knew what was coming, and he got what he deserved."

I felt tears brimming under my eyes, but I fought them off. *I will not be weak, not in front of you.*

"What exactly did you do to him?" I demanded.

"Let's just say your friend lost a few fingers." He revealed.

I felt oxygen slowly leaving my body, but there was enough left for rage to boil under my skin. Until it happened, I wasn't aware I'd splashed the rest of my drink on his face. I only knew what I'd done when everyone stopped and gasped in place. They were all shocked, and so was I.

He pulled out a handkerchief from his jacket pocket and slowly wiped the liquor from his face. When he finished, he gently folded it and placed it back where it belonged. He gave me a long and hard glare before yanking my wrist and dragging me back inside. I tripped a few times on the dress, but he snatched me back up on my feet and continued to drag me like a rag doll. We reached the foyer, and I pulled myself away and headed back outside. Wearing the stupid high heels made it impossible to run, and it wasn't long before he grabbed my wrist once again. He whirled me around, grabbed my face, and forced his tongue into my mouth. All I smelled and tasted was whiskey. The whiskey gave me strength for a strange reason I couldn't explain. I pushed him away once more and threw a punch. It threw him off balance and it satisfied me to see blood trickling down from his mouth. He turned and had a smirk on his face. I couldn't believe my eyes. The man just got punched and yet he was smiling.

"I haven't had this much fun in a while. Keep it up, Alina."

"You're an insane, delusional monster. There's a special place for you in hell, and I will make sure you get there eventually – that's a promise." I growled.

"This is just the beginning. Don't worry. It'll be fun."

"Fun? You call this fun?" I waved my hand around the mansion.

"This is evil and despicable. I'm a human being, not an animal that you can cage anytime you want. Isn't there any sympathy in your heart? Isn't there something in your brain that's telling you to stop because it's wrong?" I fought hard so tears wouldn't roll down my face.

"Then don't fight me." He simply replied.

I chuckled in disbelief. He grabbed my wrist and forced me back outside and back to the party. I composed myself so his women wouldn't see any fear in my eyes. I bet they laughed at my pain. The only face that comforted me was Lucia's. At least she had concern in her eyes, maybe even pity. At least one person had a heart.

"By the way, you can forget about the tracker. Juan already told my men about it. We've jammed the signal, so don't hold your breath for anyone to rescue you." He revealed.

Shit.

"Your life and your friends belong to me now. So, listen to me carefully. Anytime you do anything stupid like you did a few minutes ago, I'll punish both you and your friends. So, keep that in mind." He threatened me and finally released my wrist.

I could handle him hurting me, but not Ana or Juan. I couldn't even tolerate the thought of them suffering on my account. He grabbed another glass of whisky and said, "Behave and enjoy the party." He took a sip of his drink, winked, and took off to entertain his women.

I grabbed another glass of whiskey knocking it down like it was water. The aftertaste immediately slapped me, and I couldn't resist gagging loudly. The alcohol finally hit me, and I watched every step I took so I wouldn't trip and fall. I found a tall round table with no chairs and leaned my elbows down on it. I watched as Marco glided from woman to woman. Occasionally, he would grab their ass and kiss them. The sight was repulsive and made me want to vomit my guts out.

"Are you alright?" A familiar voice asked from behind. I turned to the beautiful Lucia.

I took a deep breath before responding. "Yes totally. Why?"

She placed her red wine glass down on the table and stood opposite me. "Well, we all saw what happened. He grabbed you and took you inside. Did he hurt you?" She asked.

"I mean, doesn't he do that with any of you?"

She looked at me, almost confused. "No, of course not. Well, unless we wanted to be hurt. Some women here are really into that kind of stuff."

I gently laughed in disbelief. "He is a monster."

She gently grabbed my hand. "The Marco that you know is not the man that I know. He's," she paused and then said, "sweet."

Um... what? Sweet? What the hell is wrong with her?

"You hesitated. So, I'm not sure how much of that is true, or if you're just in denial." I said bluntly. The whisky was messing me up. I was speaking in a manner that I'd never done before to anyone. Perhaps I was too harsh on her. After all, she was only trying to comfort me.

"Some women have been talking, and they said that you have a friend here?"

I paid close attention to her and stood up straight. "Yes. Her name is Ana. Have you or any of them seen her?"

She looked disappointingly away and back at me. "No, I'm sorry. That was all I heard. I'm not sure how much the others know about your friend, but I will keep an eye out for you."

I appreciated her kind gesture, but I couldn't pinpoint exactly why she was kind to me. After all, we didn't know each other.

"Why are you helping me?"

"Because I can tell that you don't want to be here. I know what it's like to be held against your will. I can only imagine the agony you're going through right now." She explained.

"You were held against your will? By whom? Marco?"

"Oh no, not him. My ex-boyfriend. We dated for a few years, and it was the worst time of my life. I never really knew what freedom was because of him. It took a long time before I could escape and when I did, I felt like I was reborn. And then I met Marco, and it was honestly one of the best things that happened to me."

If Marco wasn't a psychopath, I would have told her it was a sweet story.

"But anyway, I'm sorry you're in this predicament. I wish there was more I could do to help."

"It's alright. This is a battle that I have to fight on my own."

"Well, well, well," another familiar voice said from behind me.

I turned to Catalina in a stunning, metallic body-con dress that went to her feet, and hair in a high ponytail. Lucia, with worry in her eyes, immediately excused herself and left. I wasn't afraid of her, not anymore.

"Who would have thought that I'd run into you here?" she said calmly and then continued, "I'm quite impressed. Not only did you seduce Adrian, but it looks like now you've also gotten ahold of Marco. It takes skills to do that. I can't even hate on you."

"I'm not seducing anyone. Your crazy brothers targeted me and my friend."

"Well, your presence here says something different."

"I'm not here by choice. Your psycho brother kidnapped my friend and now is holding both of us, and Juan, against our will."

"If I remember clearly, your friend stabbed Marco. I mean, did you think he was going to let that go unpunished?" She asked.

"Well, if I remember correctly, one of his men slapped me, and I almost drowned. Then Marco nearly choked Ana to death. Or was all of that erased from your clouded memories?"

She sneered. "Marco never does anything without reason."

"Reason? So, what's his reason for beating up Jason? The guy you supposedly called your boyfriend."

Her smirk vanished, and she became quiet. I'd struck a nerve, and she wasn't pleased with my new boldness. A server with a tray of red wine stopped in between us and she grabbed a glass and gently sipped the drink. Never once did she take her eyes off mine.

"I didn't realize an ugly duckling could turn into a swan. But I have to say, Camila and Juanita did a pretty fantastic job."

I sensed she purposely avoided the conversation about Jason.

"Does it make you feel better about yourself? Insulting me?" I said, my eyes locked with her intensely.

Her smirk returned, but not as fully as she had previously displayed.

"You're brave when you're drunk. Let's see how long you last here. Marco can be ruthless, especially when he fucks. So, you better be careful not to get ripped apart." She warned.

What? I thought to myself. "How would you know?"

"Ask any of the women. They'll be more than happy to tell you."

I had no intention of asking them about their sexual activities with that monster. Plus, even just thinking about it made me shudder with disgust.

"Were you aware that he took Ana?"

"I'm his sister. No one knows him better than I do. I have to say you're bold to come after her. I am intrigued by why he kept you around. It can't be all because of *her.* "

"I thought you knew him better than anyone."

She sipped some more of her wine. I couldn't read her expression. I couldn't tell whether she was mad or sad or happy or just blank.

"Your family is part of the Gustavo cartel, right?"

My question must have interested her.

"You're naïve. It's almost cute. It's better to stay stupid than to ask questions that have nothing to do with you. Perhaps you should watch and learn from these women. That's what they do." Catalina winked and walked away. Even though all I wanted was for her to leave a few minutes ago, after our brief encounter, I had so many more questions circling in my head. I pushed myself away from the table and followed behind her.

"Where's Adrian?" I asked.

"Seriously? One brother is not enough?" She continued strolling through the crowd.

"Adrian doesn't interfere with Marco's business, so don't count on seeing him here."

I looked at her with determined eyes. "I'll get out of here. Watch me."

She stopped and finally turned to look at me. "I would love to see that. Good luck."

I turned around and walked as far away from her as possible. The ridiculous and unwelcoming party was enough for me. I started heading back inside when a hand grabbed my wrist from behind and pulled me into a corner behind the stairs, away from prying eyes.

"Adrian," I said, shocked to see him in casual dark jeans, a white shirt, and a black leather jacket. He scanned around to ensure no one saw us.

"Are you alright?" He asked quietly when our eyes met.

I looked at him with wide eyes. "What do you mean if I'm alright? I'm one of your psychotic brother's *whores*. Do you think I'm alright?" I asked, furious. I had to remind myself to keep my voice down so no one would hear our conversation.

"I know, I know I'm sorry. I should have never gotten you involved."

"You can say that again. You need to get me, Ana, and Juan out of here." I demanded.

I studied his face as he thought for a moment before answering.

"I will think of something. But please, in the meantime, obey him. It won't turn out well for you if you don't." He warned me.

"So, I'm just supposed to let your brother rape me whenever he wants?" I asked, almost in a sarcastic tone. I sometimes hid my pain behind snarky comments.

"Please, Alina, behave, and I promise I will get you out of here."

"And Ana and Juan?"

He clenched his jaw tightly and ran his hand through his hair. "I don't know if I can get all three of you out at the same time."

"I'm not leaving without them. So, you better figure something out."

"Alright, I will try. Now go back before Marco notices you're missing."

Before he took off, I grabbed his hand and stared at him with the most serious of eyes. "I beg you, please. Get us out of here."

"I'll try my best, I promise." He shot me a half-smile before disappearing around the corner.

To avoid looking suspicious, I went back to the party and stayed for a few more minutes longer. I made my way past the crowd and found a quieter spot on the stone balcony that overlooks the entire city. I rested my hands on the cold stone rail. *What a beautiful sight*, I thought to myself. *How could a horrible place like this be on such a beautiful mountaintop?*

"Your ass looks great in that dress," Marco said from behind me.

I turned around so he wouldn't be staring at my ass. He had both hands in his pocket.

"Enjoying the party?" He asked.

I laughed. "Are you seriously asking me that question?"

He strolled toward me calmly and stopped at my side. His eyes latched onto the view ahead.

"I rarely bother paying attention to just one woman, but I don't know what it is about you. I got concerned when I couldn't find you. What a strange feeling." He said, almost surprised at himself for saying that.

I wanted to jump off this balcony so I wouldn't have to hear any more nonsense from his mouth.

"I really don't care about your feelings. I came up here because I wanted to be alone. Away from you and your crowd of women. Is that too much to ask for? You know what? Don't even answer that." I walked past him to leave, but he grabbed my hand and pulled me back to his side.

"I didn't say you could leave." He looked displeased, and his voice was cold.

"Marco, if you don't let go, I will..."

He interrupted me, "You will what, Alina? Please go on, say what's on your mind. I'm very interested in what other remarks you have to make."

I knew if I said what I was thinking, there would be a punishment. So instead, I kept my mouth shut. He smiled with satisfaction. I thanked the skies when a short, blonde-haired woman approached us. Marco's eyes went dark. He wasn't pleased. The woman sensed his displeasure and hesitated at first but then said, "Darling, some of us are horny." She had a heavy Russian accent.

I only knew that because I met a few exchange students from Russia while in college, and they had very distinct accents. Of course, she was an exquisite woman with a curvy body that I wished I had. Our eyes met, and it was awkward. Marco was still holding my hand.

I turned to look at him and mockingly said, "*Darling*, you better go and entertain your guest."

He half grinned and let go of my hand. Before leaving with the woman, he turned and gave me a smirk, and disappeared into the crowd. I sense an orgy was about to happen, and I was not staying to watch that. I'd rather poke my eyeballs out with my bare hands. Just as I was about to walk back inside, an unfamiliar man with short black hair and a slender build, wearing a black suit appeared from among the crowd.

He walked straight to me and said, "Hello, my name is Diego, your private security. Marco instructed me to escort you back to the room and keep an eye on you," he said, clear and stern.

I didn't bother to converse back—my expression was raw and distant. He led the way, and I followed behind.

CHAPTER THIRTEEN

When I woke up, my head was throbbing. The dress I wore from the party was still on. I couldn't fully remember what happened after Diego brought me back to the room. Everything was a haze. I pushed myself up with my elbows, and immediately the room spun in a circle. The whiskey was very much still in my system, and I regretted every sip. I rested my head back on the soft pillow for a few more minutes before forcing myself to get up and go to the bathroom.

I brushed my teeth and scrubbed the makeup off my face. The cold water was refreshing on my face, and it woke me up. For a moment, I thought I needed to vomit, but it turned out it was a false alarm. I looked up and stared at the woman in the mirror and nearly didn't recognize who she was. My face was skinnier and so was the rest of my body. I'd only been at the mansion for a few days, yet I felt like I'd lost over twenty pounds. I couldn't decide if I was happy or not.

I unzipped the back of the dress and finally realized why I couldn't breathe when I woke up. It was the damn dress. I welcomed in a few deep breaths before grabbing a white cloth to dry my face. I turned on the silver shower faucet and hopped in the shower. My dry skin welcomed the warm water cascading down my body. I stood still under the shower and tried as hard as I could to clear my mind. That was easier said than done.

A half-hour later, I stepped out and wrapped my body in a white towel. I searched the black cabinets, hoping to find a T-shirt and shorts, but they were all empty. The bathroom was too massive to not have at least one piece of clothing. After a while of disappointing search, I gave up. Frustratingly, I strolled out of the bathroom to an unpleasant presence. Marco was resting upright on the bed against the headboard, half-naked and wearing only black joggers. His arms were folded over his chest, and he had a wicked smile on his face that made me very uncomfortable.

"The nude dress compliments your olive skin beautifully," he said with a satisfied grin.

I dismissed his compliment and instead coldly said, "I need clothes to change into."

"I don't think you'll need any clothes for what's coming next," he said. There was a cruel intention behind his eyes. *Oh no, not this again.*

"I think you should get used to the word no because unless you strap me down and force yourself on me, I will obey nothing."

"Or you can drop the towel and put on a show for me."

"In your dreams."

"Speaking of dreams, I had one last night of you."

I mirrored his demeanor and folded my arms across my chest as well.

"Is that supposed to be a pickup line? Because if it is, it's a shitty one."

"Take it as a compliment. I never dream about any women, ever."

"Um no. I think I'd rather jump off the balcony than accept your compliment."

He pushed himself off the bed and calmly strolled towards me like a predator. He halted in front of me, and it was too close to my liking.

"I don't understand why you fight so hard. You know that either way, I can do whatever I want with you, forcefully or not."

"It'll be a sad day when I willingly give myself over to you." I nudged him away from my personal space and steered towards the bed.

I lay under the duvet and prayed that he would leave me alone. Instead, he hopped into bed next to me. I pushed myself away, but he grabbed my hips with both hands and tugged me back. The next thing I knew, I was pinned underneath him.

"I like when you fight. It makes my dick harder. And when that happens, all I want to do is fuck you hard. I want to make sure you won't be able to walk for a few days." His black eyes drilled holes into mine.

"Ana should have killed you when she had the chance." I fought to separate myself from his firm clutch while praying that the towel wouldn't fall off my body.

He had a grimace and smiled. "She should have, but she didn't." He said and, with one swift motion, flipped me onto my stomach with ease.

Marco ripped the towel off my body, and suddenly I was naked. I felt his moist tongue on my neck and shoulders. My struggle was useless against his strength. The event had only started, but it felt like an infinity of misery. He turned me over to face him as he sat astride me with his cock swelling through his joggers. I was naked, vulnerable, and at his mercy. I closed my eyes and prepared for the worst.

I waited for him to assault me, but he hopped off and stepped away from me. Marco ran his hand through his hair a few times and clenched his jaw. He paced back and forth in the room, and I was left puzzled. I lay paralyzed as tears rolled down my cheeks. He intensely roamed his eyes up and down my body. His breathing became harsher and harsher and there was an intense sexual frustration on his face. I couldn't comprehend why he didn't finish what he'd started.

He took a deep breath and ran his hand through his hair a few more times. I snatched the blanket and encircled it around my body. I tightly clenched the blanket with both hands for protection. He glared at me with dark eyes, and there was an unbearable, awkward, and terrifying silence. I wished I knew what he was thinking about. Marco turned his back to me and chuckled in disbelief to himself. "I can't believe this," he said.

I remained still under the blanket, confused by what he meant.

He finally turned back to look at me and said, "I'll have Camila bring you some clothes." Without another word, he vacated the room.

I paused, mystified yet relieved at the same time. *What just happened? Why didn't he rape me? Why did he change his mind?* His actions did not reflect his supposed threats. The man, who I thought could and would do anything, changed his mind and decided not to rape me. Perhaps there was still some slight of humanity left in him. *No, Alina. He's a monster. You thought your father had a piece of humanity too, but he proved you wrong, remember?* Whatever his reasoning was, the nightmare was over, at least for now.

****

I woke up to Camila in her short black and white maid outfit.

"Good afternoon. I hope you had a good nap. I have prepared an outfit for you for the day. Master Marco would like for you to change and meet him for lunch outside." She said calmly.

She lay the clothes on the bed before excusing herself. As she walked out the door, I sat up. It satisfied me to see that it was a pair of gray sweatpants and a white tee. I couldn't handle being in another dress.

Once fully clothed, the door swung open, and Diego strolled in.

"Whenever you're ready," he said.

I sighed and hesitantly nodded my head. He walked me down the stairs and along the same path as the party and back to the same spot, but only this time, the other women weren't around. There was only Marco in a chair at the table, focused on the newspaper in his hands. *Who reads the newspaper anymore?* It was the twenty-first century, for crying out loud. As I approached closer, I realized he wasn't wearing a shirt, only white joggers. *What is it with him always being half-naked? The world knows you have a perfectly chiseled body, Marco, no need to display it to everyone every second of the day.*

Once I arrived at the table, Diego pulled out a chair across from him, and I sat down. I stared at the tremendous amount of food laid out in front of me. I wasn't sure where to look first. There was seafood, cherries, strawberries, bread, and grapes. There were some fruits that I wasn't sure I recognized. My head was spinning, and my stomach growled at the assortment of food. I hadn't properly eaten since I'd been at the mansion of hell. Marco was so focused on his reading that he didn't notice I was there. He only noticed my existence after my stomach growled for the second time. Finally, he folded the newspaper and set them down on the table.

"Eat," he commanded.

Though I was famished, I disobeyed his demand.

"I won't repeat myself, Alina. It would be best if you eat so you can have the strength to continue to fight me."

I stayed stubborn. Marco slammed his hand on the table aggressively and startled me.

"Do you want me to strip you naked and fuck you at this table right now, or do you prefer to eat?"

I finally picked up a cherry and slowly bit it. He sneered with satisfaction as I chewed the sweet and juicy fruit. *Bastard*, I thought to myself. I took my time eating the one cherry. I thought he'd be pleased that I was eating, but his irritation emerged once again. I knew I provoked him, but I didn't give that much consideration.

"I want to see Ana," I said.

"No," he said dryly.

"Why not?"

"Because you haven't done anything to deserve that privilege."

"Being able to see my best friend should not be a privilege, asshole." I regretted it as soon as I said it.

He did not take well to the insult and placed his silverware on the table and leaned back in the chair. I knew he was contemplating what he wanted to do to me. He crossed his arms and locked eyes with mine. *Be strong, Alina. If he wanted to rape or kill you, he would have done it already.*

"If I remembered correctly, you can't swim, right?"

I looked at him, confused. "What?"

He stood up from his chair and pulled me to my feet.

"What are you doing?" I asked.

Marco dragged me to the other side of the mansion, a place that I hadn't been to before. I fell to my feet a few times, but he pulled me back up and continued to drag me. My anxiety and heart rate increased, but once I saw where we were going, I panicked. "No! Let me go!" I yelled.

We stopped a couple of feet away from a vast and eloquent, square-shaped pool. *Oh shit!* After a few seconds, he resumed pulling me toward the water. I tried to plant my feet steady on the ground to make it difficult for him to drag me, but he was too strong. The closer we got, the faster my heart rate increased inside my chest.

"Marco, what are you doing?!"

The man didn't answer and tossed me into the water. *Shit, shit!* I yelled on the inside as I sank. Immediately, my body was in panic mode, and I struggled to emerge above the water. *Mom, help me!* The last thing I saw was his calm, shadowy figure staring down at me. Where was Adrian when I needed him? But then I had a crazy realization. If I died, I'd be free of him. And so, I accepted that fate and allowed my body to relax. I closed my eyes and sank to the bottom.

I thought Adrian had come to my rescue again when I felt a hand grabbing and pulling on my shoulder. I gasped for air once we broke the surface. When my vision returned, I saw it was Marco that pulled me up, not his brother. He held my body in his arms and kept me afloat, his expression empty.

"Are you insane!" I screamed and splashed water on his face.

"Every action has consequences. Insulting me is one of them."

"So, calling you an asshole is comparable to being thrown in the pool to drown?" I asked hysterically and in disbelief.

"That's still not enough, Alina." He forced his mouth on mine. I fought him off and slapped his face. Marco released his grip and let me sink again. My life was a game for him. He pulled me back up once more. I went to slap him again, but he caught my hand this time and pushed me against the pool wall. He pressed his entire body on mine, forcing me to feel his unwanted, hard cock on my stomach as his tongue ravaged mine.

After a few days with little food, a hangover, constantly battling with him, and nearly drowning twice, I didn't have much left. I stopped fighting because I knew I would most likely pass out from exhaustion if I continued. As soon as I did, he stopped and pulled away as if I had taken his excitement away. We remained in the water and stared at one another. I was bewildered when he gently caressed my face with his hand, something he hadn't done before. His expression turned soft. *What the hell is going on?*

"What are you doing?" I asked, perplexed. Then I realized he was thinking about Isabella. The mysterious woman that no one seems to want to tell me about but kept bringing up.

"It's your eyes. It's the first time I've seen you afraid."

"Of course, I'm afraid. I can't swim. Wouldn't you be if someone forced you to do something you can't do?"

"I fear nothing." He said sharply.

"That's a load of bullshit. Everyone is afraid of something. Nobody is invincible."

I will find your fear, Marco, I thought to myself.

"I realized why I'm… intrigued by you. It's not only because you remind me of Isabella, but it's your resistance and fighting. Do you want to know something? You're right. Although all those women you saw in the basement willingly stayed, there have been a few that didn't want to stay. Juliet and Carmela. They resisted too, but unlike you, they became excited by the games and eventually gave in and willingly offered themselves to me. It turns me on so fucking much knowing that I finally had power not only over their bodies, but their minds. Sadly though, that thrill only lasted a few months before I grew bored. At least with them, I knew that eventually they would submit. But with you, I can't sense anything. And that unknown is both frustrating and exhilarating." He explained as if it was supposed to make me realize and understand why he did what he did.

"You want to know why you can't sense anything? Because I hate you, and I find you revolting. I think you're a monster, and I will never submit to you. You might as well kill me now because you'll never get what you want."

He gave me a devilish smirk. "I'll break you, eventually." He lifted me and sat me on the hot concrete at the edge of the pool.

I immediately stood up to leave, but Diego blocked my way. *Has he been standing there the whole time just listening?* Marco pulled himself out of the pool. Camila ran out of nowhere and came to his side with a fresh white towel for him to dry off with.

"Take her to my room," he ordered Diego.

Wait, what? His room?

I turned to face him. "Your room? I'm not going there."

He beautifully dried his hair and tossed it around a few times like a supermodel at a photo shoot for some high-end magazines.

"You can either go to my room or go back to the pool."

Diego gently took my hand and slowly pulled me to walk after him. I hesitated at first, but then my eyes glanced over to the pool, and instinctively my feet moved on their own. I didn't want to revisit the water.

****

His room was bigger and brighter than the room I was imprisoned in, and the sunlight beamed through the enormous windows. There was a massive bed with a beautifully carved bed frame and white bedside tables. I saw a reflection of myself in the big square mirror at the end of the bed. I was instantly ashamed of the strange woman, whom I no longer recognized. My hair was messy and tangled, and my eyes were red from the pool.

"Why am I here?" I asked.

"You'll find out," he said, smiled, and left.

I wandered around the room. The white blanket was soft and smelled like fresh detergent. I strolled into the bathroom, noticing the white marble floor. It was half the size of my apartment. The walk-in shower had a glass door and could probably fit ten people or more. Between the double sinks and the shower was a giant, white oval bathtub that shone bright like a star. I'd never imagined a man's bathroom could look like that. I turned on the sink and splashed ice-cold water on my face. I needed it to wake myself up from this nightmarish reality. I gave myself a good stare in the mirror before walking back into the room.

I made my way to the bed and sat down on the edge. It was quiet, but that quickly ended when Marco entered through the door and closed it behind him. He didn't say a word. Instead, he pulled down his wet joggers and exposed his gigantic cock. I turned away to avoid the sight of it. Even though I had my back to him, I knew he was watching me.

"I was going to wait, but I realized I want you more than I expected," he said.

Shut him out, Alina. I felt a frigid chill course through my spine when his hand touched my shoulder. He stood me up on my feet and wrapped his arms around my body from behind. I felt his naked body pressed closely against mine and his hard cock brushed against my ass. Marco took in my scent like an animal. I felt his nose brush against my hair and neck. I wanted to run, but where would I go? His fingers trailed along my back, slowly and sensually. I lost control of my fear, and tears flowed down my face.

"Kill me, please," I begged quietly.

He stopped himself and turned me around to face him. For the first time, I didn't see the face of a cold-hearted monster but a strange look of concern. He took a few steps back.

"You would rather die than be here with me?" he asked.

"Is that a real question? Are you delusional or insane, or both? You've abducted me and my friends and then held us against our will. You won't allow me to see Ana unless I sleep with you, and you've tortured Juan like he's nothing. You've violated and tried to kill me multiple times. How am I supposed to feel? Happy? After everything, you dare to ask me such a stupid question. Do you even have a heart?"

He stayed silent and paced back and forth slowly, running a hand through his damp hair.

"Why don't you just kill me now? It'll be so much easier for both of us. And let's get one thing straight. Whatever sick and twisted game you and your brother are playing, I am not Isabella."

Death meant all of my problems would vanish. I wouldn't have to feel anything anymore. I wouldn't have to fear that he would rape me. There wouldn't be any more nightmares for me. Everything would be peaceful.

"I will never hurt you," he whispered. "I'm not the monster you make me out to be."

What?! I'm so confused. Did this man just do a complete 180 on me? I laughed at his moronic statement.

"The fact that you can stand there and say that tells me that's exactly what you are. Only a monster wouldn't realize that he is one. You say you won't hurt me, but you've nearly drowned me twice. Do you know the definition of a monster? It's you. Earlier, you casually talk about kidnapping two other women and raping them. You even said how proud you felt they submitted to you. Does that sound like something any normal human being would say? No, it doesn't."

"I never touched them, not until they allowed me to." He tried to explain.

"That doesn't matter. You still kidnapped them. Just because you didn't touch them until they told you, doesn't mean you weren't wrong. You know what, wrong isn't even the right word, it's criminal. You're a criminal."

"Be careful how you speak to me, Alina." He warned.

I ignored his threat once more. "And what about the women in your *creepy, luxurious* basement?"

"I've told you those women willingly agreed to be in the position that they are in right now."

"And what about me, Ana, and Juan?"

Marco came toward the bed and sat down on its edge. He tightly clenched his fists and avoided eye contact. That was a first. He never looked away from me. I was always the one to do so. But I was glad he did, because I didn't want to look into his eyes.

"This is strange," he said, avoiding the question. "I've never had to explain myself to any woman before. I guess there's a first time for everything in life," he said, amused at himself.

My body became engulfed with fire.

"You are a sick person. You need serious help. No, you need to be in prison to pay for all your crimes and have some serious therapy while you're there. That's what you need."

He nudged himself back up and closed the distance between us. Then, with one hand, he picked up my chin and forced me to gaze at him. He tried to plant a kiss, but I turned my face to the side and shoved him away. *I can't believe the nerve of this man.* His breathing grew louder, and I sensed his continued sexual frustration as we locked eyes. I took a few steps back, moving further away from him.

"Not only are you and Isabella similar in features, but I can see that you have the same heart and strength as her; perhaps that's why I can't see myself fucking you without your permission," he said.

What? What?!

"Stop comparing me to her. I am not her. I am Alina. And if I remind you so much of her, why not go back to her? Why trap me here?"

A look of despair and grief fell on his face. I couldn't believe my eyes. He actually *felt* something. I wondered if learning more about Isabella would be the key to my escape.

"You're right about one thing. You're not Isabella."

Marco left the room, naked.

I released a big breath of relief. It felt like someone had lifted a massive boulder off my chest. I knelt and pressed my back against the end of the bed. I brought my knees to my chest and hung my head between them. *Why me?* What have I done in life that was so bad that landed me in such a predicament? Perhaps it was because... *no, Alina, don't even go to that dark place. You had to do it and there was nothing wrong with it.* I counted from one to ten five times and inhaled, then exhaled three deep breaths. That was the only thing that kept me sane.

A soft knock at the door startled me. I looked up, and it was Camila.

"May I come in?" She asked in a gentle voice.

I nodded my head. She entered with a new set of clothes in her hands. She made her way to the bed and placed the clothes on it. *I wonder if she sees me suffer.* Right after I had that thought, she unexpectedly knelt beside me.

"Are you alright, señorita?"

"I-I'm not okay," I said, and tears rolled down like a waterfall.

She took my hand in hers and said, "Everything will be okay. Master won't hurt you. He may not be gentle in the beginning, but I think he feels something else for you."

I looked at her, bewildered.

"What feelings? Because I remind him of this mysterious Isabella? It's not right. I just want to leave this place with my friends." I pleaded.

"Is this... normal to you? How can you be sure he won't hurt me and those I care about?" I asked with genuine curiosity.

"Master brings no woman into his room. You're the first. That's why I said that he may feel something different for you." She replied.

"Not even Isabella?"

She looked down at her knotted fingers and then back up at me.

"Look, I don't want to get in trouble. He forbade us to speak about her. I think the best person to ask is the Master himself." She suggested. If only she knew I'd tried many times and failed.

"How long have you worked for him?"

"My mother and I started working for the Gustavo family about five years ago."

"Do you like it?"

"The Master treats us very well, contrary to what you may believe," she said and continued, "I know you're hurting, but trust me, things will get better." She stood up and said, "I have to go, but I hope you find the clothes to your liking. Is there anything else I can help you with before I leave?"

I shook my head from side to side. Camila gave me a half-warm smile and left. Though brief, the interaction made me feel slightly better. At least I had someone to vent my pain to. I changed into a pair of black leggings and a white sweater. I realized the clothes were mine. Marco must have gone back to the resort and grabbed my luggage, or at least his men did. The man planned everything.

I stepped back into the bathroom and thankfully found a blow dryer. I spent the next fifteen minutes blow-drying my thick black hair. Once finished, I pace back and forth in the room, bored out of my mind. At least twice, I checked if the door was unlocked, and each time it wasn't. Finally, I turned and leaned my back against the door in disappointment for the second time. *When will this nightmare end?*

A sudden scuffling and thumping outside the door startled me. It sounded like someone, or something had fallen to the ground. I pressed my ear against the door and at first heard nothing. It was dead silent. I leaned in more carefully and there it was again, the sounds of a struggle. I grew fearful and took a few steps back. What the hell was going on out there? The unknown was eating me up on the inside. The door suddenly burst open, and I'd never been happier to see a familiar face.

"Adrian?"

He put out his hand and said, "Come on, we've got to go!"

I gladly grabbed his hand and followed him. I stepped outside and saw Diego lying on the ground, unconscious. Holy shit, was he dead? We ran down the long hall as fast as we could. But then I remembered something, stopped, and pulled him back, "Wait, what about Ana and Juan?"

"They're in the car waiting. Now come on!"

I was so relieved to hear that they were safe. I happily bolted behind him as fast as my two feet could take me. We jumped and skipped down the stairs, and there were four big men in dark gray suits at the bottom. Initially, I thought they were Marco's men, but I soon learned they were Adrian's. We all ran through the foyer. I had to look away when I saw many of Marco's men unconscious on the ground. We headed toward the front entrance and outside. The driveway itself took about five minutes to run down. We finally reached the tall metal black gates, and I had to stop and take a breath before I passed out.

"Alina, we don't have time to rest. We need to leave before my brother catches us!"

I took a deep breath and continued. There were two black Cadillac Escalades parked outside the gates. All four men hopped into the first car while Adrian opened the second car door and prompted me into the back seat. I looked around, and there was no sign of Ana and Juan. As soon as he jumped in the passenger seat, the driver pressed the gas, sending my whole body flying backward.

"Where's Ana and Juan?" I asked him.

He turned to look at me with guilt in his eyes and said, "I'm sorry. I knew that if I told you the truth, you wouldn't have come."

"What! You mean they're still in there?!" I asked angrily.

"I'm sorry," he said apologetically.

"We have to turn back now!" I demanded. I tried opening the fast-moving car door, but it was locked.

"Will you shut up before I regret this?" The driver said.

I recognized that voice anywhere. It was Catalina. Our eyes locked in the rearview mirror. What on earth was she doing? I blinked in confusion.

"Why are you helping me?" I asked, genuinely curious.

"Trust me if it wasn't for my little brother begging me," she turned to look at Adrian and back at the road, and continued, "I would have left you there to be one of Marco's possessions. This changes nothing. I still hate you," she said dryly.

The feeling was mutual. Though I wouldn't say that I hated her.

"We have to go back," I demanded.

"We can't. When Marco finds out you're gone, he's going to come looking for you. Trust me. I know my brother. He doesn't like when his possessions are taken from him. We've arranged for a private jet to take you back home." Adrian said.

I couldn't keep my thoughts straight. I sat back and took a few deep breaths to avoid going into a panic attack. Ana and Juan were still in the mansion of hell, but there I was, fleeing away. *No, just no.* I refused to leave my friends. I started hyperventilating.

"Alina, I need you to breathe, please," he begged.

He sounded like my mother. *You can't panic now. What good will that do?* I said to myself. I counted from one to ten and spotted everything I could outside, using all five of my senses. All my therapists would be proud if they were present. Finally, my breathing slowed down.

"I'm not leaving without them."

"You don't have a choice," Catalina said, clearly annoyed by my persistence.

There was no luck when I checked the lock again. Marco and his family have once again trapped me. I would have jumped out and ran back to the mansion if I could have. I turned my head to stare out the back window. The estate became smaller and smaller the further down we drove. Marco only kept Ana to use as a pawn against me. What would he do to her now that I escaped?

"Is he going to hurt them?" I asked, my voice scared and trembling.

The sibling duo remained silent, and I wasn't too fond of it. *What if he rapes Ana and then kills them both? Or what if he chopped her fingers off like he said he did to Juan? What if he sells Ana as a sex slave?* All the dark thoughts magnified my fear. I was nauseous. How was I supposed to look her parents in the eye and tell them what happened to their daughter? How would I tell Juan's family that he was gone? Tears boiled under my eyes and soon rolled down my face uncontrollably. I hopelessly watched from inside the car as the world slowly passed. I closed my eyes, hoping I'd wake up, and it was all a terrible dream.

About an hour later, we finally arrived at a small airport in the middle of nowhere. There was a small private jet waiting for me. Catalina jumped out of the car while Adrian and I remained seated, silent. I watched as she approached a bald man standing by the jet stairs.

"You lied to me," I said, upset.

He turned around and looked at me.

"I am truly sorry, Alina. I never meant for any of this to happen, ever. When I first met you, I should have left you alone."

"Why did you seek me out so badly?"

He remained silent, contemplating what he should say next.

"You reminded me of someone that I used to know. The similarity you two share was so uncanny that I found myself drawn to you immediately. I couldn't help myself, and I had to get to know you. I should have known better to leave you alone." He explained.

"Isabella?" I asked quietly.

"I'm assuming my brother told you."

So, once again, all the events that had unfolded within the last few days all came back to *her*.

"Who was she?"

"If we had time, I would gladly tell you. But right now, I need to get you out of Mexico."

He hopped out of the car and opened the back door for me to get out. I remained still, unwilling to move.

"Please, Alina. It is not safe for you to stay here any longer. You have to get on the jet now and go home."

I ignored everything he just said. The only sound I heard in my head was Ana and Juan's scream.

"Hurry up!" Catalina yelled.

He placed out his hand and said, "Please."

I hesitated at first, but then slowly grabbed his hand and stepped out of the car. He walked me toward the jet.

"Everything's set?" he asked the bald man.

"Yes, sir, everything is all set. We are ready to jet," the man responded in a deep voice.

Before I stepped onto the plane, Adrian handed me my wallet, phone, and the keys to my apartment.

He gently grabbed my face and said, "I wish we could have met under different circumstances. I never thought I would meet someone who could remind me of what it meant to feel again after so many years. For the short time that we had together, I am forever grateful. As much as I want to see you again, I hope that we never do, for your own sake," he lightly planted a kiss on my forehead.

It left me with more questions than answers, and I didn't like it for one bit.

"I don't want to go," I heard myself say. "Not without Ana." More tears cascaded down my face.

"I know, but you don't have a choice. I won't allow anything to happen to you."

"Please, I'm begging you, please save them."

"I can't guarantee you anything, but I truly promise that I will try my best to get them out."

I grabbed his hand and brought it close to my chest. "Repeat it."

"I promise, okay?" He reassured me.

I briefly glanced over at Catalina. She had a look of boredom and annoyance on her face. I was certain at one point she rolled her eyes in disgust at our conversation. She was indeed a cold-hearted woman. She and Marco were of the same breed. But even though I disliked her greatly, I was appreciative that she helped me escape.

"T-Thank you, Catalina." I didn't realize those two words could be so challenging to say.

With a blank expression in her eyes, she said, "I didn't do it for you."

"Trust me, I know, but I still appreciate that you assisted him in helping me escape."

"Let's hope you don't find yourself back here again."

The bald man gently grabbed my hand and escorted me up the stairs into the jet. He led me to a comfortable black leather seat before disappearing into the cockpit. I looked out the window. Adrian and I locked eyes the whole time until the plane started moving, and he was no longer in view. I turned my head until I couldn't anymore. Finally, the plane took off.

CHAPTER FOURTEEN

I opened the door to my apartment, stood outside, and breathed in a sigh of relief at the familiar setting. After a few seconds of solace, I stepped inside, closed the door, and leaned my back against it. I tossed my keys and wallet on the tiny wooden table by the entrance and wandered to the couch, slumping down into it. I'd concocted various ways to break the news to Ana's parents during the jet ride. However, none of them had a decent outcome. After a while, my brain stopped functioning. I knew I couldn't prolong it any longer, so I grabbed my phone from my back pocket and dialed Mr. Davis. My palms were sweating profusely as the phone rang. I couldn't even understand the anguish he would feel once I broke the news to him, but he deserved the truth. I know I would if I were a parent. He answered on the fourth ring.

"Hey kiddo," he chirped, unbeknownst to what I was about to inform him.

I remained silent for a few seconds. I took a deep breath and began, "Hi Mr. Davis." My voice was trembling more than usual.

"Hey, so glad to hear from you. I've been trying to reach Ana, but she texted me she was having too much fun, so she couldn't talk on the phone. You guys must be having a blast, huh?" He asked and laughed.

I sat up straight on the couch, confused at what he meant. "What do you mean?" I asked.

"Well, after realizing I missed three of her calls about three days ago, I called her back immediately. But she didn't respond. I only got a text saying she was tired and was going to bed. I got a text from her the next day and she said you guys were going to explore the city and probably wouldn't have the best service. My wife showed me all the pictures Ana texted her. It looks like you guys are having a blast."

Marco must have coerced Ana to deliver those text messages to her parents.

"Alina?" He asked after I remained silent and trapped in my thoughts.

"Mr. Davis, there's something that... I have to tell you," I said, scared.

"What is it, sweetheart?" he asked, his voice softening.

I took a deep breath and rambled about everything that had happened since we arrived in Cancun, to the moment I was on the phone with him.

After my lengthy explanation and repeated rambling, Ana's parents told me to stay put as they jumped into their Mercedes and drove over.

I sat impatiently waiting for their arrival. About thirty minutes later, I heard a knock on the door. I hopped out of the couch and hurried to the door. Mr. And Mrs. Davis stepped in with Detective Walter, a long-time friend of theirs. He was the lead investigator in Sofia's disappearance. They became close and kept in touch afterward. Over the years, Detective Walter stopped by the house to visit and check in on the family. Although I hadn't seen him in months, he still had an enormous belly, a thick mustache, and a head full of messy, silver hair.

Mrs. Davis embraced my weak body immediately upon seeing me. She always had a motherly touch. That was why I adored her so much. Her hugs reminded me a lot of my mother. Though I was delighted to see her, I felt guilty that I was the one hugging her and not Ana.

She separated from me, gently caressed my face, and said, "We're so glad you're safe."

I couldn't hold my tears any longer as I stared at them both. How could they not be furious that it was me they were embracing and not their daughter?

"I'm so sorry," I said as tears rolled down.

Mr. Davis took me in his arms and stroked my back. "Oh, sweetie. It is not your fault. Never think for one second that it is. We are glad that you're here with us right now."

I wanted to believe their words, but it was hard to. I couldn't imagine not feeling some type of way if somebody else's daughter was in front of me and not my own. I knew they didn't want to exacerbate the situation, but I wish they were more honest and yelled at me or something. Perhaps I was overthinking the situation.

I turned my attention to their dear friend. "Good to see you again, Detective," I said and wiped my tears away. It was no time to cry.

"Yes, and you as well, Alina. I'm glad you're okay. Now, why don't we sit down, and you walk me through everything, okay?"

I nodded my head. We all settled down on the couch. I prepared myself for all the questions that were coming my way. He had done this before with Ana and her parents. I knew I had to be emotionally ready. It helped that Mrs. Davis was clasping my hand.

"And you said his name is Marco?" he asked.

I nodded my head.

"Do you know his last name?" He asked as he was jotting down notes in his small brown notebook. That was what an actual detective looked like, not like the two scumbag officers in Mexico that didn't bother to do anything.

I shook my head but then remembered. "Well, my friend Juan mentioned the Gustavo Cartel, but I'm not sure if that's the last name."

Detective Walter's face fell suddenly after hearing the last name. He knew something. I studied him carefully, awaiting what he had to say.

Mr. Davis clasped my hand tightly. "Do you know something, Walter?"

"Law enforcement knows Gustavo's name very well. Their leaders have been on the top ten most wanted list for many years. They're one of the most powerful and dangerous cartels in the world. I will reach out to the police force in Mexico and notify them of the situation," he explained. There was a lack of confidence in his voice, and I didn't like it. Detective Walter was always confident.

"Those scumbags," Mr. Davis began, his voice trembling. "Walter, I can't lose her, too. She's all we have left." Tears rolled down his face.

Mrs. Davis rested her head on his shoulder. She caressed his arm lovingly and delicately.

"I promise, Mark. I will do everything in my power to find her."

For the next ten minutes, I provided him with as much information as I could. I hesitated at first to mention Adrian and Catalina. They helped me escape, after all. *No, no. This all started because of them.* The rational part of my brain shouted and instructed me it was the right thing to do, especially since any knowledge could help find and save Ana. So, I told him everything and left nothing behind... well, except for a few minor details. I was too ashamed to speak of it. After nearly an hour, I was both mentally and physically exhausted.

"Thank you for all the details. You did a great job."

I gave him a weak smile. Mrs. Davis came back from the kitchen and handed me a cup of warm English Breakfast tea that she made. I gladly took the cup in my hand and sipped the warm beverage.

"No matter what you are thinking right now, we do not blame you. We are so glad that you are sitting right between us now." She said once again.

"She's right. I know you fought hard and did everything for our baby, and that's all that we could ask of you. We can't imagine losing both of you." Mr. Davis said.

"What about the tracker?" Detective Walter asked.

"As soon as Alina told me what happened, I checked, but it got disconnected." He reported.

"Marco told me he found out about the tracker and had his men jammed the signal," I said.

"That evil son of a bitch," Mr. Davis said, furious.

Even though he was putting on a strong face, I knew he was in pain. I knew he couldn't panic because he had to be strong for his wife. He was always the cool-level-headed one in the relationship, and his wife was the more anxious one. He always helped keep her calm. I admired their relationship.

"How can people be so evil?" Mrs. Davis said, finally shedding tears she'd held back since coming to my apartment. Her husband took her in his arms and delicately smoothed her hair and rubbed her back with gentle hands.

"I will do everything in my power to find Ana, Margret," the Detective said. Then, he took out his wallet, grabbed a card and handed it to me, and said, "If you remember anything else, please call me, alright?"

I took the card. "Of course."

Before they left, Mr. and Mrs. Davis held me tightly in their arms once more. I didn't want them to go, but it'd be selfish for me to ask them to stay the night in my cramped home.

"Get some rest. We'll call you tomorrow." Mrs. Davis said and kissed me goodbye on the cheek. I gave them a half-smile and watched as they descended the stairs and into their car.

The darkness outside reminded me it was getting late. I quickly jumped in the shower, changed into the soft black pajamas that Ana got me for my 20th birthday, and curled up in bed. I fell asleep once my head hit the pillow.

I run and run in the never-ending halls of the mansion. I try to find an exit door, but a brick wall appears everywhere I turn. Then I hear him calling my name and his footsteps heading my way. I continue to run, but the more I try to move faster, the slower my legs are. Finally, I come to a dead end, and there is nowhere else to turn. I turn around to Marco with a wicked smile.

I sprung up in fear. My breathing was erratic, and my forehead was drenched in sweat. The room was a scorching sauna. I pushed the blanket off my body, hopped out of bed, and headed toward the kitchen. I'd never been so thirsty in my life. My throat was dried like the Sahara Desert. The instant air cooled my body as soon as the fridge door opened. I grabbed a water bottle and drank. I felt like I had been denied water for days, and I finished the entire bottle in seconds. *Great Alina, good luck trying to sleep now without waking up twenty times to use the bathroom.* Oh well, it was worth it. I leaned my back on the kitchen counter and stared at the microwave clock. Damn, it was only two in the morning. I wasn't surprised that I had a nightmare about him. If I weren't so tired, I would have stayed awake until the morning. I strolled to the bathroom and relieved myself before jumping back into bed. I hesitated to turn off the side table lights. *Grow up. You're not a child anymore,* I scolded myself. So, I turned it off and covered my head under the blanket.

  When something touched my face, I thought I was having another dream. I gradually open my eyes to a menacing presence. I jolted awake with terror and panic. Marco calmly stood at the side of the bed, leaning against the wall with both hands in his pockets. He was in a white, long-sleeved button-down shirt and black suit pants. His dark pants matched his black eyes. I wanted to scream for help, but my throat was closed shut. I scooted to the further side of the bed and wrapped the blanket tightly around my body.

  "Did you think you could run away from me?" He asked with a frigid voice.

  "How...how did you find me?" I asked. My whole body was quivering with terror. I'd never been so frightened of him until that moment.

  He walked toward me and stopped at the end of the bed. "It wasn't hard. I have people for everything. Finding you wasn't that hard. The better question is, did you think I was going to let you escape? You think I wouldn't come for you?"

I glanced over at my phone on the other side of the bed and launched to grab it, but he was quicker. He clenched my ankle and hauled me towards him. He maintained complete control once I was underneath him. I scrambled and struggled as hard as I could.

"I spent the entire plane ride asking myself, why did you leave? Do you know how frustrating it was not knowing the answer?"

"Are you serious? I left because you're a psychopath. You're sick, and you need help. Let me go!" I declared as I tried to fight away from his clutch.

"You belong to me, and when I say you're mine, you are mine. There's no choice."

Am I in a terrible horror movie or something right now? This can't be real.

"I don't belong to anyone!" I shouted in his face. "HELP!" I finally yelled out.

Before I could scream out for help again, he used his mouth to cover up my voice. He forced his tongue into my mouth aggressively as I fought, effortlessly. I tried to move away from his furious roughness, but it was impossible to do so with his body heavily pressed on top of mine. Once he finished devouring my mouth, Marco looked down at me. I was afraid to look into his eyes. They were unusually blacker than normal.

"Scream again and your friends will be punished," he warned.

"If you're going to kill me, then do it. I'm tired of all the games." I surrendered.

"I will never hurt you, but just so we're clear, no woman leaves me unless I tell them to. Is that understood?" He asked me.

I remained silent underneath him.

"I'm tired of your disobedience," he ripped the shirt off my body, and it left me half-naked and exposed. It was humiliating.

I tried to yell for help again, but he grabbed my shirt and stuffed it in my mouth. After that, I no longer had a voice. Marco untied his black tie and bound my hands above my head. Once satisfied, he stood up, ripped my shorts, and tossed them on the floor. I was fully naked and hopeless. Even my father wasn't that evil. He never felt the need to dominate my mother by binding her hands or stuffing fabric in her mouth. Perhaps it was because she was obedient. Maybe that was why he never felt the need to do it.

He took a step back and trailed his eyes up and down my vulnerable body, and his manhood was bulging through his pants. He clenched his jaw and ran his fingers along his bottom lips. Not knowing what he was thinking was the scariest part.

"I told you, every action has a consequence."

He strode atop me and trailed his fingers from my face to my neck and breasts. He carefully fondled my nipples and as much as I tried to control my body, they hardened on their own. It disgusted me that my body reacted in that way. It was wrong. His slow and sensual motion frightened me to the core. I wanted to vomit. I looked up at his eyes and there was desperation and hunger in them.

"I'm going to remove your shirt from your mouth. If you scream, I will force my dick into your mouth to shut you up. Understood?"

I nodded my head in obedience for the first time.

"Good girl," he pulled the fabric away.

I took a massive gasp of oxygen into my lungs.

"See, it's not bad when you listen. If only you could continue to do that, then I won't have to be this person who you don't like me to be," he said.

"I'm sorry that I don't have that much obedience in listening to a psychopath," I said sarcastically.

"I don't think a psychopath can feel the way I feel about you."

"Really? And what's that?"

"I almost went crazy when you left me. That's when I knew I needed to have you. I knew you needed to be mine." He said possessively.

This man is batshit crazy.

"You can't just have someone like that, Marco. We're living in real life, not a movie. You can't just say stuff like that and expect me not to loathe you. It does the opposite. Every minute I spend with you, I feel angrier and angrier, and my hatred toward you grows every day. I hate everything about you."

"I'm not giving you an option. I'll turn that anger into lust and desire. Eventually, you'll come to me, and you'll want me. However, I can't guarantee that I won't be able to touch you without your permission until then. Especially now, you look so helpless and desirable."

"What are you going to do?" I said, terrified.

"It's best if I show you,"

Right away, his mouth dug deep into mine. I felt every unwanted desire and sensation that he had for me. His lips were demanding and firm on mine. He moved his lips from my mouth to my neck and kissed every inch of my upper body. I stopped fighting because it did me no good and instead held my breath. He expertly sucked and licked my breasts with his tongue. His movement sent an unwanted message down to my sensitive area. I was pissed at myself for feeling that way. I was too weak to experience that emotion.

Marco's lips met mine once more, and it was gentle for the second time. I was frozen in place, and I hoped he felt he was making out with a corpse. He moved his hand down to the most sensitive area and slipped his middle finger inside my sex. It took me by surprise. He slid it in and out, slowly and digging deep inside me. I tried my best to contain my emotions. But once he circled my clitoris with his thumb, I nearly let out a moan. His fingers ravaged my sensitive spot. I closed my eyes and avoided his animalistic glare. Though I couldn't see his face, I sensed his satisfaction. He continued with the motion. I unwillingly arched my back and pushed my head back at the mercy of his fingers. He licked my neck up and down. Finally, he pulled his finger out and allowed me to breathe. My heart was beating erratically and uncontrollably. He remained on top of me. A small teardrop rolled down my cheeks.

"I told you I would break you," he whispered in my ear.

A sudden thought dawned on me. *What if I pretend to submit? What if I allow him to fuck me until he gets bored? After all, that was what happened with Juliet and Carmela.* He mentioned he let them go once he was bored if I remember correctly. So perhaps that was my only way out. Maybe if I could fake pleasing him, he'd also let me see Ana and Juan. *Use your survival instinct,* mom used to say. I stopped contemplating and latched my eyes to his. Marco observed me carefully. I lifted my head and leaned in to kiss him, a gesture that caught him off guard. He slightly pulled his head back and, with confused eyes, said, "What are you doing?"

"Isn't that what you wanted? This whole time, for me to submit and finally give myself up to you? Well, I'm giving that to you now. We can agree that I'll fuck you or I'll continue to fight until I can't anymore. Pick." I said in a stern voice.

He looked shocked and amused. The choice wasn't hard for him as he brought his lips to mine. I played along and kissed him back—our tongues danced together with passion. Marco untied my hands and pulled my body up straight, and closely embraced me in his arms. *It's only a game.* I chanted in my head. Finally, he grabbed my hair and pulled my head back as his tongue devoured my neck. I stared up at the white ceiling in shame. He pulled my face back down and once our eyes locked, I took a deep breath and said, "F-fuck me, Marco."

He was stunned and aroused at the same time. He gently set me on my back and hopped off. Marco unbuttoned his pants, and his hard cock sprung free from his pants. As he paced around the bed, he watched me intensely. He stopped between my legs and knelt on his knees and spread them into a missionary position. He kissed my legs and thighs and then moved his soft lips to the sensitive area. I took a massive breath in and prepared myself for the assault. I didn't look down at him. He mercilessly ate my wet sex, and I nearly convulsed. My toes naturally and unwillingly curled. I made the mistake of looking down at him between my legs. *Holy shit.* The sadistic psychopath was so hot as he swirled his tongue in and out. *No, Alina, no!* I fought internally, and it hurt as much as I was pleased. Finally, I lost the battle and gasped out loud. He stopped and took away the gratifying feeling when I was close to climaxing. He stood up and said, "You like that, don't you?"

"Can you shut up and just fuck me and get it over with?" I said, ashamed.

He gave me a grim smile and without hesitation slammed his cock inside me. *Shit!* His cock was buried deep inside, and I felt every inch. I understood why those women signed a contract to be his whores. He was not gentle, and I was afraid. He viciously thrust in and out while letting out animalistic groans as he pounded me non-stop. Marco tilted his head back in pleasure and savored every moment. I'd never felt such a full sensation in my stomach before.

"Tell me to fuck you," he demanded.

Ah, are you shitting me?

"Please… f-fuck me," I begged.

What the hell was I doing? Was I still pretending, or was a deep part of me enjoying it?

He pulled out suddenly and flipped me onto my stomach. He grabbed my hips with both hands and pulled my ass up, my face buried deep in the bed. He knelt once again and devoured my sex from behind. How did I go from not having sex for years to being eaten out by the son of a powerful drug lord?

"Holy shit," I heard myself say.

When I was close to exploding, he stopped and stood up, backing away from me. Confused, I turned on my back with heavy breathing and looked at him. He pulled his pants back on and leaned against the wall with both hands in his pockets.

"Why did you stop?"

He gave me a devilish smirk and said, "That's your punishment. I will not allow you to come until I say so."

Motherfucker. I knew I should have continued to fight his ass. I covered myself under the blanket like a complete loser. *Why Alina? Why did you do that?!*

"Get dressed. We're leaving now." He demanded sternly.

"Leaving? To where?"

"Back to Mexico."

Though I didn't want to return to that place, I knew that was where Ana and Juan were, which reminded me, "Please tell me Ana is alright?"

"I thought about letting my men fuck the shit out of her, but I thought about you. I knew you wouldn't be pleased. So, for now, she's safe."

I was relieved. If she was safe, that was enough for me.

"You're courageous, Alina." He said as he grabbed some clothes out of my closet and tossed them to me.

I grabbed black joggers and white crop top and changed.

"I'm impressed that you got my siblings to help you escape," he returned to his favorite spot on the wall and leaned against it.

"Are they alright?"

"Should they be? They betrayed me. I don't like betrayal, especially from family members," he said with bitterness in his voice.

"What did you do to them?" I asked curiously.

"Nothing that you need to worry about, but if you're wondering, I can't kill them. But that doesn't mean I can't punish them in other ways. My father wouldn't be pleased if he found out I killed them."

"Have you... killed anyone?" Why was that even a question, of course, he had.

His stillness and silence answered my question.

"Actually, no, don't tell me."

"I like the way you taste." His voice was raw and disturbingly disgusting.

I had no response. Instead, I just sat awkwardly on the bed. *Holy hell, I allowed him to fuck me.* My head was spinning in a circle. I wanted to kill myself.

"Why now?" He asked.

"Why now what?" I responded with a counter-question.

"Why suddenly surrender yourself to me? You've fought so hard ever since the first day we met. And now suddenly you decide you want to fuck me too? I'm curious why." His eyes were fixated on my body.

I wasn't stupid enough to reveal my plan to him, but I wondered if the answer was too obvious. What if he had already suspected that I was only pretending to surrender? Did I just turn into the idiotic character in movies that everyone hated, including myself? I had to be smart with my response.

"I just want to see my friends." That was the best I could mutter out.

"I think you're slowly falling for me, and you don't even know it, or you're afraid to admit it to yourself. I think you've been horny for a while, but you've been telling yourself no because you think I'm a monster that you shouldn't be fucking. When I was inside you, I felt your need and desire. But you're afraid that if people were ever to find out, they'd judge you for your choice. You wonder who would ever stand and sympathize with a woman that fell in love with someone like me, especially after he took her best friend."

I smiled in disbelief. It was good to know that he suspected nothing out of the ordinary. He was more blinded than I thought, which benefited me.

"You think I have feelings for you? Wow! I wish you could read my mind. Then you would know my exact thoughts about you. I'm doing what I need to do to survive, nothing more."

"Well, I don't believe that you're willing to fuck me now because you want to see your friends. If that's true, you would have done it since the first day you were at the estate."

I stood up and folded my arms across my chest. "Believe what you want. If you want to continue to fight, then I will. But know one thing," I took a few steps closer, "I will never fall for you, ever."

"We shall see. Now let's go." He grabbed my hand and walked me out the door, down the stairs, and into a black Cadillac Escalade. Diego was the driver. Had he been waiting in the car this whole time?

"It's good to see you again," he said to me as I settled down.

I ignored his greeting. I sat in silence as he drove away. Shortly after, we reached the airport, hopped into a private jet, and headed back to Mexico.

CHAPTER FIFTEEN

My face fell in despair when I saw the estate gates open. I was silent throughout the car ride, and so was Marco. It was wonderful because I didn't want to hear anything out of his mouth, anyway. Finally the car pulled up to the driveway and parked in front of the mansion. He had to yank me out of the car because I refused to move. Diego drove the car away and left us standing at the front entrance. He took my hand and dragged me inside, straight to the elevator. I was filled with dread as he pressed the "L" button. We were going to the basement. I'd preferred to stay in the darkroom.

As soon as the door opened, he dragged me out, and shortly after, we were in the presence of his women. They were enjoying themselves but stopped everything once they saw their so-called Master at the door. The women's eyes gawked with desire and thirst. It was a sickening sight.

"Mariana," he called out.

Mariana, a stunning black woman with naturally curly hair and beautiful blue eyes, in nothing but black lace lingerie stood up from the white couch. Her body was voluminous, and it astonished me at how perfectly fit and toned she was. *How can anyone be born with such a blessing?* She looked like she could walk in a Gucci or Versace fashion show. She ambled up to Marco with a glass of champagne in her hand and greeted him with a lusty kiss on the lips. I stare with disgust.

"It's good to see you again, darling," she said with a British accent.

"I love those luscious lips of yours. I could suck on them all day," he said to her.

They were eye-fucking each other, and it was apparent. Finally, too disturbed, I snatched my hand away from his firm grip.

"This is Alina. She's new, and she will stay down here with everyone for a few days. Take good care of her for me?"

She looked at me with icy eyes. I already knew she wasn't too fond of me. There was nothing but negative judgment behind those piercing blue eyes. She gazed back at her master. "Of course, anything for you."

Marco turned his attention to all of the women in the room. "And no one is to touch or hurt her. Is that clear?"

All of them nodded their heads in obedience, and I had thought watching him and Mariana tonguing one another was sickening. He kissed her once more before pushing me towards her and leaving the room. Once he was gone, she walked around and scanned me like a predator. She took a slow sip of her drink and brought her other hand to her hips. Then she took a few steps back and re-examined me again. *What is this, a circus show?* Finally, she finished her drink and instructed one of the women to pour her another glass. And they did, without hesitation. I understood then that she was the alpha female of the group. She moved with such confidence and elegance it wasn't difficult to figure out.

"There's only one rule you need to know while you're down here. You must do everything I say, and if you don't," she giggled to herself and continued, "Well darling, don't even try, and you won't get hurt." She turned around, strolled back to the couch she came from, and sat down. She signaled for a blonde-haired woman to rub her feet, and to my astonishment she did just that.

The other women were still looking at me, so to escape their unpleasant glares, I made my way to a small white couch in the corner, far away from everyone else. I sat down, lay my head on the couch's arm, and counted to ten to control my anxiety. *Could this day get any worse?* Just as I was about to close my eyes to take a nap a young woman, probably around my age, with black hair to her shoulders, approached me. She had two glasses of wine in her hands and with a smile, said, "Hi Alina, my name is Stella."

I hesitantly took the glass she offered. She placed her hand in front of me. I pushed myself up and slowly shook it. She had a genuine, warm smile on her face. It was refreshing compared to the other women. She looked way too innocent to be in a place like that. She reminded me of Lucia, and I wondered where she was. I hadn't seen her yet since I was dragged back to this horrible place. She sat down on the other side of the couch. I thanked her for the kind gesture.

"Where are you from?" she asked.

"Rhode Island, and you?"

"Florida. I came down here for a vacation a few months ago at one of the many luxurious resorts." She sipped her drink.

"How did you end up here?" I asked with curiosity.

"Well, on the last day of my vacation, I ran into Marco and his men, and I quickly fell in love."

I arched an eyebrow and thought to myself, *how can anyone fall in love with that monster?*

"I know it sounds ridiculous, but I believe in love at first sight. He was the most attractive man I have ever seen. I was too shy to ask for his name, but I was surprised when he approached me in the restaurant and told me about his unique hobby." Stella saw the look of confusion on my face and giggled.

"I know it's crazy. How can any woman agree to be a whore? When he first told me about it, I wanted to run to the airport and fly back home and forget about everything, but then I realized that the riskiest thing I've ever done in my life was to come here for a vacation by myself. I have no family or friends back home, so what's the worst thing that could happen?" She finished her wine.

I looked down at my glass, which was still full. I didn't even have the chance to drink any of it because I was so shocked by her revelation.

"You can have mine." I proposed, which she gladly accepted.

"So, you're okay with him fucking other women and abducting those that don't agree to his *hobby*?"

"At first, the idea scared me, but when I became open-minded and tried it, I enjoyed it more than I thought. Abducting women? Of course, I'm not okay with it, but I also know that he won't do anything to them until they permit him to."

It seemed like Marco had truly brainwashed her. She made it sound so normal it was frightening. I regretted offering her my drink because now I needed that wine more than ever after what she said. Was she delusional? Maybe she was experiencing Stockholm syndrome.

"Look, he's not a bad guy. He treats us very well here. We have everything at our disposal, and we get to wear elegant and expensive gowns, go to parties, and travel all around the world. I could never in a million years have imagined the things that I've been able to do and experience here. I would have never done so if I were still back home. Honestly, my life was pathetic until I came here." I watched as she chugged the entire glass of wine in one massive gulp. And then she said, "What about you? What's your story?"

I paused for a few seconds to absorb everything she said. Then, after counting to ten in my head, I responded, "I came for a vacation with my best friend. I ran into his brother and sister and, shortly after, him. Some shit went down with a friend of ours, and we intervened, not knowing that it would put us into the crossfire. We tried to leave, but Marco's men came to our hotel room and kidnapped my best friend."

She had a look of pity on her face. "I'm sorry that happened. How did you end up here?"

"I tracked her phone, and it brought me here. It wasn't a well-thought-out plan. His men found us, and the next thing I know, I'm here."

"Wow, I wish I had a friend as devoted as you are. She must be a fortunate person to have someone like you."

"I'm the lucky one to have met her. She saved my life." I said, and it was the truth. If it weren't for Ana, I wouldn't be alive.

"Wow, brave and humble. You're one of a kind." She praised me.

"There's nothing brave about me at all. I think you're brave for putting yourself in such a dangerous position."

"Oh, this isn't dangerous at all. Marco never lays a finger on us. He's the first man who has never physically put his hands on me. I've had too many of those shitty relationships. That's why I don't have any friends. They grew tired of telling me to leave those terrible relationships, and I wouldn't listen. After a while, one by one, they disappeared. I was alone for the longest time. I came for a vacation alone, hoping I would find myself again, you know." She explained.

"Well, then they're shitty friends. A genuine friend would have stayed by your side no matter what."

Her eyes lit up with delicate warmth. "Thank you, Alina. Those words mean a lot to me."

"You're welcome."

"And I'm sorry that Marco kept you captive. I believe you're the third person he has held against their will. I know that the first two eventually gave in, but he got bored and let them go. So, what are you planning to do then, since you don't want to be here?" she asked.

I had to be careful not to expose my plan, so instead, I said, "I don't know. I guess I'll escape from here somehow."

"Well, good luck with that. Perhaps play the same game as the first two women. Maybe then he'll lose interest. There's one thing that I know about him is that once you're in his grasp, it's impossible to get out. The only way to be free is if he allows you to be free." She said with a straight face. *Trust me, I know.*

"Stella, enough small talk with the new girl. Come and give me a neck massage." Mariana ordered.

"I lied. There's one thing that's unpleasant about being here, and that is living with that bitch." She whispered in my ear before getting up and leaving to attend to the alpha female.

I slumped down on the couch and closed my eyes, hoping that I'd be able to find some peace and fall asleep.

A loud groan and scream woke me from my deep slumber. I slowly pushed myself up and rubbed my eyes to clear my vision. Once I had, what I saw was truly disturbing.

The room was empty except for me, Marco, and Mariana, and he was pounding her in the missionary position while her back was on the couch. I had no idea a woman's leg could spread that far apart. He flipped her onto her stomach and took her from behind. He was thrusting into her hard as she screamed in pleasure, then he grabbed her hair in his hand and pulled her head back. At one point, I thought her head would touch her back. However, she was the alpha and took his cock like a champ. He smacked her butt multiple times, which made her moan even louder. When Marco let go of her hair, her face went straight into the couch. He turned to look at me with fire and need in his eyes. The scene was both erotic and disgusting. I turned around and had my back to them. Though I couldn't see, I could hear the aggression in his voice as he pounded her. I covered both ears with my hands, hoping to drown out the noise.

"Fuck me harder!" she begged.

"You like it when I slap your ass?" he asked her.

"Yes, Daddy, slap my ass harder," she begged him, and he did.

All I heard was screaming and moaning for another five minutes. Was that another one of my punishments for escaping the compound?

"Fuck I'm coming. I'm coming!"

"That's its baby. Come all over my dick. Fuck, that's so creamy," he said, and then he exploded. "Fuck!" he growled.

Finally, it was over. I breathed a sigh of relief. And even though they were done, I didn't bother to turn around. But that didn't stop Macro from grabbing my shoulder and turning me around to face him.

"Next time when I fuck another woman, you will watch the whole time. Understand?"

To ensure that he wouldn't suspect my plan, I slowly nodded my head.

"Where are the other girls?" I asked, diverting my attention to something else.

He pulled up his gray joggers and ran a hand through his messy black hair. Marianna stood up from the couch, naked, and strolled toward a wine rack, grabbing a bottle. She poured it in two glasses, and then walked back to the couch and handed a glass to her master. The two of them sat down comfortably on the sofa, enjoying their drinks. Marco drank his wine in one big gulp and placed the empty glass on the enormous rectangular glass coffee table. He turned to her and said, "Leave the room. I want to talk with Alina, alone." he ordered.

Marianna looked at him with a surprised expression. She briefly looked over at me and I knew her dislike of me grew tremendously. She placed her glass on the table and said, "Are you sure? We always hang out for a few minutes afterward."

He shot her an ice-cold glare and his expression was dry. "Do not make me repeat myself." His voice was ruthless.

Immediately, I saw fear in her eyes. She knew she had crossed a line by not obeying his command the first time. She lazily lifted herself to leave the room, but not without eyeing me down the whole time.

Great, now I'll have to deal with her later.

"Come and sit next to me," he instructed.

I pushed myself up, strolled towards him, and sat down on the couch. It was still wet from their sweaty sex. *Ew!* I sat still, as far away as possible, and paid no attention to him and his half-naked body. I focused my eyes on the flat-screen TV mounted on the wall in front of me. But even though I wasn't facing him, I could feel his burning stare on the side of my face. I reminded myself to stay calm. His hand gently tugged my hair back so that he could get a better look at me.

"I'm curious about you," he said suddenly, breaking the silence.

I remained still.

"Why did you surrender yourself so fast to me?"

I had to be careful how I answered his question. "Like I said before. I wanted to see my friends, and besides, I've grown tired of fighting with you. There's no point because I lose either way."

"Or perhaps you're hoping that I'll get bored and let you go?"

Damn it. Is the plan that obvious?

"How long have you guys been friends?" he asked casually.

"Almost ten years."

"It must be nice to have such a good friend as Ana. I admire the friendship you two share. It makes me envious sometimes. But being who I am, having friends is not possible."

I turned to look at him with pity. He sounded lonely. I knew what it felt like to be alone before I met Ana. "But you have Adrian and Catalina." I reminded him.

He spread his arms out on the couch. "Siblings can be… annoying sometimes. They have their ways of provoking me from time to time. For example, when they helped you escape."

I wouldn't know what he was talking about because I had no siblings. I always wanted a brother or sister. Someone that could have gone through what I went through as a child with me. But I realized it was a selfish thought. Why would I ever want anyone else to experience the pain I suffered?

"What about all the women here? I'm sure they keep you company." I said, slightly irritated to think he had so many women at his disposal.

"They keep me occupied, but I grow tired of just fucking these women sometimes. At some point, I want to know what it feels like to make *love* to someone that I truly care for."

Who was this person sitting next to me? I barely recognized him. One minute he talked about gagging and fucking women, and then the next minute he talked about making love. *Perhaps if you stop with all this ridiculous bullshit, maybe one day you can find someone to love.* My sympathy dwindled after I reminded myself of who he was.

"What about you? Have you fallen in love with anyone?"

What was it with both brothers wanting to know about my love life?

"I don't remember agreeing to disclose my personal life to you," I said, annoyed.

He gave me a grim smirk. "That's fine. Maybe we should fuck instead of talking then?"

I had a feeling that would come out of his mouth at some point. I turned to look at him with an arched eyebrow. "Really? You just had sex and you already want more?"

"I've always wanted *you* more."

Why does his compliment feel both violating and erotic at the same time? Perhaps because he was a sexy man. I doubt I'd have these conflicting feelings if he were ugly.

"Who are you, exactly?"

Perhaps the more I get to know him, the more I can figure out his secrets and weaknesses. Then maybe I could use that against him and beat him at his own game.

"I thought you didn't want to talk about your personal life, so why do you think it's ok to ask me about mine?"

"Well, perhaps because I would rather talk about it than have sex with you."

He sat back on the couch and didn't respond to my initial question. Maybe with all the time spent fucking those women and being a boss, he never had time to sit with someone and talk about personal things. Perhaps he didn't even know how to begin the conversation.

"My father is the head of the Gustavo cartel that expands into multiple other countries in the world. We've been the most feared, and most wanted, cartel for the last fifty years. My father is getting older, so I've been handling most of the business as the head of the organization. My grandfather was the man who started all of this. We own businesses, resorts, casinos, strip clubs, and much, much more. You name it; anything major in Mexico, we have a hand in."

I absorbed the information he disclosed. I felt like I was reading a book or watching a documentary. It was scary, but almost intriguing to learn.

"Are you proud that people fear you?"

"I wouldn't say that I'm proud. There are many things that I've done in my life that make me wish I was normal sometimes, like you. Perhaps your innocence is another reason I have become so drawn to you. Whenever I'm around you, I feel a small sense of normalcy. Something that I don't feel with any of the women in here." His voice was meek and soft.

"What about Isabella? Whenever you mention her name, there's a change in your tone and eyes. I can already tell she was special. Right?"

"You have good intuition. Yes, you're right. She was very special to Adrian and me."

"What made her special?"

"Isabella saw the real me and never once judged or criticized anything I had done in the past. She understood me."

Every time Marco spoke of her, he became a different person. He was vulnerable, and someone you would never guess in a million years was a sadistic psychopath.

"What happened to her?"

He remained silent.

"She's not important anymore." He responded, and suddenly his voice was back to the same, bitter man I had grown used to.

"That's not true at all if talking about her brings you such pain."

"She's not important anymore because she's dead."

Woah. I was not expecting that at all. I feared asking him the next question, but my need to know was irritatingly annoying. "Did you...kill her?"

"Does that matter?"

I instinctively stood up from the couch and took a few steps away from him. Before I could go any further, he grabbed my hand

and pulled me back down, close to his body. He grabbed the back of my head, pulling my face close to his, our lips just barely touching. I felt every breath he inhaled and exhaled. I trembled.

"I can sense your fear. But that's not what I want you to feel."

"How should I be feeling, then? You killed the woman that was supposedly the most important person in your life."

"I never said I killed her. There are things you shouldn't be so quick to judge."

"Why shouldn't I judge you? You're the son of a drug lord who kidnapped my friend because she defended herself against you. You tortured Juan like he was nothing, and you've done nothing but violate my mind and body without my permission." I was full of rage as I reminded myself of everything he'd done in such a short time.

"Did I violate your body? If I remember correctly, you finally submitted yourself to me. Then, you allowed me to fuck you. I don't think that's a violation when I had your consent."

His audacity was astonishing.

"I wouldn't have to do anything if you had just let us go." I pushed him away from my body and slid to the other side of the couch, as far away from him as possible.

"You're not fooling anyone, Alina. I know exactly how you want to play this game. You want to let me fuck you until I get bored. The only flaw in that plan is that I feel something for you. Something that I can't even explain myself."

Shit, well, there goes the plan. I guess I shouldn't be surprised. It wasn't even that elaborate, anyway. Perhaps deep down, I wanted Marco too. *No, Alina! Stop that thought right now!*

"That's not true." Was all I managed to say.

"I want you to *want* and *desire* me. So, I will convince you sooner or later. But since you are in denial about pretending, why don't we just continue this game?"

He sat back on the couch and spread out his arms and legs. Instantly his hard cock was bulging out of his joggers. I turned my head away. I carefully waited for what would come out of his mouth next.

"Since you finally submitted yourself, I want you to suck my dick. Right now."

I remained calm, but I was screaming in protest on the inside. He sat patiently, waiting for me to obey him. Do I continue with my flimsy plan, or just give up? After debating internally, I slowly got off the couch and knelt between his legs. He watched me hungrily. I pulled down his pants, stopping slightly above his knees, and watched as his dick sprang out. It had been five years since I last had a dick in my mouth. And quite honestly, I was never any good at it; perhaps that was why some guys weren't interested after our first attempt. How was I supposed to do it to a man who probably had his cock sucked every single day? The thought that I was going to do it wrong made me nauseous.

I grabbed his cock with both hands and moved myself slightly up to suck the tip. The second my lips touched his cock, he groaned. He raised his hips so his cock went deeper into my mouth. My jaw hurt as his large cock invaded my mouth. *How should I feel about this?* I asked myself. *Perhaps I should be savage and bite his dick off. That way, he could never use it again. Woah, Alina, that's a bit too dark.* I snapped myself back to the present, although the thought of him suffering in unbearable pain was definitely appealing. He grabbed my hair with both hands and moved my head up and down. Marco was not gentle; I felt the head of his cock hitting the back of my throat. The more I choked, the hungrier he became. He proceeded to fuck my mouth viciously.

"Fuck" he groaned.

I couldn't decide what was more messed up, pretending to submit, or seeing an image of my mother once doing this to my father in my head. My mother acted like she enjoyed herself because she knew that would please him, but more importantly, she knew it would stop him from forcing me to do it. I remembered it like it was yesterday. My mother and I made eye contact once, and all I saw were tears rolling down her face. I was about seven years old and didn't fully comprehend what was happening. I didn't understand until she sat me down and told me what she was doing and why she had to do it. *"Remember, everything I do, I do because I love you. And I will do whatever it takes to protect you from harm. One day, you will understand what it means to do something that you do not want to survive. I pray you will never have to, but just in case it happens, you'll know and understand."*

Her angelic voice rang loudly in my head. I fought emotionally, but deep down; my body was fighting against me. Once satisfied, he pulled his dick from my mouth and sat up straight. He released my hair and delicately pushed it out of my face. Marco pulled me up by my shoulders to his level and passionately slid his tongue into my mouth. I resisted the kiss for as long as I could. He pulled my shirt over my head and unhooked the back of my bra. He tossed both pieces of clothing onto the fluffy, white rugs. Then he had me straddling him on the couch, half-naked. He gently ran his thumb along my lower lips.

"You have the softest lips of any woman I've ever tasted." His eyes never left mine.

He glided his fingers over my breasts and stomach, and slid them inside my shorts, into my sensitive folds. It tickled a bit before it felt good. He slowly circled and rubbed my clit with his fingers, and I nearly combusted. I realized I'd made the first move and slid my tongue into his mouth. He slipped a finger inside, and I groaned against his breath. The moment went on, and I surprisingly didn't want it to end. Marco broke the kiss and stared into my soul.

"I want you…*so* badly."

He moved his tongue to my right breast and licked, gently biting and sucking on my nipple. I never felt so turned on and wet in my life. I knew it was wrong, and I knew I had allowed myself to be in over my head with this poorly constructed, fake plan. I questioned my morality, and my sanity.

He placed both hands under my arms, picked me up like I weighed nothing, and laid me on my back on the soft rug. He swiftly pulled my shorts off and spread my legs wide before him. Then he stood on his feet and scanned every inch of my naked and vulnerable body on the floor.

"You're beautiful," he said roughly.

My legs instinctively spread wider at his comment. He kneeled between my legs and his lips slowly kissed my thighs. He didn't miss an inch of my skin. I refrained from looking at him because I knew if I did, I would orgasm. But the monster was good with his mouth. The woman enjoying this wasn't me, and I contemplated killing myself after. I was Alina, the girl who judged female characters in movies that got abducted and somehow magically fell for their captor. I used to laugh profusely because the content was so comical and unreal. Yet, there I was, fucking Marco, the son of a powerful drug lord.

I nearly convulsed when his skilled, wet tongue slid in and out of my pussy. *Fuck,* I said to myself. I made a mistake when I looked down at his dark eyes and devilish smirk. He ate me out with his soul—the bastard knew what he was doing. My head tilted back, and my back arched like it never had before. I grabbed his hair hard with one hand while the other was tightly gripping the rug underneath me. I felt it coming.

I was close to exploding into a million pieces when he stopped. "Beg me to fuck you," he demanded.

With every fiber of my being, I wanted to say *yes, please fuck me,* but I knew what I was doing was wrong. I didn't need to pretend to submit and allow him to fuck me until he got bored. He had no right to decide that; I did. And even if I had to fight him until my very last breath to escape the horrible place, I would.

"No," I said, my face calm and straight.

"What?" he said, confused.

I pushed myself up, away from him, grabbed my clothes, and quickly slipped them back on. Marco stood up and stared at me. I couldn't tell if he was angry, upset, disappointed, or all the above.

"You gave yourself to me, Alina. You're mine," he said, as his possessive look and voice returned.

"I guess you're right. It's all a game. I won't continue to pretend to surrender myself and allow you to do whatever you want with my body. I'm going to continue to fight you, and even if you rape me, at least I'll know that I haven't lost my integrity." My face was calm.

He strolled towards me, and I backed up until my back pressed against the wall, and I had nowhere else to run. He took my face with both hands, his eyes holding a predatory look that I hadn't seen before. I didn't back down. I was no longer scared, and I was ready to fight. The old Alina was back.

"No woman has played me before," he said. I could hear the frustration in his voice.

"Well, get used to it. The longer I'm here, the more you're going to regret keeping me. You took my friends and my freedom, so I'm going to take away the one thing you desire." I said with confidence.

"I can have you either way," he said coldly.

"As long as I'm alive, I won't make it easy for you," I told him. My eyes were just as bleak as his.

"We shall see." He pushed himself away from me and walked to the door. Before exiting, he turned to give me a chilling grin, and then he was gone.

As soon as he disappeared, I slowly slid my back down along the wall. I put my hands in my hair and then my head between my knees. I made myself as small as possible. Perhaps then the pain would also shrink. *Holy shit, Alina, what did you do?*

CHAPTER SIXTEEN

I awoke to a chaotic scene of women preparing themselves for something. I blinked to clear my vision. Many of them wore dresses in shades of black, maroon, and nude. *What in the world is going on here?* Finally, a familiar face appeared in the chaos. I took a few strides towards Lucia, who was sitting in front of the vanity table. She glanced at my reflection in the mirror as she applied red lipstick.

"What's going on?" I implored.

She turned to face me in the chair. "We're going to the club."

"The club?" I arched an eyebrow.

"Yes, we usually get invited to be in one of his clubs once a month. I think this is a new place that they just bought," she reported with an ecstatic voice.

So, I guess hosting parties for the women in the enormous backyard wasn't enough. He also took them to clubs. *Disturbing, yet fascinating,* I thought.

"Aren't you going to get ready?" she asked as she zipped the back of her short black dress.

Me, at a club? It was a funny thought.

"Yeah, I think I'm just going to stay down here and relax. I'm not into that sort of thing," I said awkwardly.

She looked at me, alarmed, "I'm not sure how well Marco is going to take that. I'm not sure if that's wise. He doesn't like when women don't obey his orders," she warned.

I appreciated her concern, but I didn't care about his rules, or his punishments. "Well, it's a good thing I don't care what he thinks," I said, slightly sassy. Unquestionably, a new Alina - I wasn't sure if I liked her yet. She made hasty, dumb decisions, for example, faking submission to Marco and having sex with him, only to regret it later.

"Suit yourself," she said and trotted into the walk-in closet that was twice the size of my apartment and full of designer clothes and shoes.

I went back to my little corner and sat down comfortably in the soft, round chair. I was adamant that no one would persuade me to change my mind. Plus, I didn't care to partake in another one of his freak shows. I observed as the other women swooned over Mariana in her fitted, fiery red gown that hugged her curves in all the right places. I couldn't lie, she was a gorgeous woman. Of course, the others were beautiful too, but there was always one woman more captivating than the rest, and she was it.

If it weren't for the clock mounted on the wall in front of me, I wouldn't have realized that it had been three days already since he tossed me in the basement. Stella made the time pass by more quickly and almost made it tolerable. She had been babbling nonstop. I didn't mind though, because her talkative nature took away my need to think of something to say. The girl loved chatting about herself and how extraordinary her life had become since abandoning her life in Florida. It was disturbing to see her face light up every time she talked about her sexual activities with Marco. I'd never seen a woman so excessively infatuated by an abuser like him.

I watched the poor girl struggle for the third time to pick the perfect dress to wear for the evening. Her last option was a long silver gown that I thought was lovely. It confused me that she wasn't too fond of it. It fit her pear-shaped body flawlessly. Once she saw I had been watching, she moved toward me in her nude, lace lingerie. In her hands was a black and silver dress. Frankly, the two were indistinguishable. The only difference was the color.

"Which one do you think I should wear?" She asked, holding both up for me to judge.

I analyzed both gowns and said, "The silver one. It looks good on you."

She grinned. "So glad I have at least one person here that I can trust. Are you sure you're not going?"

"I'm sure," I said with utter confidence.

"That sucks. It would have been fun to be with at least one person I like."

Good attempt, but that won't work, Stella, I thought to myself.

"It's time, ladies." Mariana declared and directed the sheep out the door. Stella hurriedly jumped into her dress, plopped her tiny feet into black pumps, and ran out the door.

"Bye, Alina," she yelled before bolting out.

The room was empty, the quietness was almost pleasant. Hopefully, leaving for the club would become more frequent, so they could leave me unaccompanied. I stood in the middle of the room alone and savored the peaceful moment. I hadn't relaxed since being back. The basement was undoubtedly better than waiting in the darkroom or Marco's room. If he thought tossing me down here was a punishment, he made a mistake. In the new space, I had the satisfaction of drinking as much champagne and wine as I wanted. I could watch TV whenever I wanted, play pool or even relax in the jacuzzi.

I strolled toward the bookshelf mounted on the wall behind the pool table. It was full of every piece of literature you could think of. I was not bored. I skimmed my finger through each book, searching for the right one to distract my mind until they returned.

The door unexpectedly opened, startling me. I turned around, and it was Diego. He stepped in, wearing his usual black suit. "Why aren't you dressed?" He asked, dissatisfied to find me still in my black shorts and a tank top.

I ignored his existence and continued my search for the perfect book, but even though I couldn't see his face, I felt his glare of disapproval.

"Alina, if Marco finds out you're not going to the club, he will not be happy."

I heard the desperation in his voice as if he knew he would get scolded by his master.

"Well, then he won't be happy. That's not my problem." I said, my voice raw.

"Your friend will be there."

It grabbed my attention. I swirled to face him, struggling to comprehend whether it was a ploy to get me to go. I'd been lied to before about the whereabouts of Ana, and I didn't want to fall for another scheme again.

"Are you lying to me so that I'll go with you?"

"I do not lie. Ana will be there. I suspect she has already left, along with the others." He said dryly.

I thought to myself for a few seconds. *Should I trust him?* After a long ten seconds debating with myself, I decided I had no choice but to put my confidence in him if I wanted to see Ana. Without further hesitation, I grabbed the black dress that Stella was holding earlier, ran into the bathroom and slipped it on as quickly as I could. There was no time to do my hair or makeup, so instead, I threw it into a high ponytail and applied a nude lipstick I spotted on the bathroom counter. Finally, I grabbed one of the many black heels lying on the white marble floor, and to my surprise, they fit perfectly. Aside from my perky breasts, the only other quality I genuinely liked about myself was the ability to change and be ready at short notice.

"Impressive," he said once I stepped out of the bathroom.

Damn right, I thought to myself proudly. I followed him as we headed to the elevator and up to the foyer. It was as vacant as Marco's heart.

"Where are the others?" I asked as I looked around.

"They've already left. You'll meet the women at the club, including your friend."

"I swear Diego, if you lied to me about Ana, I will…" I struggled to articulate an intimidating threat, "Spend the rest of my time here trying to kick you in the balls."

My harmless words did nothing to him. Why would they? It was an amateur warning that even a bully in elementary school wouldn't be afraid of. Instead of being terrified, he chuckled, and that was the first time I ever saw him smile. He looked so young when he did.

We strolled outside to a black BMW SUV, waiting. I let out a sigh of relief at the sight of the vehicle. The thought of walking in heels from the driveway to the gates sent a pinch of phantom pain to my feet. He opened the back door, and I stepped in. Then he got into the passenger seat, and the driver turned on the ignition, the car roaring to life.

We drove down the long, steep mountain. The car descended with each minute of the ride. I glanced at the clock, and it was a quarter past ten at night. Somehow when I woke up, I thought it was earlier. It disappointed me that it was pitch black as I looked out the window. I wanted to view the thick, luscious green trees. That view kept me occupied the day Marco brought me back to Mexico. Since I couldn't see the trees, I tilted my head up to the sky filled with shiny bright stars. I remembered when my mom used to bring me up on the rooftop at night to watch the stars. One of the nights was also the first time I saw her bruised wrist as she pointed up to the sky. I was seven and clueless, so I thought little of it. She used to tell tales of each star and what they meant. Those lovely memories helped me cope throughout the years without her. Sometimes at night when I wanted to feel closer to her, I'd sit outside the balcony of my apartment and stare up at the sky.

After about thirty minutes, we seemed to have leveled out. It took another half an hour to drive through downtown. It was a beautifully lit night filled with majestic old brick buildings on either side of the road. Each building had its own story, hopefully not as sad as mine. There were people all around, laughing and smiling with their friends and families. There was lovely Spanish music playing in the background as the car drove through the crowded street. The city was saturated with color, history, and culture.

The car finally came to a halt and parked in front of a tall black gate. Diego hopped out and opened the door for me to exit. He was a gentleman, and I realized I had become fond of him. The gate opened, and he led the way inside with two men behind us. I felt important for a brief few seconds. As soon as we reached the club, more upbeat Spanish music played in the background, blasting into my ears. The club smelled like expensive perfume, cigars, and alcohol. We walked along a narrow hall where some people stood and stared curiously. Although there weren't really that many people, it felt overcrowded. We descended the stairs and finally reached the club, entering a massive, open floor full of people. My heart pounded instantly at the sight of so many humans in one spot. There were strippers barely wearing any clothes dancing on poles. They were twirling and performing impressive tricks. Ana convinced me to join a pole dancing class once, and I nearly died.

We continued navigating through the crowd. There were people gathered around high black tables and leather chairs, while others were on the dance floor, drunk and dancing. There were powerful-looking men, mostly in dark suits, sitting in the VIP sections, protected by large, muscular security guards. Most of them had a woman on their lap or at their side. Some of them snorted white powder from the table. As we made our way through the crowd, I stared blankly at Diego and avoided eye contact. I had no clue where he was taking me, but I prayed it was to Ana. I looked around, but she was nowhere in sight, and neither was Marco.

"Where's Ana?" I asked, but it went unheard because of the loud music.

Before attempting to ask again, a soft and cold hand grabbed my wrist and pulled me back. I turned around. It was my beautiful best friend.

"Ana!" I screamed and pulled her into a tight embrace. I held on to her as if it was the last time I'd be able to. A sense of relief washed over my body as I took in her familiar scent. Once we separated, I looked her up and down at arm's length. She still looked like herself, and healthy. There were no visible scars or bruises that I could see.

"I missed you so much!" I exclaimed, my voice trembling with happiness.

She gently grabbed my face and kissed both my cheeks. "I missed you more. I thought I would never see you again."

"I know. When I escaped, I was afraid Marco would hurt you. I couldn't shut my eyes without seeing an image of you in pain. Ana, I was terrified." I felt warm tears falling from my eyes.

"He came into my room right after you escaped. He was furious. I thought he was going to kill me immediately, but he didn't. I was so relieved when he told me you had disappeared. I thought at least one of us needed to make it out."

"I'm so sorry. Adrian lied to me. He said you were in the car, and I stupidly listened and followed him. I tried to come back to you, but I couldn't. They made me get on a jet and fly back home. I told your parents everything, and by now they probably realize that I'm missing again. Detective Walter is working on the case."

A slight sense of relief appeared on her face.

"That's good. I'm sure Dad tried to track me, but that asshole had it jammed."

"Did he hurt you at all?"

"Thankfully, no. I've been mostly kept in the darkroom. The only time I saw another person was when they brought me food."

"He is a sick, twisted man. I don't know how the hell we ended up in this position."

Although I had a theory in mind, I couldn't fully make any conclusions until there was more information.

"What about you? Has he done anything to hurt you?"

I looked down at my knotted fingers, ashamed.

"Alina, what is it?"

I could barely lift my head to face hers. *Why do I feel this way?* She had been with me through everything. I had no reason to hide what I'd done.

"Alina, you're scaring me," she said, her voice soft.

She grabbed my hands in hers.

"You know you can tell me anything."

I finally lifted my head and faced her. "I did something that I'm not proud of."

She waited for me to relax and speak when I was ready. That was another admirable trait about Ana. She knew when to push and when not to. Finally, I took a deep breath and exhaled through my nose.

"I had sex with Marco."

Ana remained calm.

"Did he force you?"

"Not exactly. I pretended to submit, hoping he would eventually get bored and let me go. I was hoping that if I did what he wanted, he would let me see you. I tried to follow through with the plan for as long as possible, but I couldn't."

Before I could utter another word, Ana pulled me in for another hug. She gently caressed my back.

"Oh, love. I'm so sorry."

Ana had a way with words, even when she didn't say much.

"I hate myself," I said, my face buried in her hair.

She pulled me away, "No, you will not do that. You did what you had to do to survive. People have done far worse things to survive, and there is no shame in that. He may have us physically trapped in his prison, but he will not have us mentally. I refuse to let that happen; do you understand me?"

I nodded my head and said, "I love you so much."

"Ditto." She said with a warm smile.

I hadn't realized that Diego had left, which surprised me. I didn't think he would leave me alone like that. Perhaps he wanted me to have my moment with her. Whatever the reason was, I was glad to have the time.

"Who was the man in the black suit that was with you?" She asked.

"His name is Diego. He's one of Marco's men, assigned to monitor me."

"Have you seen Juan?"

"No. He wouldn't tell me anything other than...." I paused.

"Other than what?"

"They tortured him for information."

There was invisible smoke bursting out of Ana's ears. She slowly paced back and forth in a rage.

"I'm going to kill that bastard."

Suddenly, *"Hawaii"* by Maluma and The Weekend played in the background, and her face turned gloomy. It was a painful reminder of her and Juan's first-time dancing together. She tried her best not to shed any tears, but on the inside, I knew she was slowly crumbling.

"Hey," I said, and stopped her. She had to calm me down earlier, and now it was my turn.

"We will find him, and we will escape."

"Promise?"

"I promise."

As the night continued, more people showed up. Here and there, I made eye contact with some of his women. I searched for Stella and Lucia, but they were nowhere in sight. I looked around for Diego and Marco once more and still had no clue of their whereabouts. Finally, I grabbed Ana's hand and pulled her to a corner by the bar where the music wasn't as loud.

"I have a plan. Why don't we find someone and ask for help?" I suggested.

"I was thinking the same thing."

We scanned around to see if there were any men in black suits, but there weren't. I assumed we had only a few minutes to locate someone who might help. My eyes glanced around the room and stopped on an elegant, older woman in a silver gown sitting at the bar. She stood out amongst the others for reasons that I couldn't explain. Perhaps it was her age? From afar, she seemed harmless, and frankly, her composed and straight posture reminded me of my mother. I stopped Ana from taking another step.

"I think I found someone," I said, pointing to the woman. She approved of my choice, and we immediately approached her.

"Excuse me, ma'am, do you speak English?" I asked.

She turned to look at us with familiar black eyes. She placed her wine glass on the table and said, "I do."

"Oh, thank god," I said, relieved. "Please, a man named Marco Gustavo kidnapped us, and we need help. Can you please help us?"

Her eyes lit up when she heard Marco's name like she knew him. As if that wasn't odd enough, what threw me off even more was the fact that her demeanor was calm and collected. I'd expected her to react with horror after learning about our abduction, yet she had the opposite reaction. The woman didn't reply, which only made my anxiety spike further. I had no clue what she was thinking about, but I feared Diego could show up at any moment.

"Ma'am, please, we need your help!" Ana begged.

The woman stood up gracefully and said, "Of course, I will help. Follow me," and led us to the nearest exit by the bar.

I thought I would feel a sense of relief that someone was helping us, but something about her made me uneasy. I hesitated to follow her lead.

"Hey, why are you just standing there?!" Ana asked after realizing my feet weren't moving.

I pulled her close and said, "I have a bad feeling about this woman."

"What do you mean?"

"I just have this feeling in my stomach that we shouldn't trust her."

"Alina, this may be our only chance to escape, we have to take it." She reminded me.

I looked at her, then at the woman. Finally, after finishing the most exhausting battle in my head, I went against my intuition. Perhaps being held captive has made me more paranoid. We slowly followed her as she opened the door. We walked through a dark alley to the back parking lot of the club. Once there, we saw a black SUV already turned on and waiting. I felt a pinch in the back of my spine, something was wrong. A man with his hair in a bun, wearing a dark gray suit under a black trench coat appeared from inside the car. He left the car door open and stood patiently by the vehicle. Two other men in similar uniform appeared from behind, startling us. One had short blonde hair, while the other was bald. They surrounded us like we were their prize.

"What's going on?" I asked, confused.

As soon as the woman stepped away, the bald man grabbed my arm, while the other snatched Ana up and tossed her over his shoulder, both taking us in the direction of the car.

"Let us fucking go!' Ana yelled as she struggled to fight the big man.

I took off my heels to give myself a better chance at steadying my feet on the ground. I channeled my strength and worked my way out of the man's grip, elbowing him in the chest as hard as I could. It momentarily knocked the wind out of him, but I wasn't done yet. I used my dominant leg, kneeing the other man in the groin, successfully bringing him to the ground. He dropped Ana with him, and I ran to her. The man near the car rushed to aid his friends. I fought as hard as I could, but my strength was no match to his. He knocked me right to the ground, picked up Ana over his shoulder, and rushed her to the car. He threw her inside and shut the door. I hurriedly pushed myself back up. The man with the bun composed himself and came back towards me. I briefly looked at the woman. She stood calmly, watching everything unfold.

"Why are you doing this?" I yelled.

She remained stoic, telling me that it wasn't her first time doing something like this. I screamed as loud as I could for help, but no one heard me. Ana banged aggressively and attempted to open the door. She kept calling my name. I took a few steps back as the man kept walking toward me. His other two friends started getting back up on their feet. Soon, all three of them lurked towards me.

"Why don't you make this easy and get in the van." the man with the short blonde hair threatened.

"Go to hell."

I stopped and planted my feet firmly on the ground. Right as the men launched forward to grab me, Diego, Marco, and three other men bolted through the back door and rushed our way. Diego immediately fired his gun and hit the man I elbowed in the chest. His massive body slammed into the ground. There was blood dripping from his mouth, and I watched as he took his last breath. Marco hurried to my side and pulled me into his arms, out of range as the men started a shoot-out. He dragged me to the nearest dumpster and tossed me behind it.

"Keep your ass here!" He ordered.

He pulled out a gun from his belt and fired it alongside Diego. The man I had kneed in the groin grabbed the older woman and shoved her into the car. The other one stayed behind to shoot back. I sneaked my head from behind the dumpster and made eye contact with Ana from inside the car. My body jolted up away from the hideout and towards her, but Diego grabbed my hand and dragged me back.

"Stay put!" he yelled and continued firing his weapon.

"Ana!"

It wasn't long before the last man was shot and fell to the ground. Marco and his men killed the three of the others but failed to stop the car as it drove away and disappeared around the corner.

"What the hell were you doing out here?!" Marco yelled.

He made me feel like a child who had misbehaved. He had no sympathy, no heart. I just watched my best friend get kidnapped again, and he dared to scold me. My blood boiled with rage, so I pushed him back.

"This is all your fault!" I shouted at him, tears running down my face uncontrollably.

I kept pushing and pounding at his chest, which he allowed me to do until finally he had enough and grabbed me in his arms. His embrace was so tight that I couldn't move to get away. The continuous fight exhausted me, and once in his arms, I released tears of defeat onto his chest. The harder I sobbed, the harder he squeezed my body in his arms.

"Sir, it's Lorena," Diego reported.

The pain was far too great. I became lightheaded and my vision blurred. My heart was palpitating, and I started hyperventilating. My body was numb. The last thing I remembered was darkness.

CHAPTER SEVENTEEN

I slowly opened my eyes, my vision foggy. There was something wet and soft on my forehead. I reached my hand to pull whatever it was away. It was a white cloth. My head was throbbing, but I placed the cloth on the bed and attempted to get up. My body didn't agree with that idea, so I laid back down.

I sensed someone watching me. I turned my head to the side and there he was, crouching on his knees next to the bed. I thought it was a dream, but once he stood up and sat on the bed, I realized it wasn't. He was in the same black attire as last night. There was a glimmer of wrath mixed with concern in his black eyes. He had a glass of brown liquor in his hand, which I smelled right away- whiskey. The potent smell made my headache progressively worse. Marco finished the remaining alcohol and set the empty glass on the bedside table. I tried to push myself up with my elbows once again, but he wouldn't let me, so I let my head fall back onto the white cotton pillow.

"What happened?" I asked, still dazed.

"You fainted last night," he said coldly.

My discomfort evaporated once my memories returned. Instantly, I sprung up in a panic—my headache temporarily disappeared.

"Ana! Where is Ana?" I asked frantically.

I leaped out of bed, but my dizziness returned immediately, and I nearly lost my equilibrium standing up. Marco jumped out of bed and quickly came to my aid, softly holding me in his arms.

"You need to sit." He gently led me down to the bed. His touch was sweet and delicate.

Tears promptly rolled down my face.

"It's all my fault." I said and proceeded, "I was the one that suggested we escape from the club last night. I should have listened to the voice in my head when I sensed something was off. Because of me, Ana is gone. Again."

He stooped down in front of me and gently wiped the tears away with his thumb. His gesture was simultaneously soothing and strange. Though his eyes exhibited warmth, I still saw a hint of frustration. I knew it did not satisfy him to learn I'd tried to escape again. I instantly regretted blurting out the truth. I was confident he would pick me up and haul me back to the basement as retribution, but he didn't. Instead, he helped calm me down.

"Right now, I suggest you rest."

It sounded more like a demand than a suggestion.

"I can't. I can't sleep knowing she's out there somewhere with another psychopath." I said uneasily.

"You won't be able to do much if you're weak."

Though frustrated, I knew he was right.

"I heard Diego say Lorena. Do you know her?"

Marco stood up and stepped away with his back to me. He placed both of his hands in his pockets.

"She's my aunt," he revealed.

"What!?"

He turned back to face me.

"Lorena used to be close with the family. But something happened between her and my father a few years ago, and she abandoned the family. After leaving, she joined the Martinez cartel, one of our longtime rivals. Besides dealing drugs, they also trafficked women into sex slavery and prostitution."

If I weren't already sitting down, I would have almost lost consciousness again. My mind went to the worst-case scenario. *What if they sell Ana? What if those men rape her? What if she kills Ana out of spite?* All the what ifs made me nauseous. He tentatively observed me to ensure I wouldn't faint again.

I felt my resentment return, and though I was furious at what occurred, the only person I could blame was the same man that took care of me. He was the culprit—the one who began all of this turmoil

196

and suffering. I looked up at him with a straight face and blurted out, "I blame you."

"Me? Alina, you escaped last night. If you had stayed put, none of this would have happened," he said back, his voice unsatisfied.

"I wouldn't have tried to escape if you hadn't kidnapped us."

"Don't waste your breath fighting me. It won't do you any good."

And once again, he was right. I needed to regain my strength to battle him and his lunatic aunt.

"If Lorena is your aunt, can't you ask her to release Ana?"

Marco took in a massive breath and exhaled through his nose. He paced back and forth.

"It's not that simple. There's a lot of history and bad blood between her and the rest of the family. My aunt is cunning, stubborn, and like me, she doesn't like when her possessions are taken from her."

I stood up again, this time I managed to keep my balance.

"Ana is nobody's property! She is a human being. How could you people kidnap and torture people, and act like everything is normal?!"

"You need to calm down before you faint again," he commanded.

"Calm down? I despise you and your family."

I picked up the empty glass from the side table and flung it at him. Marco promptly moved and avoided being struck in the face. The glass shattered into tiny pieces as it smashed against the wall. I instantly regretted my hasty action. He forced me onto the bed on my back and climbed on top of me.

"Don't do that again," he demanded angrily.

"I told you, as long as I continue to breathe, I will fight you, every second."

"You're lucky. I have allowed *no* woman to be this brave and bold around me. If you do that again, I will throw you back in the underground prison with the rest of the rats." He pushed himself up and took a few steps back, allowing me to sit back up.

"I won't sit here and do nothing. Either you get her back, or I will do it myself."

"You think you can escape again?"

"I think I've gotten away from you twice, and maybe the third time will be the charm."

He crossed his arms over his chest. "Well, look around the room. I had cameras installed in every corner. My men will monitor you 24/7."

"Wonderful," I said sarcastically under my breath.

"From now on you'll sleep in this room with me," he ordered.

"What? No, I'd rather you throw me back in the basement with the other girls or stay in the underground prison. I'm not sleeping in the same bed as you." I said sternly.

"That wasn't an option, Alina. You'll sleep in this room next to me, or I can strip you naked and fuck you in the basement while the others watch."

And suddenly, his gentle side disappeared, and the only thing that remained was the monster that preyed on the innocent. I wanted to bring my knees up to my chest and sob quietly.

"Get some sleep. We will discuss the matter of your friend more when you wake up," he said coldly and left the room.

I curled into a ball and cried myself to sleep.

I grab Ana's hand as she dangles over a cliff. There's fear in her eyes as she screams for me to pull her up. "Alina, help me, please!" I use all of the strength in my body, but I can't seem to pull her up to safety, no matter how hard I try. I feel her hand slowly slipping from my grasp. She falls and is swallowed by the sea. "ANA!" I scream.

"Ana!" I cried out, jumping awake from my nightmare. I felt a hand on my shoulder, and it freaked me out. I tried to fight off the person lying next to me.

"Get off me!" I yelled.

"Alina, it's me!" Marco said.

He grabbed my face with both hands and instructed me to mirror his breathing. Right away, my breathing turned steady, and after counting to ten, I was back to my normal self. He helped ease me down, and I didn't like it one bit. I didn't want to see his soft side. He was cruel, and I wanted him to continue to be that way. Then it would be easier to continue to hate him.

"Did you have a nightmare?"

Though I was calm, I still couldn't find my voice to respond to his question. Instead, I nodded my head. He took my face into his chest and gently caressed the back of my head. I heard his heart thumping. His skin was warm, and I realized he was shirtless. I remained steady for a few minutes until I remembered who Marco was. I slowly pulled my head away from his chest and moved a couple of inches away.

"Do you want to talk about it?"

What are you, a therapist? I asked myself. I'd had plenty of counseling in the past, yet my problems persisted. No amount of talking helped relieve my pain. One therapist even forced me to process my traumas because she said it would be good to do so. Unfortunately, she failed to realize doing so only re-traumatized me. Only one therapist helped me throughout my life, and she was my mother. I never understood how she was a therapist helping clients with their problems yet couldn't solve her own. It boggled my mind for years until I realized that sometimes in life it was easier to guide and help others than yourself.

"No... I don't want to talk about it. I need my journal."

"Alright. I'll have Camila bring it to you tonight. It's late afternoon, and you haven't eaten anything all day. There are clothes on the side table; get dressed so we can have lunch." He got out of bed and wandered into the bathroom.

I remained in bed for a few minutes, inhaling and exhaling deeply through my nose. Once I was fully stable, I stepped out of bed and took off my short romper, tossing it on the bed. Marco strolled back out and stood frozen as his eyes trailed up and down my naked body. *Shit, Alina! How can you be so careless?* I scolded myself. I immediately jumped under the covers and hid myself.

"You should be more careful getting naked around me. I can be impulsive, especially around you," he warned.

I ignored his comment and continued to stay hidden under the covers. He stood for a few more awkward seconds, deciding what he would do with me. There was hunger in him, and his manhood already showed through his black joggers. I wish I could read his mind.

"I'll see you outside," he said and left the room abruptly.

I plopped back on the bed and sighed in embarrassment.

Really? A long-sleeved, knee-length bodycon dress? I looked at the dress lying nice and neat on the bed in front of me after finishing in the bathroom. Well, at least it was black. I would have thrown a tantrum if it was pink or yellow or something bright. I lazily slipped the dress over my head and walked toward the door, where Miguel was waiting outside. He led the way to lunch in the backyard.

Juanita poured water into my glass while Marco sipped down his whisky like it was juice. I played with my steak and asparagus, but I had no appetite. Even with the assortment of food exquisitely laid out in front of me, I wasn't hungry. All that was coursing through my mind was Ana. It wasn't long before he noticed my lack of appetite.

"Please eat," he begged.

"I can't eat knowing that your aunt kidnapped my friend. Why can't you ask for her release?" I asked, growing impatient.

"Lorena and I don't talk. We used to have a good relationship, but then she left."

"You said something happened between her and your father. So, tell me what happened?"

"She fell in love with Andres Martinez, head of the Martinez cartel. It was against the family rules. Once my father found out about the affair, he forbade her to see him again. But of course, my aunt didn't care and disobeyed. The two cartels have always been at war with one another, but the love between them only made it worse. After senseless bloodshed and millions of dollars lost, my father and Lorena called a truce and ended the war."

"All this started because she fell in love?"

"It's not about love, Alina. It's about power."

"I despise your aunt because she took Ana, but I can't understand how your father can punish her for loving someone. We're in the twenty-first century, for crying out loud. People should be able to love whoever they want."

"Maybe where you're from, it's different. Here in Mexico, that kind of love is considered a betrayal, and the family will not forgive it."

"But how would you feel if you fell in love with someone that your father forbade? What would you do?" I asked curiously.

"My father will treat me in the same way he did Lorena."

"You didn't answer my question."

"Why is it important to you? Are you hoping I fall in love with you?"

I chuckled in disbelief. "I'd rather jump off a bridge than fall in love with you."

"Why would it be such a bad thing? You'll live a life of luxury, and everybody will be envious of you."

"You don't fall in love with someone so you can live a fancy life. You fall in love because you found the right person. I could never fall in love with you because you're a sadistic psychopath with no sympathy or regard for anyone but yourself. Your family trafficked drugs, kidnapped, and tortured people. You're all killers."

"Tell me how you *really* feel, Alina."

I struggled internally. I wanted to spit out all my hatred for him and his family, but I knew doing so would awaken the monster in him, and I would lose my chance of getting his help. To get my way, I had to play nice.

"Is she going to sell Ana?"

He avoided eye contact and remained silent.

"I don't know. My aunt likes to play games. Getting your friend back will not be as simple as you think."

I didn't like his response, and I pushed myself off the chair to walk towards the pool, standing close to the edge. Marco hurried from his seat and stood close behind me. It was as if he was afraid, I would jump in and drown myself. Which was ironic, because he had no problem throwing me in before. It would be a lie to say the thought didn't cross my mind. All of my problems and pain would fade away for good. I wouldn't feel sad, trapped, or guilty anymore. He placed his hand on my shoulder and turned me around to face him. He grabbed my face with both hands and rested his forehead against mine. I'd promised myself that I wouldn't shed any tears, but it turned out to be more complicated than I thought.

"Why does it hurt me to see you cry?" He asked, confused at his own emotions. He tried to plant a gentle kiss on my lips, but my mind reminded me of who he was, and I pulled away.

"Why are you playing games, Alina?" he asked, bewildered and frustrated.

"Games? I'm not playing any games with you. You're to blame for everything. I asked you to release Ana, Juan, and me a long time ago, but you refused. All of us could have been home and safe by now."

"You've allowed me to fuck you, yet you're denying that you're playing games with me."

Remember what Ana said? I did what I had to do to survive, nothing more.

"I did those things because I needed to survive. Not because I feel something for you. I didn't have a choice."

His raging black eyes were bright under the scorching sunlight. He tightly clenched his jaw in frustration.

"The worst thing you can do right now is to play with my feelings. It's hard for me to be gentle. Remember that." He warned.

"If you wanted to kill me, you would have done it a long time ago."

Marco gripped my face tightly and brought it close to his, our lips nearly touching. His breathing was ragged and harsh.

"Don't piss me off. Because if I want to, I can force you to watch my men behead your friend in prison."

Just like a light switch, his cold demeanor returned once again. It was challenging to keep up with his mood swings. One minute he was gentle, and the next he was sadistic. *Remember, play nice. You need his help,* I reminded myself. I mustered up the courage and opened my mouth and said, "I-I'm sorry."

His eyes softened lightly, and finally, he released his grip and said, "You're what?"

I rolled my eyes in my head.

"I said I'm sorry."

I looked down at my knotted fingers and avoided eye contact. It was awkward to say those words while our eyes met. I wondered if he knew it wasn't a genuine apology.

He let out a small laugh. "I didn't think those two words existed for you."

"I just want Ana back, that's all."

"I know."

The plan worked. I realized once my attitude changed, so would his. He was back to his softer side.

"Nothing is guaranteed, don't get your hopes up."

At least it wasn't a solid "no", which gave me a sense of hope.

"Though the chances are likely not great." He admitted.

I finally looked up at him. "But I thought you're the son of one of Mexico's most powerful drug lords. A few minutes ago, you threatened to behead Juan, and now you're saying it will be difficult to do something as simple as bringing my friend home. Are you really the great and dangerous Marco Gustavo that your women raved about?"

Marco didn't take my snarky disrespect well. He clenched my neck with one hand while the other was on the back of my head. He was so quick I had no chance to back away. *Are you really that idiotic? You just agreed that you needed to play nice, and then less than five seconds later, you insult the most dangerous man. Again, stupid, stupid.*

"Don't insult me ever again. And here I thought we were getting along. I'm not usually kind to women, so consider yourself lucky that I've been giving you more attention than the others. But that doesn't mean it won't change. There's a lot you still have to learn to be here," he said and continued, "Am I making myself clear?"
I nodded my head. He released his grip.

"Now, I need you to eat. You have eaten nothing since yesterday. I don't want you fainting on me again."

He grabbed my wrist, dragged me back to the table, and sat me down. I had no choice but to force myself to swallow the tender steak and perfectly grilled vegetables. When finished, I excused myself to the room to rest.

The bright daylight coming through the floor-to-ceiling windows woke me. As soon as I opened my eyes, Marco's unmatched, half-naked self was resting next to me. He looked so young and peaceful while he slept. He almost looked... normal. I stared as his chest rose and down. Then, I felt like a stalker, so I compelled myself to look away.

My journal and pen were on the side table when I rolled over. I immediately grabbed it and brought it close to my chest. I'd never been so ecstatic to hold this little book in my hands. I felt whole again. I opened a blank page and wrote all that happened over the last few weeks.

I was so deep in my thoughts and writing that I hadn't realized he woke up. I closed my journal as soon as I noticed he was fully conscious and leaning his back against the headboard. He ran a hand through his beautiful, messy hair. I hastily hid the journal under the pillow, and he let out a small chuckle

"You realized I just saw you hide that notebook under your pillow, right?" He asked sarcastically.

"Well, I guess I'll have to wait until you're gone to re-hide it."

"Good luck with that. Just remember, there are cameras everywhere. I'll know where you'll hide it."

Shit. I rolled my eyes at him and attempted to get out of bed. He clasped my wrist and pulled me back in, forcing our eyes to meet. I attempted to wiggle myself out of his firm grip, but my efforts failed.

"You know that I've had that journal for a while, right?"

I glared at him with vast eyes. "Did you...read my journal?"

He jerked my body even closer to his and said, "Every page."

Instant rage circulated throughout my body like a forest fire. I slapped him in the face and shoved myself away, falling onto the cold, marbled floor. I didn't remain down for too long, and I lifted myself to my feet and darted for the door. For once, it was unlocked. I turned the knob, opened the door, and dashed away. There was invisible smoke fuming out of my ears as I bolted along the hall. My thoughts weren't coherent; I was so furious.

I heard his footsteps following behind me. *How dare he read something so personal?* I descended the stairs and passed two of his men in their usual annoying black suits. They didn't step in to deter me from leaving the mansion -Marco had signaled them not to. I walked through the foyer and headed outside. I guess that was my boundary, since he grabbed my wrist, turned me around, and stopped me from going any further. He grabbed my face and brought it close to his. Close enough that our lips and noses were touching. *Again, with the invasion of personal space, who does this asshole think he is?!* I attempted to back away, but he gripped my body with his other hand. We stood still and silent.

"I know you're mad, but you belong to me now. And everything that you possess is also mine. All your pain, your suffering, are also mine. You can't hide from me like you do from the world."

"I should have suffocated you to death when you were asleep," I said, my voice cold.

The old Alina began to re-emerge. I was both electrified and terrified. It was electrifying because she always stood her ground and fought against bullies. However, when she was angry, she could destroy everything in her path. I changed at least five schools throughout my childhood—each one stated they couldn't control my behaviors and subsequent fights. As a young kid, I didn't care about all the transitions; it was more irritating than anything. Not only was I bounced from school to school, but also between foster homes. I'd lost count after my fourth foster home. When I was fourteen years old, I overheard my foster mom informing the social worker that I was impossible to be around, and that she saw me as a danger to her biological children. I was reckless with my mouth and didn't care who I hurt at that age. I was delighted to leave each foster home. As I grew older, I realized how lonely and isolating it was to have nobody. For the longest time, I thought that was what I desired, but as an adult, I recognized that was me pretending. I didn't want to appear pathetic to the world. But then I met Ana, and she changed my entire perspective on life. Throughout the years, she supported me through repeated suicidal ideations. She taught me to live with my inner darkness. It wasn't the easiest journey, but my very existence was proof that I had survived. I shuddered at the thought of returning to my old self. She could be as bad as Marco.

Diego appeared behind him suddenly with a cell phone in his hand.

"Sir, it's Lorena."

I tried to grab the phone, but he held me tightly in his grip.

"You'll only make matters worse. Stay quiet. I will speak to her."

It was grueling to comply with his demand, but I hesitantly nodded my head anyway. He took the phone from Diego's hand.

"Lorena, what a surprise to hear from you." He said coolly.

I pinned my ear close to the phone, but I couldn't hear anything she was saying.

"You've taken a woman that belongs to me. Is she alive?" He probed.

I heard a small whimper in her voice on the other line, but I couldn't make out what she said.

"Why don't we meet at our old spot and discuss this important matter?" He suggested.

I heard only one word "sí" which I knew meant yes in Spanish. Aside from that, the rest of their conversation was in Spanish. I reckoned he did that on purpose. Finally, Marco hung up the phone and tossed it back to Diego.

"Is Ana alright?" I asked anxiously.

"She is fine, but there are a few high-profile clients that are interested in buying your friend. Lorena and I will discuss it when I meet with her tonight."

I was relieved that she was safe, but my chest tightened when I heard that one of my worst fears could come to pass.

"I want to go with you," I asserted.

He released me from his grip. "No. You will stay here with Diego, and don't even think of doing anything stupid. I will know. If you disobey, I will make sure you get punished far worse than before."

"I will not sit in this room and do nothing. I want to go with you, and I want to talk to your aunt." I said firmly.

"Alina, listen to me. You coming along will be a liability. Should anything go wrong, I want to ensure that you are nowhere near any danger. So, I would rather you stay put so that I know you'll be safe."

"You're so confusing! One minute you're threatening to kill me, and then the next, you want to protect me."

"It's not that confusing. If anyone were to kill you, it'd be me."

"Like you did with Isabella?"

I knew I was treading on dangerous territory. Diego awkwardly withdrew himself from the conversation. Even his most trusted man didn't want to associate with that so-called complicated relationship.

"This will be the last time that you bring up her name," he warned.

"Oh, so you can bring her up and compare me to her whenever you want, but I can't. How is that fair?"

I wondered whether he knew how confusing he was sometimes.

"The world is unfair, and you don't have a choice but to deal with it," he said dryly and then continued, "Now, I will allow you to roam around the mansion, but Diego will be with you at all times."

He took my hand and forced me back inside.

I sat on the bed cross-legged and watched him button up his white shirt and tuck it into his black dress pants. Now and then, I had unwanted thoughts about how gorgeous Marco really was, which was really unnerving. When he turned to look in the mirror, I saw how well the pants fit his nicely toned ass. Though the alluring view was distracting, a slight tingling reminded me he had read my journal. And even though I had clothes on, I felt naked knowing that he knew the darkest parts of my life. I reminded myself that he only read one of my journals, and that was mainly about my nightmares, horrendous days at work, and uneventful everyday life.

"Camila will bring you some food later tonight. If you want to eat on the balcony or by the pool, you're free to do so. If it gets too quiet, you can go down and chat with the others."

How generous of you, I thought sarcastically.

"Will Ana come back with you?"

"I don't know. You'll find out tonight." Marco finished tying his black tie and shrugged on a blazer to match. He walked toward me and sat at the edge of the bed. "I'm confused," he said, as he looked into my eyes.

"What are you confused about?"

"I don't know why, but I don't want to leave you alone. I worry you will try to run away from me again."

Well, if you don't want to leave me alone, then take me with you. I stayed silent. I wasn't sure how to respond without pissing him off again. Without my permission, he kissed my forehead before leaving the room. Strangely, the unwanted goodbye kiss felt marvelous. I seized my journal from under my pillow and started writing about the unusual feelings I was developing, and how I was both baffled and appalled at how little control I had over them.

CHAPTER EIGHTEEN

"Diego!" I called out to him from the bedroom for the third time.

He promptly opened the door and looked at me. "Yes," he said, knowing exactly what I was about to inquire from him.

"What time is it?" I asked, ignoring his annoyance.

He glanced down at his watch, looked back up at me, and said, "It's a quarter to ten. Is there anything else?"

As soon as he asked, my stomach growled mercilessly. "Actually, yes. I'm kind of hungry. Can I go into the kitchen and grab something to eat? Please," I begged.

"Alright, let's go."

I bounced out of bed and followed behind him into the hall and down the stairs. We walked through the hall leading to a spacious, grand kitchen with white marble countertops and stainless-steel appliances. I skimmed my fingers over the countertop, and it was so smooth. Diego led me to the refrigerator on the wall. If he hadn't shown me, I probably never would have found it. It was filled with an assortment of food, but a bowl of cherries caught my attention immediately. I grabbed the bowl and settled down on a high, white bar stool. I ate a handful before speaking.

"I never thought that I would grow to like you," I said.

Diego did not react to my statement and stood still like a statue. His expression was blank. Well, that was awkward and a miserable failed attempt at starting a conversation.

"I'm glad you have." He spoke suddenly.

It caught me off guard slightly.

"I'm sorry. I didn't mean to come off as a bitch. It's just been difficult being imprisoned here. I haven't exactly been myself." I explained, feeling a flood of guilt for my attitude towards him; he had been nothing but kind.

"Don't worry. I am not offended." He said with a straight expression.

"So, are you always this serious?" I joked, trying to lighten him up. It was also a way for me to distract myself from constantly thinking about Ana.

"My line of work does not allow me to be anything other than serious."

"Have you always wanted to work for the cartel?"

"I don't think most people come into this world wanting to work for the drug organization."

"So why did you?" I asked with curiosity.

When I was a teenager, my dream job was to become a criminal interrogator. Crime shows and walking through the steps of solving mysteries always fascinated me. I often imagined myself walking into the interrogation room with a black binder in my hands, wearing an all-black suit, and combat boots. I played out a scenario in my head where the suspect looked confused when I stepped into the room. The female character I created knew how to fight. The best part of this imagined scenario was that she always won the fight, even against the most dangerous of criminals. But life had other plans for me. At least for now, I could pretend I was a detective interrogating a criminal. Aside from my natural curiosity, I realized I knew nothing about the man who had always been at Marco's side.

"My family and I were struggling. Here in Mexico, it can be very hard sometimes to survive, especially when you're poor and have a wife and kid. When my wife became pregnant, she experienced many complications, and I didn't have the money. The doctors didn't help unless I gave them money first. I ran out of options, so I joined the cartel to help support them."

His story made me sympathetic towards him. I mean, if I ever had a family and they were struggling, I'd do anything to make sure I could provide for them.

"That's actually very... admirable," I said with a soft smile.

"Thank you for your kind words," he said and returned a warm smile.

It felt good to know that I could put a smile on someone's face at least.

"How long have you worked for him?" I sought further.

"Three years, and before that I worked for his father."

"Wow, that's a long time to be around someone like him," I said, impressed.

Diego let out a small laugh and said, "I think you have him misunderstood."

I arched an eyebrow in confusion and asked, "Misunderstood? How?"

"Marco has always treated me and my family well. Because of him, I never have to worry that they won't have food on the table. Because of him, my daughter went to a private school, and my wife can live a comfortable life. He has helped many families in my small town. The people there are loyal, and they respect him. That's more than I can say for our own government, who does nothing for their people."

Marco, helping people? I couldn't see it no matter how hard I tried. I felt like I was living in the twilight zone.

"How do you feel about him kidnapping women and holding them as his prisoners?"

He sat down in the chair next to me. "Those women are here because they want to be."

"But not Juliet and Carmela." I reminded him, slightly irritated that he didn't mention them himself.

"Those women were here before my time, so I cannot speak to that. But I believe Marco does nothing without reason."

What reason could he have to justify kidnapping and forcing women into submission? *I liked you, Diego, don't ruin it.*

"You really are loyal to him."

We sat silently and listened to the subtle yet noticeable air dashing from the vents. I hadn't realized how cold it was until I noticed there were goosebumps all over my body. Being so invested in learning about Diego made me forget about the cool air continuously brushing against my skin. I had a million other questions coursing through my head, but I kept coming back to one daunting question. I wasn't sure how to ask it; I just knew I needed to know. Maybe just being blunt about it was the way to go.

"Have you killed anyone for him?"

He looked straight ahead with his coppery eyes. I studied the side of his face as he contemplated precisely how he would respond. The anticipation was killing me. I counted to at least fifteen before he opened his mouth to answer my invasive question.

"I do whatever Marco tells me to do."

Was I astonished by his answer? No. But I was still slightly shocked. I was sitting next to a literal killer. His response was not a direct "yes", but it was enough confirmation for me.

"Are you alright?" he asked with a soft and concerned voice. My silence was easily detected.

"I mean, I guess. I'm not really sure how to feel about it."

"What's going through your mind?" he asked, returning the interest.

"Well, I mean, I've been surrounded by nothing but danger since I've been here. I guess I haven't really gotten used to this new life." I said, defeated.

"Don't worry, he won't let anything happen to you." He said with confidence.

Diego had a strange way with his words that made me feel comfortable. I nearly trusted him when he said his boss would keep me safe.

"Are there other questions running through your mind?" He asked, almost playfully.

"Do you know where Adrian might be?"

He went to speak but paused, as if thinking to himself, *I must be careful before speaking.*

"Marco ordered him to go away on vacation with his sister as punishment. They will be gone for a few weeks."

"It doesn't sound like a punishment, if you ask me."

"If you are concerned about their safety, you shouldn't be. Adrian and Catalina go on these vacations a lot. It's normal for them, and the rest of the family." He explained.

It pleasantly surprised me how easy it was to talk to him. He was respectful and had more awareness of the real world than his boss. We continued to talk more about his family, job, and life in Mexico for the next hour. I was more interested in his life than my own, and I preferred it that way. I appreciated that he didn't probe too much of my personal life. The most basic details I disclosed were my current job and a few hobbies. Besides, his life story was way more interesting than mine. There were a few laughs along the way, and it was lovely.

The sound of a car door closing made me jump to my feet. I hopped off the barstool and ran towards the foyer outside. The black Cadillac pulled away as Marco stood and watched. I looked around for Ana.

"Where is she?" I asked with hope in my voice.

He turned to look at me and ignored my question. He walked past me, towards the stairs inside. I followed behind, trying to catch up as he strode away.

"Marco, where is she?" I asked again, agitated that he wasn't responding. I ran three steps ahead and stopped in front of him, blocking him from going any further. Our eyes locked with a shocking intensity. His eyes had a hint of guilt and defeat in them. A look that I hadn't seen before.

"We will talk about it tomorrow." He finally spoke.

I refused to back down. "No! We are talking about it right now. Where is she?"

Frustratingly, he grabbed my hand, dragged me to the bedroom, and shut the door behind us.

"Sit down, Alina." He suggested.

"I'll be fine. Now stop stalling and just tell me." I demanded.

Marco took off his blazer and tie, then unbuttoned the first two buttons of his shirt. He tossed his blazer onto the bed. His jaw clenched, and he slowly took a deep breath.

"Lorena will only release your friend on one condition."

"Ok, what's the condition?"

"She'll let her go, but only in exchange for you." He said, his voice unsatisfied with her condition.

Without hesitation, I said, "I'll do it."

He didn't react well to my quick agreement. His eyes grew emotionless and bitter. "That will not happen."

"Fuck Marco, I don't care. All I want is for Ana to be safe and return home. I'm begging you, please agree to this." I pleaded in desperation.

He overlooked my plea and turned away, attempting to walk into the closet, but I stopped in front of him once more.

"Agree to your aunt's terms," I insisted.

"I can't do that."

"That's not your choice. Tell your aunt that I agree to her terms and take me there. Ana's life is more important than mine, and I'll be damned if I let her suffer any longer."

With his eyes locked on mine, Marco said, "Your life is important to me. So, whether you like it or not, you're staying here."

Infuriated, I stormed out of the room. My disgruntled footsteps could probably be heard all the way outside. I descended the stairs to where Diego was standing at the bottom.

"Call Lorena!" I demanded of him.

He stood still, and just like his boss, ignored me. *Damn you.* I thought we were close after the hour-long conversation.

"Diego?"

"I'm sorry," he said and just left.

The blood inside me was simmering with rage. I staggered towards the main door to go outside.

"Alina!" He called after me as he descended the stairs.

I dismissed his call just as he had mine. I yanked the doorknob, and of course, the damn door was locked. I searched for anything I could throw and spotted a vase of beautiful white lilies on a high table near the door. I quickly grabbed the vase and flung it at the door as hard as I could. It shattered into hundreds of tiny pieces, but the door remained unscratched.

"That door is bulletproof. You will not break it with a vase."

"Then I'll just have to continue to keep throwing everything I can at the door." I walked around looking for more things to throw.

Marco didn't permit me to roam for too long. Once he saw I was making my way into the kitchen, he stopped me.

"Alina, enough." He ordered.

I pushed past his defense. He grabbed my wrist and twirled me around to face him. Tears rolled uncontrollably down my face. There was a sharp pain in my chest, like someone was poking needles into my heart. My resentment toward him grew, and all I kept thinking about was stabbing him in the chest with a sharp knife and twisting it, so he could feel my agony.

"Let me go," I begged in despair.

"No."

He wiped away my tears with his thumbs and moved in for a kiss. I turned my head away from his lips. Instead of aggressively forcing me to face him as he did before, he planted a soft kiss on my cheek.

"Look at me," he ordered.

I refused.

"Look at me, or I will fuck you right here, right now," he threatened.

Bastard, I thought to myself and turned to glare him in the eyes. My lips were quivering with anger. I wanted to kill him so badly.

"Come back to the bedroom,"

"No. There's no way in hell I'm going back in there with you. I would rather sleep in the living room or in the basement. Hell, I'd rather sleep with the rats in the underground prison than with you."

"That wasn't an option."

"I don't care. I don't care about your stupid rules or orders or any of your other shit. I only care about Ana."

"Alright then, since you want to make this difficult. You leave me with no choice." Marco picked up my body, flung me over his shoulder, and headed up the stairs. I screamed until I couldn't anymore.

****

When I opened my eyes, the room was quiet. The sunlight reflected through the room in an undisturbed manner. I jolted up quickly after hearing a soft moan. Marco slept peacefully in only his gray boxers. *Why can't I remember anything that happened from last night after he brought me upstairs?* I peeked under the covers, and thankfully I was wearing shorts and a T-shirt. I thought hard, but I couldn't remember a thing. *Did he do something to me, and I just completely blocked it out of my head to protect myself?* That was the only explanation I could think of. I'd read enough stories of rape survivors sometimes claiming they had no recollection of what happened to them. When I was in college and studying psychology, I read a study that discussed how the human brain sometimes blocks traumatic events as a coping mechanism to protect the host from painful memories. Could that be what happened to me? The thought that he possibly assaulted me sent a chill down my spine.

I lightly stepped out of bed and went to the bathroom to shower. The dirtiness Marco made me feel needed to be washed away. I twisted the showerhead, stepped under the refreshing spray, and allowed the water to cascade down my body. I grabbed the white loofah, poured jasmine body wash on it, and harshly scrubbed myself. After aggressively cleaning every inch of my skin, I lowered to the floor in a fetal position and bawled.

Once exhausted from my tears, I nudged myself up on my feet, grabbed a towel, and wrapped it around my body. I stared at my reflection and was appalled at the stranger glaring back at me. She looked pale, dazed, and drained. I wanted to throw something at the mirror, so it would shatter. That way, I wouldn't have to continue to look at myself. I was a disgrace. All my sins were being punished at once. I lowered my head in despair.

Enough with the pity party, Alina. Wipe your tears, suck it up, and move on with your life. I straightened back up and stared at my reflection once more. I dried my tears, took a deep breath, and sauntered out of the bathroom.

Marco was in a dark gray suit when I stepped out of the bathroom. He watched my every move like a hawk. I avoided meeting his glare and strolled straight to the new set of clothes on the bed that was brought in while I was in the shower.

"I'm sorry," he said unexpectedly.

I turned around and hurled the clothes at his face.

"You're sorry? For what? For keeping me prisoner or for raping me?!" I shouted at him, more tears dripping down.

He picked up the clothes off the floor, folded them neatly, and placed them back on the bed.

"I never intended to hurt you."

I laughed harshly.

"You didn't mean to rape me? Well, I'm so glad you explained it." I said in utter disbelief.

I grabbed the clothes and slipped into a black high-waisted jean and a long-sleeved, V-neck sweater. I neatly tucked the beige sweater inside my jeans.

"You thought I raped you last night?"

"Are you serious? You raped me, and now you're questioning my sanity?"

"Alina, I didn't lay a finger on you last night."

"I don't believe you."

"Listen to me. After I brought you back to the room, you sat on the bed and cried. And then, eventually, you fell asleep. Nothing more. I watched you sleep peacefully, even with all the chaos that happened. And if you haven't noticed, you didn't have any nightmares last night." He explained cautiously.

"Taking advantage of me wasn't enough? I had to see it in my dreams too?" I asked, disgusted by his ridiculous explanation.

"Believe what you want. I already explained myself."

I knew he was fabricating the truth. Every fiber of my being told me he was.

"You must despise me as much as your father."

I gave him a nasty scowl. If he didn't realize that by now, I had no clue what else to do or say to make him understand how much I detested him.

"You know, we have more in common than you think. My father used to rape my mother as well." He said with a hint of sorrow in his voice, one that I had not heard before.

There was a sense of vulnerability in his tone, but my feelings for him did not waver upon his declaration. If he believed that somehow, I would feel sorry about what happened to his mother and forgive him, he was mistaken.

"Am I supposed to feel sorry for you now?"

He clenched his jaw and weaved his hand through his hair. "No, I want to be open and honest with you."

I rolled my eyes. "I honestly do not care what you want. Just because you went through the same shitty experience as I did as a child changed nothing. I still despise you. And if you died today, I would happily dance on your grave."

I snatched my journal from the bedside table and headed for the door. It was locked. I turned and frowned at him. Marco willingly came to the door and unlocked it with a passcode, and I took off. I was shocked that he allowed me to leave. I ran down the stairs to Diego, waiting at the bottom.

"I want to eat," I said to him.

"I will have the maids prepare you some food."

I made my way toward the backyard. The backyard had a gazebo with black stones and a firepit in the center. I made myself comfortable and sat down. I opened the journal and began releasing my anger through words. I was so lost in my emotions I wasn't aware that food had been brought and set there for me. My stomach groaned as soon as I saw the sausage, bacon, and eggs on the golden plate. I set my journal aside and ate.

I must have fallen asleep after, and when I opened my eyes, Catalina was sitting in front of me, cross-legged and wearing a stunning black suit with a white tie. It appeared that she was watching me while I slept. I lifted myself up with my elbows.

"What are you doing here?" I asked, still wary, but regaining my awareness.

"My punishment is over, so I figured I would come and visit the woman that got me in trouble in the first place," she said coldly.

"I didn't ask for your help. I asked Adrian."

She chuckled, "Please, Adrian could never help you escape from Marco without my help. I don't understand why both of my brothers are so obsessed with you. Yes, you bear a striking resemblance to Isabella, but aside from that, I mean, there's nothing special about you from what I can see." She said in her regular, brooding tone.

If only she knew that I had asked myself that same question repeatedly.

"I don't know. Why don't you ask them and let me know?" I answered back, uninterested in any further dialogue. Though I did have one question I felt I must ask.

"Where is he, by the way?"

"He's not allowed back here for a while. His punishment is considerably longer than mine. So don't hold your breath for him to rescue you again."

It was disheartening to hear her say those words. A small part of me hoped he was okay.

"Don't look so disappointed. You should be happy to live a life of extravagance with Marco. I mean, look at the mansion and the beauty that comes with it. I'm sure you've never seen such luxury before. Isn't that every woman's dream? To live a carefree, spoiled life? Why do you think so many women agreed to be one of his whores?"

"That's the difference between them and me. I don't care about the mansion, the money, or the designer clothes. I just want to be free and back home with my best friend."

The sudden thought of Ana brought tears to my eyes, but I wiped them away immediately. She was the last person I'd ever want to see me cry.

"I heard about your friend," she paused and continued, "How unfortunate that she got kidnapped twice."

I couldn't decide whether she was being genuine.

"Are you here to gloat even more at my pain?" I asked, annoyed by her existence.

"As entertaining as that sounds, no. I didn't come here for no reason. I came because Adrian wanted me to check on you; to make sure you're still alive. So now that I have, I don't have to be here anymore," she said as she stood up to step away.

"Wait," I blurted out to her.

She stopped her steps and turned back to look at me.

"Will you...be able to help Ana?" I took a risk.

I needed to exhaust all of my options. Catalina narrowed her eyes and gave me a half-smirk, which confused me. I couldn't determine whether that meant yes or no.

"What do I get helping you again? The first time I did, I got sent away. If I do it again, Marco will kill me."

"I'll disappear from your life forever. You'll never have to see me again. I can guarantee you Marco wants me around for a long time from the look of things. Which means we will see each other more often than you'd like."

I knew my bargaining game was weak, but that was all I had to offer.

"The thought of never seeing you again has its appeal. What do you have in mind?"

"Your aunt will trade Ana for me. Get me out of here and take me to her to make the trade."

She appeared impressed. "You're willing to sacrifice yourself for your friend, again?"

"She is more than my friend; she's my sister, and I will do anything for her, even if it means giving up my life."

"I think I might have figured out another reason why Marco is so enamored with you. It's that annoying self-righteousness. It's more than annoying, it's infuriating. How do you say stuff like that and not cringe at yourself?" She placed both her hands on her hips and waited for me to speak.

I stood up and looked her straight in the eye. "I don't care about what Marco thinks or feels. And I certainly do not care how you feel about my character. So, are you going to help me or not?"

"Impressive. Well, this could be fun." She had a wicked smile.

We shook hands to close out the deal.

Marco had left for the evening for a business meeting with his father, and I didn't care for further clarification because I knew I wouldn't like the answer. I was ecstatic when he left. It was perfect timing for my third escape.

I sat in bed waiting impatiently for Catalina. I looked at the clock for the fifth time. After asking Diego so many times, I requested a bedside clock. It was half an hour past nine and she was still absent.

I was hopeful for the first hour, but after two hours had passed, it became discouraging. I tried to remain still, but I was growing more restless and had to stand up and pace back and forth to keep busy. Maybe she lied to me as part of her sick, twisted mind games. I bit my nails one by one- a habit I developed when I was young.

My heart nearly burst out of my chest when the door finally opened, and she strolled in casually in the same outfit from earlier in the day. She was calm, unlike me, and I was confused to see Diego behind her. She failed to inform me of that part of the plan.

"Why is he here?" I asked, uneasily.

"Diego is fine. He won't do anything. Now, are you coming or not? There's this awesome club in the city that I want to show you." She gave me a look of you-better-play along.

So, I did. "Of course. Let me just throw on some clothes quickly." I ran into the bathroom, slipped on a little black dress that I requested from Camila earlier, and brushed my hair to tame the tangles. I finished in less than five minutes.

"Alright, I'm ready."

We walked outside to a suspicious Diego. "I think it's best if myself and a few other men follow along."

"Whatever makes you feel comfortable." She said flirtatiously.

At that point, I had no clue where she was going with this plan. Catalina barely told me anything when she'd agreed to help. She only mentioned that I needed to play along. Diego pulled out his cell phone and dialed a number, speaking in Spanish as we waited.

"Alright, we are ready to go."

I was confused. Why hadn't he opposed my leaving? He knew Catalina had helped me escape before, yet he still allowed me to leave with her. Even though he was tagging along, it made no sense. There were many questions without answers, and it killed me on the inside. We walked through the long hall and down the stairs.

There were two black SUVs and three men in black suits waiting outside for us. Diego stepped into the passenger seat of the first car while we got in the back. The three men stepped into the car behind us.

After what felt like an eternity of awkward silence, we arrived in the city where we'd been to a club previously. Though this time, we approached a different club. The car came to a halt, and Catalina and I waited for Diego to open the door. We stepped out in front of a brightly lit gate entrance. Of course, it was as fancy as Marco's club, but this new one was grander. Diego led the way inside, along with the three men following behind. The entrance was dimmer, and music blasting in the background made it hard to hear or focus. I tried my best to be as calm as possible.

The entrance felt like a long corridor that just didn't end. Finally, I saw bright lights as we walked out into a high-ceilinged, circular room with stripper poles, tables, and chairs. It was empty. Diego turned to look at Catalina, but before he could open his mouth to say anything, five men in gray suits appeared from different angles and attacked them. It was clear Diego had no clue what was happening, and the element of surprise knocked him and his men down relatively quickly.

Everything happened so fast. I looked down at his unconscious body, face down on the ground, and instantly felt a sense of guilt.

"Well, that worked better than I thought," she said.

I turned my attention to Catalina, who stood calmly and gracefully with a soft smirk on her face.

"You should have told me the plan," I said, annoyed.

"I needed you to be as clueless as possible. Who knows how you'd act if I told you what the plan was? Besides, I knew he wouldn't have let you come with me alone, especially after what happened the first time. I knew having him follow along with his men was a better plan. Plus, he didn't expect a surprise attack, and that's why it worked. Now come on. We're going to meet my aunt at her place."

She turned her attention to one of the men and said, "Tie them up and watch them."

The man nodded his head. She led the way to the back of the club, and I followed. Another black SUV waited for us as soon as we exited. I didn't hesitate to jump in.

"Thank you for doing this," I said.

She didn't look at me, but said, "Don't thank me yet. When Marco finds out, he'll come looking for you. I've never seen him this possessive of anyone before."

Possessive. I was not fond of that word. I lived most of my childhood watching my father possess my mother, and I couldn't do anything to help her.

"I hate him," I said.

"You don't have to tell me. I can tell from your eyes that you hate him."

I played out various scenarios in my head about how things might unfold during the drive. Every single one of them resulted in my exchange with Ana, and I accepted that fate. I looked out at the world as the car drove by and tried to remember how beautiful it was. We drove far out of the city and entered a dark forest up the mountain. The car drove up the hill and continued deeper and deeper into the dense forest. It was so dark, and the trees were so high and thick that they shielded even the moonlight from us. I rolled down the window and listened to the silence of the trees and night sky. Ironically, it was beautiful. As quickly as the window was down, it automatically rolled back up.

"I wouldn't do that if I were you," Catalina warned.

"Why? We're in the middle of nowhere."

"My aunt is a very paranoid woman. You may think there's no one outside, but trust me, there is always someone watching."

"But it's the forest, and we're in the middle of nowhere."

"It'll do you good to listen once in a while."

We finally came to a stop in front of a tall, black gate. The driver lowered his window, spoke Spanish into a speaker box, and showed his face to a camera. The gate opened, and we drove down a long driveway until we reached the front of an enormous glass mansion. How ironic that a supposedly paranoid woman lived in a see-through house. I needed to stop with all the unnecessary questions. It did nothing for me and only brought more questions.

We stepped out of the car and Catalina led us to the front door. It opened automatically to an open-concept house with a black marble floor, a massive kitchen, and a living room. We stepped into the spacious living room. It held a giant, white sectional sofa decorated with black and gold pillows, and a square black coffee table. There was a massive gold and white chandelier above our heads. Behind the living room was a stainless-steel kitchen, a gigantic, black glass dining table, and leather chairs to match. Opposite the living room was a terrace that overlooked the forest.

Catalina casually strolled in as if it was her own home. I was in awe of the beauty of the house. I turned my head to the right and there was a floating staircase with black railings that led up to the second floor. Briefly, after we entered, I heard heels clicking down the stairs. Lorena walked down with grace and elegance in a black, long-sleeved pants suit. She was more beautiful than the first time I met her.

Catalina made herself comfortable and sat down on the sofa with her feet stretched out on the coffee table. I remained still in my current position.

"We meet again," she said once she took her last step.

"Where's Ana?" I asked.

"Impatient, aren't we?" she said and walked towards the bar near the kitchen.

She grabbed three glasses, and poured the rich wine, and continued, "Why don't you sit so we can talk?"

"I'm not here to talk. I'm here because you wanted to exchange me for Ana. Where is she?" I asked once again, my patience thinning.

Her niece stood up, grabbed a glass, and returned to her original position.

"It's rude to refuse a drink while in my house," Lorena strolled towards me and handed me a glass.

I hesitated but took it, anyway.

"That's much better," she said after I took the glass.

I didn't drink it though.

"How about this? When you finish that wine, I'll bring your friend into the room." She offered.

"You promise?" I asked.

"Of course."

After hearing her proposal, I downed the whole drink in one big gulp. It had a bitter, yet smooth taste. Both Lorena and Catalina looked at me, amused.

"I like you, Alina," she said with a grin.

She wandered toward the front door and spoke to a speaker box attached to the wall. "Bring her in here." Then she walked to the living room and sat down on the arm of the sofa. "I have to admit, I don't come across brave women like you often. Most cry and beg for me to let them go. It's insufferable after a while," she said, sipping her wine.

"You find women who beg for their life insufferable? I guess cruelty runs in the family." I snapped.

"Yes, it's pathetic. But, I mean, come on, the least they should do is fight for their life. Am I wrong?"

"Human lives mean that little to you?" I questioned.

"Of course. Why else would I be in the business? Those women mean nothing to me."

"Those women are somebody's daughter, sister, friend, or wife, and yet you see them as nothing. How can anyone be so cruel? Do you have no soul?"

She chuckled. "You are adorably naïve. In this world, you do whatever it takes to survive. And if that means selling whores to men, so be it."

"I may be naïve, but at least I have a heart. Something that none of you people will ever understand."

I felt uncomfortable as Lorena stare me down like I was her prey. There was an odd desire in her eyes. Either I was going crazy, or I was tipsy. I realized then, all of them had that same look on their face—cold and soulless.

The front door opened behind me, and a man in a black suit walked in with Ana at his side. I dropped the empty wine glass and rushed to her side, grabbing her bloody, bruised face in my hands. She looked unrecognizable.

"Oh my gosh, Ana!" I said and took her body in my arms. She was fragile and could barely stand. I held all her weight in my arms.

"Alina?" she said, her voice weak and tired. She cried on my shoulders.

"I'm so sorry."

Once we separated from our embrace, I turned to glare at Lorena and asked, "What did you do to her?!"

The evil woman pushed herself off the sofa's arm and placed one hand in her pocket. "It's a shame. I tried to keep that pretty face of hers, but she wouldn't stop screaming. So, to shut her up, I ordered my men to slap her a few times," she explained in an eerily calm tone.

"You're a despicable woman," I said harshly.

She gave me a crooked smirk and sipped her wine. I turned back to look at Ana and gently caressed her face. I'd never seen her so beaten down. It took a lot to break her spirit, but they had done it.

"You shouldn't have come," she whispered.

"You know I would follow you to the end of the world."

"You're always so stubborn," she smiled weakly.

"And yet you love me anyway." I kissed her forehead.

Even though I was relieved to see her, I dreaded saying goodbye. I couldn't stop my tears from falling uncontrollably.

"Alina, save yourself," she said as she gripped my hand.

I pushed her hair away from her face and with a smile said, "It's okay, Ana, you're going home. Catalina will take you to the airport, and you'll fly back to Rhode Island. You'll be with your family soon, okay?"

She looked at me, dazed and displeased, and said, "Wait, what? No, I'm not going anywhere without you. I won't."

"You have to, and you will. Please don't come back for me. I don't want to risk losing you again. So, please do me a favor and live your life to the fullest. I hope that you'll get married and have a lot of children. You will be the *best* mom a child could have. I love you so much." I said and kissed both her cheeks.

When I attempted to step away, she held onto my hand, "Alina, no."

I gently tugged my hand from hers, turned my back, and looked at Catalina. "Please take her."

She finished her wine, set it on the table, and wandered toward us. She grabbed Ana's arm, lifted her, and started walking out the door. Before they walked out, I clasped Catalina's wrist and said to her, "Please make sure she gets home safely."

She looked at me and nodded her head. I watched as they walked to the car, got in, and drove away. A massive sense of relief seeped through my body as the door closed. I wiped my tears away before facing this evil woman again. Even if I died tonight, I'd still rest easy knowing that she would be safe and back home with her parents.

"That was almost beautiful," she mocked.

"You wouldn't understand the true meaning of friendship," I said.

"Well, we shall see how much longer you continue to keep your bravery. Come, I'll show you to your room." She led the way to the spiral staircase.

I took a deep breath and followed.

CHAPTER NINETEEN

It was midnight when I woke up with an intense need for water. I felt so dehydrated, and my throat was dry and scratchy. I pushed myself out of bed and walked toward the black door. Lorena's favorite color was black. Everything in the room was black, and it only amplified my already depressed mood. I banged on the door. A few moments went by before a man with short blonde hair and blue eyes opened the door.

"I'm thirsty. Can I please go downstairs and grab some water?"

The man approved, to my astonishment, and directed me down the stairs.

The sight of Lorena lounging on the sofa holding a glass of wine startled me. I glanced over at the table and there were three empty bottles. She was wearing the same outfit as before, the only difference being that she was now barefoot. She motioned her hand for the man to go away, and he did.

"Want to sit and drink with me?" She asked as if we were friends of some sort.

"No thanks. I'm thirsty. Can I grab some water?" I inquired.

"Help yourself," she permitted.

I went to the kitchen and straight to the refrigerator. I grabbed the gigantic pitcher of water, placed it on the kitchen counter, and looked around for a cup. After finding one, I poured the water almost to the rim and drank it all in one go. I couldn't believe how thirsty I was. The water was ice cold and refreshing. Once finished, I put the pitcher back in the fridge and went back upstairs.

"You're a courageous woman," she said as I passed her.

I stopped and looked at her, perplexed.

She proceeded, "I wish I had friends who are willing to sacrifice their life for me like you. You do not know what it's like growing up in a family full of criminals. I admire you, Alina."

It was obvious she was drunk. She attempted to stand on her feet but wobbled around. I watched her struggle to maintain an equilibrium. It was almost comical. She somehow moved toward me, but she was too close, and I took a step back.

"Are you afraid of me?" She implored.

"I've been through the worst with your nephew. This is nothing compared to the things he has done to me."

"There it is. That confidence you exude, it's sexy."

I lifted an eyebrow and asserted, "You've had too much to drink."

"Tell me, was it worth it?"

"What was worth it?"

"Sacrificing your own life for that useless piece of shit."

"The only piece of shit in this room is the woman who kidnaps and exploits women and is drinking alone," I said.

She chuckled and kept stumbling toward me. I kept stepping backward until I met the wall.

"What are you doing?"

"You belong to me now," she said.

"You're a sick woman," I said and turned to walk away.

She grabbed the back of my head and twisted me around to face her. She then tried to plant her lips on mine. I freaked out and pushed her body away from mine. But she kept pushing back. So, I took advantage of her intoxication and smacked her in the face. She fell straight to the ground. *Shit.* She flashed me an angry glare, her eyes the same as Marco's when he was furious.

"You stupid bitch!" Lorena hoisted herself up and moved toward me with difficulty. She clenched my face and forced her tongue into my mouth, much like her nephew had. She clasped a handful of my hair and threw me to the floor. "You shouldn't have done that," she said, then shouted something in Spanish.

Four men in black suits burst through the door, grabbed my arms, and yanked me to my feet. I tried to fight the four of them, but one of them clenched his fist into a ball and punched me in the stomach. That knocked the wind out of me, and I landed on my knees. The hit subdued my aggression and will to fight further. As I was on my knees, she marched back and forth in vexation.

"That was idiotic. I don't like disobedient women. Do you think you're brave? Do you know what I do to women that pisses me off? I punish them. You and your friend are alike. She, too, was foolish. I had to show her the consequences of her actions. But don't worry; you're about to learn and know exactly what I mean."

I stared at her. "What does that mean? What did you do to Ana?" I asked. I struggled to get away, but two men held my arms in place.

She scowled at me, spiteful, and ordered, "Place her on the sofa."

They hauled me up and tossed me on the sofa like I was a sack of potatoes.

"Maybe after this, you'll learn to be more cooperative." She said and took a few steps back, enabling the other two men to grab me.

I kicked my feet and backed away as far as I could until the bald man grabbed my ankle and dragged me closer to them.

"Let me fucking go!" I yelled.

Another man with short spiky hair walked behind the sofa, snatched both of my arms and heaved them up and over my head. Another bald man pulled down my white shorts and threw them to the ground. Then he ripped my white tank top away, exposing my sports bra and underwear. I'd thought it frightened me when Marco violated my body, but the fear I had looking up at the four men staring down at me paralyzed my spirit. The two bald men grabbed my legs and spread them apart. I'd never felt so mortified in my life. Lorena beamed as I panicked.

"Allow me to tell you what happened to your friend. I had her strapped to a bed while five of my men beat and raped the shit out of her. They fucked her mouth, pussy, and ass all night long. But that wasn't all; after my men finished, I had a fuck machine pound the shit out of her even more. It only stopped when I was satisfied." She explained with a wicked grin on her face. "But I won't do the same thing to you as I did to her. I'm going to make sure that you suffer slowly. Tonight, I'll let these four fuck you. Tomorrow it will be five, and the day after that six, and well, you get the idea. Each day that passes by, I will add another one of my men to the list until *I* am satisfied."

She took a few steps back, sat down on the opposite sofa, crossed her legs, and watched. Then she signaled for them to begin my torture. As they ripped the only remaining clothing I had, I screamed loudly and aggressively. I wiggled back and forth with all the strength I could find, but it wasn't enough. I was no match against four men. Finally, after I realized that the fight was over, all I could do was close my eyes and prepare myself for the inevitable.

The entrance burst open, and Marco stepped through the door with a gun, firing at the men. Diego came through behind him with more men. Lorena dove behind the sofa to protect herself as her men struggled to pull out their guns to shoot back. Marco's sudden appearance was an advantage that took all of them off guard, and the two bald men were shot and killed immediately. The remaining two men grabbed Lorena and attempted to take her through the back door. In the brief time they were out in the open, Marco shot them both in the back and his aunt in the shoulder. Even with the injury, she somehow escaped, disappearing into the dark woods. I stayed frozen on the sofa. Diego was closest to me, and once he saw I was naked, he immediately took off his blazer and covered me. Marco rushed to my side, took me in his arms, and carried me to the car.

I remained immobilized in the car. Even though I was physically out of danger, my mind wasn't. I wanted to cry, but I couldn't. I tried to howl but couldn't. I felt nothing. Marco held me tightly in his arms; I could hear his heart thumping loudly.

"There will be consequences," Diego said from the front passenger seat.

"I don't give a shit about the consequences right now. Just drive as fast as you can, call the doctor and have him meet us at the estate." He ordered.

"Your father will not be pleased," he said.

"I will deal with him," Marco said back, irritated.

"Thank...thank you," I forced myself to say under my breath. The three simple words took my remaining strength.

"Don't talk, just sleep." He demanded, and so I did.

"Please stop!" Ana screams. One by one, Lorena's men are taking turns violating her bruised, naked body. They all laugh like a bunch of barbarians. I stand in the dark and watch as the horror unfolds. I want to run and help her, but my feet are stuck to the floor.

My swollen eyes opened as soon as the car came to a stop at the front entrance. I never thought I'd be glad to be back at his mansion.

"I'm going to carry you inside; let me know if anything hurts, okay?" he said, his voice warm and delicate.

I nodded weakly. He carried me inside and straight to his bedroom. He laid me down gently on the soft bed. Diego came in shortly after and reported, "The doctor will be here soon."

Marco didn't pay him any attention but said, "Thank you."

"Of course," he said before leaving the room.

Once I was comfortable and settled, Marco stood up and away from the bed and paced back and forth in frustration. He clenched his jaw tightly and had both fists balled up.

"How could you do this?" he asked, furious.

I wanted to respond, but I couldn't move the muscles in my mouth. Marco was distressed, that was certain, and I knew if I weren't beaten up, he'd punish me himself somehow. I bet he would do it anyway once I was fully recovered.

"Do you realize what could have happened?" he asked, frowning at me with fierce eyes.

"I-I'm sorry." That was all I could muster out.

"You have no idea what you did to me, do you?" he asked with an ache in his voice.

I had a sense of what he was talking about, but I prayed it would not become a reality. I didn't want it. Eventually, he sat by my side and wove his fingers through my hair. There was a new expression of pain and confusion in his eyes. I saw an internal struggle as if he wasn't sure how or why he felt the way he did. Marco gently stroked the side of my face. My guard gradually crumpled down.

"I never thought I could ever feel this way about anyone. When I found out you left the first time, I was angry, and all I wanted to do was punish you. But this time, I thought I was going to die. I couldn't understand why I felt this way. I couldn't bear the thought of you getting hurt. Every second that passed by not knowing where you were, I couldn't breathe. Every time I closed my eyes, I saw your face. I realized then that your very existence is my downfall." He said in agony.

Every word he said struck me intimately. The man next to me was a completely different person. The way he caressed my skin was so genuine I nearly forgot my current predicament. I almost forgot who Marco was for a brief instant.

"Why would you care about me? I'm nobody. I'm not beautiful like the women you have at your disposal. I'm a plain girl from a plain town." I said truthfully.

"You don't know what you've done to me," he said.

"Marco, I have done nothing. The only thing that I've done is fight and disobey you. I think the only reason you're feeling any emotion for me is because I remind you so much of Isabella. You've told me plenty of times that was the reason I'm still alive. Whoever she was and whatever feelings you had in the past for her, I am not her. It's clear you still love her, and that's why you're trying to use me to fill a void. Because even though I am not her, it's still enough to satisfy you. Everything about this is a lie smothered in darkness, and that's all we have. Nothing else." I said with brutal honesty.

"But what if we made it more than just darkness?"

The thought of being with him was both bewitching and terrifying, but I had to remind myself of the absolute truth. And although his gesture was kind, falling for him was not an option. He was my abductor, Ana's abductor, and likely Juan's murderer.

"Nothing will ever change between us."

His eyes were no longer delicate. Instead, they were mixed with disappointment and frustration. Marco pushed himself off the bed and crossed his arms.

"I've spoken my truth and yet you deny me. What more can I do to prove to you I have intense feelings for you?"

"Nothing. There's nothing that you can or need to do. You only need to accept the truth."

"No. I don't believe it. I know you feel something for me, too. I'll make you mine."

And the dominant and selfish Marco was back. I knew it wasn't long before his authentic self-emerged. The door opened again, and Diego walked in with an older man in his late fifties, wearing a dark blue suit, sporting white hair and glasses. The doctor came in prepared with a black medical bag in hand. Marco went to him, and they shook hands.

"Thank you for coming, doctor," he turned to look at me and said, "Alina, this is Dr. Rodriguez. He has been both a friend and doctor to my family for over twenty years. He will take good care of you."

"Nice to meet you," I said.

"The pleasure is mine. Now, let me check your injuries." Dr. Rodriguez came to the side of the bed, placed his bag on the table, and sat next to me. "I need some privacy," he said.

Marco hesitated at first but followed instructions and left the room. The doctor was a gentle soul, and he made me comfortable instantly. He reminded me of Mr. Davis when he spoke. They both had that calming and soothing voice. He was a rare man to find in this place. I wanted to ask him a million questions about Marco and his psychotic family, but my energy was drained.

"You'll live," he said with a smile and playful tone.

"Thank you," I said, returning his smile.

Once he finished checking me, he suggested I get some rest. I didn't fight against his recommendation. He was the doctor. I covered myself completely under the blanket and watched as he walked out the door and vanished. Once the door was closed, I shut my eyes and fell asleep.

"Please let me go!" I beg as four men rip away my clothes. "Please!"

The graphic scene in my mind jolted me awake, gasping in fear. It disappointed me that the sleeping pills I'd requested from Dr. Rodriguez didn't work. My body was burning up due to my panic, so I removed the covers. I stared at the ceiling above my head and counted every tiny dot I saw. I closed my eyes, counted to ten, and took a few deep breaths. *You're safe,* I reminded myself. Once my breathing slowed down and my heart rate leveled out, I propped myself up on my elbows. It was a bright day, which lightened my mood slightly. Even though I was fully awake, I was still tired.

I wanted to see the damage done to me, so I lifted my white T-shirt to look at my stomach. It was black and blue, though the pain had slightly subsided. My strength, however, was not one hundred percent yet. I felt stiff when I pushed myself up and leaned against the headboard. I turned to the side table, where there was a tray of sausage, eggs, bacon, and a glass of orange juice. My stomach growled at the sight of the food. I grabbed the tray, placed it on my lap, and started eating.

After eating the whole plate, I felt so much better. I grabbed the juice and drank it all. Marco walked through the door as soon as I placed the empty glass back on the table. He had a blank expression on his face when he saw I was awake. He strode to the bed and didn't hesitate to plant an unwanted kiss on my forehead.

"Good morning," he said with a warm smile.

He sat on the bed next to me and took my hand in his. "How did you sleep?" he asked, gently caressing my knuckles.

"Good. How long have I been asleep?" I asked.

He smiled. "You've been asleep for over sixteen hours."

Sixteen hours? That has never happened in my life, but why was I still fatigued if I'd gotten that much sleep?

"You should have woken me up."

"How could I? I knew you needed rest. Plus, you look so peaceful while you sleep. I didn't have the heart to wake you up."

"You watched me sleep?"

"Well, you are sleeping in my bed, in my room."

"You should have left me with the girls downstairs, then."

He brought my hand to his lips, gently kissed it, and said, "You'll never be down there again."

Marco grabbed the glass carafe filled halfway with water and poured it into an empty glass. He handed me the cup, and I took it but didn't drink it.

"You need water. Your body is very dehydrated, according to Dr. Rodriguez. He recommended you drink as much water as you can when you're awake." He explained.

I trusted the doctor's advice, so I drank the entire cup of water. He took the empty glass from my hand and set it back on the table. He was back to his gentle side. We sat silently and our eyes met silently. The quiet reminded me of what he'd disclosed after he rescued me from Lorena.

"You said you've never felt the way you feel about me with anyone before." I started.

"Is that all you remember?"

"I don't know. I'm pretty sure getting beaten up and nearly gang-raped will probably fog up anyone's memory."

"Those bastards paid with their lives. I should have chased after Lorena and killed her." He said, his eyes returning to their original darkness.

"Why didn't you?"

"Because I couldn't leave you alone."

"Well, Diego was there. I wouldn't have been alone."

"It's not the same, Alina. Those men's deaths were a mercy after what they'd done to you." He stood up and stepped away from the bed, his back to me as he stared out the glass window. I felt his rage radiating from where I sat.

"Are you mad I left?"

"You have no idea. There was a moment where I wanted to rescue you so that I could kill you myself," he turned back to me, "You have a gift of arousing and pissing me off at the same time."

I wrung my hands under the bed sheet. Marco's words were crawling under my skin. I still hadn't figured out the annoying voice inside my head that kept screaming in excitement. There was no reason for me to feel ecstatic. No reason at all. He returned, sat next to me, and took my face in both of his hands.

"You make me want to be a different man, Alina, a better man, whether you believe it or not. You do not know what it's like to live the life I have. My very existence scares the world. Everyone in Mexico only knows me as Marco, the oldest son of the most powerful drug lord. When people hear my name, they only hear fear. But when you're around, I feel different, and I don't want to be that monster. I knew how much you meant to me when I nearly lost you. Please don't leave me again."

I stared at him in awe, and for the first time since I met him, I saw a genuine vulnerability in his eyes. His intoxicating words seeped their way into my heart.

"I'm sorry. I just can't." I looked away.

He promptly removed his hands and body from mine. I couldn't allow myself to be distracted. He had his back to me, and I wished I knew what was running through his mind.

"I have to take care of some business. You're free to roam around as long as Diego is with you." He said and simply left the room.

I rested my head back down on the soft pillow. Everything that transpired a few minutes ago replayed in my head until my mind shut off and I fell asleep.

I jolted awake when the door unexpectedly opened, and Camila entered. In her hands was a new set of outfits for me to change into. She carefully laid a white pantsuit with a deep V-neck and black pumps at the end of the bed.

"Good afternoon. I hope you find these to your liking." She said politely.

"Yes, they're beautiful. Thank you," I said with a tight smile.

"Of course, we are glad that you are back, Miss Alina," she said with a welcoming beam.

"Oh please, call me Alina. No need for formalities." I said, slightly embarrassed. No one had ever been that polite to me before.

"Master Marco instructed all of us to address you in that way. It would be disobedient not to follow the rules." She explained.

"Oh, well, I guess I will have a conversation with the *master* then," I said, annoyed.

Marco stepped through the door wearing a loose, short-sleeved white shirt nicely tucked into his black pants.

"You can leave," he ordered less politely.

Camila slightly tilted her head down in obedience and left the room, closing the door behind her.

I felt awkward in his presence and wrapped the blanket tightly around my body.

"What's wrong?" he asked when he saw my body tense up in his presence.

"Alina?"

"Nothing, but that was unnecessary," I said.

"What was unnecessary?" He said, his voice genuinely confused.

I rolled my eyes, but it did not surprise me that he was oblivious to his behavior. "Camila is a charming woman. And she has been nothing but kind to me. Would it kill you to be kind to her occasionally?"

He took a few steps toward me and stopped at the end of the bed. "You should know by now that I don't know what that means."

"Trust me, I know, and the second I asked you that question, I realized that there's not an ounce of kindness or decency in you. So why bother?"

"But you could teach me." His gaze was burning through me.

Teach you? I barely know how to teach myself anything most of the time. How am I supposed to turn a psychopath into a decent human being? His request was too much to ask of one person. Besides, I didn't care about him enough to waste my energy helping change him into a better person. *But perhaps you could, Alina? No, stop it! That will never happen*, I scolded myself.

"It's not my job to teach and change you. If you want to be a better man, then you need to figure out how to do that on your own." I may have sounded harsh, but it was the truth. My mom used to tell me tales of how she tried to fix and change my dad. But unfortunately, her sacrifice and agony got her nowhere, and he became even worse.

"Perhaps you're right, but it wouldn't hurt to try, right?"

"That will not happen."

"There's always hope, Alina. And when you believe it enough, one day it will become a reality."

I stared at him in disbelief.

"Get ready, and meet me downstairs," he demanded and left the room.

I took a massive breath, sighing before taking my lazy ass to the bathroom to prepare myself for whatever plans he had for the day. I dragged my feet, curling my long black hair. I brushed out my eyebrows, moisturized my face, and applied a matte nude lipstick to match my olive skin. Finally, I slipped into the pantsuit and sprayed on the Chanel No. 1 perfume sitting on the counter. I stared at my reflection in the mirror and saw two different versions of myself. One version believed she could change Marco, and the other version screamed at me to get as far away from him as possible.

Am I going insane? I spun away from my reflection and yelled at the voices in my head to shut up. I took a slow, deep breath, and walked out of the bathroom and out of the room. Marco waited for me in the foyer like he was Prince Charming, and I was his Cinderella. His eyes did not leave mine the entire time I descended the stairs. I was surprised to make it down without tripping.

"You look beautiful," he said as he took my hand and kissed the back of it.

"Thank you." I forced out a smile.

As we were about to head out the door, I heard loud, furious heels clicking from behind. Marco and I turned at the same time to see who it was. Mariana approached with a death glare aimed at me. She appeared exhausted, with dark circles under her eyes. It looked as if she hadn't slept in days. Her eyes were swollen, red, and puffy like she had been crying.

"What the hell is going on, mi amor?" She looked directly at Marco.

I shifted my attention to Marco. Clearly, her sudden disruption displeased him. For a brief moment, I feared for Mariana. He had that murderous look in his eyes.

"Take your ass back downstairs," he ordered, his voice dry.

She grabbed his arm and knelt before him. *Holy shit!* I couldn't believe my eyes. She was practically begging.

"Please, I need you. I can't live without you." She cried out hysterically.

I was never fond of her but seeing the desperation in her eyes made me sympathetic toward her. She was too exquisite a woman to be begging for love from a man like Marco.

"You have less than five seconds to remove your hands from me," he said, his voice ice-cold. His patience was thinning.

She instantly removed her hands but was still kneeling on the ground. I couldn't take it anymore, so I stepped away from them.

"What's wrong?" He asked, completely ignoring the woman on her knees.

"This is madness," I said to him. I turned my attention to Mariana and said, "Please, stand up. Marco is all yours." I walked out the front door. I needed to breathe in some fresh air to clear my mind. But it wasn't long before he joined me outside. He made it challenging to breathe alone in peace and quiet.

"Alina," he called out behind me.

I stopped at the front of the lawn because even if I wanted to stagger away, I wouldn't get far in these black pumps. Marco stopped in front of me and tried to grab my face with his hands. I turned away.

"I can't do this," I said to him.

There was a tense silence between us.

Mariana fumbled out behind us. "Mi amor, tell me what you want. Whatever you want, I will obey. I will be your good little whore, just like you like."

"I want you to shut your mouth and go back down to your room." His voice turned from ice-cold to rage.

"What is so special about her? What does *she* have that *I* don't?"

I turned around to face her. "Please, leave me out of this. I don't want to be involved in whatever fucked up relationship you guys have, okay?"

She made her way to me with crazy eyes. "You little bitch," and she raised her right hand in the air, and it quickly came back down. But Marco caught it before it connected with my face. He gripped her wrist tightly, and I saw the pain rising in her eyes. His eyes were black as coal.

"Marco, let her go," I said, but it was as if he wasn't here anymore. After a few moments, he still hadn't let go, so I did the only thing I could think of. I bravely grabbed his hand with all my strength and pulled his hand from her wrist. Of course, I wasn't dumb; I knew it only worked because he allowed it to. However, either way, I was relieved.

"If you ever try that again, I will kill you." His tone meant business, and I knew he was sincere. By the look on her face, she knew she had crossed a line.

"I-I'm sorry. I don't know what has gotten into me." She said as tears cascaded down her cheeks.

"Now, go back to your room." He commanded. She looked at him with pain in her eyes, turned around, and walked back into the mansion.

Marco turned back to me and lifted my chin with his fingers to look at him. "Are you alright?"

He had a talent for shifting between murderous and gentle within seconds. I had no clue how he did it.

"I want to go home," I said.

Marco turned away from me, placing both his hands in his pockets. "You know I can't do that."

"Can't or won't?"

"You're the only thing that makes sense in my life; I won't let you go."

I closed the distance between us and stopped in front of him.

"This is insane, Marco. We are not lovers. We are not soulmates. We are enemies and nothing more."

He turned his face away, unwilling to hear the truth. I followed his gaze and refused to let him ignore the conversation.

"I can't fix you. I refuse to fix you. Ignore me all you want, but I will never stop fighting. I will escape and run far away from this place, and you." I said sternly.

He finally looked at me with narrow eyes. "Well, it's a good thing I will never let you escape from me again." He grabbed my hand, dragged me toward a black Range Rover, forcing me into the back seat.

CHAPTER TWENTY

I couldn't tell how long we had been in the car, only that it had been a while. I was in complete darkness. Marco had blindfolded me at the start of the drive. I tried to yank it off my face, but he threatened to strip away my clothes and fuck me in the back seat. It was disturbing to hear how easily those words rolled out of his mouth. Instead of risking it, I remained in the seat and stopped fighting.

"Would you like to listen to music?" Diego asked suddenly.

"I would like to run away from your boss. Is that a possibility?" I said like a smart ass.

"We're almost there," Marco spoke.

"Where are we going?" I asked, slightly curious.

"You'll find out when we get there," he said simply.

"Is the blindfold really necessary?"

"With you? Of course."

"You know, it's ironic that you said you want to be a better man and then you turn around and do something like this. It doesn't seem to be the actions of a man who wants to change."

"Perhaps you need to be more open-minded." He suggested.

Be more open-minded? It often baffled me the way his mind worked.

"Really? That's your way of trying to convince me to believe that you want to change. And here I thought you were the son of Mexico's most powerful drug lord. I'm sure you could have come up with a better negotiation than that."

Even though he'd deprived me of my sight, I could feel that he had moved his body closer to mine. I felt his warm breath on my cheek, and an intense glare on the side of my face. Marco trailed his fingers from my face to my neck and down my right arm. His touch transmitted an uncomfortable chill down my spine. He gently planted a kiss on my cheek without consent.

"Your body is tense, Alina. Tell me what you're thinking about," he whispered in my ear.

I turned to face him in confusion.

"I don't know what you're talking about."

"I sense sexual frustration from you." He said confidently, and even though I couldn't see his face, I knew he was grinning with satisfaction.

I remained silent, unsure of how to explain to him it wasn't true.

"That's ridiculous. How can I have sexual frustration for someone who has brought me nothing but pain and misery? You really think that highly of yourself?"

Marco gently caressed my shoulder with the back of his fingers. "I don't believe you for one second. I think you're in denial."

"You couldn't be more wrong."

"I watched you sleep, Alina. You said my name during your sleep." He revealed.

"You watched me sleep? How disturbing," I said.

"I know you want me even if you deny it. Otherwise, you wouldn't have said my name in your sleep."

"That's where you're wrong. I said your name in my sleep because it was a nightmare."

"I will make sure that one day you come to me, and you will beg me to fuck you."

That will never happen, and I will do everything in my power to ensure that it doesn't, I thought confidently to myself.

"Please, leave me alone." I requested. I was done with the conversation.

He grabbed my chin and gently planted a kiss on my lips. I turned my head away. He moved back to his original spot but was holding my hand in his. I attempted to remove it, but he had it tightly gripped. I quit resisting after a few tries and accepted the placement of my hand for the remainder of the ride.

I enjoyed it when he stopped speaking. It allowed me to have a moment of solitude. I'd accepted that I would be in the dark for the rest of the drive, so the only thing left for me to do was think about the exchange between Marco and Mariana from earlier. He was cruel. All she wanted was his love. For crying out loud, the woman knelt on her knees and begged. But he treated her as if she was just another one of his toys that he could play with and toss away anytime he wanted. He had given me so many reasons why I could never fall for him. I knew the reality of the situation. Eventually, Marco would grow bored, and eventually, he would treat me the same way he did her. Besides, if I remember correctly, Mariana had bragged multiple times that she was the so-called "favorite mistress" and yet he dumped her like trash. So, how long would I be his *favorite* until he found somebody else?

"You didn't have to mistreat Mariana like you did earlier," I heard myself say suddenly.

I heard a soft sigh under his breath. "It wouldn't have happened that way if she would have just listened. All of my women know to never test my patience. It never ends well for them."

"Clearly she's in love with you."

"Well, I don't love her. I do not love any of the women at my disposal. At least not until you."

There was no chance in hell I believed a man like him could love. But, more importantly, no one could ever love me. I didn't deserve it. Who could love a broken person like me? I believed myself to be unattractive and clumsy, and my life had no real purpose. I was a lonely soul, always had, and always would. When I was a child, my father repeatedly screamed into my soul that I was a force of destruction sent by the devil. I was the reason he had become the man he was. If the most important man in my life couldn't love me, what man could?

"What you're doing to me isn't love. Love shouldn't hurt this much. I may not have a lot of experience, but at least I know love should be gentle."

"You're right, and I'm hoping that you can teach me how to be gentle and loving in the right way, for you."

"We're here," Diego announced.

My heart briefly stopped. I wasn't fond of the unknown, especially with him. Finally, the car came to a halt, and the engine turned off.

"Can I take off my blindfold now?" I asked.

"No," Marco said. Instead, he grabbed my hand, slowly helped me out of the car, and shut the door behind me.

Once we were out in the open, I felt a powerful wave of wind slamming against my body. It didn't take long for me to recognize the sound of the ocean's tides hitting against the shore.

"Do you trust me?" Marco asked.

"Is that a serious question?"

"Don't panic, but we are going to walk down some stairs," he informed me.

We descended the concrete stairs, and I counted twelve steps. Once we hit the last step, my heels sank into what I could only imagine was sand. He knelt before me and removed my black pumps; then we stepped into the soft, warm sand.

"Are you ready?" he whispered in my ear.

I hesitated at first, but then nodded my head. Marco finally took the blindfold off of my face. Once my vision cleared, the view of the majestic blue sea captivated me. It was a magnificent, never-ending horizon. My gaze drifted from the water to the tall cliffs with luscious green trees to my right. I'd only seen beauty like that on social media, and never in my life had I imagined I would be standing only a few hundred feet away from it. It was a surreal moment of peace and serenity. I took a few steps forward.

"Wow," I said.

"You like it?" he asked from behind.

I turned to look at him. "I do. It's absolutely breathtaking."

The scenery was so stunning that I almost forgot where and who I was with.

"Why did you bring me here?"

Marco walked to my side and grabbed my hand. He, too, took a moment to savor the sight before pulling my hand, a silent demand to follow him. As we strolled further down, I realized nobody was around - we were the only two people in sight. How could a glorious place like this be so empty?

"Why are there no people here?" I asked.

"I own this beach," he said casually.

Of course he did.

"What does your family *not* own?"

"That's a tough question, but maybe for another time."

We continued our walk along the ocean shore, the destination still unknown to me. I glanced back at the car atop the hill, with Diego standing outside, waiting like the loyal bodyguard he was. He became smaller and smaller as we ventured further.

"This is my secret, private beach. I come here when I want to be alone."

"I can never imagine you being alone. You always seem to have business meetings, clubs to go to, and women to entertain."

"There's more to me than meets the eye, Alina." He stopped and turned to look at me. "I'm... trying to let you in so you can get to know me."

"I'm not sure what you want me to say. I've already told you how I feel."

"Shhhhhh," he said with his index finger to his lips, "Do you hear that?" He closed his eyes and tilted his head to the sky.

I looked at him, confused at first, but once I mimicked his behavior, I heard nothing but the sound of the waves.

"You're the first woman I've ever brought here." He said and turned his attention to the sea.

I turned my head to look at the confusing man next to me. He appeared so ordinary that it frightened me. I didn't want to believe my eyes, to think that he could be real. The only thing that helped ensure that I wouldn't form any emotional bond with him was the constant reminder that Marco was nothing more than a monster. I'd used that logic to survive and not fall prey.

"Why haven't you brought any woman here?" I asked curiously.

"Because I have met no women worthy of bringing here. I never thought I would ever meet anyone that I could share such a special place with," he said, and turned his head to me and continued, "You're the first woman to break me."

"Break you?"

I was dumbfounded.

He let out a small, adorable laugh, "I have very strong feelings for you, as you already know. Something that I've never felt before. Every fiber of my being wants to have you and protect you at all costs. These feelings confuse me sometimes."

"Well, what about the other two women that you took against their will, or the mysterious Isabella? Didn't you have strong feelings for them?"

He took my hand, and we continued walking.

"I don't think what I felt for those women were true feelings. I think it was more lust and control. I saw how beautiful they were, and I had to have them. I know it's fucked up, but it's what I grew up with. My father did the same thing. He had hundreds of women. I know it's not enough to excuse my behavior, but I want you to at least know where it started." He explained.

"So, am I also another object of lust, or is it because I remind you so much of *her*?"

"In the beginning, I was stunned by the physical similarity you shared with Isabella. In fact, you two looks so similar that when you first ran into me, I thought you *were* her. I became intrigued. But then

250

you showed me something else that caught my attention - bravery. I'd never seen someone risk their own life to save their friends."

"I really remind you of her that much?"

"Yes, to both Adrian and Catalina as well. If it weren't for my brother informing me, he had met someone that reminded him of Isabella, I wouldn't have walked into the restaurant."

"Did you ever love her?"

"I was young. I'm not sure I knew what love meant back then. Perhaps I did, perhaps I didn't."

We came to a stop, and there was a white table with two chairs in front of us. The table had an assortment of snacks, fruits, and champagne. It was perfect because I was starving.

"I had this prepared for us. I figured you would be hungry, and there's no better place to eat than on the beach."

Marco pulled out a chair for me, and I sat down, watching as he opened the bottle of champagne. He carefully poured it in two glasses, then handed one to me. I took the glass but didn't drink it. Instead, I set it down on the table and grabbed a cherry. He sat across from me sipping his champagne. He was right. The view of the beach made the food taste better.

"I have a few questions," I started.

"Ask away."

"What happened to Juan?"

He sat back in his chair. "You're concerned about him?"

"Of course I'm concerned, he's my friend."

"He's still alive." He stated simply.

A sense of relief coursed through my body. I realized I had been so concerned about Ana and escaping Marco that I forgot about the other person who helped me. Juan had no clue that Ana was no longer in danger. I needed to tell him.

"I want to speak with him," I requested boldly.

"I don't think that's such a good idea," he said, and sipped his drink again.

"I need to let him know Ana is safe now. He deserves that much after all the torture you've inflicted on him."

"I said no," he said.

I felt like a small child being told no like this. I stood up from my chair and angrily walked away. He followed behind.

"Alina," he called out my name.

Even though I didn't know where I was, I ignored him and continued walking. I didn't think too much. I just needed to get away from him. *Who am I to believe that he would be lenient and allow me to ask such a thing from him?* I foolishly assumed that I would have the advantage because he had confessed his love for me. *How can I be so stupid?* I chastised myself.

"Alina," he finally caught up to me, grabbed my shoulder, and turned me around. "You can't run from me."

"I wouldn't have to if you would just let me see him."

Marco released his hand from my shoulder and ran it through his hair a few times in contemplation. I remained hopeful that he'd miraculously change his mind. I stood and waited for his decision.

"Alright, I will allow you to see him, but only for a short time and with my supervision. Is that clear?"

I disliked that he made the ultimatum to be present, but at that point, I had to take what I could get. I nodded my head in agreement. Maybe there was hope. Marco insisted I needed to eat more, so he grabbed my hand and waddled me back to the table.

"Any more questions?" he asked as I ate more cherries.

"When I was in the basement with the girls, all of them, including Mariana, said that she was your favorite. Is that true?"

"For a while, she was. She was the main woman I fucked before you came." He revealed.

"So, you haven't slept with any other women? That's hard to believe, since they're all so beautiful."

He nodded his head. I stared at him in contemplation, deciding whether I should believe his words or if it was just a sweet ruse to lure me in, as he did with Mariana, only to dump her like she meant nothing.

"The answer is simple. I just didn't want to. When I'm bored, perhaps, but Mariana usually provides me with the most pleasure."

I suddenly had an image of them fucking on the couch in my head. I cringed.

"Sometimes, I wish I could read your mind so I could know what you're thinking," he said after noticing my gaze elsewhere.

"Then how come they're still in the mansion?"

"You just ruined the surprise." He said, slightly annoyed.

I gawked at him, bewildered by his words. "What surprise?"

"I brought you here so that when we go back, you'll see that all of the women are gone. I arranged for all of them to return to their normal lives." He declared.

I composed myself. I didn't want to look like an excited fool after his revelation. *Could it be true? Did he really let all of them go because of...me?*

"You did that for me?" I asked out loud. I needed to hear him confirm it once more.

"I told you. I want to be a better man for you, and I will do anything to show you that," he said.

His actions were promising, but I continued to battle within myself. Just a few minutes ago I angrily bolted out of my chair and staggered away for him to agree to let me see Juan. If Marco truly wanted to show me, he changed, my request should have been granted without that.

"I apologize for how I reacted when you asked to see your friend. I should have been more understanding. Sometimes my actions betray my words, but I promise to try harder."

I was flabbergasted. It was like he had just read my mind. I didn't want to, but I couldn't control my heart as it skipped a few beats. *Don't do it, Alina. Remember, Marco is a psychopath who kidnaps and imprisons women, claiming them as his whores. More importantly, he kidnapped Ana and tortured Juan.* The two versions of myself drove me insane as they continuously fought against one another.

I was glad when he stood up from his chair, grabbed my hand, and led me further down the beach. The voices had finally ceased for the moment. We stopped under a giant, hollow cave with the perfect view of the ocean. It was an excellent spot to be, under the shade and away from the scorching sun.

"Wow, this place is so surreal," I said, amazed at the ancient structural carving of the cave. I understood why he called it his secret hideout. We settled down on the sand beside one another.

"You're so beautiful," he said.

I turned my head, and our eyes met. My face became warmer than usual. The word *beautiful* was an unfamiliar term in my vocabulary. In fact, I couldn't recall the last time a man had genuinely said that word and meant it from their heart. Usually, it was so they could get inside my pants. Even when Jason said it, it felt more like a cheesy pickup line rather than an actual compliment. We stared into one another's eyes intensely. Marco made me nervous, but it wasn't because I was fearful of him. Instead, it was more of a butterflies-in-your-stomach feeling you get when you're a teenager and about to kiss the boy you secretly had a crush on under a tree, or in the basement of his parent's house.

"Marco, I…"

"I love you."

My heart stopped beating inside my chest. I looked at him, dazed and unsure of what just flew out of his mouth. I flushed in embarrassment. The only thing I wanted was to bolt away and hide.

"Are you alright?"

"I-I'm fine," I lied. I was relieved to find my lips working.

"Are you sure? Because it looks like you've just seen a ghost?"

"I'm not sure what to say. You realize what just came out of your mouth, right?" I questioned him, still baffled.

"I do."

"You can't possibly mean it. I mean, this is all sick." I spoke.

"But I mean it. If only you could read my mind, then you would know exactly how I feel. You would know that it's real."

"It may be real for you, but for me, it's a nightmare. I'm sorry." I turned my attention back to the ocean.

CHAPTER TWENTY-ONE

The sound of chattering woke me up. I blinked a few times before realizing what I heard wasn't a dream. To my surprise, Marco wasn't present. When I looked at the clock on the side table, it was already 11 AM. I propped myself up on my elbows and stepped out of bed. Slowly, I stretched my whole body and yawned. For the past two nights, I realized I'd been sleeping well. But more excitingly, I didn't need to journal about any nightmares. I debated whether I should write about my conflicting emotions for Marco a few times, but I feared he would find the journal and read it. It was safer to keep those thoughts locked in my head.

As I was about to head into the bathroom, the chatter became louder. It was coming from the backyard. I opened the giant glass door and stepped onto the balcony that overlooked the yard, and the beautiful city of Mexico. I recognized Marco's voice immediately, but I didn't recognize another man's voice that was much deeper, and perhaps older. Slowly and carefully, I walked closer to the edge and secretly listened to their conversation. I peeked through and saw Marco and an older man in a gray suit, a white tie, with mostly gray hair. He was well-built and good-looking for his age. If I had to guess, he was probably in his late sixties. When I glimpsed his face, it was strikingly like Marco's. *Could that be his father?* I asked myself.

As I continued to listen, the man's voice became harsher and louder. It was difficult to comprehend precisely what they were talking about because the conversation kept switching between Spanish and English. However, I was confident that they were talking about me. I heard my name at least three times as they spoke.

"Marco, she is one woman. She is not worth this family going into war with Lorena." The older man said, unsatisfied.

Marco had his back turned to the man and said, "I love her. And I will not give into Lorena's demands." He said, stern and uncompromising.

"Love? You just met her a few weeks ago, Mijo. That is not love. Have you ever thought that it's perhaps lust that you're feeling for her? Or that it's because she looks like Isabella? There are plenty of other women for you to enjoy."

Marco paced back and forth and ran a hand through his hair. I didn't need to be near him to sense his frustration. He turned back to face the older man.

"It's not the same. Yes, she looks like Isabella, but she's not her. I know how I feel about Alina, and I will not compromise what we have together."

"Do you think she loves you, son? You took away her freedom and forced her to stay here. Before that, you kidnapped her best friend and tortured another one. You think any woman would be crazy enough to fall in love with their captor?"

"I'm trying to change for her father. I want to."

"Marco, she is not Isabella. Isabella has been dead for many years, and no matter how much you try, Alina cannot fill that void."

"It's not like that, not anymore. Alina is nothing like Isabella. She's different in so many ways, and so innocent. She's what I need in my life."

"Mijo, trust me, she will leave you the minute she gets the chance."

"She won't run away. I won't let her." He said, determined and possessive.

"You're willing to risk breaking this family apart for one woman who doesn't even want to be with you?"

Marco struggled to say the right thing. Finally, the man walked up close to him and placed his hand on his shoulder.

"Lorena wants her dead. And if she doesn't get what she wants, there's no avoiding war between the two cartels." His father warned him.

Marco looked at the old man intensely.

"Then I will step away from this family and the cartel and take Alina far away from here."

The man, furious, slapped Marco across the face.

"Are you out of your mind?! You would dare turn your back on the family for a *woman*. Listen to me, carefully, I will not allow it."

He muttered something in Spanish, and suddenly two of his strong-looking men in dark gray suits grabbed Marco's arms and brought him to his knees. I watched in horror as he tried to fight them off, but they were too strong for him. The great Marco was subdued for the first time in his life.

"This ends right now." Marco's father said and left.

The door to the bedroom abruptly swung open, and Diego rushed inside and straight to me.

"Alina, we need to leave right now!" He grabbed my hand and dragged me out the door and down the long hall.

"What's going on?!"

"Marco's father is here, and he's going to kidnap and kill you to avoid the upcoming war between the two cartels. I need to get you to safety." He explained hastily.

We ran down the stairs and found ourselves blocked by his father and three men with guns. Diego held my sweaty palm tightly in his hand and positioned his body in front of mine.

"Diego, move aside." The man ordered.

"Sir, I can't do that. It's my responsibility to protect Miss Alina."

The man closed the distance between us and was quickly only a few feet away.

"I will not repeat myself. Move, or I will move you," he threatened.

Diego stood firm in his place.

"Very well then," the old man returned to his original place, grabbed a gun from one of his men's hands, and without hesitation, shot Diego in his right leg. He fell to the cold hard floor with blood trickling out steadily.

"No!" I screamed.

I knelt and tried to cover and press my hands down on his wound.

"You should have moved!" I yelled at him.

I glanced up at the man's face. "What is wrong with you people?"

"Run," he said, his voice was meek.

I looked back at him. "No, I'm not leaving you."

One of his men grabbed my hair and jerked me to my feet. He dragged me to face his boss. Marco's father looked me over, up and down. Unlike his son, his eyes were full of confusion, almost as if he couldn't understand his son's infatuation with me.

"All this trouble because of *you?* I will not allow a whore like you to break my family."

If anyone was a whore, it was his son. His insult enraged me, and I did the only sensible thing and spat in his face. I provoked the beast within, and I saw the wrath in his eyes. He calmly grabbed a handkerchief from his blazer pocket and wiped away my saliva. Then he slapped me hard across my face.

"Go to hell!" I yelled at him. I was so mad that I didn't feel any pain.

He grabbed my face with one hand, tightly squeezed it, and said, "So brave for a tiny woman. In Mexico, bravery gets you killed. I've killed many men who thought they were brave, but they were just stupid."

The old man released his grip, looked at his men and ordered them to drag me away. A black Cadillac Escalade was outside as I struggled to fight my way out of their grasp. One of his men walked behind me and placed a cloth over my mouth. I fought some more until my vision turned foggy, and then everything went dark.

****

A splash of water jolted me awake, entering my nose and making me choke. It was ice cold. I cleared my vision to get a better look at my surroundings, and realized I was in an unfamiliar room with nothing but dark walls and a tiny dim lightbulb above my head. It wasn't Marco's underground prison; I was sure of that. There was a musty metallic smell that I couldn't make out what it was. They had tied me down to a chair with my hands behind my back. I struggled to move, but the rope was tight. My effort to free my hands was useless. The only thing I could do was study my surroundings. However, the dimness made it hard to see anything. The room was quiet, and I jumped in fear when my eyes caught a dark silhouette lurking in the room's corner.

"Where am I?" I asked.

The shadow said nothing and remained as still as a statue. The door in front of me opened, and Marco's father walked in. His stride was full of power and ego. Marco was almost an exact copy of his father. The old man stopped before me and then ordered his man in the shadows to leave.

"Tell me where I am!" I demanded, as if my courageous voice would make any difference.

He grabbed an old wooden chair from the corner and sat across from me.

"You are a fiery one; I can understand why my son is so infatuated with you. I know you want answers and I'm the type of man who doesn't like to play around, so here it is. You, my darling, are an unfortunate woman that's been caught in a long-time rivalry between two of the most powerful families in Mexico. Now, I know it's not your fault, but at last, here you are. I take no pleasure in killing a young and beautiful woman like yourself, but I have to do what is right for my family." He explained.

"I didn't ask to be caught in anything. It was your sons that got me into this position. I just want to go home."

He sat back in the chair and crossed his arms and legs.

"I know everything. My men keep tabs on all my children. It's unfortunate, but it's our way of life here."

"A way of life? Kidnapping, drug trafficking, and exploiting women is a way of life? You and your family really are evil."

The old man studied me carefully with his black eyes. It was uncanny how much Marco's demeanor and mannerisms reflected his father's. They both had the same mentality and were oblivious as to why their actions were wrong. I couldn't fathom how such a family came to power. But then the more I thought about it, the more I realized it was because they were cruel. They viewed life as nothing more than a transaction and money in their bank account. They took advantage of those that couldn't fight for themselves, and they enjoyed watching others suffer.

"Your name is Alina, right?"

"I thought you knew everything," I said like a smart-ass.

"I do, but my son has so many women that it's hard to keep track of all of them sometimes. Tell me *Alina*, do you have a family?"

I ignored his question and remained silent.

"That's alright. You don't have to talk. But I want to let you know again that I'm only doing what's best for my family. I hope you can understand that. Unfortunately, I can't allow you to live. My sister wants you dead, so that is what must happen to keep the peace."

"Human life means that little to you?"

"Any life means nothing to me if it means protecting those I love. Surely you can understand. You willingly sacrificed yourself for your friend, and so I will make that sacrifice for my family."

I didn't think I could loathe anyone more than Marco. There was nothing in his eyes; there was no soul or spirit, only darkness. He reminded me of my father, and the thought made me shiver in fear.

"So, what's next then? You're going to call your sister and execute me in front of her?"

"Execution is an understatement. My sister wants to see you suffer first before she kills you. And that is exactly what's going to happen. We agreed that your death will subdue the feud."

"Go to hell," I said and turned my head away.

"Lorena is on her way. Use these last few moments you have and think of all the things you've accomplished in life; maybe that'll help ease the pain that will soon come." He stood up, left the room, and shut the door behind him.

How was it possible to think of everything I had accomplished when I had done nothing? Most of my life was pain and suffering. I couldn't even explain the definition of true happiness. For years, I'd been frightened and lost. I'd never wanted to live.

"Alina, please, baby, come back to me. Please!" My mom yells as she tries to resuscitate me after I took an entire bottle of prescription pills she accidentally left on the kitchen counter.

I remembered that moment like it was yesterday. When I was ten, I tried to kill myself. I recalled the shock in my mom's voice, but I wasn't shocked at all. Death had always been on my mind, even before that moment. I knew I wanted to die; it was only a matter of when. I'd become trapped in my mind, and I couldn't escape from the horrible reality I was living in. I saw no hope for a future and made a conscious decision that I would be nothing more than a "useless" and "soul-sucking" daughter—those were exact words used by my father.

"Please save her, please!" She begs the paramedics when they arrive, tears streaming down her face.

The door swung open again, and a big bald man with a thick mustache and beard appeared in the room. Once he was in the light, I noticed a giant skull tattoo on his neck. Was he the one that splashed water on me earlier? It was hard to guess. The man didn't speak but pulled out a cell phone from his back pocket to snap a picture of me.

"What are you doing?" I asked, dazed by the flashing lights.

He looked at the picture, seemed satisfied, and left the room. The only explanation I thought of was that perhaps they needed a photo as proof for Lorena.

The long silence continued, and it was oddly comforting. I stopped counting in my head after I'd reached over a thousand. After that, my brain gradually stopped functioning. I dozed off a few times, and soon, I was out like a light.

A loud popping outside the room startled me awake. When I opened my eyes, it was still dark, and silent. I'd heard that sound before, and I knew right away it was a gunshot. The noise triggered an unwanted memory.

"Alina, look at me!" my mom said as she brought my face close to hers. Tears and blood were cascading down her face. Seconds before everything happened, my dad struck her in the head with an empty Jacks Daniels bottle, but mom is so numb to all the physical pain and feels nothing. "Everything will be alright. I promise," she said, kissing my forehead.

The door burst open, aggressively hitting against the wall. A dark silhouette holding a handgun appeared in the darkness. I immediately recognized who it was.

"Adrian?" I whispered.

He rushed to my side and pulled out a pocket knife and began to free my hands from the rope. I stared at him with utter disbelief, and a million questions flew into my head.

"Come on, we have to go!" He said, helping me to my feet. We bolted out the door and I had a moment of déjà vu.

I counted five dead bodies on the ground outside. I had no time to react before adrenaline kicked in, and all I could think about was getting the hell away from wherever we were. Adrian placed his hand on my shoulder when we came to a corner. It was pitch-black outside, and our only source of light was the full moon. He cautiously peeked out to ensure none of his father's men were around. Once he felt certain that it was safe to leave, he grabbed my hand, and we ran like our lives depended on it, which they did. The night sky made it challenging to decipher where I was. I was only sure of the tall, dense trees everywhere, so we were likely running in a forest. Adrian seemed to know the way, so I followed behind without hesitation. After a few minutes of running, we finally came to a road, and a black Range Rover was waiting for us. He opened the door and I jumped in with him following right behind. Once the door was closed, the driver stepped on the gas, sending the two of us flying back into the seats.

"H-how did...you...find me?" I asked, struggling to breathe.

"I know my family," the driver said and turned to look at me.

It was Catalina. It amazed me at how they kept finding me, and I was even more shocked that she was always involved in my rescue.

"Like my father, we have eyes and ears everywhere," Adrian said as he settled more comfortably in the seat.

I took advantage of Catalina's presence and asked an important question that had been on my mind since arriving at Lorena's.

"Ana, did she make it?"

She shot me a glare through the rearview mirror.

"You really are annoyingly pure. You were only a few minutes away from being executed, yet you're worried about someone who's not even in Mexico anymore." I heard the irritation in her voice.

"Is she ok?" I asked again. I wasn't giving up that easily.

She sighed, "Of course, I made sure she arrived safely back in your shitty little apartment."

I felt a huge sense of relief flooding through my entire body. After leaning back in the seat, I closed my eyes and smiled. I felt safe around the two of them for reasons I couldn't explain.

"You've been quite a problem," she said.

I stayed quiet because I didn't know how to respond to her.

"The feud between the two families had been contained for many years. You've only been around for a few weeks, and everything went to shit."

"I didn't want any of this. I've told all of you this since the beginning."

"Doesn't matter what you want. A war has already started, and now it needs to end."

"Catalina, enough," Adrian interrupted.

"What? I'm only stating the truth. None of this would have happened if she never showed up."

I was grateful that she had helped me for the second time, but that gratitude quickly vanished. I was stunned that she dared to blame me for all of this bullshit. She was a cold, wicked, and heartless woman.

"None of this would have happened if your lunatic brother didn't kidnap my friends and me. I don't know what your problem is, but you need to shut the fuck up."

I was mean, and I couldn't care less about it. I'd spent too much time in my life holding back, hiding, and being afraid of the world. It was time to end that. Her brother looked at me, impressed, and gave me a proud grin, which I returned.

"It's about damn time," she said.

Her statement bewildered me. I remained silent, hoping that it would prompt her to finish her sentence.

"I was wondering when you were going to stand up to me."

"Wait, what?"

"To be involved in this family, you need to have skin as hard as a rock. Because if you don't, you'll be nothing more than a rotting corpse in a shallow grave somewhere in the desert." She clarified.

So, all those snarky remarks and the sassy attitude were what, a test?

"I don't understand. I don't plan on being involved in your family. After everything I went through, I think I've had enough."

"If only it were that simple," she said.

The phone rang, interrupting our conversation. She grabbed it from her pocket and answered.

I turned my attention to Adrian instead and said, "Thank you for saving my life, again. I don't know how I could ever repay you."

"All of this started because of me. If I hadn't told Marco about you, none of this would have happened. So, if anyone needs to apologize, it's me."

I appreciated that he took full responsibility and acknowledged his mistake.

"For a moment, I thought I was going to die. I almost accepted it and gave up."

"But you didn't. That's what makes you special, Alina. You don't give up."

If only he knew my history, then maybe he would change his mind. But for the time being, I took the compliment. Catalina finished speaking to whoever was on the phone and said something in Spanish to her brother.

"That's good to know. Everything should be good now."

"Thank you, Catalina." I forced myself to say.

She remained quiet and contemplated what to say next. "I can't fully say that I dislike you. Instead, I should thank you."

I raised an eyebrow in confusion. "For what?"

"I haven't had this much fun in a very long time," she said. Her tone was soft for the first time.

"All of this is fun to you?"

"Why not? It's fun going against Marco and my father. By the way, if you're thinking about him, don't - he doesn't know that we rescued you again."

"So, where are you guys taking me?"

"Somewhere safe and far away from all of this." Adrian chimed in.

I was relieved that I'd be safe from their father and psycho aunt, but I couldn't exactly pinpoint my feelings for Marco. It shouldn't be difficult - I should be happy that I was safe from him, yet there was a small part of me that wasn't. I couldn't explain why.

"Get some rest. We have a long ride." Adrian said.

I took his suggestion, closed my eyes, and fell asleep.

CHAPTER TWENTY-TWO

A bump in the road shook me awake. I opened my eyes and was slightly disoriented before remembering my whereabouts and that I was safe. We were still driving, to my surprise. I looked out the window, and even though it was still night, I could see that we were going up a mountain slope. I looked out at the stunning bright city lights of the country beneath us. Adrian was still asleep when I turned to look at him. He looked strangely comfortable with his head awkwardly resting on the car door.

"I've never seen him sleep so peacefully," she said.

"How long have we been driving?" I asked.

"A little over three hours. I had to take a few different routes to make sure no one was following us."

"Where exactly are we going?"

"To a safe house that my brother and I bought a few years ago. No one knows about it, not even Marco," she said proudly.

"A safe house? Why would the two of you need one?"

Catalina looked at me through the rearview mirror.

"There's a lot that you don't know about my family. Don't worry, we'll have plenty of time together in the house to talk. You've only slept for a few hours, so try to sleep some more."

She was right. I was still tired. I didn't think twice about her suggestion. As soon as I closed my eyes, I fell back into a deep slumber.

I felt a light rub on my shoulder and a soft voice calling my name. I opened my eyes to Adrian's warm smile and the bright sunlight. The car had stopped. Catalina parked it in front of a massive, unique black, wooden house with glass walls. I saw everything inside the house, looking in from the outside. The house was similar to their aunt's. *What is it with these people and glass walls?* I asked myself.

Adrian helped me out of the car. I looked around the estate and noticed the vast, dense green trees that protected the house. It was eerily quiet. The siblings led me to the house, where Catalina pressed a few numbers on the door lock. The door opened to a high, vaulted ceiling and an open concept living space.

"This house is beautiful, but why does it look so similar to Lorena's?"

She turned to look at me and said, "I like the design of her house, so I took it as inspiration to build one of my own."

She unzipped her jacket, took it off, and tossed it onto the giant black sectional sofa. She made her way into the kitchen, but quickly returned with a bottle of red wine and a glass. She settled on the couch and poured herself a glass of wine. I couldn't blame her after how long she'd driven to get us here; I'd do the same thing if I was her.

Adrian stood beside me and said, "I'll show you to your room."

I followed behind him up a floating staircase. We walked down a narrow hall with white walls and many black and white portraits of Adrian and Catalina. I was mesmerized by how stunning the two looked in each picture. We reached the end of the hall, which I assumed was my room. He pulled out a key from his pocket and unlocked the door. It opened to a luxurious, massive space with a floor-to-ceiling window, a gigantic white bed, and a stunning chandelier. Above the headboard was a massive portrait of the Egyptian Queen Nefertiti, who I recognized right away from an obsession of Egyptian history I'd had since I was a child. As we entered, I noticed that there was a gorgeous view of the lush, green forest.

"I thought this was supposed to be a safe house. How come it's so open?" I asked, curious.

"Don't worry. Like my sister said, no one knows about this place. We built it under a different name. Even if my father and Marco wanted to, they wouldn't be able to find us here." He said, confidently.

"There are a lot of clothes in the closet. Catalina had it all set up for you. You're probably still pretty tired, so I'll leave you alone to relax."

Before he walked out the door, I called out his name. He turned to look back.

"Thank you again."

He flashed me a half-smile and shut the door behind him. I walked around the room and slowly explored everything. The room decor was simple and modern. I stepped into the closet opposite the bed and thought I was in another room with how massive it was. The white marble drawers matched the white walls, and there was a gigantic floor-to-ceiling mirror at the back of the closet. There were designer bags and clothes from Gucci to Chanel and Louis Vuitton. All the top brand names in the fashion industry were in this closet. The fabrics were soft and expensive. I was happy to see only neutral-colored clothing, and everything was neatly organized. I'd thought Ana's closet was enormous, but this closet definitely took the win. My eyes stopped at the sight of a white V-neck T-shirt and black sports leggings. The familiarity of the outfit caught my attention. I pulled it off the hanger and went into the bathroom to change. The bathroom counter matched the closet's white marble design, and there was a giant tub in the middle of the room. Next to it was a glass doored, walk-in shower with black walls. I turned on the water and waited for it to warm up. Once the temperature was desirable, I hopped in and washed all the dirt away from the last twenty-four hours.

After showering, I wrapped a towel around my body and plopped onto the bed. I inhaled and exhaled a few deep breaths. The room was quiet, and that was how I liked it. I rolled onto my side and stared out the window. I wished Ana was here to witness the magnificence of this view. She would love it. Besides shopping at designer stores, enjoying nature was her second favorite hobby. I missed her so much it hurt.

After half an hour passed by, my stomach reminded me loudly that it was time to get some food. I pushed myself up from the bed, got dressed, and walked down the hall and to the stairs. I walked into a bizarre sight of the sibling's preparing food in the kitchen. They looked like professional chefs as they worked together in unison. They didn't notice my presence, and I didn't want to interrupt them. After a few minutes, Adrian noticed me awkwardly standing and watching them.

"Hey, I hope you're hungry."

"Starving," I said and strolled toward the black leather bar stool and sat down.

"You guys cook?" I asked, still slightly baffled.

Adrian placed a silver skillet on the stove, turned on the heat, and said, "Of course. Are you surprised?"

"Honestly, I figured since you guys are so rich that, you know, you never needed to learn how to cook. I'd thought you always had a chef cooking for you." I said awkwardly, slightly embarrassed that I had judged them before asking that stupid question.

Catalina gave me a dirty look and said, "Of course we have chefs that prepare meals for us, but that doesn't mean we don't know how to do it ourselves. In fact, my brother and I love to cook. It's one of our favorite things to do together."

"Yeah, I'm sorry about that. That was a horrible assumption, and I shouldn't have judged you."

"No need to apologize. I assumed many things about you, so, I guess we're even," she said and continued cutting some asparagus.

"Do you guys need help with anything?" I offered.

"We're fine. Why don't you relax in the living room and I'll let you know when food is ready," Adrian said with a warm smile.

I didn't want to sit in the living room and be alone while they cooked, so I stood there and watched instead. Catalina washed the asparagus, laid them neatly in a pan, which she then tossed with black pepper, minced garlic, and olive oil. I felt foolish for offering a hand when I didn't know how to cook. I tried cooking an egg many years ago and sadly burned it. After that, I mainly survived on take out and fast food. It baffled me how I stayed this tiny, even though I barely worked out.

"I hope you like the clothes," Catalina said as she dried her hands with a white towel.

"They're perfect. I like that it's not colorful clothing, thank you."

"I'd figure a girl like you wouldn't like too much color. I guess we have more things in common than we thought."

"I guess so."

Adrian placed three medium-sized steaks on a wooden cutting board and seasoned them with salt and pepper. Then he gently laid the meat in the skillet and allowed it to cook as he washed his hands. The show was fascinating to watch until they exchanged conversations in Spanish here and there. I scolded myself for not paying more attention to Spanish class in high school. However, I was relieved because they did not mention either Lorena's or Marco's name.

After a while, Adrian noticed my defeated posture. So, he suggested I help set up the plates and silverware on the dining table. I happily agreed, and suddenly I wasn't so useless anymore. He showed me where the plates, silverware, and wine glasses were, and I carefully grabbed them, neatly placing everything on the table. After that, Catalina informed me where the wine cellar was.

I stood frozen staring at the racks, which were never-ending on each side of the walls. It was well-stocked with every wine from around the world. The room was well insulated, and the lights were dim. I was overrun with anxiety, trying to decide which one to choose. Finally, after a few minutes of contemplation, I grabbed the Château Lafite Rothschild because it was the closest one to my right hand.

The siblings had already prepared the steaks and asparagus on our plates. I felt terrible that they had to wait for me. Once I reached the table, Adrian stood up from his chair, took the bottle from my hand, and helped me to my chair. He grabbed the corkscrew, swiftly opened the bottle, and poured the exquisite smelling wine into three glasses. He handed a glass to his sister and to me before sitting back down at the head of the table.

He raised his glass in the air and said, "Cheers to a beautiful evening."

Catalina and I raised our glasses in unison and toasted. I took a sip of my drink, and it was the most delicious wine I'd ever tasted. The texture was smooth and rich, and I had to take another sip. My stomach reminded me once again that it was time to eat, and I didn't waste any time digging into my food. The steak was medium-well and perfectly cooked to my liking. The meat was tender, and the asparagus was crunchy.

"How's the steak?" he asked.

"It's perfect. You guys really know how to cook." I said, impressed.

"Perks of having a wonderful mother that knows how to cook," she chimed in as she sipped her wine.

"Well, she is one lovely woman, then. You guys are lucky to have her. It's too bad I'll never get to meet her in person."

The siblings looked at one another in silence, and their expressions transitioned from pleasant to sorrowful. I pondered whether I had said something insensitive or offensive.

"Did I say something wrong?"

"No, you said nothing wrong, Alina. It's just that conversations about our mother are more difficult for us." He explained.

I didn't quite understand what he meant, but I knew better not to pry. I could tell that their mother was a topic that brought sadness, and I could relate to their feelings because talking about my mother had never been a simple thing to do. Most of the time, I'd just cry.

"I apologize."

"Don't worry about it." Adrian assured me.

The awkward silence quickly filled the massive, open space, so I steered the conversation elsewhere.

"How long will I be staying here for?"

"Probably a few days. We need to make sure we can safely secure a private jet for you to go somewhere that's not…What's that tiny state called again, Rhode something," Catalina stopped to think.

"Rhode Island." I assisted her.

"Ah yes, that. Honestly, I don't know how people can live in such a small state."

"It's actually very peaceful and beautiful."

"Well, you won't be going back there," he asserted.

I shot him a confused look. "Why wouldn't I?"

His sister looked at me like the answer was so obvious.

"Did you not see what happened last time? Marco found you in less than a day. So going back there is not wise. You have to stay somewhere else."

"I don't have anywhere else to go."

"Don't worry. We have a few other properties across the country. You can stay in one of them until we're sure you're safe." Adrian said.

"Why are you risking so much for me?"

He remained silent and avoided eye contact. So, I looked at his sister. Catalina wouldn't hesitate to tell me the truth.

"I guess Marco isn't the only brother who's in love with you," she blatantly spat out.

I regretted asking. My face warmed, and my legs were uncomfortably stiff under the table. I picked up my wine glass and took a sip to avoid saying anything. Adrian and I refused to look at one another, instead, he ate his food and pretended as if there was nothing shocking about what Catalina had said.

"Well, this is awkward," she pointed it out.

She grabbed her wine glass and excused herself to the balcony that overlooked the mountains.

We both sat still in our seats. I did my best to avoid his gaze, because at that moment I'd rather be hit in the face by a ball and knocked unconscious. I needed to do something, so I cut into my steak and picked at it.

"I'm sorry," he finally said. His apology caught me off guard.

"For what?"

He placed the silverware on the table and said, "Everything that has happened is because of me. I should have just left you alone. You and your friends could have been back home and safe a long time ago."

"You've apologized already. But you're right. If our paths never crossed, life would be so much better right now," I said truthfully. I saw the hurt in his eyes, but I knew I had to speak my truth.

"I saw the way he looked at you at the party. It's a look that I've never seen on him before. I knew you were special to him."

"Special? I can't really see why, though."

He remained quiet.

"Your brother told me that the only reason you approached me was that I reminded you of Isabella. But he wasn't willing to tell me much else about her. Will you?"

He grabbed his wine and drank it all in one big gulp, then set the empty glass on the table.

"She was your girlfriend?"

"She was a maid at the mansion when we lived with our father about ten years ago," he began but stopped and contemplated whether he should continue.

"And?" I prompted him.

I had an annoying desire to know about the mysterious woman everyone referred to, but never talked about in depth.

"She came during a difficult time for my family. Our family relationship was… I guess you can say it was complicated. There were a lot of fights, especially between Marco and I. Most of the time, we fought for our father's attention. After a while, our relationship became strained. We could barely speak or look at one another without fighting. Our issues nearly broke the family apart. But then one day, Isabella walked through the door, and she instantly drew us both to her. She was the most beautiful woman I'd ever seen, and she was delicate and kind. Unbeknownst to the other, we both fell in love with her."

Of all the different scenarios I'd thought of since I learned about Isabella, none of them involved her being a maid. The story was intriguing, but I felt like I was watching a cheesy, dramatic movie.

"Two brothers fell in love with the same woman. What could go wrong, right?" I said sarcastically.

His reaction was the opposite of mine. I removed the stupid smirk from my face. My comment was insensitive, and I'd overstepped my boundary.

"Sorry. I didn't mean to be a smart ass." I took another sip of my wine.

"It's okay. It's not something that I like to talk about with anyone. But long story short, you were right, things became complicated, and ultimately we both lost her."

I heard a hint of regret, or perhaps despair, in his voice, but I couldn't pinpoint it.

"Do I remind you that much of her?"

He looked me directly in the eyes. "Yes. When we first met, I thought my eyes were playing tricks on me. You both share the same soft brown eyes. It took me a moment to realize that you weren't actually her."

I knew I wasn't someone special. Although, there were some brief moments where both brothers gave me a glimpse of hope that perhaps I was a person worthy of love. I thought I was the extraordinary woman that changed a beast into a prince. It turned out the only interest they had in me was because of *her*. She must have been a remarkable woman. Or maybe completely insane.

"It sounds like you and your brother are still in love with her."

"Even after ten years, my brother and I still fight because of her."

"That's a long time to fight for a woman who's dead."

"How do you know she's dead?"

"Marco told me, but he wouldn't tell me how."

Adrian shifted uncomfortably in his seat. He picked up his fork and played with the vegetables. It was obvious he knew how she died but wasn't willing or ready to tell me.

"Did you seek me out because you thought I could replace her?" I asked blatantly.

I studied his face as he debated internally on how to respond to my straightforward question.

"Once I realized you weren't her, I thought long and hard about whether I should approach you. Of course, I knew about the danger if I did, and I should have known better, but my curiosity got the better of me. The only thing I remembered after that was that I needed to know who you were."

"I hated you for a while, but then I realized you weren't the one that took my friends and me. It was your brother. So, I accept your apology."

"You're very kind. I understand why my brother fell in love with you. He found me the night we helped you escape back home. I'd never seen him so angry. I thought he was going to kill me that night." He revealed.

I stood up from my seat and moved to the one next to his. I took his hand in mine and said, "I appreciate everything that you've done for me," and flashed him a smile.

He pulled my hand to his lips, gently planted a kiss on the back of it, and said, "I'd do anything for you."

For a moment, I believed him. Our eyes met for a little while before my anxiety screamed at me to release his hand before I gave him the wrong idea. I released his hand, scooting away from him.

"Well, I'm out of wine, and your sister took the bottle. I'm going to get some more." I said but only because I wanted to remove myself from the situation and not have to look into his beautiful eyes anymore.

I pushed myself up from the chair, grabbed my glass, and headed to the balcony. I slid the glass door open and stepped outside to an angelic Catalina staring into the beautiful sky. Carefully, I made my way to her.

"You guys really know how to pick the best place."

"Thanks. More wine?" She asked and raised the bottle.

"Please,"

I raised my glass, and she poured the wine half full before placing the bottle back on the small table beside her.

"The best time to be out here is during sunset," she said and then sipped her drink.

"I can only imagine how beautiful that must be. I didn't think someone like you would like to live in a place like this," I said, and took a big sip of my wine.

"Why does that surprise you?"

"Well, you freaked out because I ruined your Gucci swimsuit. I assumed you were one of those girls that likes luxurious, materialistic things. This mansion is top-notch, but it's in the middle of nowhere. I assumed you were somebody who would want to live, you know, in the city where all the other rich people live."

She raised an eyebrow at me and said, "Just because I like expensive clothing doesn't mean I don't like peaceful places like this. I specifically picked out this location because our mother used to bring us here when we were little."

"Honestly, you're not what I expected."

"Trust me, you're not the only person to say that to me. People always assume they know who I am when they first meet me. I'll admit I don't always make it any easier. You surprised me, though."

"How?"

"When I first met you, I thought you were a timid person. But everything you've done so far shows otherwise. Even though I thought certain things you did were foolish, I can't deny the fact that you're braver than most women I've encountered in my life. I can understand why both my brothers are fascinated by you. Even Isabella didn't have the guts to do what you did to save Ana."

Hearing her name caused me to tilt my head. Adrian had disclosed some details, but I suspected there was more to the story than what he told me. Perhaps she'd tell me. After all, she never had problems speaking the truth.

"Adrian told me a little about her. I know it was painful for him to talk about her. What really happened between the three of them?"

"Why are you so invested in knowing about her?"

"Shouldn't I be? I mean, my resemblance to her is the reason I am standing right next to you right now."

"You have a point. I never understood why both my brothers fell in love with her honestly. She was unbearably annoying."

"How so?"

Catalina turned her body and leaned her back against the balcony's black metal rails.

"She wasn't as innocent as Adrian and Marco portrayed her to be. She had them both wrapped around her finger like little puppets, and she enjoyed every minute of it."

She paused and sipped her wine. I listened intently—my stomach twisted in excitement. Finally, I was about to learn the whole truth. I took another sip of my drink.

"Adrian and Marco used to fight a lot when they were younger, and Isabella showing up didn't make it any better. First, they fought for our father's attention, then it was all about her love. She made their relationship even more strained, but she immersed herself in it instead of feeling bad about it. She was a pathetic little housemaid who enjoyed the attention of two of Mexico's most powerful men fighting over her. Eventually, she had to choose, and when she did, the family turned upside down."

I took another big gulp of my drink, my attention entirely invested in the story.

"What happened after that?" I asked after a few long moments of silence. She needed to finish, but I had a feeling that she was hiding something, which caught me off guard. She was never afraid to speak the truth. Her silence had me debating whether it was wise for me to know the ending.

She looked at me and asked, "Are you sure you want to know?"

I nodded my head, but not without hesitation at first.

"She chose Marco. So, Adrian shot her," she revealed in an unusually nonchalant voice.

My eyes bulged widely, and I nearly dropped my glass on the deck. That revelation wasn't even a possibility in my head. But was I at all that surprised? I couldn't decide truthfully. Even though Adrian had a soft side, I hadn't forgotten who he was. Catalina saw the pale look on my face, took my wine glass and refilled it to the brim.

"I think you need more wine," she said and handed me back my drink.

She was right. I drank half of it in one big gulp.

"He k-killed her?" Finally, I spat out the words from my dry mouth.

"I asked if you wanted the truth, and you insisted."

"I know. I just didn't expect that to be the ending. I thought he loved her?"

"He did. My little brother couldn't handle the rejection. He thought that if he couldn't have her, neither should Marco. When Marco found out what he did, he beat him nearly to death. If our father hadn't intervened, Adrian wouldn't be here today. After that day, Marco swore to take away any woman he held dear to his heart. So now you know."

"He took me to spite his brother. You realize how messed up that shit is, right?" I asked, still in disbelief.

"Marco always keeps his promises. Adrian didn't believe him at first. It wasn't until he took Carmela and Juliet that he realized he wasn't lying. After that, Adrian closed himself off. Well, at least until after he met you. I warned him about the danger if he approached you, but my little brother rarely listens to me."

Every cell in my body boiled with irritation and confusion. All this started because of a feud over love. *How unbearably cringe*, I thought to myself. I gripped my wine glass tightly in my hand. The only thing that calmed me down was the soothing sight of the mountain ahead of us. It helped distract me slightly. I turned my head and looked toward the dining room, but he wasn't there.

"Adrian was young. And when you're young, your emotions are heightened, and rejection isn't the easiest thing for most of us to handle." Catalina said after a few long moments of silence.

I turned my head back to gaze at her.

His brutal reaction to the rejection made me recall when Ana did the same thing to the football team's quarterback during senior year. His name was Donovan, and he'd had a massive crush on her for months. But she knew he was a womanizer. She wasn't interested in being one of his many women. She became his first-ever rejection, and he didn't react well to it. After that, he became obsessive and would secretly follow her home. But the nightmares didn't end there. On multiple nights, he stood outside her house and stalked her. And when he wasn't watching her, he would leave notes on her porch and call her from various numbers throughout the day. His stalking continued for weeks until Ana noticed, and eventually, he was arrested. Because she was from a prestigious family, she had no issue getting the best lawyer to build a strong case against him. He got what he deserved.

"Why are you defending him? Your brother murdered the woman that he supposedly loved." I said, disturbed that she defended his action.

"Because he is my blood, and no matter what he did, I will always defend and protect him," she said firmly.

I guess I wouldn't understand since I was an only child. I finished the rest of my wine.

"So, now what?"

"What do you mean?" I asked.

"You just learned the truth. What are you going to do now?"

I thought for a minute. My head was numb.

"I guess I'll go back to my normal life. Whatever that means." I said honestly.

"Well, we will let you know when it's safe to do so," she turned around to walk back inside. Before she disappeared, I needed to say something.

"Catalina," I called her name.

She stopped and turned around to face me.

"Thank you for everything. I know we haven't exactly been *friends*, but you're the only one that has been honest with me, and I appreciate that."

"I almost believe you."

"I mean it. I have one more question, though. Aren't you afraid of what will happen to you for helping me?"

"I'm not afraid. Not of my father or Marco. I've never been afraid of anyone." She said confidently.

I believed her wholeheartedly.

"Why are you helping me? I know you said it's because of Adrian, but I can't help but to sense that it's more than that." The daunting question needed an answer.

"That's two questions."

"I know, but honestly, though, why?"

She looked at me. "I guess... I felt guilty."

I looked at her, perplexed. "Guilty?"

She finished her wine.

"If it weren't for me, Marco wouldn't have visited the resort. He wouldn't have learned about you from Adrian, and you and your friend would have been safe."

She was not wrong, and though I should be more upset with her, I wasn't. I surprised myself. I didn't think that I would ever change my opinion of her. However, amidst the conversation about Marco visiting her, I remembered when Adrian told me about his obsession with another man being with her.

"I have a third question," I said cautiously.

She laughed gently and returned to my side.

"I've always wondered. I mean, I get that he's your older brother and protective and stuff but beating up Jason and forcing him to leave was a bit much. Don't you think so?"

"He has always been like that. I can't see any man. Being with Jason was a risk, and I knew it. But I liked him."

"Well, I mean, he is a psychopath."

"He is, but he's only like that with women that he loves. Before you that was only Isabella and one other woman."

I peeked at her with interest. I'd learned about Isabella, but unbeknownst to me, there was another mysterious woman. My desire to know more about him was getting unbearable and yes, I was aware; however, I couldn't fully explain why.

"Who's the other woman?"

She turned and locked eyes with mine, and then she revealed, "Me."

I thought my mind was playing tricks on me. Or perhaps she was playing a prank on me. I'd read stories of incest between family members, but I'd never imagined I would stand next to someone involved in that kind of thing. I looked at her with wide eyes. What came out of her mouth was hard to process. But what was more disturbing was how calmly she revealed the truth.

"Don't look at me with such wide eyes, Alina, they might pop out of your head." She said with a wicked smile.

"I'm sorry, it's just the way you said it...like it's not a big deal. So, Marco, your brother, was or is in love with you?"

She laughed. I guess I was the only one who didn't get the joke.

"Relax. I'm his step-sister. We're not blood-related." She revealed.

I felt a tremendous sense of relief, but it was still weird. I guess my uninteresting life kept me drawn to know more about them because their lives were much more exciting than my own. It was both fascinating and dangerous. Great, I'd become that annoying character that fell for the horrible people around her.

"That's why he's so protective. It's because he loves you."

"Loved," she clarified and continued, "My mother married his father about twelve years ago. That's when Adrian and I stepped into the family and the cartel. I met Marco when he was 18 years old. My little brother adjusted to the family easier than I did. I struggled to cope with our father's murder and then, only a few months later, our mother married a new man. She thought she had found her soulmate, but she couldn't have been more wrong. My stepfather cheated on her repeatedly. And when he wasn't sleeping with other women, he beat her. You would think she was happy with all that power and money, but she wasn't. My mother knew what he was doing, but it wasn't until she caught him sleeping with another woman in their bed that she had enough. That same day, she threw herself from her bedroom balcony. My brother and I held her in our arms and watched her die. After that, I isolated myself from everyone, including Adrian. But that wasn't even the worst part. I chose not to let my brother in, but I allowed Marco in. I don't exactly remember what happened. I just remembered feeling safe in his arms. He helped me through a difficult time, and one thing led to another, and soon we fell in love."

For the first time, I heard pain and grief in her voice. Catalina was the last person on earth that I thought I could genuinely relate to. I understood and empathized with her suffering. There was a familiar sadness in her voice, one that she had hidden for many years. I wondered if I was the first person she ever talked to about this. I waited a while and allowed her to be in the moment with her pain. Then I moved in closer and placed my hand above hers. She finished her wine, and I could tell she was trying her hardest to hold back tears.

"My dad did the same thing to my mom. So many nights, I watched him beat her repeatedly, and I couldn't do anything to help."

"The world is full of fucked up people. You think family is supposed to protect and love you. But sometimes, they're the ones that hurt you the most. I envy you, Alina,"

I stared at her, bewildered. "Why? I think I'm the last person anyone should envy."

"Because you're innocent. And you maintain a pure heart, even after all the fucked-up shit you've experienced. No one in my family did."

If only she knew what I'd done, she'd probably have a different opinion about my innocence.

"We're all flawed, Catalina. No one is perfect."

We stared out into the beautiful horizon and bright sunlight reflecting against the mountain. I shocked myself. Besides Ana, I'd never talked about my past to anyone. It surprised me how natural it felt to tell her my story.

"So, did the two of you... ever sleep together?" I asked curiously.

She looked at me and then chuckled. "What did you think? We fell in love, and honestly, now that I think about it, it was probably because we were horny teenagers. It was probably more lust than anything," she said and continued, "but yeah, we fucked for about a year, until I realized I wanted more. I ended things between us, but that didn't stop him from killing any man that came near me."

"That's some crazy shit," I said out loud without realizing it. I was glad she found my comment comical and laughed.

"I like you. You have guts. Truthfully, I know what Marco feels for you is different, even from how he felt about Isabella and me. As soon as you were in his grip, I sensed a change in him. I saw deep darkness in his eyes when he found out we helped you escape. Immediately, all of the affection that he ever had for me disappeared. You're special to him. But my advice for you is to run the fuck away from our family, as far as possible. Trust me; it'll only make your life easier."

"You don't have to tell me twice. That's my plan."

Catalina closed her eyes and took a deep breath of the fresh air, and said, "It's not fun to stand here and have a heart-to-heart without getting more wine. I'll be right back." She went back inside.

I had a sudden image of them sleeping together once she was gone, and it made me shudder with revulsion. *What a mess*, I thought to myself. I felt like a character in a chaotic book with never-ending twists. In less than an hour, I learned every disturbing truth about their family. I thought I'd prepared myself, but I was wrong. Catalina came back outside, filled both glasses with more wine, and we spent the rest of the day drinking. I planned to get drunk and hopefully sleep the horror away.

CHAPTER TWENTY-THREE

A fresh new day was upon us despite this never-ending nightmare. I opened my eyes to the bright light streaming through the trees outside. I could stare out at this view forever, in complete peace. After stretching my entire body, I turned my head to look at the clock on the bedside table. It was already two in the afternoon! I drank way too much with Catalina yesterday. If I recall correctly, we finished five bottles of wine between the two of us. Surprisingly, I remembered our entire conversation, and I felt closer to her. She was almost a reflection of me, except she was more confident and immune to the cruelty of the world. After a few minutes I pushed myself up and off the bed and strolled into the closet. I grabbed a pair of white jeans and a black shirt and took them into the bathroom to change into after I showered.

I felt refreshed after my shower, but my head was still pounding slightly. I opened the door and walked out at the same time as Adrian, who was in nothing but a pair of white joggers. He looked like a Greek God with his perfectly chiseled six-packs and disheveled hair. *Who looks this perfect in the morning?* I asked myself. We both stared at each other in an awkward silence.

"Good morning," he finally spoke.

"Good morning," I said with a half-crooked smile.

"How was your sleep?"

"It was good. Quiet and peaceful."

He led the way through the hall and down the spiral staircase. I meekly followed behind like a lost puppy. Once we were in the living room, he went straight to the kitchen. I tried to grab a skillet so I could cook eggs, sausage, and bacon, but he refused to allow me to lift a finger.

"Please, let me do it. I can't have you serve me every time."

"It's alright, Alina. I like to cook," he insisted.

I'd thought about protesting, but I knew I would lose this battle. So instead, I sat my butt down on the bar stool and watched him work. He grabbed a bottle of orange juice from the refrigerator and poured me a glass. I'd never seen a man so graceful in the kitchen before. He was mesmerizing to watch, and even though he appeared perfect now, I hadn't forgotten what he did to Isabella. I debated whether it was wise to bring up that conversation, and after a few minutes, I decided it was best to wait. I would be able to concentrate better after I'd eaten a full breakfast.

"So, how much longer will I be staying here?"

Adrian placed the skillet on the stove and turned up the heat. Then he grabbed a basket of eggs from the refrigerator and set it on the counter. I patiently watched as he cracked a few into the hot skillet.

"A few more days. Until everything settles for you in LA."

I nearly choked on the orange juice and asked, "What? LA?"

"One of our private estates is there. Marco and my father will never find you there."

"How am I going to survive in LA? It's too expensive."

He went back to the fridge and grabbed a bag of bacon, and with ease, said, "Don't worry about money, we'll take care of it."

I wasn't exactly sure how I felt about a new house, and their help with money in a place like LA. I'd never been one to feel comfortable when people offered help, especially in that way.

"Also, we suggest you don't contact Ana once you're back in the States."

"Wait? Why not?" I asked, my voice upset.

"Because I know my brother. He will most likely be keeping tabs on her, and when you contact her, he will know your location."

"Well, what if he hurts Ana and her family?"

He turned quiet. I was not too fond of his silence.

"Hello?" I prompted.

"I don't know how far he will go to find you. But for now, getting you to a safe location is what's important."

His response gave me no comfort, in fact it made me more anxious, and my brain spiraled into all of the possible worst-case scenarios for my future. I was more than convinced that Marco would not stop until he found me. The man was insane, and I was his prey. A predator does not let go of its prize that easily.

"Look, I know it wasn't the response you were looking for, and I wish I could give you a better answer, but for now, that's all I can say."

The thought of not telling Ana that I was alive killed me. Knowing her, she was probably going insane searching for me now. I sighed deeply at that disappointing thought. Adrian continued with his chef skills, and I continued with my anxious thoughts as I watched him. The house was eerily quiet. It was well past two in the afternoon, and I thought Catalina would have come downstairs by now. I scanned around for her, but she was nowhere in sight.

"Where's your sister?"

"She went to the market at the base of the mountain."

"Is that safe?"

He dumped the scrambled eggs, sausage, and bacon onto a white plate with a fork and presented it to me. He had made himself a plate, but he stood and ate across from me instead of sitting down.

"She'll be fine. Now eat. I need to make sure you're fed and strong. There's something that I want to show you today." He said with a devious smirk.

I picked up my fork and began eating. After a few minutes, I stopped halfway through my meal. I wanted to finish the rest of it, but my anxiety stopped me, so I placed the fork down on the counter and prepared myself for what I was about to say.

"What's wrong?"

It was a perfect lead-in for me to ask, "You…killed Isabella?"

He stopped eating and looked at me. There was a hint of guilt in his eyes, and I could tell he was ready to close himself off again. He remained silent, then placed his fork on the plate. I waited anxiously for him to speak.

"I did."

"All because she rejected you?"

"She was my first love and the only person who understood me. It was difficult to be a stepson to a man who was the head of one of Mexico's most powerful cartels. I sought comfort in her. I thought she loved me, but unbeknownst to me, Isabella was also sleeping with Marco. And when she chose him, I lost control. I couldn't accept the truth, and I did the unthinkable. I pulled the trigger."

"What you, your brother, and Isabella had wasn't love. It was a dangerous affair fueled by lust."

"I realized that now. Perhaps she truly loved my brother, but I know now she never really loved me. So, I guess Marco was the better man."

I wanted to be brutally honest and tell him he was a horrible person for killing an innocent woman. But for some reason my feelings were conflicted. How could I judge someone when I'd also sinned? Besides, she wasn't entirely a saint. I had a feeling she knew what she was doing and probably enjoyed pitting the two brothers against each other. But she didn't deserve to die; that much I was sure of.

"Marco is not a better man. Trust me."

"And me?" he asked, his eyes peeking with curiosity.

I thought for a moment, and once I was ready, I said, "You killed someone, so neither one of you is a saint. But at least I sense that you regret your actions, which is more than I can say for your brother."

"I tried very hard not to fall for you, but I guess that didn't work out, and here we are again…."

"No, Adrian, you only love the fact that I remind you of her. And of course, that goes for your brother too."

"I think you're so self-critical that you can't realize that there are people out there who could love you for *you*. I hope that one day you'll realize there's more to you than you give yourself credit for. And whether you want to believe it or not, I didn't fall for you because of your resemblance to Isabella. Things may appear uncertain, but one thing is clear, I have to protect you."

Adrian barely knew me, yet what he said couldn't be more true. I wished it was easier to find yourself in the world. I'd learned helplessness for so many years that sometimes it was nearly impossible to get around the fact that there was more to life than pain and suffering.

"Please, finish your food. I need you fully fed for today's activity."

I stopped my pity party and picked up my fork to finish eating.

"What is it exactly that we're doing today?"

He gave me a gentle smile and, without saying anything, disappeared upstairs, leaving me bewildered. *Oh boy, what are we doing today?* A few minutes passed, and he returned wearing a gray shirt, carrying a black duffle bag in his hand. There was a huge grin on his face. He looked like an excited boy scout about to go on his first adventure in the woods. He grabbed my hand, and we walked outside and towards the forest.

"Where are we going?" I asked, intrigued and nervous at the same time.

"You'll see."

We ventured deep into the luscious green forest with its sky-high trees. Somehow, I walked through the uneven ground, with branches everywhere, without falling on my face. But perhaps it was because Adrian was holding my hand and guiding me along the path. We walked a few hundred more feet before stopping in front of a large boulder. He released my hand, placed the bag on the ground, and instructed me to close my eyes. I hesitated at first but my curiosity about what he had planned won. So, I did as I was told. The sound of light wind wrestling against the tree branches was soothing, but the anticipation was killing me. After a period of silence, I finally heard the bag unzip.

"Alight, open your eyes."

I opened my eyes to the unexpected sight of him holding a handgun with enthusiasm in his eyes.

I gaped at him, puzzled, and asked, "A gun?"

"I figured since you're involved with my family, now might be a good time to learn how to use one of these in case you need it." He said in a serious tone.

He handed me the gun, and I stared down at it, hesitantly. Adrian pulled out a red marker from his pocket and made his way toward a tall, wide tree about twenty feet in front of us. He then drew an enormous circle and a giant letter "X" in the center. Once finished, he came back to my side.

"Show me what you've got. It's ready and loaded. All you have to do is pull the trigger."

I'd always wanted to learn how to shoot but was too much of a coward to try it. I held the weapon with both hands and slowly raised it in the air, my heart beating fast with adrenaline. Once the gun was raised to my eye level, I closed my left eye and aimed at the letter in the circle. I took a deep breath and pulled the trigger. The gunshot was so loud I thought my eardrum exploded. There was a loud ringing in my ear for the first few seconds.

"Shouldn't I be wearing some type of ear protection?" I asked.

"Oh yeah, sorry, I was so excited for you to shoot I forgot to grab a headset for you." He bent down and pulled out a black headset and placed it over my ears. It was much quieter with it on.

He signaled me to shoot again, and I did. From where I stood, I thought I'd hit the target, but when we looked where I'd shot, it was nowhere near the letter, or the circle. It was embarrassing how far off I was. Adrian and I looked at each other and burst out laughing at my pathetic attempts.

"It's only your first time. Keep practicing." He encouraged me. I admired his positive attitude.

We spent the next few hours shooting at the poor tree. Adrian shot like a pro, and it discouraged me every time he hit the mark.

Finally, after over fifty attempts and still nowhere near the target, I gave up.

"I suck," I said in a defeated voice.

I could tell he was trying hard not to laugh at my continued failure and self-pity party.

I cocked my head to the side and said, "Go ahead, say it. I'm pathetic."

He smiled and said, "It's your first time. Don't be so hard on yourself. We'll practice again tomorrow."

I gladly handed him the gun, and when he finished packing everything back into the duffle bag, we headed back to the house.

"I'm grateful we met," he blurted out.

I turned my head to look at him and asked, "Why?"

"I haven't felt this happy in a long time. It's nice to feel genuine happiness again."

"I wish I could say the same." After my comment, I saw the hurt in his eyes. "I'm sorry. I didn't mean it in that way."

"It's alright. I understand what you meant."

My attitude was completely unnecessary, and I felt guilty for making him feel bad. Adrian had been nothing but generous and apologetic. He rescued me twice, gave me a place to stay and cooked delicious meals for me. What more could a girl ask for?

"I understand now why Marco is obsessed with your sister."

"About that. I should have told you from the start. I didn't want to scare you. My family is already messed up enough."

"Don't you think that it's weird? You know, him being in love with her and all? And the two of them having sex?"

"There's nothing normal about my family, but, trust me, there are worse things that you don't know about. I If I told you everything, you'd probably run and scream in horror."

"You're probably right. Don't tell me anything else," I said, and we both giggled.

A silver Porsche pulled up behind us when we reached the front of the house. Catalina stepped out in casual blue jeans and a white shirt, carrying a brown grocery bag in her hands. Only she could make a simple outfit look like it came straight from a Gucci runway show. She removed her black sunglasses and looked at the duffel bag in Adrian's hand. Her expression showed that she already knew what was in it. She closed the space between us with a smirk.

"I see you guys had a fun day."

"Well, he did. Me? Not so much." I reported like a loser.

The three of us entered the house in unison, and Catalina went straight to the kitchen to put the bag on the island. Adrian excused himself and went upstairs with the duffel bag. I sat down at the barstool and watched as she pulled out fresh green peppers, onions, and jalapeños from the bag.

"I assume he told you where you'll be staying for a while when you get back to the States," she said as she rinsed the vegetables in the sink.

"He did. I can't say thank you enough for everything that you guys are doing for me."

"Well, it's the least that we can do, especially after everything you've been through these last few weeks."

"Once I'm in LA, will I see you again?"

"It's safer if we don't meet again. I know Marco, and he will keep a close eye on us once we go back to the family. I assume Adrian also talked to you about contacting Ana?"

I nodded my head sadly. The thought of not being able to do so still pained me, and even though I knew it was for the best, it was still difficult to process.

"Good," Catalina stopped what she was doing, looked me in the eye, and said, "Look, I know it's going to be hard, but for your safety and hers, she should believe you're gone, forever."

I exhaled a deep sigh. "I know."

"You'll be okay, Alina. You're a survivor. If you can survive Marco, you can survive anything."

"I know he won't hurt you, but what about your step-father?" I asked, concerned about her safety.

She continued washing the vegetables.

"I'll deal with my father. Defying him isn't something new for me; I've been doing it for the last decade or so."

Though I admired her confidence, I couldn't shake the uneasy feeling that something terrible would happen to her and Adrian. The way I saw it, if a man could beat and cheat on his wife, he was capable of anything.

"Has he ever hurt the two of you?"

Catalina grabbed a white towel from one of the many drawers and dried her hands.

"No, he has never laid a hand on any of us. And believe it or not, his children mean everything to him," she said, and continued, "I know. It makes little sense, but nothing in the family makes sense. I stopped wondering about it a long time ago. It did me no good to wonder."

It was hard to comprehend that even the cartel's most dangerous leader didn't harm his children. It enraged me to learn he had the heart not to do so, but my father didn't. The harsh realization made me loathe my so-called father even more. Their father was the last man on earth that I'd thought would have more integrity than my own.

"Marco told me once that he raped his mother. Is that true?"

She stopped what she was doing once more and took a few steps away from the sink. She leaned her back against the opposite kitchen counter and folded her arms across her chest.

"It is. Our mother never told us whether he did the same to her, but I wouldn't be surprised if he did. I know you despise Marco, but there's one thing you should know about him, and that is he never lies, especially to the people he cares about."

I suddenly felt a quick surge of guilt at how I treated him when he disclosed that information to me. Of all people, I should have been the one person who understood what it was like to witness your mother getting assaulted by your father. Even though he was a monster, his trauma shouldn't have been invalidated.

"Do you still have nightmares?" she asked, disrupting my thoughts.

I paused and thought for a moment. "Not as much as I used to. I used to have them every single night, but I guess with all the craziness in the last few weeks, other things have distracted my mind."

"What happened to him, your father?" she said with curiosity in her eyes.

"He, um, died," I replied hesitantly. I felt my facial muscles tense up at the unexpected and uncomfortable question. I played with my hands to keep myself distracted. Catalina saw the pale expression on my face, and she knew not to push further about my father.

"Well, I'm glad he's dead. A man like that doesn't deserve to live in this world," she said coldly.

Sometimes I had thought the same of him, but other times I sobbed uncontrollably at how much I missed him. I would be furious with myself for missing such a horrible father, and I couldn't explain why. A therapist once told me it was because he was still the man who gave me life, and our relationship was complicated, but no matter how much I despised him, I'd always have a tiny spot in my heart that would always love him. I refused to listen at first, but only because I realized later that the therapist was right. I'd always love him, no matter how much he hurt us.

"Alright, enough with the depressing talk. Why don't you help with the rest of the vegetables?"

I happily stood up from the chair and helped in the kitchen.

It was near evening time when we all sat down at the dining table to eat.

"No one followed you?" Adrian asked from the head of the chair.

She flashed him an agitated look. "I've been doing this for a while now, little brother. So don't you worry." She said and took a bite of her salmon.

"What is your aunt going to do now since I'm not, you know, dead?"

The siblings looked at one another with a flat expression. I couldn't figure out what they were thinking about, but I wasn't fond of it. I wished they were cartoon characters, so their thoughts would pop up over their heads in a bubble. Wouldn't that be nice?

"Lorena is a very vengeful woman. She doesn't like when people double-cross her, especially family members. So, I know she's pissed, and she won't stop until you're dead. That's why we must be careful in handling the situation," Adrian reported.

"Marco said she fell in love with a rival cartel's leader and left the family. Is that true?" I asked, curious.

Catalina sipped her wine before speaking. "Our father has always been a controlling and prideful man. He has this need to control every member of the family. Aunt Lorena, like myself, is more of a free-spirit woman and doesn't like to be told what to do..."

Adrian interrupted his sister, "What Marco said is the truth. After war broke out, other cartels saw our family as weak, and my father wasn't happy about it. After many months of an ongoing feud, our father and Andres met and agreed to a truce, and he released our aunt. She left with him, and everything worked out accordingly for the past five years. That is until you and Ana approached her in the club. She must have known that you and Ana belonged to Marco, which makes the game more exciting for her.

Of course she knew because I was stupid enough to inform her Marco kidnapped us.

"So, because of me, the war reignited?"

"It's not your fault, Alina. You had nothing to do with any of our family's mess."

"My aunt has a history with Marco, and she could have easily ended this whole thing when he asked for Ana's return. But she saw an opportunity to hurt him, and she took it." Catalina chimed in.

"A history?"

More tales of the family? Please enlighten me. She stopped eating and placed her silverware on the table.

"It's complicated and something that you don't need to worry about. Besides, the only thing you should focus on right now is getting out of Mexico," Adrian asserted.

It was not the response I wanted, but I knew he was right. I shouldn't be so curious about their family. The only thing I could think about was my unfortunate luck in life. First, of course, I'd be the person to get imprisoned by the cartel, and of course, I'd be the same person to approach the wrong woman for help in the club. I wished for just one day life wasn't so shitty. I didn't think that was too much to ask for from whoever was in control of our lives.

"I think you've had enough for today. You should get some rest." Adrian recommended.

"You're absolutely right. Thank you for dinner. It was delicious." I stood up from the chair and grabbed my plate, intending to bring it to the sink to wash it, but he stood up just as fast to stop me. Both he and his sister insisted they'd take care of the dishes. I didn't bother to protest because I knew I would lose. After admitting defeat, I took myself upstairs.

I closed the door behind me and walked toward the bed. I sat down at the edge and stared at the wonderful view. The heavenly sunset was reflecting off the glass windows and onto the trees beautifully. But even though the room was silent and relaxing, I couldn't say the same for my brain. Various thoughts rushed through my already aching head. It had only been two days, and I heard more crazy stories than I had in my last few boring years of life. Marco, the siblings, Lorena, their father, and the cartels were all too much. I was living in a horror movie. Insanity was the only word I could think of to describe everything that had happened. Finally, after half an hour passed, I lay my head on the pillow to sleep away the pain. I knew if I continued to stay awake, my head would most likely explode into a million tiny pieces. As soon as I closed my eyes, I fell into a deep slumber.

When I woke up, it was still slightly light outside. I breathed a sigh of relief, knowing that I didn't sleep through the day. I slowly sat up and let my feet dangle off the bed for a few seconds before finally pushing myself off. I twisted the doorknob and opened the door to go downstairs. It was eerily quiet; I called the siblings' names a few times, but there was no response. I searched the wine cellar, balcony, and out front, but still no sign of them. The only thing I found was a note on the kitchen counter next to the black duffel bag from earlier. I grabbed the piece of paper and read it. It was from Adrian and Catalina - they had left after eating for some business but didn't clarify what it was. At first, I was in disbelief that they would leave me alone in the house. I guess they were that confident of my safety. They probably also knew that even if I wanted to run, I wouldn't. They were right. It was unwise for me to take off and roam in the forest alone. I grabbed the duffel bag and decided instead of staying inside, I'd go out and do some more target practice on another unlucky tree.

CHAPTER TWENTY-FOUR

Five days passed since I'd come to the safe house. I grew more and more impatient with each day. I didn't think it was possible to be bored looking at the same scenery in my room. The view was still breathtaking, but there were only so many trees I could keep looking at. When I wasn't resting in bed or eating a delicious meal, I was in the forest shooting with Adrian. Target practice was the only activity that kept me entertained. After many hours of shooting, I was pleased with how much my aim had improved.

By the sixth day, I felt safer. If Marco had failed to find me by now, he wouldn't in the future. Sometimes the idea of never seeing him again was bothersome. *Do I want him to find me?* Honestly, I had no clue. A few times, I scolded myself for missing his touch. I was aware of how messed up it was to long for him, even the tiniest bit. I consistently had to remind myself that he nearly killed Ana, kidnapped her and then Juan and me, and kept us prisoners.

Dear Diary, I started in my journal, and before I knew it, I was on the seventh page. While target practice kept me busy, journaling was the only thing that kept me sane. Of course, I had Catalina to thank for the journal. It was like she'd read my mind after the third day. It caught me off guard when she returned from the grocery store some days ago and handed me the black notebook. Weirdly enough, she was the bitchy and fashionable older sister I'd always wanted. Besides Ana, of course.

A knock on the door disrupted my deep thoughts.

"Come in," I said, slightly irritated that I had to stop my writing. I closed my journal and placed it under the pillow.

Adrian opened the door and came inside wearing nothing but tight black joggers. I couldn't help but notice his perfectly sculpted body. He looked more toned than when we first got to the safe house.

Most likely it was because he spent most of his free time lifting weights on the balcony. I moved my eyes from his abs to his face as he stopped at the end of the bed. It was late. I looked at the clock and it was one in the morning.

"Did I wake you up?" he asked softly.

"No, you're fine. I was already awake. Is everything alright?"

"Everything is fine. I just spoke with my sister. The private jet will be ready in the morning to take you to LA," he reported with a slightly defeated tone in his voice. I wondered whether it was because I was leaving.

I breathed out an enormous sigh of relief after hearing the news. Finally, I could leave Mexico. Unfortunately, I couldn't say the same to him. There was a hint of sadness in his eyes.

"Are you alright?" I asked, curious to hear his response.

He sat on the edge of the bed. "Yes, everything is alright, Alina," he said.

After spending close to a week with him, I knew he was lying. He avoided eye contact when he wasn't telling the truth.

"I know you enough now to know when you're lying, so tell me what's on your mind," I insisted.

"By now, you know how I feel about you. I'm relieved that you'll be leaving, but it would be a lie to say that the thought of never seeing you again isn't bothersome."

The feeling was mutual. Even though I wanted to tell him I'd be devastated too, I held myself back. I knew saying it out loud would make it more difficult for me to leave. So, instead, I took a different route.

"I guess since we're never going to see each other again, I should probably tell you something," I began.

"What is it?" He asked tentatively.

"I should hate you. Every part of me keeps telling me I should. But for reasons that I can't explain, I don't. Even when I learned that you killed Isabella, I still didn't hate you. I feel like I should be afraid, but I'm not. Believe it or not, I feel safe when I'm around you and your sister. The two of you have been so kind to me, and I cannot say thank you enough."

"If anyone should say thank you, it's me. Because of you, I learned to open my heart again. For years, I've been careful not to let no one in because of my brother, but with you, it was natural to allow myself to feel again," he explained.

His words were sweet. I couldn't help but feel my heart skipping a few beats. I felt my cheeks warming up, and all the muscles in my body tensed up. Adrian moved from the edge of the bed to my side. He pushed a few strands of my hair back and away from my face with his gentle fingers. His piercing eyes never left mine. He gently caressed my cheeks, and for the first time in a while, I wanted to kiss his delicate, soft-looking lips. But I knew doing so would only complicate the situation more, so I restrained myself and focused my attention away from his lips.

"I really want to kiss you," he said.

I scolded him in my head. *Why would you say that?* It didn't help with my already struggling with the temptation myself. He moved his head in closer, slowly, as if he was waiting for my permission. I wanted to say "no" but my lips weren't moving. He took my silence as consent and continued moving in. I tried to focus on his movement, but the battle in my head was stronger than his lips. I couldn't concentrate on what to do. When he was less than an inch away, I finally made my decision and tilted my head away from his advance. Unlike Marco, Adrian respected my decision and stopped.

"I'm sorry, I... I can't," I said.

He stood up and moved back to his original position at the end of the bed. There was guilt in his eyes.

"No, you shouldn't apologize. It's me who should say sorry. I shouldn't have done that."

"Don't apologize. Trust me, I want to kiss you too, but that will only make things worse for both of us. We have to focus on the real matter right now, which is getting me out of Mexico and to LA."

"Of course. I came here tonight because I wanted to see you for the last time."

I looked at him, confused. "What does that mean? You won't be coming to drop me off at the private jet in the morning?"

"No. It's safer if all of us aren't together. Catalina will take you. I'll stay behind to make sure everything is clear. Besides, I fear if I go with you, I won't be able to let you go."

It was a disappointing realization that I'd never see him again. I felt a surge of guilt for not allowing him to kiss me, at least as a goodbye. Before he got up to leave, I had to ask him a daunting question that had been on my mind for the past few days.

"I know Catalina already said it, but it still hasn't really registered in my brain. Are you really in love with me? I can't imagine falling in love with someone at a glance."

"I'd never thought falling in love at a glance would ever be possible either, but I did. You asked me before whether I fell for you because of Isabella, but after the past five days of us spending time together, I realize you are nothing like her. You're real and innocent, and you have courage that I don't even have in myself. You're a survivor. I fell in love with *you*, Alina."

My ego boosted itself up and did a cartwheel in my head. Finally, after many years of feeling unworthy of love, somebody fell for me, the real me. I held my tears back because it was silly to cry at the realization that I wasn't so undeserving of such a thing. After the revelation, he pushed himself off the bed to leave, but I made a conscious decision to grab his hand and pull him back down. He appeared confused at first but didn't resist. I tenderly grabbed his face with both hands and pulled him in closer. Our lips touched, and I felt his warm breath on my skin. Our eyes locked intensely, and then I felt his soft lips on mine, and butterflies stirring in the pit of my stomach. Our lips danced along with one another, and though it had only been a few seconds, it felt like an eternity. His wet tongue made its way between my lips, and I nearly combusted. He grabbed the back of my head with one hand while his other wrapped around my body. Adrian pulled me in closer to his body, and I felt his hard cock pressing against my thigh. After a few minutes of the best make-out session I'd ever had, he pulled his lips away, but his eyes never left mine. He had a wicked smile on his face.

"I've wanted to kiss you since the first time I met you," he said.

I'd expected him to continue kissing me, but he moved back a few inches away, almost to control himself from doing anything else. I was relieved, but at the same time conflicted. I wanted him to do more. He contemplated for a few seconds to himself. I studied him closely, and finally, Adrian planted a kiss on my forehead and stood up to leave the room.

He stopped in front of the door, turned his head to look at me, and said, "As tempting as it is to strip you naked and fuck you all night long, I'll let you get some rest. Good night, Alina." He opened the door and disappeared, leaving me hot and horny from his words. *Holy shit.* I plopped back onto the bed. My sexual frustration fogged my mind. The only thing I could think to do was close my eyes and sleep the desire away.

I felt a gentle touch on my face, and when I opened my eyes, it was Adrian. He had returned. I nudged myself up on my elbows, dazed at what was happening.

"What are you doing here?" I asked, groggy.

"I couldn't sleep, at least not without being with you one last time." He said with longing and desperation in his voice.

"Adrian," I began, but he shut my lips with his and aggressively kissed me. I followed his every move and did the same.

He separated from my lips and said, "I want you now."

The words were simple, but they ignited a spark within me. I wanted him to. We continued passionately kissing one another like we were long-lost lovers. His lips alone were enough to send a strong need between my legs. I was wet and ready for him. His expert tongue made its way into my mouth, and I welcomed it with pleasure. He pulled my shirt over my head with one swift move and tossed it on the floor. Quickly, he laid me on my back on the bed and pulled off my shorts, leaving me completely naked. He stood up and observed every inch of my body with desire and fire in his eyes.

"You're so beautiful," he said, and I instinctively parted my legs for him.

He pulled down his pants and freed his cock, already so hard for me.

"I want to taste you," he said, and without hesitation, knelt between my legs. He didn't even warn me before he pressed his warm tongue against my clit. That made me groan in shock and pleasure. As I tried to take in everything that was happening, I gripped the comforter tightly. I felt a vibration coursing throughout my body, and I nearly came undone, but he stopped. I looked at him, perplexed.

"I won't let you come, not this way. I want to fuck you until you scream my name," he said and stood back up on his feet. Adrian settled his weight on top of me, and before I could react, he slammed into me, sending electricity through my veins.

"Fuck!" I screamed.

"I'm going to fuck you, hard," he informed me before viciously thrusting his entire cock in and out. The faster his movement was, the wider I spread my legs for him, taking him in deeper and deeper with each thrust. He buried his face in my chest while I wrapped my arms around his body. I knew he enjoyed it when I dug my nails into his shoulder because his pace increased faster. I was lost in his motion, and he was lost in me. Somehow, we found ourselves on the floor, and I was on top and taking charge. I rode his cock like a porn star. When I looked at the satisfaction on his face, I felt powerful. I inserted my fingers in his mouth, and he sucked on them like an animal. He grabbed my hips with both hands and assisted me with my continuous riding.

We fucked on the bed, the floor, and then in front of the bathroom mirror.

"Fuck, your pussy is so wet," he said as he cupped both of my breasts in his hands and took me from behind.

I felt like I was in a porn movie. In every position, I felt a different type of exhilaration. He pulled his cock out, turned me around, picked me up, and placed me on the counter. Adrian inserted himself between my legs and slowly kissed me with affection and possession. Then, just as I was about to explode, the sound of loud banging woke me up.

The loud noise jolted me awake from the exhausting dream. *What the hell, Alina? What is happening to me?* I wanted to vomit. My heart was thumping vigorously, and my vision was fuzzy. I had little time to think when the door burst open and startled me. Catalina ran inside in a panic.

"Alina, get up. We have to go now!" she commanded and hurriedly disappeared into the closet.

I quickly jumped out of bed, dazed, and ran to where she was. She grabbed a fully packed black duffle bag from the shelf and disregarded my presence by the door.

"What's going on!?" I asked, panicking myself.

I'd never seen her so disheveled and disgruntled. She turned to look at me with fear in her eyes, one that I hadn't seen before. Something terrible was happening; I felt it.

"He is close by."

"Who's close by?" I asked, even though I had a small inclination of who she was referring to.

"Marco. We placed cameras and sensors around the house and the surrounding areas. One of the alarms was triggered. Now let's go. Adrian is waiting for us downstairs."

She tossed a few more pieces of clothing into the bag, zipped it up, grabbed my hand, and dragged me out of the room. We ran downstairs and Adrian was waiting with a gun in each hand. They were the same handguns from target practice.

"We need to create a distraction," she said as we took the last step.

He handed me a gun. "Do you remember how to use it?" he asked.

I nodded my head.

"Good. When the time comes, pull the trigger."

The sibling wasted no time and bolted outside. There were two black SUVs waiting outside. Both vehicles were ready to go. Catalina grabbed my hand, pushed me into the passenger seat, and threw the duffel bag in the back seat. Adrian jumped in the car in front of us. As soon as she stepped into the driver's seat, she stepped on the gas, sending me flying back against the seat. I'd thought we would follow her brother, but she steered in the opposite direction once we were out of the driveway.

"Why are we separating?"

"We need to create a diversion."

I looked at the clock, and it was a quarter past three in the morning. The world outside was pitch black, and even though the headlights guided us, I had no clue how she could drive so smoothly. She was like a professional racecar driver. She swiftly twisted and turned the wheel on the narrow, bumpy road. Finally, I realized we weren't on the freeway but on a path along the forest. Everything was a blur. If I was the driver, I'd probably have hit a tree by now.

"How did he find us?" I asked, trying my best not to go into a complete anxiety attack at the thought that he could be nearby.

"I don't know. I honestly didn't think he would find us here," she said in disbelief.

"When you went to the market, did you notice anything odd or out of the ordinary?"

She thought to herself for a few seconds. "Not that I can recall. Everything was normal," she answered. But I heard a hint of unease in her voice.

"Well, maybe one of his men spotted you, and you just didn't notice?"

"I don't know. It could be. Right now, we need to focus on getting off this mountain and to the jet," she said, focused.

"It's pitch-black outside. How do you know where we are going?"

"Don't worry. I've practiced driving around these woods for many years. I know what I'm doing."

Against all odds, I believed her.

"We need to get on the main road at the bottom of the mountain. Once we're there, we'll have a better chance of losing him."

Though the situation was futile, Catalina remained calm and collected. I had no clue how she did it. I, on the other hand, was struggling to control my breathing. I couldn't focus on counting from one to ten in my head. My anxiety increased with every second that passed, and my body slowly turned numb. Suddenly everything spiraled rapidly, and I knew that if I didn't act quickly, I would pass out. I lifted my right arm to my mouth and bit down on it, hard. Catalina turned halfway and looked at me, bewildered.

"Why are you biting yourself?"

"I'm trying to keep myself from passing out."

"You are an intriguing and strange thing," she said.

Her comment lightened the mood in the tense atmosphere. I didn't know how it was possible, but we both flashed a smile at one another. Even though it was bizarre, it worked. I regained awareness of my surroundings, my body functioned, and my erratic breathing decreased. We continued driving for another ten minutes, and for a brief few second, I thought we were finally out of danger. That serene thought quickly vanished when Catalina slammed on the brakes, and the car came to a harrowing stop. Both of us stared at the headlights of a vehicle blocking us. Soon after, another car appeared from behind, trapping us.

"What do we do now?" I asked, my panic returning.

"I'll try to hold them off. They won't hurt me. When I say go, get out of the car, and run like hell and use that gun. Understand?" She said and glared at me with the most serious looks.

I nodded my head and tried to hold off my tears. It was no time to sob; it was time to survive. All four doors of the car in front of us opened simultaneously, and four men in black suits stepped out, one of them being Diego. I recognized the other three because I'd seen them around the mansion. They closed the doors in unison as if they had practiced this for years. Catalina reached over to the glove compartment and pulled out a handgun. She prepared herself, and before anything else happened, she yelled, "Go!"

We both opened the door, and I ran into the darkness, fast as hell. Besides my heavy breathing, the only other thing I heard was multiple gunshots. I shuddered at the thought that Catalina might be hurt. I wanted to turn around and go back to make sure she was safe, but I knew I had to keep running. Warm tears rolled down my cheeks as I continued sprinting. It was bad enough I could barely see, but I had to be careful not to slam into a tree or trip on something stupid like a tree branch.

"Alina!" Diego yelled behind me suddenly.

His voice made me pick up my pace. I imagined he was a scary monster chasing me and it helped with my adrenaline. He continued to call my name, and I continued to run in the dark with no guidance. It surprised me that I hadn't tumbled to the ground. Perhaps I was doing better than I thought. His voice became more and more distant, and soon I no longer heard him at all. Just as I was feeling a slight sense of victory that I'd gotten away, I fell down a hill, fast. I tried to grab onto anything, but I was rolling too fast. I thought I had fallen off a cliff. My body stopped when I slammed into something hard. I laid motionless and couldn't move. Shortly after, I saw a glimpse of light and heard footsteps approaching my direction.

"Alina!" Diego yelled as he stopped at my side.

His face was blurry as he picked up my head with one hand and flashed the small flashlight behind my head. I felt something warm trailing down my neck. He took off his blazer and placed it behind my head. The harder I tried to look at his face, the blurrier he became. I wanted to open my mouth to utter some words, but my lips refused to cooperate.

"It's alright. I've got you," he whispered. That was the last thing I heard before I lost consciousness.

CHAPTER TWENTY-FIVE

I slowly regained consciousness, and everything was blurry as I opened my eyes. I went from dazed to startled when I saw Marco sitting with his legs crossed and arms spread wide across from me. He was holding a glass of brown liquor in his right hand. His eyes never left mine, and I knew they were full of fury. I felt slightly afraid when his eyes turned darker than normal as he continued to glare at me. It felt like I was staring into a black hole, so to avoid making eye contact, I looked around to see where I was. I was back at the safe house.

"What's going on?" I heard myself ask the question.

He didn't say a word, only clenched his jaw tightly. I didn't need to be close to him to feel his rage. I slowly pushed myself up and immediately felt my head throbbing. There was a small bandage on the back of my head. I looked around the room and noticed no one else was here. It was daytime, and the light shone through the glass door of the balcony. My gaze stopped on a half-empty whiskey bottle on the coffee table. Oddly enough, I wanted to finish the remaining alcohol and fall back asleep. I wasn't ready to deal with his wrath. *Screw it.* I reached to grab the bottle but was interrupted when he threw his glass into the fireplace. I retreated further on the couch.

"Did you know I almost died?" he finally spoke, his voice a mixture of anger and pain.

I should feel sorry that he suffered, but I didn't. Instead, I was pissed. How dared he say that he almost died? I was the one who nearly died on multiple occasions since meeting him. I straightened my posture and prepared myself to respond.

"You almost died? Your crazy father took me and was going to kill me to appease your lunatic aunt. I nearly died multiple times in the last few weeks. The only person who's allowed to be upset is me," I said boldly.

The audacity that this man had to be upset with me. I'd been through hell since I met him, yet he dared to be angry. I rolled my eyes in disbelief.

"Why didn't you come back to me? You stayed with Adrian and Catalina for nearly a week, and you never once thought of coming back to me. I almost went crazy looking for you. For a moment, I thought… I thought you were dead," his voice quickly changed to despair.

"Why would I go back to you? From day one, all I wanted was to get away from you."

"You still hate me?"

I raised an eyebrow in disbelief. *Is this man serious?*

"Is that a serious question?"

"When we were at the beach, I thought something had changed between us. I thought you had changed your mind about me," Marco said, disappointment flooded in his voice.

"I didn't, and I never will," I said, slightly deceiving even myself.

I knew deep down that I had conflicting feelings for him. I knew it was wrong because it made no sense to form any emotional bond with him. He was the son of a criminal. And not just any criminal, but the worst kind.

Marco stood up from the couch and stuck his hands in his pockets. He strolled towards the fireplace with his back to me and stared intensely at the burning flames. I cautiously observed and waited to see what he was going to say next.

"I'm glad you're safe. Not knowing if you were dead or alive nearly broke me. I was lost for days, Alina. You do not know the pain I felt." He said softly.

"I need you to let me go. I've never done this before, but I am begging you. Please, just let me go. We can forget about everything that happened within the last few weeks and move on. I can go back to my regular life, and you can go back to being the son of the most powerful drug lord in Mexico. We'll all be happier that way." I pleaded.

With his back still facing me, he said, "I... can't do that."

My breath fluttered, and my heart was beating erratically. I reminded myself to breathe and remain calm. The last thing I wanted was for him to be furious again. Besides, I fought against him so many times, but it did nothing for me. Perhaps I needed to be more amicable. Maybe then he'd let me go. Maybe.

"I know you're only doing this to hurt your brother because he killed Isabella. But what's the point? You can't keep doing this to each other. You two are *brothers*."

He finally turned around to face me.

"This is not about Adrian or Isabella. Not anymore. I've fallen in love with you, Alina. And now you have to take responsibility for that."

I stared at him, shocked at his words; they were possessive and cruel. *When did his feelings become my responsibility?* If I heard him correctly, it sounded like he was blaming me for everything. I couldn't stay calm after that; he had become the definition of a narcissist.

"You're insane. I want to leave." I stood up and turned to walk to the front door, but Marco's feet were quicker, and he stopped me by wrapping his arms around my waist.

"Let me go!" I demanded, but the harder I tried to fight his grasp, the tighter he gripped my body.

"Stop fighting. You're bruised all over already and you're going to hurt yourself even more."

I ignored his concerns and kept struggling to free myself. Finally, he twirled me around to face him, and we locked eyes. He leaned in, bringing his lips close to mine, but before he had the chance to kiss me, I turned away to face the fireplace. He let out a sigh of frustration.

"So, you learned the truth about Isabella," he said.

I remained silent and unmoving.

"As much as I don't want to, I'm going to release you. But don't bother running; my men are everywhere outside," he warned.

Still, I said nothing, and Marco released his grip, walked me back to the couch, and sat me down. He sat across from me on the other couch.

"I know you want to know more about her, Alina. You don't have to pretend that you don't. I know you well enough by now." He said calmly.

It was irritating every time he was right about me. I learned about her from his brother and sister, but it would be intriguing to hear him talk about her. I wondered if their stories would align. Although, I knew I had to prepare myself. I looked at the whiskey bottle and contemplated whether I should toss back a good amount of it before he began. After a few seconds, I was convinced that I was about to go on a roller coaster ride, so I took the bottle in my hand.

"I'm going to need a drink first."

"I'll grab you a glass." He stood up, went into the kitchen, and came back with a glass.

I took the glass from his hand and poured the whiskey for myself. Immediately, the potent smell slapped me in the face, and I instantly regretted it. I pinched my nose, took a small sip, and gagged. I felt the burning sensation in my throat as it struggled to slide down. It was disgusting. I made the ugliest face, and Marco let out a small giggle under his breath. I set the drink on the table.

"So, what do you want to know?"

"Do you still love her?" It was the first thing that popped into my head and out of my mouth.

"I did until I met you."

"You could just be in love with me because I remind you of her."

"I thought that was the case at first, but then I got to know you as a person, and you two are nothing alike."

"Your brother said the same thing. I still don't understand why. You can't expect me to fall in love with someone who kept me trapped against my will. That's not how love works."

"So, you feel nothing for me at all? Because I don't believe that."

"Believe what you want, Marco. I just want to go back home to my friend. I don't want to be involved in this crazy mess with your dangerous family anymore. If *you* loved *me*, you wouldn't put me in this kind of danger. Everywhere I go, either your father or aunt try to kill me. That's not a life I want to live in." I explained calmly.

"I won't let anyone hurt you," he said confidently.

I chuckled in disbelief.

"Really? Because if I remember correctly, your father abducted me less than a week ago. Is that the life that you want for me? To always be worried and looking over my shoulder?"

Marco sat straight and thought to himself. He clenched his jaw tightly. I wish I could read his mind and know what he was thinking. He took his black blazer and tie off and tossed it on the other couch. He slowly unbuttoned the first two buttons of his shirt, revealing his defined chest. I tried my hardest not to be distracted by it, but it was easier said than done. Despite my hatred for him, I couldn't deny that he was an attractive man.

"I will deal with my father." He said sternly.

"And how will you do that? Surely you can't kill him, he's your father."

"Leave that for me to worry about."

I'd always hated his short answers. It was frustrating to play these guessing games. I remained quiet, hoping that it would pressure him to keep talking, but he didn't budge. I understood now why some therapists sat quietly and stared at me. It was awkward, and I often felt obligated to utter random words to fill the silence. Finally, after I grew too uncomfortable with the silence, I picked up my glass and took another sip of my whiskey. *What to do, what to do? Think Alina, think. Screw it; I'll break the silence.*

"What about your aunt? Adrian and Catalina told me you guys have a complicated past. Care to share that?" I prompted.

I saw a change in his eyes. A few minutes ago, it was rage, sadness, and then desperation. After my question, there was a hesitance, like he didn't want to share their history.

"So?"

"I was 14 when it started," he began quietly.

Immediately, I was ready to listen, and I felt my stomach stirring with both excitement and fear. Knowing his family history, I was about to hear some crazy shit. I gripped the glass tightly and held on for dear life.

"She asked for my help in her bedroom. She lost a diamond earring and couldn't find it for a few days. At first, I thought it was strange that she asked for my help when the house had countless maids. But I quickly got over that and thought nothing about it. It wasn't until I was in the bedroom that I realized what she wanted."

My skin was crawling like invisible ants were moving up and down my entire body. I had a sense of where he was going with the story, but I didn't want to assume, so I let him finish.

"I was a horny teenager, and Lorena, well, you can say she was an attractive woman. She was in her late thirties at the time. Before she met Andres, she was married to Javier. He was a shitty husband because he was constantly out sleeping with other women, and they never loved each other. My father and his father arranged the marriage as a truce between the two rival cartels. He left her in the mansion for nearly two years to roam alone. I didn't realize how lonely she was until that day, and I was confused and aroused when she started unbuttoning her shirt. Shortly after, she stripped me naked and pushed me onto the bed. She got on top of me, and that was the first time I'd ever had sex."

I nearly dropped my glass onto the fluffy white rug. *What the actual fuck?* His aunt raped him. For so long, I thought my upbringing was horrendous, but Marco's wasn't much better. It would explain why he was so messed-up when it came to sex. Perhaps he was never

315

truly evil, and his family members were the ones who created the monster in front of me. I sat in silence, unable to form any words.

"Say something, Alina," he requested gently.

I took a deep breath in and exhaled.

"That's definitely some crazy shit and I'm sorry that happened to you. No matter what, you didn't deserve that." That was all I mustered out.

He grabbed the bottle of whiskey and drank a considerable amount in one gulp. Watching him made me want to vomit. Even though this revelation was disturbing, I wanted to know more.

"What happened after that?"

"We continued fucking until I became bored. I was 17 when I ended our relationship, or whatever you wanted to call it. Since then, my relationship with her hasn't been the same. I guess she never forgot." He said and then took another substantial drink.

My head was spinning viciously. Marco and his aunt fucked for three years. I had no right to complain about my life anymore. I wondered if he realized that she had taken advantage of him.

"You realized your aunt raped you, right?"

"It took a long time for me to come to that realization. For many years, I thought I was also in the wrong. After all, I didn't say no."

I straightened my posture. "But you were young, and your aunt took advantage of that. She knew what she was doing. Just because she was lonely doesn't mean she can have sex with her nephew. I'm really sorry that happened." I said genuinely.

"That's not even the worst thing that happened in my family," he said almost sarcastically.

Holy shit! There's more? I really need to get out of here.

"Did you... love her?" I asked.

"I was a horny teenager fucking his aunt. Whether or not I loved her wasn't really the focus. I only remember that it felt good."

I took another drink.

"Wow, I have no words."

"You wanted to know the truth so badly," he said with a half-smile.

I looked at him with a crooked smile. "You're right, I did. I just wasn't expecting that to be the truth. Then again, I wasn't all that surprised either; your whole family is messed up."

"I'm sorry. I know it's almost unbelievable to think it's real."

"At least that's something we can agree on. Perhaps your aunt fell in love with you, and that's why she's still harboring deep hatred for you. I mean, that's the only explanation that I can think of."

"Perhaps, however, I don't intend to find out."

"And I thought my family was a mess," I let slip, and I instantly regretted it. There was a spark of interest in his eyes.

Marco stood up from his seat and came towards me. He sat down next to me, and his face was far too close to my liking. I wanted to move back, but my body refused to cooperate with my mind. He pushed a few strands of my hair away from my face. His manly scent mixed with the alcohol was intoxicating. He gently caressed my cheek, and I wasn't sure why I didn't push him away.

"All families have issues, Alina."

His intense stare almost burned a hole in my head.

"I think I need more whiskey," I said, breaking away from his gaze.

I grabbed the whiskey bottle on the table and refilled my glass. I moved to the opposite couch and settled down. Without thinking, I took a massive gulp as I held my breath. This day was already too much for me, and it wasn't even halfway over yet. I realized I wasn't leaving, so I figured if I had to deal with him, I might as well be drunk. I knew it wasn't the wisest decision I could make, but what else could I do? The alcohol finally kicked in and disrupted my deep thoughts. I thought it would make my headache even worse, but it went away instead. My head was lighter, and I felt more relaxed. I drank again until the glass was empty. I grabbed the bottle once more and poured the rest into the glass. There was a moment where I thought Marco would stop me, but he just watched as I kept drinking.

"What are you doing?" He finally spoke.

"Wow, he speaks." I teased him.

Shit, I was drunk.

"Really? You wanted to drink that bad?" he asked in disbelief, but also with a playful tone.

I placed the empty glass on the table and glared at him. "It's only fair; I mean, can you blame me? I've been through so much shit these past few weeks. I feel like I've been in a horror movie that never ends. So, do *not* judge me because, for once, I just want to get drunk and not feel sad."

"I apologize for everything that happened to you. I never intended to hurt you in such a way. I didn't think I'd fall for you in such a short time." He said apologetically.

"You know what? Don't even say you're sorry. I mean, this whole thing isn't even the worst thing I've been through in life," I said honestly. Right then, I figured out why I avoided alcohol for most of my life. It brought out emotions that I had suppressed for many years.

"So, tell me then," he whispered and leaned his body forward, his arms resting on his legs. He clasped his hands together like he was a professional therapist preparing to hear my childhood traumas. Then I remembered that he should already know parts of my story. After all, he read my diary.

"You've read my diary. There's no point in repeating it. It's not anything exciting," I said, slightly irritated. The thought that Marco had invaded my privacy made my anger seep out.

"To tell you the truth, I only read the first few pages. After I saw how upset you were, I made sure that I didn't do it again."

The whole time I'd thought he read every page of my diary. And because of that assumption, I harbored a tremendous hatred towards him. I felt like the biggest idiot.

"Oh, well, I appreciate that a lot. My story is nothing compared to yours."

"That's not the point. Every story matters, and I want to know more about yours, Alina."

"Um, okay, well, where do I start? My mother experienced a lot of abuse from my father during their marriage. And I watched pretty much everything, and that's about it."

I felt tears brimming over my eyes, and an overwhelming wave of sadness and resentment thanks to the damned whiskey. It intensified my feelings tenfold. Shortly after, warm tears rolled down my cheeks. I promised myself that I'd never cry in front of him, but I couldn't control it. I quickly wiped them away and composed myself. *Be strong, Alina. You have survived through worse things.* Marco pushed himself off the couch and made his way to my side. He grabbed the glass from my hand and gently placed it on the table. He put his fingers under my chin and turned my head to face him. His gesture only made my tears roll down faster.

"It must have been hard to witness such a thing as a child." He said and then wiped away my tears with both thumbs. "It's alright. You're safe now."

"Do you ever have nightmares about what your mom went through?"

"No. I guess I was lucky. Truthfully, I've never been bothered by it. I don't know why. Perhaps it's because I've buried it so deep inside."

Oh, how I wished that was possible for me. Even the slightest chance of never having another nightmare sounded so wonderful.

"That sounds nice. I've always wondered what life would be like nightmare-free. I imagine it would be peaceful."

"You're stronger than you think. I've seen firsthand how resilient and persistent you are."

"I wish I felt that way, but I don't. I dwell so much on the past that I've lost sight of who I am."

"So, tell me, who is the real Alina?"

I looked at him with profound uncertainty. No one had ever asked me that question before, and even worse, I'd never asked myself. Who was I? I turned my head and stared at the beautiful orange flames dancing back and forth. I thought hard and deep within myself, but I got nothing. I turned back to face him.

"I really don't know. I don't know who I am."

Marco grabbed my hands in his and said, "Well, I can tell you that Alina is stubborn and brave. She's willing to risk her safety for the sake of others, especially those she loves. She stood up to a man who, in the beginning, only wanted to torture and punish her. And what's most impressive about her is that she made someone like me fall in love with her."

I'd never thought of myself as brave or courageous. When I tried to rescue Ana, it was out of pure adrenaline and desperation to save my best friend. But the way he described me as a person made me believe in his words, even if it was for a short few seconds. Was it a trick so that I'd fall for him? Was he taking advantage of my drunkenness?

"I think I need more alcohol." I stood up, but quickly lost my balance.

Marco caught me in his arms before I fell to the floor. Once I was in his arms, he didn't let me go. I felt his muscles tensing up, and his breathing was heavy.

"You do not know how I felt thinking that I had lost you," he said sadly.

"I know. You already told me," I reminded him.

"I know, but I need you to know again how important you are to me."

"Marco…"

He interrupted me, "You don't have to say anything. I know. You can't love me. But just know that I will do anything for you to fall in love with me. That's a promise, and I won't stop until it happens."

"Anything?"

He nodded his head.

"Alright then. I want you to release Juan immediately."

Marco released a sigh and clenched his jaw. I knew he was unsatisfied that I was still thinking about him. But then again, I didn't care that much.

"Fine. I'll let Diego know."

I felt an immense sense of relief. Finally, both Ana and Juan were safe. Marco released me from his arms and prepared to walk away. I grabbed his hand. He looked at me, confused.

"Thank you. I'm going to pass out now."

Everything turned black.

CHAPTER TWENTY-SIX

When I opened my eyes, it was daytime again. There was a massive rush of pain in my head, and I wanted to push myself up, but my body was physically unwilling to move. I had no idea alcohol could make me feel this sick. I felt like an elephant was sitting on my body. It served me right to be so irresponsible. I remained under the sheet for another hour, but eventually, I pushed myself off the bed. I headed to the closet, grabbed some clothes, and made my way to the bathroom to change. After twenty minutes, I was out. I debated whether I should head downstairs. I knew who would be waiting for me, but as much as I didn't want to, my stomach growled and reminded me I needed to move my ass down and get some breakfast. Once downstairs, Diego was waiting in his usual black suit in the living room.

"Good morning."

I ignored his morning etiquette, walking right past him. There was no one else here, and I felt a slight sense of relief. Finally, I could breathe again.

"Where's your boss?" I asked, finally acknowledging his presence.

"He has some business to attend to with… his siblings," he reported.

I wasn't fond of the fact that he paused. I had a feeling something terrible was happening. *What if he kills them?*

"What business?" I asked, scared of what might come out of his mouth.

"I think it would be best if you ask him yourself when he comes back. Which should be soon."

Damn you.

"I've prepared you some breakfast." He said and pointed to the plate on the dining table.

My stomach growled again, so I went to the kitchen and stared at the giant plate of bacon, eggs, sausages, and a glass of orange juice. He pulled out the chair, and I sat down.

"How's your head?" He asked as I was midway through my food.

I sipped the juice.

"You'll have to be more specific. If you're referring to the bottle of whiskey, it's pounding like crazy right now. But if you're referring to the fall, it hurts like a bitch."

"I didn't mean to scare you last night. I was only following Marco's orders," he explained.

I continued eating my breakfast and suddenly remembered that Marco's father had shot him.

"How's your leg?"

"Much better. Thank you for your concern."

"Thank you for trying to protect me. I realized I haven't had the chance to tell you that."

"No need for a thank you. My job is to protect you."

"Well, that doesn't matter. It had to be said. By the way, how did Marco find this place?"

"We have resources and people everywhere, and given his worry about your absence, it didn't take long to locate the safe house."

I stopped eating.

"Did I say something wrong?" he asked after noticing my silence.

"Tell me, is it true that your boss is in love with me?"

Diego pulled out the chair opposite me and sat down.

"This is the first time I've seen him worry about another person. Marco is a powerful man. He's also the type of man that does not show emotion. A part of that has to do with who he is and the family he was born into. If he's not strong, his enemies will not be afraid of him. However, with you, he's different. He's gentle. I know you may not believe so, but I saw how afraid he was when he thought he lost you. You're special to him."

"I can't imagine how that could have happened. There's nothing special about me. I'm just a regular girl from Rhode Island." I said, once again, degrading myself.

"Well, to him, you're more than that."

I resumed eating and bit into the crispy bacon.

"I'm sorry for giving you an attitude earlier," I said, feeling guilty for the behavior I displayed.

He gave me a light smile. "You have nothing to apologize for. I'm just glad you are here and safe."

"But that's where you're wrong. I was safe with Adrian and Catalina. They were going to send me home, away from all of this." I said, disappointment flooding through my body.

"Given the problems brewing between the two families, I believe you wouldn't have been safe back in the States. It wouldn't be long before Lorena found you."

"Am I wrong for wanting all of this to be over?" I asked him out of curiosity.

I studied his expression closely as he pondered about a response.

"No. I don't blame you. Unfortunately, you're trapped between the two families. I have a daughter, and I couldn't imagine what I'd do if she were in the same position as you," he said.

"What's her name?"

"Gabriela. She is the love of my life." He said with a smile that was bursting with pure love.

"That's a beautiful name. How old is she?"

"17. She'll be 18 in two months."

"Any special plans for her?"

"No, nothing too big. My wife and I plan to take her out to a nice dinner and celebrate the occasion as a family."

I beamed brightly at the thought of him and his family being together. I was happy, but I was also envious of them. Even though he worked for the cartel, he still took care of his daughter. I realized more and more how useless my father was. Some men weren't meant to be fathers.

"Your daughter is lucky to have such a devoted father," I said without realizing I'd said it.

"It's me who's the lucky one. My daughter changed my whole life."

I gave him a half-grin and then remembered something.

"Oh, I have a question. Why did you let me leave with Catalina that night, knowing that she and Adrian had helped me escape before?"

He looked at his hands on the table. Then he looked up at me and said, "As I said, I have a daughter, and I would hope that at least one person has a soft spot in their heart to help her if she was ever in danger."

My eyes went wide in astonishment. So, Diego knew what he was doing, and he did it anyway. It explained why I could leave the mansion without issue. I guess Ana wasn't my only guardian angel after all.

"You were in on the plan?"

He nodded his head.

"Catalina came and talked to me earlier that day. She asked for my help, and I couldn't say no. I hope that this conversation will stay between us. If Marco ever finds out what I did, he will most likely kill me." He said sternly.

"Trust me, he'll never find out."

We exchanged smiles, and I continued eating. Diego and I conversed for the next thirty minutes. He went into further detail about the night of my rescue. I learned that not only was he loyal to Marco, but he was also equally loyal to Catalina. He explained how she had saved his family multiple times during financial difficulties, and how much she adored his daughter. After I learned more about Catalina, I felt guilty for assuming she was nothing more than a rich airhead. There was far more to her than expected.

Our conversation was interrupted when I glanced outside at a car approaching the front entrance. Marco stepped out in a perfectly fitted, black, long-sleeved button-down shirt, dark gray pants, and black sunglasses. He moved gracefully toward the house and through the door.

"I'll leave you two," Diego said, stood up, and disappeared outside.

I turned my head away and pretended to eat my breakfast, even though I was full. His presence immediately made me anxious. Marco pulled out a chair and made himself comfortable.

"Did you sleep well?" he asked.

I cleared my throat and said, "It was fine."

"Do you remember what happened last night?"

I remained silent, embarrassment flooding me. I continued to avoid eye contact and stared at my nearly empty plate.

"Alina?"

Finally, I perked up at him and asked, "Where are Adrian and Catalina?"

He let out a sigh of annoyance. "You won't be seeing them ever again," he said, his voice cold.

I placed the fork on the table and looked up at him. I needed him to clarify what he meant.

"What did you do to them?"

"Nothing that you need to know or worry about," he said dryly.

"I don't believe that you could kill Catalina since you love her."

"She told you?"

I leaned back in the chair and folded my arms across my chest. "She did. Honestly, it is disturbing. She's your sister."

"Step-sister," he corrected me.

Frankly, I didn't care; it was still unsettling.

"I loved her a long time ago. But why are you bringing it up now? Are you jealous?"

I laughed. "Jealous? Why would I be jealous?"

"Your eyes say it all, Alina. You wouldn't have brought it up if it didn't bother you," he said with confidence. He couldn't be more wrong.

"I only brought it up because it's gross. Plus, I'm not interested in talking about what happened last night."

"Why is talking about what happened so terrible? It was nice finally getting to know the real you."

"I was drunk. So, it doesn't count." I pushed myself out of the chair, irritated, and walked towards the door. I needed some fresh air, but the door wasn't unlocked. I turned around and Marco was leaning against the back of the couch with his hands in his pockets.

"I thought we made progress," he said.

"What progress?"

"We talked about some really serious matters. I thought we connected at a deeper level."

"Again, I was drunk. Even though we had the conversation, it was purely out of me being intoxicated, not because we clicked in some ways."

"That's not how I see it," he said with a wicked smirk that I despised.

I straightened my posture and folded my arms across my chest. I needed to set this man straight so he wouldn't get any crazy ideas.

"You're right. It didn't matter whether I was drunk. But just because we talked about personal issues doesn't mean that I have any feelings toward you. I haven't forgotten what you did to me and my friends. So, remember that."

His smirk vanished, and he ran a hand through his hair in frustration at my boldness. We glared at each other in silence.

"How do you do it?" He asked suddenly.

I looked at him, perplexed.

"How is that you make me want to fuck and kill you at the same time?" He asked.

I rolled my eyes in disgust and ignored his question.

"I don't care about your insane thought process. The only thing I'm worried about now is my safety. I don't trust that you'll be able to keep me safe from your family."

"You think you'll be safe without me? You don't know Lorena then. She won't stop. Everything is a game for her, especially when I'm involved. Staying by my side is the safest place for you."

I sighed angrily. It was clear I would never go back to my old life. I was so angry and so frustrated, and the sight of him only made me more upset. The process of acceptance was daunting and depressing. I walked away from the door and towards the stairs, but he stopped in front of me. He tried to caress my face, but I turned my head away. I was in no mood for his touch.

"I'll keep you safe from now on. I promise."

I finally turned my head to face him and said, "All I want from you is to leave me alone."

As I walked past him, I bumped his shoulder. I was relieved when I didn't hear his harsh footsteps following behind me. I opened the door to my room, plopped down on the bed on my stomach, and closed my eyes.

****

The next day, Diego woke me up early and instructed me to get dressed and ready to ride back to the mansion. I dreaded it the whole time I was changing. I moved as slowly as possible to prolong my stay at the sibling's safe house. A small part of me did it to provoke both him and his boss. That was their punishment for waking me up so early. Diego was waiting when I walked downstairs in a white pantsuit with my hair in a high ponytail. He led me to the black Ranger Rover outside. When he opened the back door, Marco was waiting inside, wearing a dark navy suit and a white tie. I jumped in but sat as far away from him as possible. Diego hopped into the driver's seat and began our drive.

Thirty minutes later, we were still descending the mountain slope. Marco was eerily quiet, which I didn't mind.

"You won't be leaving my sight from now on," he blurted. His voice was cold and dominant.

Though he was brooding, it didn't surprise me. Nothing that came out of his mouth surprised me anymore. I stayed silent, and I planned to remain so for as long as possible. Maybe then he'd eventually grow bored and decide to either kill me or let me go. It was wishful thinking, but one could always hope.

"Did you hear me?"

I ignored his question. He grabbed my arm and dragged me onto his lap.

"You're stubborn, Alina. But don't worry, from now on, I won't do anything without your consent."

I laughed in disbelief.

"You say that, but then you force me onto your lap. I don't think you understand what consent means." Fighting the same battle repeatedly was exhausting.

He released my arm, and I moved back to my original position. The two of us sat in silence as the car continued to move.

When I woke up the car had stopped, and we were back at his mansion. Diego hopped out and opened the back door for us. I stepped out behind Marco, and we headed inside.

"Stay here," Marco ordered.

Both men disappeared upstairs, and they left me alone in the foyer. They returned after a few minutes, each holding a black duffel bag in their hand. I didn't even want to know what was in those bags.

"What's going on?" I asked, still aggravated that they had left without explanation.

"This place is not safe for you anymore. We'll stay somewhere else for a while," Marco said.

I looked at him, confused. "Where are we staying, then?"

"You'll find out when we get there," he said, grabbing my hand, and we went outside to the car once more.

I used to enjoy car rides. I found them peaceful, but after the last few days of being stuck in the car for hours, I wasn't so fond of it anymore. We drove for another hour before stopping at a small airport field. I hesitated to walk up to the private jet. Marco grabbed my hand and dragged me up the stairs. Diego and two other men followed behind. He led me to a black leather seat and forced me down. He attempted to buckle me up, but I forced him away. After realizing that he would not win, he stopped and sat down across from me.

A young man with short blonde hair and green eyes approached us with a tray that held a bottle of whiskey and two glasses. I shuddered at the sight of it. It triggered an unpleasant memory from two nights ago. I kindly declined the drink and asked if I could get water instead. The young man politely nodded his head and disappeared into the back of the plane. He promptly returned after a few minutes with a glass of ice water.

The plane started moving, and soon after it took off for an unknown destination. Marco crossed his legs as he sipped his whiskey. He had said nothing, and I prayed he wouldn't. Diego unbuckled his seatbelt and came to sit next to his boss. The two communicated in Spanish, and though I didn't understand, I heard my name here and there. After realizing they wouldn't speak in English, I turned my head to stare out the window to distract myself from my brewing anxiety. It was a beautiful sunny day with a bright blue sky. I was so distracted by the breathtaking view I hadn't realized Diego had gone back to his seat.

"What is on your mind?" he asked suddenly.

Of course, he had to interrupt my serene moment. Without turning to face him, I said, "Home."

I wanted him to feel guilty.

"You can make a home here with me."

He made it sound so easy. Even though I lived a life of nothing but pain and misery, I wouldn't exchange it for a life with him.

"That won't happen."

Finally, I turned to look at him.

"I won't give up. I'll continue to do whatever it takes to make you fall in love with me. You mean too much to me to let you go."

"You know, in America, we call that abuse. What you're doing to me isn't love; it's abuse and control. You're a man who has a lot of power and has always gotten what he wants: women, money, drugs, sex. But I'm the one thing that you'll never have, ever." I explained and turned my attention back to the clouds underneath us.

A little over two hours later, the captain spoke and informed us that the plane would be descending soon. Once the aircraft breached the clouds, I realized where we were going. I looked down at the exquisite tropical island below, surrounded by deep blue sea. I'd never seen anything more beautiful in my life. A massive, magnificent glass mansion stood in the center of the island. I turned and gaped at him in shock. He looked at me with devilish eyes.

"We're staying on the island?" I asked, baffled.

"We are."

The plane landed safely, and the door opened. I walked down the stairs in awe of the fresh scenery of the forest and ocean. Marco stepped to my side and admired my stunned reaction. I saw a glimpse of a smile on his face, but I ignored it. A silver Bentley pulled up, and we got inside. The car drove along the road, and all I saw was the vast blue ocean with no end in sight. After about twenty minutes, I realized I hadn't seen one other car, house, or person.

"Are we the only ones here?" I asked.

"This is my island, so yes," he said like it was nothing.

The wind hit my face and hair after I rolled down the window. I loved the smell of the fresh ocean breeze. I lay my head on my arms and stared up at the bright sun shining down on my face. Ironically, when I was a child, I often wrote in my journal wishing that one day I'd get lost on an island, away from people and society, and live alone with no cares in the world.

We arrived in front of the house, and he jumped out, reaching his hand out for me to grab. I hesitated at first, but I took it and got out of the car. Diego and the rest of the men drove the car away. We walked inside to the most futuristic home I'd ever seen in my life. A giant white sectional couch and marble coffee table sat in the middle of the living room. A giant white chandelier hung above the coffee table. Next to the living room was a massive kitchen with a white marble island and dining table that could fit over twenty or more people. The house was practically all glass. There was certainly no privacy.

"This house is stunning," I said under my breath.

"I'm glad you like it."

"How long are we staying on the island?"

"A while. Until I figure out exactly what to do with Lorena," he said.

"Are the other girls here?" I asked.

"It's just you and me. All those women are gone. You don't have to worry about sharing me with them ever again."

I chuckled. "Not exactly what I was thinking. You can sleep with whoever you want. I don't care." I reminded him.

"I'm trying to be patient with you. But you are not making this any easier."

I ignored his emerging rage, walked past him, and sat down on the couch. My stomach immediately started growling.

"I'll have the chef prepare you some food." He took his blazer off, tossed it on the couch, and disappeared into the hall.

Diego walked in through the door with three large suitcases. I stood up and offered to help, but he refused. I made my way toward him and pulled one of the bags from his hand, anyway. He looked at me, almost with fear that I was carrying something I shouldn't.

"Why do you look like you've just seen a ghost?" I asked, looking around to ensure there wasn't anybody else in the mansion but us.

"You're not supposed to do any type of work," he responded.

I look at him in disbelief. "Well, good luck with that. I won't sit with my arms crossed and watch while you struggle."

"You're too kind, señorita."

Marco reappeared in a white T-shirt and black joggers. Diego immediately grabbed the luggage from my hand, struggled to the corner, and disappeared.

"I've called the chefs. They should be here soon to prepare dinner." He said and walked past me and straight to the bar near the balcony. Marco grabbed a bottle of Don Julio and poured it into a glass for himself. He stared at the view of the ocean from the floor-to-ceiling glass windows as he sipped his drink.

"Where's my room? I want to shower."

Right then, Diego showed up behind me.

"I can show you," he said and led the way.

The room was simple but full of light. It had a giant white bed and two bedside tables decorated with simple, rectangular gray lamps. A gold and silver chandelier hanging above the bed added a small touch of color. My favorite part of the room was the balcony that overlooked the blue water and the rest of the island. I walked into the bathroom near the corner of the balcony, which was completely open - no walls, just the air hitting my face as I stepped out. The only thing here was a sink and a giant oval white tub under a tall palm tree. I'd never seen a bathroom out in the open before. *I guess when you live on an island by yourself, there's no need for privacy.* Showering later would be interesting. I stepped out and sat on the edge of the bed.

"If you need anything, let me know," Diego said before leaving the room.

The only thing I wanted was to strip out of my clothes and jump in the tub. After he left, I undressed, tossed the pantsuit on the floor, and went back into the bathroom. I turned on the tub faucet and waited until it filled halfway before stepping in. I watched the surrounding palm tree dance in harmony with the gentle wind. It was serene. A moment that I wished would last forever. The water came a little bit above my breasts. I leaned my back against the tub wall, tilted my head back, stretched out my arms, and closed my eyes.

"It's hard to take my eyes off of you," Marco said, startling me.

I opened my eyes, and he was standing with his back against the door, his arms crossed over his chest. His eyes trailed up and down my naked body and then fixed on my eyes. I covered my breasts with my arms and brought my knees to my chest.

"Can't I relax in peace?" I asked, annoyed.

"Care if I join you?" He asked politely.

I glared into his dark eyes and said, "You can use the bath, just without me."

His eyes turned cold. He didn't like my response. I waited to see what he'd do next. He exhibited a half-smirk, pushed himself off the door, and left. I didn't think he would go, but he surprised me.

Half an hour later I stepped out of the tub, grabbed a towel, and wrapped it around my body. I walked out to Marco, asleep in the bed. He looked peaceful and innocent. I liked that he was unconscious. That way, I wouldn't have to talk to him. I walked into the massive walk-in closet next to the bathroom, grabbed a short, white spaghetti strapped romper, and slipped it on. My stomach reminded me again that I needed food.

I left the room and went to the kitchen. The dining table was filled with an assortment of food: steak, chicken, sausages, salmon, cherries, asparagus, and more. I was so hungry I was ready to eat everything. Before sitting down, I looked around for Diego, but he was nowhere in sight. I sat at the head of the table and, without hesitation, dug into my food. I stayed away from the bottle of champagne, and instead poured myself a glass of water. After my experience with whiskey, I decided not to drink again for a while. Diego walked through the front door as I spread butter on some warm, soft bread. He looked exhausted. It was like he had just come back from a jog.

"Are you alright?" I asked, after taking a bite of the bread.

"Yes, of course. I had to run some errands."

"Errands?" I asked curiously

"Nothing of importance." He reported.

"Why don't you come sit and relax for a bit?" I offered

I observed as he debated internally whether he should.

"Please, I'm bored," I begged.

He smiled and walked over to sit in the chair next to me. I offered him food and was glad he didn't deny it. The two of us ate and talked like two good friends.

"What do you think I should do?" I asked, sipping my water.

"What do you mean?"

"When I was in the bathtub, I realized that I'll probably never go home to my old life and see my friends. As much as I wanted to deny it, something in my head told me I couldn't. I'm trapped."

"Marco is not a bad guy. He may not properly show it at times, but he has a good heart. I understand why people are afraid of the cartel because of all the horror stories they've heard on the news and in movies. I don't blame them. But the truth is, Marco didn't choose to be born as the successor of one of the most powerful cartels in Mexico." He explained passionately.

Until that moment, I'd never thought of or looked at Marco from that perspective. I understood there was truth to his explanation, but even though I respected what Diego said, it still wasn't easy to look past everything he had done. He didn't choose to be born into the family, but he had the freedom to choose a different path for his life, and he didn't.

"I understand where you are coming from, Alina. Sometimes our feelings come from our experiences, and I know you haven't had the greatest of experiences with both families."

At least one person understood my feelings and what I was going through. I appreciated the fact that he listened and didn't pass judgment.

"Is it true that all the women in the house are gone?" I asked.

"Yes. Marco is a man of his word."

I wasn't sure why I felt relieved to hear that confirmation. I guess I didn't honestly believe he would let go of that many beautiful women for someone like me.

"Do you have doubts?"

I took a sip of my water to clear my throat before speaking.

"I mean, yes. Those women were beautiful. Like beautiful, beautiful."

"So are you," he said with a kind smile, which made me flush.

"You're too kind, Diego."

We continued eating until I was stuffed. I'd never eaten so much food in my life. I moved from the dining chair to the couch, stretched out my entire body, and fell asleep.

CHAPTER TWENTY-SEVEN

I grab the handgun from the toolbox in the basement and run upstairs. My mom is lifeless on the bed as he continuously enters her from behind. I get to the room, crack the door open and watch as warm tears roll down my face. I slowly and quietly push the door wider. He can't see me because his back is to me. He is too busy to notice his daughter standing behind him, pointing a gun at him. I stand at the door with my finger on the trigger, deciding what to do.

I jerked awake from the nightmare that haunted me most nights, the dream paralyzing my body in bed like a corpse. I could only move my eyeballs in the dimly lit room. My heart was thumping in my chest, and I felt like a little girl all over again, hopeless. I tried reminding myself that I was safe, but then quickly realized I wasn't. Marco and I were under the same roof.

One, three, ten, twenty.... I blinked a few times and wiggled my fingers slightly. After a few seconds of great effort, my limbs started working again. I inhaled and exhaled a few deep breaths before falling back asleep.

When I woke up again it was morning, and the sun was rising from behind the ocean, shining through the floor-to-ceiling glass wall. It was spectacular scenery. I raised myself out of bed and headed for the bathroom. After brushing my teeth and washing my face, I changed into black shorts and a tank top and left the room. I was slightly disoriented and nearly bumped into Ernesto, a tall and lean man with short brown hair and brown eyes. The door was being guarded by him. He stood still, like one of the Queen's palace guards at Buckingham Palace. He politely greeted me, but without a smile. All of Marco's men were always so serious.

I walked down the hall, and of course, he followed behind. I left the house and walked down the driveway toward the beach.

For the past two days, I spent my mornings strolling along the shore and watching the sunrise. Each time, it was soothing. I hadn't tried to run because I'd still be on the island no matter where I ran. This new reality I was living in slowly crept through my tormented soul. Marco, to my astonishment, kept his word. He had done nothing that would warrant a fight from me. What was more shocking was that he had been sleeping in his bedroom. He didn't once attempt to welcome himself into my room.

As soon as my bare feet touched the sand, every worry I had slowly melted away, and even though it was for only a short while, it was enough to keep me sane.

I liked Ernesto. He allowed me to roam the beach by myself, observing from a distance. Another reason I liked him was the fact that he only talked when spoken to. I made my way near the shore and sat down. I brought my knees to my chest and allowed the water to lightly cover my feet. The nightmare was unforgettable. I remembered the events of that night like it was yesterday. As it played out in my head once again, warm tears rolled down my face, and I wiped them away. My poor, fragile mother didn't deserve all that pain. No one did. I closed my eyes and felt the soft breeze dancing on my hair and skin. Taking in the ocean's smell helped take my mind away from that horrible night.

"Good morning," a familiar voice said from behind.

I turned my head to see Marco approaching me in his usual black joggers. His body was more defined than it was two days ago. I suddenly realized what he had been doing instead of bothering me. He'd been working out. Both brothers were more similar than I expected. I wished I could lift weights and become toned and defined in two days. He sat down next to me without asking if he could. But it was Marco. What more could I expect?

"I've missed you," he said without looking at me.

I stared at the side of his face and said, "We've been living under the same roof for the past two days. It's not like you haven't seen me in years."

"I know. But I missed having you next to me in bed. I sleep better when you're next to me."

"I can't say the same. I sleep perfectly fine alone. Can I ask you a question?"

He turned to face me and cautiously nodded his head.

"Do you ever think what you did to my friends and me is wrong?"

Without hesitation, he said, "I know it's wrong."

I didn't expect him to acknowledge his wrongdoing so quickly and in that way. I thought he was going to explain and justify his actions.

"Do you ever feel guilty about it?"

He thought to himself in solace.

"Of course, but then I remember my actions led me to fall in love with you. And when I think about that, I regret nothing at all," he paused and then continued, "and that helps me to feel less guilty."

"Love? The same way you love your sister and Isabella?"

"No. It's not the same. The more I think about it, the more I realize I was lonely and just needed somebody to cure that loneliness. I thought what I felt for Catalina and Isabella was love, but my intense feelings for you prove that I never knew what love truly meant." He explained.

"But what you're feeling for me could just be lust. Your father is right. I think your subconscious is looking at me like a new toy. Something that's new and shiny and you must have."

"I think you'll do and say anything to ensure that you won't fall for me. I know my feelings for you are different because when I met you, I lost interest in the other women. The more time I spent with you, the more I realized how similar we are. We're both strong-willed and short-tempered. Then, when I read the first few pages of your journal, I learned what a tortured soul you are, just like me. We saw our mothers get beaten and raped by our fathers and were both helpless to do anything about it."

There was great pain in his voice. He never spoke about his mother. So, it was the perfect opportunity to learn more about her.

"What happened to her?"

He turned his head back to the sea.

"She left when I was ten and I never saw her again."

His silence exuded agony and grief. For once, he was a genuine human being and not a dangerous man.

"I'm sorry that she left you," was all I could mumble.

"I know the reason she left. Sometimes I was upset that she abandoned me, but then I remembered everything my father did to her, and I couldn't be angry at her anymore. She was in a lot of pain. Pain that was caused by the man she called her husband. The same man that she loved with all her heart. How could I be mad at her?"

"Are you angry with your father?"

"Of course. I hated what he did to my mother, and I wish I had been stronger and helped her when she needed me, but what could I have done? He was my father, after all."

More and more, I heard the aching in his heart release, and I suspected he never talked to anyone about his trauma.

"It's difficult to realize the person who's supposed to love and protect you was the one that hurts you the most. Your mother didn't deserve what your father did to her, and neither did you. You can spend the rest of your life blaming yourself, but it will not change the fact that there was nothing that you could have done. You were a child." I explained from my heart.

"Is that what you tell yourself?" He asked with novelty in his voice.

I took a deep breath in and exhaled slowly.

"Not for the longest time. I spent most of my life blaming myself for my mother's abuse. She used to tell me my father wasn't always like that. He was a loving husband until they had me. One day something changed in him, and our family was never the same again."

"What do you think happened that caused him to change?"

He asked a question that I had wondered about for many years myself.

"I don't know. My mother wouldn't tell me. I've spent many years wondering the same thing."

"He was a shitty father. No matter what the circumstances were, there is no excuse for his behavior and his treatment of his family. I hope you realize that."

We stared into one another's eyes for a long while. For the first time, we exchanged a smile that signified warmth and passion. I never thought I'd be able to have such a deep and vulnerable conversation with him. Marco was still a monster, but I had to remind myself that he was a person too. And like any human being, he had a story.

He grabbed my hand and gently squeezed it in his palm. We sat silently.

After a few minutes he said, "Please stop hating me."

I turned to gaze at his delicate, dark eyes. *What do I even say? Sure, I'll stop hating you and start giving myself entirely to you? Or hell no?* The inner battle was debilitating.

"Say something," he pleaded.

"I... don't really know what to say."

"What else can I do to change the way you feel about me? To let you see the real me?" He asked gently.

The questions were too much. I was stuck. I had no answer no matter how hard I tried to force myself. *The real question is, can he change into a decent human being?* My mother used to tell me that my father would often apologize and say he would change. But he never did. What made Marco any different?

"I'm not sure there's anything that you can do or say to change the way I feel. I've hated you since the day we met, and I don't know how to change that. Yes, there were moments where I thought maybe I felt something for you, but that could be my vulnerability playing tricks on my mind. You've hurt me, but most importantly, you hurt my best friend and Juan. Maybe one day I can forgive everything that you've done to me, but I can never forgive what you've done to them. I can pity you, but I can never love you. I'm sorry," I said.

I tried my hardest not to allow the depressing emotions to take over, and then continued, "I've seen how many times my mother tried to change my father. To turn him back into the man that she once knew, but in the end, she still got hurt in the most unimaginable ways. And I can't risk repeating the same mistakes she made."

I gently tugged my hand away from his and pushed myself off the sand and strolled back to the house. My words cut him deeply, but they had to be said. I was proud that I stood my ground. I could only hope that one day he'd realize that I could never permit myself to fall for him and let me go.

A black Bentley Bentayga drove up behind me as I walked up the driveway. The car stopped and Diego jumped out from the driver's seat. I hadn't seen much of him since we arrived on the island. Especially yesterday. He was gone all day.

"Good morning," he greeted.

"Good morning," I said and smiled.

He dropped the keys on the ground, and when he went to grab it, I noticed his right hand was shivering. When I stopped in front of him, his face was paler than two days ago. He did his best to avoid eye contact. Something was off about him, and I couldn't help but worry.

"Are you alright?" I asked.

He looked at me with empty eyes, "Yes… of course, why?"

"Your right hand is shaking." I pointed it out.

Diego looked down and tried to cover the shaking with his other hand.

"Where did you go yesterday?" I said as we both walked inside the house.

"I flew back to Mexico to run some errands." He reported.

"What kind of errands?" I inquired further.

Perhaps I was too nosy, but I couldn't shake the feeling that he was not himself. There was a hint of nervousness in his voice when he spoke. He was always calm and collected, and every time he spoke it was with sternness and confidence. Whatever happened yesterday or the day before made him different.

"Just personal errands. Nothing of importance."

"For your family?"

"Uh, yes, for my family."

Right after he said that his phone rang loudly in his pocket. He took it out, looked at the caller, and turned his phone off. I tried to peek at who it was, but he was so quick with his hands that I couldn't make out any numbers or letters.

"Are you sure everything is alright?" I asked again, growing both concerned and suspicious.

"I promise I will tell you if something isn't alright." He smiled, but it was a forced smile, not the genuine one I'd seen on his face before.

The two of us stood in the living room, awkwardly. I hoped the silence would make him more nervous, and that he would eventually disclose what was bothering him. Instead, he excused himself and disappeared, leaving me by myself. *That's odd,* I thought to myself. Maybe I was overthinking the situation. Maybe he was stressed from his duties. He would have told me if something was wrong. Or at least I hoped he would.

I walked to the kitchen and straight to the fridge. I pulled out a basket of eggs, bacon, and sausages. There were so many cabinets that it took me five minutes to find a skillet. When I found one, I placed it on the stove, turned it on, and waited for the pan to heat up. I found an empty bowl, cracked three eggs and whisked it until it was smooth. I tossed two small butter cubes in the pan and gave them a few seconds to melt before pouring the eggs in. I finished the scrambled eggs and started with the sausages and bacon. My new cooking skills were all thanks to Adrian. I found a plate for the food, poured myself a glass of orange juice, and sat on one of the white bar stools.

As I was finishing up, Marco entered the house. He was soaking wet, and I watched as water dripped off his body and fell to the floor.

I stared at him, bewildered. "Why are you soaking wet?"

"Is it that obvious?" He playfully teased me, then continued, "I went for a swim in the ocean."

"Why?"

"Why not? It's hot outside. Plus, I needed to clear my mind, especially after your hurtful words. Also, the ocean usually calms me down. Unfortunately, you left before I could ask if you wanted to join."

"That's nice, but I can't swim, remember?" I reminded him.

He looked slightly embarrassed that he had forgotten a crucial fact about me.

"My mistake. How could I forget?"

Damn right! I loudly thought to myself. How could he forget the important event when one of his men knocked me into the pool and I nearly drowned? Yet he claimed to love me. I imagined a man who says he loves a woman wouldn't forget such an important detail.

"Forgive me," he pleaded.

"I cooked breakfast for myself and there are some leftovers if you want some."

"I would love that. But first, let me jump in the shower."

"I'll have a plate ready when you're done. In the meantime, I'm going to explore the forest, if you don't mind."

He looked disappointed. "Do you mind if I come along? We haven't really spent much time together since we got here."

I guess that was a reasonable request. At least he didn't ask me to join him in the shower. I nodded my head, and he gleefully left for his room. I hopped off the barstool and went to sit on the couch.

Four of his men tagged along as I ventured into the forest. I did my best to ignore them as they followed behind us. I mainly focused on the sky-high palm trees, delicate flowers of all colors, and the scorching heat. The flat surface made it easier to walk. Ana and I used to go on hikes and explore caves a lot. Thinking about those times made me miss her desperately. I hoped she was healthy and happy. After half an hour of walking, we stopped in front of a small, clear pond and an enchanting waterfall. I knew the men weren't fond of the experience, but I didn't care. Marco leaned his back against a tree and stood silently.

"Wow," I said.

"It's beautiful, isn't it?" he asked from behind me.

I turned to face him and said, "I can see why you bought this island. It's so beautiful."

"The island's beauty wasn't the only reason I chose this place."

"What do you mean?"

"When I realized you wouldn't be safe in Mexico, I knew I needed to find someplace else for you to stay. So, I bought the island the day after your encounter with Lorena. I knew then that something bad would happen," he explained.

"How was the house built so quickly?"

"It was already here when I bought it."

Oh, duh, Alina, what a stupid question that was.

"You didn't have to do all of that."

"Of course, I did. Your safety is all that matters to me now."

I turned back to look at the majestic waterfall in front of me. *That's a sweet gesture.* I'd never thought in my life a man would buy me an island, but here I was. After a few more minutes of observation, we continued to venture deeper into the forest and came across a cave. The sight of it made me excited. I always had a natural curiosity about nature. I walked right inside with no hesitation.

My mother was to blame for my interest. When I was little, she read books about caves and tropical forests, and anything related to nature. For whatever reason, I remembered being so fascinated by it.

Marco ordered his men to wait outside and followed me inside. He stopped me and handed me a small flashlight that one of his men had given him. I politely thanked him, turned it on and continued moving forward. I carefully stepped over the uneven surfaces and rocks underneath my feet. The ground inside wasn't as smooth as the outside, but I didn't mind.

Marco struggled with his steps, and I found it hilarious. I assumed a powerful and dangerous man like him had never gone cave exploring. I wanted to burst out laughing, but I didn't want to be an ass. After about a hundred feet, I stopped and pointed my flashlight at the wall. I'd hoped to see bats hanging from the wall, staring at us. I could only imagine what that would do to him. Ana hated it when I used to do that. Though she loved to explore nature, she wasn't fond of being up close and personal to the creatures of the earth.

"Now I know how I can impress you," he blurted.

I turned to look at him and said, "I guess so."

"What made you so interested in stuff like this?" He asked, genuinely interested.

"My mom. She used to read to me books about nature and earth's wonders every night before bed."

"What happened to her, your mom?" He asked with a careful voice.

The personal question slightly took me back. I asked Marco about his mother, so it was only fair that it was his turn. Though I wasn't ready to talk about her, especially not to him. Even Ana didn't know the whole truth of what happened to her.

"I don't enjoy talking about what happened to her. It's a memory that I would like to keep to myself," I said meekly and politely.

"Fair enough. Well, I hope one day you'll feel comfortable enough to open up to me about her."

Respectful Marco was definitely a new look on him, and I liked it.

"Thank you. Now shall we venture deeper, or is this too much for the great Marco?" I asked playfully.

"I'll follow you anywhere," he said.

"Alright then, let's go," I said, leading the way, even though I had no clue exactly where I was going. I figured I would just keep walking straight.

After a while, the cave became smaller and tighter to navigate, so I agreed to stop and relax on a large rock. I hadn't realized it, but Marco brought a lantern for extra lighting. Once it was lit, I could see sweat dripping down his face and body like the water was earlier when he was fresh out of the ocean. I couldn't help but grin like a fool. Clearly, he was out of his element.

"What are you smiling about?"

"You look like you're about to pass out," I said, unable to control the smirk on my face.

"How is it you're not sweating? It's so hot in here." He said and wiped the sweat off his forehead.

"I don't know. Ever since I was a little girl, I don't sweat as easily as everybody else. I guess it's a blessing in disguise."

"Lucky you," he said and pulled his shirt over his head, using it to wipe his body.

Under the dim lights, his body was glistening. I turned my attention elsewhere so he wouldn't catch me staring. We both sat on the rocks opposite of each other in silence. It wasn't long before we both heard a familiar sound.

"You hear that?" I asked.

Marco listened carefully, "Yes. It's the ocean."

I stood up, grabbed the lantern off the ground, and followed the sound. He quickly followed behind. The cave became narrower, but the further we walked, the more I saw a glimpse of light at the end of the tunnel. I followed it with excitement. Finally, we exited the cave to an open, glorious ocean view and the whitest sand.

"This is crazy," I said excitedly.

Marco came to my side. He tossed his shirt and flashlight on the sand and ran toward the ocean, straight into the harsh waves. It brought a smile to my face. I placed the lantern and flashlight next to his and walked closer to the shore. It was nothing but pure serenity. I made myself comfortable on the sand and watched him swim, carefree. I wished I had faced my fears and taken the swimming lessons Ana arranged for me a few years ago.

He emerged from the water and made his way back to me.

"One day, I'll teach you how to swim," he offered.

I looked into his eyes and gave him a warm smile. We spent the next hour talking more about his family and the history with his aunt. He told me about how his grandfather started the cartel, the type of operation they ran, his siblings, their enemies, and the ongoing feud with Lorena. It was both riveting and terrifying. I listened intently, hoping to learn more about him.

"You know if someone were to tell me a few weeks ago that one day I'll be sitting next to the son of a drug lord in Mexico, I would have laughed at them," I said.

"I know that no matter how many times I apologize, it won't make a difference, but I have no regrets about you coming into my life. I would do this all over again if I had to."

"Well, perhaps maybe under different circumstances, things could have been different between us."

I'd never mentioned it to anyone, but deep down, I'd always found myself attracted to bad boys. I found them to be thrilling. That was why high school was such a horrible four years for me. I always fell for the jerks. I learned my lesson when one of them played a prank on me. The boy asked me on a date and then ditched me in the middle of it. I couldn't believe how gullible I was. I cringed every time I thought about it.

"Perhaps one day," he said with continued hopes in his eyes.

"Maybe. Now come on, I think it's time to go. Your men are probably wondering where we are."

We both forced ourselves up, grabbed our lights, and headed back.

During the silent walk back, my thoughts ran wild. I learned so much about his family history in the hour we chatted. His family did so many horrible things; however, I could honestly say I somewhat understand why and how they came to be. The more I learned about Marco, the more I felt sorry for him. I saw a real light-hearted man who became trapped in a legacy that he didn't wish upon himself.

"You're quiet," he pointed out.

"So are you."

"Yes, but I feel it's easier for you to read my mind than for me to read yours. I can't even guess what you're thinking about most of the time."

"You think you're easy to read? I recall many times when I didn't have the slightest clue what you were thinking about."

Marco grabbed my wrist and stopped me from walking.

"What are you doing?" I asked.

Marco nuzzled my hair back and gently caressed my right cheek with the back of his fingers. He trailed his thumb along my bottom lip sensually and moved his body closer to mine. I watched as his lips made their way closer to mine. When I felt his breath on my skin, I took a few steps back, and my clumsy self-tripped on a rock and I almost fell straight on my ass. But Marco was faster, and he grabbed my waist and held me close. His eyes were full of need and passion.

"I've never wanted anyone so much in my life," he said seductively.

His passionate words delivered a tingle down my spine.

"Can I please kiss you?" he asked.

I gently tugged my body away from his grip. I was surprised he allowed me to move away. He took a step back and cleared his throat. My hands were shaking.

"I'm sorry," he said.

The cave was getting hotter with the second that passed by.

"Are you alright?" He asked.

My heart was pounding inside my chest.

"Yeah... I'm fine." I said and turned to continue walking.

"Are you sure?"

"I said I'm fine," I said with an attitude and continued to walk away.

We finally reached the entrance of the cave, and his men were waiting like statues.

We headed back to the house. My legs became weaker and weaker with each step I took. I was falling behind, so Marco stopped walking and came to my side.

"Are your legs hurting?" he asked.

"Just a little. I haven't gone on a long walk like this for a while. So I'm just a little tired. I'll be…,"

I couldn't even finish my sentence before he picked me up.

"Marco, I can walk, it's fine," I said, though I didn't struggle to get down.

"Relax, we'll be home soon."

CHAPTER TWENTY-EIGHT

That night it was difficult for me to fall asleep. The fear of closing my eyes kept me awake. I feared if I did the nightmare from the previous night would reappear. I continued tossing and turning. Though, the nightmare wasn't the only thing that kept me awake. It was difficult not to think about the conversation I had with Marco. I tried my very best not to sympathize with him, but he was genuine and open. If he wasn't involved with a criminal organization, would I have fallen in love with him? Truthfully, I had no clue.

I turned to look at the clock, and it was already a quarter past three in the morning. I sighed in frustration, pushed myself up, and leaned my back on the headboard. No matter how much I tried, I couldn't shut off my brain. *Marco, the siblings, the cartels, Ana, Juan.* It was too much for one brain to bear. My thoughts were disrupted when I heard soft footsteps outside the room. *Who's walking around at this late hour?* I asked myself. I listened carefully to ensure that it was real. There was a tiny, soft voice, and I was confident someone was outside. I stepped out of bed quietly and strolled toward the door. When I pressed my ear against the door, I heard Diego's voice. I couldn't understand what he said because it was all in Spanish. I cursed at myself once again for not paying more attention in Spanish class.

After a few minutes, he wasn't talking anymore. I carefully opened the door and slightly peaked my head out. He wasn't in sight, and neither was Ernesto, which was odd because he was always guarding the door. I wasn't upset about it, though. His absence allowed me to step outside cautiously, while slowly closing the door, but not all the way. I made my way toward the living room and stayed behind the corner where I could see him. He was pacing back and forth, whispering to someone on the phone. Even though I couldn't understand the conversation, I could sense that he was in distress. From afar, I saw a hint of fear in his eyes. Could he be on the phone with his wife or daughter? My theory quickly shattered when I heard a familiar name: Lorena.

"Please, I have been doing everything that you've asked of me," he said in a panic and then continued, "Hello? Hello?"

Diego looked at the phone, frustrated. I assumed whoever was on the other line hung up. When I saw he was heading in my direction, I bolted back into my room and shut the door. I leaned my back against the door, and so many thoughts rushed through my head. Why did he mention her name? Was he working for her? It would explain why he was nervous and out of character the other day. But it wasn't possible. Diego was one of Marco's most trusted men. There was no way he would betray him, or at least I hoped he wouldn't.

I paced back and forth in the room, contemplating what to do. Would Marco even believe me? The unknown mystery behind the phone call drove me nearly insane. I plopped into bed like a failure, grabbed one of the big, fluffy white pillows, covered my face, and screamed. I forced my eyes to close and counted until my mind was exhausted, and finally I fell asleep.

When I opened my eyes, I was in the same position at the end of the bed as when I fell asleep. I pushed myself off the bed and went to the bathroom. I needed to shower to clear my head. After twenty minutes of straight cold water soaking my head, I slipped into gray sweatpants and a white T-shirt. I looked homeless, but I didn't give too much consideration to it. I opened the door and walked out of the room. When I turned the corner, Marco was sitting at the dining table in his usual black joggers and white T-shirt. From afar, his hair was disheveled, but still looked good. Better than I could ever look early in the morning. While I looked like I just woke up under a bridge, he looked like a Greek God.

He stood up as soon as he heard my tiny footsteps approach him. Without saying a word, he took me in his arms and gave me a gentle kiss on the forehead. I didn't hug him back. My reaction wasn't to be an asshole, but it was because I had too many things on my mind.

"What's wrong?" he asked after noticing my unusual silence.

I pulled out a chair and sat down. He followed behind.

"I'm fine." I lied.

"Are you hungry?"

"I am."

He poured me a glass of orange juice as I slowly ate some pancakes. Even though I told him I was hungry, I wasn't. My head continued to replay the phone conversation Diego had last night.

"Is everything alright?" He asked once again, his voice filled with concern.

I peeked up at him and forced out a half-smile and said, "Of course. Why wouldn't I be?"

"I don't know. You seem distracted. Not that it's new, but it's different right now. You have an unfamiliar look on your face."

As soon as he finished his observation, Diego appeared around the corner.

"Good morning," he said calmly. He was back to his usual self, calm and confident. Was my mind playing tricks on me? He approached the table, and I noticed a small brown notebook in his hand. I recognized my journal immediately. I jumped out of my chair and grabbed it from his hand. The instant it was close to my chest, I felt relieved.

"I sent Diego to Mexico to grab it for you. I know how important that little thing is to you." Marco said with a smile on his face.

I looked at Diego and said, "Thank you so much."

"Of course."

The two men spoke in Spanish, and shortly after, Diego left the house. I was irritated that they kept speaking in a foreign language, especially when I was around.

"Sit down. You barely ate anything." He suggested though it sounded more like a demand. Some things never change.

I sat back down but didn't eat. Though I was slightly relieved, the thought of him being on the phone still bothered me. *Why can't I just forget about it and move on with my life?* The way my brain functioned annoyed me. Anytime there was something bothersome, it was difficult to let go of.

"I know something is bothering you, Alina. So, speak," he said in his dominant voice.

I placed the notebook on the table and looked around briefly to ensure Diego wasn't in sight.

"I have a funny feeling." I straightened my posture and continued, "Last night, I heard Diego talking on the phone. It was mostly in Spanish, but I heard... Lorena's name."

He sat up straight in his chair, listening intently.

"I'm getting a different type of energy from him. I feel like he hasn't been the same for the last few days."

He took in every word I said, which made me less paranoid. He placed his left hand on the table while his other hand was on his thigh and thought to himself. I waited as patiently as possible to hear what he'd say.

"You think he's working for my aunt?" He finally spoke.

I hesitated at first, but then slowly nodded my head. He slowly tapped his fingers on the table. These were the few times that I wished I could read his mind. I couldn't stay quiet any longer and said, "I'm just concerned about him and his family."

Marco raised an eyebrow. "How do you know he has a family?"

"Well, whenever you aren't around, I have to talk to somebody. But that's not important. Could it be possible your aunt has something on him?"

"Alright, will it put your mind to ease if I investigate further?"

I nodded my head. He pulled out a cell phone from his pocket and dialed a number. He spoke in Spanish, and within minutes, Ernesto walked in through the front door.

"Sir," he said once he was at his side.

He spoke in English and instructed him to keep a close eye on Diego. Ernesto followed orders and left.

"Let's see if you're right," he said.

I felt terrible, but I knew that if I didn't voice my concerns, it would continue to bother me all day. After that, I continued eating breakfast.

Once I finished, Marco stood up from his chair and said he needed to take care of some business and left. I watched him hop in the black Cadillac Escalade, along with Ernesto. Once again, they left me alone. Since there wasn't much for me to do, I grabbed my journal and stepped out onto the balcony. I made myself comfortable and wrote about everything that had happened within the last few days.

A few hours had passed, and Marco still hadn't returned. Diego was absent too. My butt was numb, so I stood up and stretched my entire body. I made my way back inside and out the front door. I ran into Carlos, a middle-aged bald man with a sharp jawline and was built like a mountain, strong and sturdy.

"Where is Marco?"

"He has some business to attend to back in Mexico." He said in a deep, hoarse voice.

What?! Mexico?! I thought loudly to myself. He never once mentioned anything about going back to Mexico. I wondered why he didn't.

"What about Ernesto and Diego?" I inquired further.

"They're also in Mexico."

"Thanks for letting me know."

I walked back inside and aggressively sat on the couch with my arms folded across my chest. I wished I had a phone to call Marco and yell at him for not telling me about his whereabouts. The door opened, and I turned my head, thinking maybe it was him, but it was Carlos.

"Is there anything I can get you, senorita?" He asked politely.

"No, but I have a question. What else can I do on this island besides sitting by the ocean?"

"I could always accompany you to explore the forest again," he offered.

I debated whether I should, but then decided against it. I needed to recover from last night's lack of sleep.

"No, it's okay. I think I'm just going to take a nap."

Before leaving, he informed me to call him if I needed anything. I thanked him and lay comfortably on the couch, closing my eyes.

I woke up in bed, and the room was dimly lit. Someone had moved me. It was already seven o'clock and I felt energized. I was proud that I managed not to sleep until the next day though. I stretched out my body as far as I could and pushed myself out of bed. As I made my way toward the bathroom, I heard a scuffle outside. I walked away from the bathroom and headed towards the door instead. I walked out into the dark hall and headed into the living room. It was silent and empty. Where was the noise coming from?

I opened the main entrance, and it was clear the noise came from outside. Carlos was standing guard, so I carefully waited until he turned the other direction and then quietly bolted past him. I followed the noise to the beach and walked into a horrific scene. Ernesto and Don held down Diego, and Marco had a gun in his hand. He spoke in Spanish and punched him in the face. Diego's entire body collapsed into the sand. Ernesto grabbed his shoulder and forced him back on his knees and in front of his boss. Marco raised his gun and pointed it at his face. My feet moved on their own, and I hurled toward Diego.

"Stop!" I screamed and shielded him. I had no clue how I shoved Ernesto and Don out of the way, but I did. Marco was not happy with my actions. There was a bright flame burning in his eyes. He clenched his jaw tightly as he glared at me.

"Alina, move." He ordered. His voice was cold and dry.

"What the hell is wrong with you?" I shouted angrily.

Marco grabbed my wrist, yanked me up on my feet, and pulled me close to him. He turned his attention to his men and said something in Spanish. After he finished speaking, they grabbed Diego and dragged him back to the house. Finally, he let go of my wrist and put the gun behind his belt. He ran a hand through his hair and paced back and forth in frustration.

"Will you tell me what the hell is going on?" I demanded.

Marco stopped in his tracks and looked at me. He waited a few seconds and then said, "You were right. He's compromised."

I hated the fact that I was right, but I was more distressed about what he would do to him.

"Were you going to shoot him?" I asked.

"I don't have a choice, Alina. He was feeding information to Lorena. The island is no longer safe for you. We have to leave."

"Was he working undercover this whole time?"

"No. When he returned to Mexico, Lorena's men grabbed him. She kidnapped his wife and daughter and threatened to kill them if he didn't follow her orders."

My heart dropped. Diego's whole family was in danger because of me. I'd already destroyed my family. I couldn't do it to his.

"He's only doing what is right to protect his family. I would have done the same thing." I explained.

"You don't understand. I have to protect you."

"None of this would have happened if you had just let me go! How am I supposed to feel if Lorena kills his family?" I snapped as tears rolled down my face.

Marco stepped closer and gently took my face in his hands. He delicately wiped away my tears with his thumbs. I reached up and grabbed his hands away from my face. Comfort was not what I needed. I needed him to figure out a way to save Diego's family.

"You need to do something," I demanded harshly.

He stepped away and looked toward the sea. I walked up next to him. There was no time to think. There was only time for action.

"Please," I begged in a softer voice.

He turned to look at me with frigid eyes and said, "I have to protect you." He strolled away and toward the house. I promptly followed behind, and once we reached the front of the house, he ordered Carlos to hold me.

"Let me go!"

I staggered to get away.

Marco looked at me with sad eyes and said, "I'm sorry Alina," and entered the house.

I continued to struggle and demanded a release, but Carlos wouldn't budge.

"I'm sorry, senorita."

"I don't need your sorry. I need you to let me go!"

I struggled some more and finally pulled one of his arms close to my mouth and dug my teeth into his skin. He whined and released his hold, allowing me to run into the house. The living room was empty when I scanned it. I heard more scuffling in the basement and bolted toward the door. I skipped the stairs as I descended, nearly tumbling to my death. I made it down without falling and turned the corner to where they were. Diego was lying unconscious on the cold, hard floor. Once again, I sprinted toward him and used my body as a shield to protect him from further harm.

"If you're going to shoot him, you might as well shoot me too!" I yelled, my voice firm.

Marco once again grabbed my arm and jerked me to my feet.

"What the hell are you doing?" He screamed. His face was so close I felt every breath when he spoke.

"I won't let you kill an innocent man because of me. I won't." I said, determined.

There was an unfamiliar anger in his eyes, one that I hadn't seen before. He looked like a complete murderer. It frightened me slightly, but I knew I needed to stand my ground. There was immense tension between us.

"Don, take her upstairs." He ordered and released my arm.

Don grabbed my wrist and dragged me away. I punched his arm repeatedly, but my efforts were useless. As he was about to yank me up the stairs, a familiar sound coming from the living room halted us in place. It was a gunshot. Immediately, Marco bolted to my side.

"I-I'm sorry," Diego said faintly. There were tears in his eyes.

Marco grabbed my wrist and pulled me close to his body.

"Go upstairs and check." Ernesto nodded, pulled a gun from the back of his pants, and disappeared.

Marco turned his attention to Don and said, "Go through the cellar door and prepare a car. We'll meet you outside. Call Antonio."

"Yes, sir," he said and was gone in an instant.

"What's happening?" I asked. I tried my best not to panic.

More gunshots went off. Now I was panicking, and Marco started up the stairs quietly with me behind him. After the fourth step, something stopped me from moving. I turned to Diego.

"Wait, we can't leave him."

"Alina, this is not the time to test my patience. Lorena is here and we need to leave now." He said, irritated.

We emerged upstairs and met Ernesto by the door. Marco said something in Spanish and moved further down the narrow, dark hallway cautiously behind him. I meekly followed behind. My heart raced as the tension continued to build. The realization that this night could be my last on this earth was surreal and terrifying. We stopped at a corner. Ernesto sneakily peeked his head to view the living room. Without hesitation, he raised his gun and pulled the trigger. There was a thump, like someone had fallen to the ground. I knew he had shot somebody. I wanted to see who the unfortunate victim was, but Marco gripped my wrist. He was unwilling to allow me to move from behind him. Ernesto swiftly moved to the other side of the hall for a better view. Marco and I moved further down the hall. I briefly peeked behind Marco's shoulder, and there she was, sitting on the couch in a black suit with sky-high, red heels. Four largely built men surrounded Lorena. They had armed themselves with guns and were ready to kill. Carlos' lifeless body was near her feet. There was blood spewing out of his mouth and stomach. I covered my mouth with my hand in disbelief. I had to remind myself to remain quiet.

"I know you're here, nephew, and I know your little whore is here too," Lorena said calmly.

Marco signaled Ernesto with his hand, and they rapidly opened fire. I crouched on my knees and covered my ears with both hands. Bullets were flying everywhere. If it weren't for the walls protecting us, we'd be dead already. Although their effort was great, it was two guns against four. Marco emptied his clipped. He screamed something in Spanish to Ernesto. The next thing I know, Ernesto tossed him a new clip of bullets. Marco reloaded his gun and continued firing.

"Enough!" she commanded, and they all stopped firing.

She reappeared from behind the couch in disarray.

"I want the two of you alive." She composed herself and walked toward the wine bar and grabbed herself a bottle of red wine. She gracefully poured the drink into a glass and paced back and forth, slowly. The room was silent.

I stood back up on my feet. Marco turned around to look at me.

"Are you alright?" He asked gently.

It was too chaotic for me to speak, so I nodded my head. He softly cupped my cheek before turning back around. I continued watching from behind his shoulder.

Lorena made her way back to the couch and sipped her wine. She looked way too comfortable. It was frightening.

"Alina, darling, did you think I wouldn't be able to find your precious friend, Ana?"

Hearing Ana's name was enough for my body to jerk away from Marco and jump out into the open. Her men immediately pointed their guns at me. I didn't need to turn around and look at Marco's face to know that he was furious at my action, but I didn't care.

"Where's Ana? What did you do to her!?"

She grinned at me with satisfaction in her eyes.

"What a loving relationship the two of you share. It's very admirable." She said mockingly.

Marco and Ernesto rushed out from behind the corner. Marco then jumped in front of me and pointed his gun directly at his aunt.

There was no fear in her eyes. I moved myself to his side instead of being shielded behind him.

"There are so many women out there that you can have. Why her?"

"Your anger is towards me, Lorena. It has nothing to do with her. Why don't you let this go and nobody else will get hurt?"

"I loved you and you left me. I will make sure you'll know what it feels like to have someone you hold dearly suffer and die in front of you. And trust me, I will make sure your precious whore suffers slowly."

She turned her attention to me and said, "But before I kill you, I will make you watch your friend suffer until she begs my men to kill her. She won't be the only one. I will make sure her parents suffer too. And that, my dear, is a promise."

I wanted to remain brave, but all that was coursing through my head was Ana and her parents' screaming in agony. The thought shook me to my core. They'd suffered because of me. Everyone I loved suffered because of me. My father was right. I shouldn't have been born.

Lorena leaned back on the couch and crossed her legs.

"Where are they?" I asked as tears brimmed over my eyes.

She had a despicable smirk on her face. "I'm curious. You act so protective of Ana, yet you've stayed with a man who knew about her rape and torture. No, that's not entirely true. Did you know that he could have saved her from the torture?"

The room turned silent. I was confused.

"All he had to do was agree to exchange you for her. But he refused, and instead watched as my men ravaged her in every way possible," she revealed.

I suddenly lost control of my breathing. The room spun in a circle, and I felt as if I was moving in slow-motion. I reluctantly turned my head to look at the side of Marco's face. He didn't turn to look at me. Warm tears cascaded down my face uncontrollably, and my body started shaking.

"You... you knew?" I asked, almost not wanting to believe it could be true.

After a few moments of silence, he slowly turned to face me and softly said, "I'm sorry."

I balled my fists in rage.

Lorena clapped her hands at the show that was unfolding in front of her.

"Bravo, bravo, bravo. I take it that your beloved Marco never told you the truth. That is very sad. Very sad. It's almost painful to watch."

I turned to glare at the evil woman. "You're really enjoying this, aren't you?"

"I am. It has been quite a while since I've had this much fun. But the show is just beginning."

The front door burst open and a slim, copper-skinned woman with shoulder-length black hair was tossed into the room. I didn't recognize who she was.

"Please, let me see my husband and daughter!" she pleaded hysterically.

It was then I knew she was Diego's wife. Her face was bruised and bloody. The state of her body was all too familiar to me. She was terrified and fragile. I wanted to run to her and hug her tightly in my arms, but my body didn't allow me to move.

She crawled a few more inches closer to the center of the room.

"Please, I am begging you. Let me see my family." She pleaded with an ache that was too painful to hear.

Lorena grabbed a gun from one of her men and walked toward the tiny woman. She tried to scurry away but the man that brought her in blocked her passage.

"I won't be needing you anymore," she turned to look at me and continued, "Alina, say hello to Luisa," then she turned back to look at Diego's wife, pointed the gun at her head and without the slightest of hesitation, pulled the trigger.

"NO!" I screamed. My feet finally moved, but Marco grabbed my waist and held me in place.

"Now you get to say goodbye."

Lorena turned around and pointed the gun at me. Marco shoved me aside and stood in front of me. Ernesto tried to defend his master, but two men fired their weapons, and they instantly killed him. I watched as his body collapsed onto the white rug. It was slowly turning red.

"I won't let you hurt her," he said firmly.

"Drop your gun, nephew. Right now, it's you against four of my men. With one simple word from me, you'll both be dead."

He looked around with defeated eyes. He was no longer the confident and unbeatable Marco Gustavo. After analyzing the situation and realizing Lorena had beaten him, Marco lowered his gun to his side.

"Now drop your gun," she demanded.

He tightly clenched his jaw and finally tossed the gun on the floor. One man with massive shoulders and the mane of a lion bent down and picked up the weapon and held it in his hand. He gladly returned to his boss's side.

My head was numb, and everything was foggy. The only thing that was clear was the fact that Marco knew about what happened to Ana and he chose not to tell me. How could he not have told me? How could he claim to love me, yet keep such a secret from me? But that wasn't enough. Diego's wife was dead. *Shit, Diego.* I couldn't imagine the pain and heartache he'd felt once he learned of her death.

"How does it feel to be so powerless?" She asked him directly.

"If anyone is to get hurt, it should be me. You hate me, not her. What you and I did was wrong, and it should have never happened."

"That's not true. Your judgment is clouded because of this look-alike whore. Admit it, Marco, you only care for her because of Isabella. You can lie to yourself, to her, and the world, but you can't lie to me. I know you better than anyone."

"I'm sorry that I hurt you, but it doesn't have to end in this way."

"You did more than hurt me. You abandoned me. The time that we were together held some of the happiest moments of my life. And you just left as if I meant nothing."

Lorena slowly paced back and forth. She unbuttoned her blazer, took it off, and flung it on the couch. There was a mixture of wrath and sadness in her crazy eyes. I assumed that wasn't the only time Marco rejected her.

I observed her movements and wondered what insane things were running through her mind.

"I'm done with you," she turned to her men and said, "Take them. We're leaving for Mexico right now."

As the men prepared to grab us, multiple gunshots traveled through the glass doors. One by one, Lorena's men got hit, and they all fell to the floor. There was blood and bodies everywhere.

I crouched down behind the coffee table while Marco grabbed one of the many guns on the rug amidst the chaos. He fired the gun multiple times, killing whoever was still breathing. Sharp glass shattered everywhere.

One, two, three, four, five, six, seven, eight, nine, ten...

Everything suddenly stopped. No more gunshots, no more broken glass. I peeked my head from behind my hands. It was over. My hands were shaking uncontrollably. *It's over. It's finally over.* I lifted myself up on my feet. I'd never seen so many dead bodies in my life.

Just breathe.

Lorena stood up from behind the couch. There was no one else with her. She turned to look at me. She wasn't as confident as she was five minutes ago. Marco shot her in the chest after she tried to point her gun in my direction. She gasped in shock.

"You... you shot me," she said meekly. The gun fell from her hand, and she dropped to her knees. She brought her right hand to her chest, and her body slowly crumpled to the floor.

I watched as she struggled to breathe in her last breath. It was satisfying to watch her die. I barely recognized who I was. I stared into her eyes until they were no longer alive. Marco tucked his gun in his belt and took me in his arms. I didn't embrace him back.

"I'm so sorry," he said.

I'd no clue because I grabbed the gun, but I did. I pushed myself away from his arms and pointed the weapon in his face.

"What are you doing?" He asked, confused.

I took a few steps back. It was clear I wasn't in the right state of mind. I no longer saw Marco. I only saw an evil man who kidnapped Ana, tortured Juan, and physically and emotionally abused me from day one. There was nothing pure about him. He had a heart, but it was black and cold as ice. He was the son of a criminal who murdered, tortured and exploited people for money and power.

I briefly glanced over to Luisa's lifeless body and saw her brain tissue splattered all over the rug. She was an innocent woman, murdered because of me. I thought of her daughter, who was only a teenager, who was now motherless, because of me. All because of me. My chest tightened, and it was difficult to breathe. If he had let me go, she would still be alive, and Gabriela would still have a mother.

"Alina, please," he pleaded softly.

"Why didn't you tell me about Ana? You knew. You watched as your aunt's men raped and tortured her and you did nothing. All you had to do was agree to her one condition. You had the chance to save her, but you didn't. We spent days together and never once did you think to mention exactly what happened that night. Why?" I asked as tears rolled down my face.

"I didn't tell you because I didn't want you to be hurt any further. I was trying to protect you. I couldn't lose you. You're too important to me." He explained.

"No. You weren't trying to protect me. You only wanted to protect yourself."

"Alina, please. I love you." He said with an ache in his voice.

"Love?! Marco, you know nothing about love! You have no right to say that word. You're nothing but a heartless bastard. All of this was a sick game between you and your brother. Ana and Juan got hurt because of me. Luisa is dead because of me. Everything happened... because of me."

He took a step toward me, but I backed away, keeping my distance so he wouldn't be able to grab the gun from my hand.

"I'm sorry I kept the secret about Ana. I realize now that I should have told you. I-I just couldn't bear the thought of how much it would hurt you. But I was wrong. I know that deep down, you feel something for me. But you are afraid to bring yourself to admit it because you know it's wrong to love me. You're a good person and you won't hurt me."

"You're wrong. I'm not who you think I am." I paused, took a deep breath, and continued, "On my thirteenth birthday, my dad came home drunk. He was always drunk, but that night, for whatever reason, he was fucked up more than usual. I guess the day of my birth was too much for him. He was angry. My father grabbed my mother by her neck and dragged her into the bedroom. He beat her badly that night, and when he was done, he ripped off her clothes and raped her. I couldn't listen to her cries anymore. I decided it was enough. So, I ran down to the basement and grabbed his gun from the toolbox. He'd no clue that night was about to be his last." I stopped.

"What did you do, Alina?"

My mouth quivered in fear. "I... I killed him."

That was the first time I'd admitted the truth out loud. I'd been to multiple different therapists over the years, and none of them knew of what happened that night. I had no idea why I told him. Perhaps because in my mind, I had already decided what I was going to do within the next few seconds.

"That night, I protected my mother, and now I have to do it again. I must protect Ana. As long as you're alive, we'll never be safe. That ends today."

"Alina...,"

I pulled the trigger and shot him in the chest. Marco looked at me, stunned. He couldn't believe what I'd done. His white shirt turned red, and he fell to his knees. I dropped the gun from my hand and watched as he gasped for air. My body went numb. The room was spinning, and instead of seeing Marco, I saw my father. That haunting night replayed like a slow-motion picture in my head.

I remembered my mother jumping out of bed, half-naked and covered in his blood. She grabbed the gun from my hand and embraced me in her bruised arms. I remembered how she tried to shield me from looking at my father as he took his last breath. I listened to his desperate breathing. He was fighting to live, but then suddenly, he stopped making noise. I remembered what she said to me then, word for word.

"Listen to me, Alina, you did nothing wrong. Do you understand me?" She took me out of the room, sat me on the kitchen chair, and said, "I love you so much. Don't you ever forget that." Then she grabbed the home phone and dialed 911.

Marco's agony snapped me back to the present moment. My actions horrified me, but I didn't know what to do. His body collapsed to the floor. He reached out his hand to me. I took a step forward, but then stopped.

He needs to die, so you and Ana will be safe.

I stared into his eyes and saw his life slowly draining out of him.

"Alina…" he said meekly.

I dropped to my knees and said, "I'm sorry."

Everything came back full circle.

ACKNOWLEDGMENTS

I am forever grateful to the following people for their encouragement and support:

To my fiancé, Mitchell, thank you for believing in me and never once giving up on my crazy journey.

To Kristie Wagner for editing the book and believing in my story.

C.C. Y

C.C. Y is a proud Mental Health Therapist with a secret passion for writing and imagining the craziest of stories. She graduated from Mount Union University with a bachelor's in Psychology and later earned her Master's in Clinical Mental Health Counseling at Johnson and Wales University. At a young age, C.C. Y dreamed of becoming a writer, but due to fear and barriers with her English, she deterred herself from pursuing her passion. *Full Circle* stems from her love for romance and thriller novels with a dark twist. Certain events and traumas in the book were inspired from her work with individual clients throughout the year. She is a strong advocate for mental health and wanted to write a story where the main protagonist is haunted by her traumatic pasts but somehow managed to survive.

Printed in Dunstable, United Kingdom